# END AS A MAN

# End as a Man

BY CALDER WILLINGHAM

THE VANGUARD PRESS, INC. NEW YORK

Designed by Stefan Salter

Manufactured in the United States of America
by H. Wolff, New York, N. Y.

# TO HELENE

PART

*1* September is a hot month in certain parts of the South, but Maurice Maynall Simmons arrived at The Academy in a heavy wool suit. He wore a vest with watch chain; and a candy-stripe shirt that had attachable collar and cuffs. There was a fuzzy brown hat mashed down over his ears. He had on a pair of shoes that laced up above the ankles. Simmons was covered with sweat; his clothing was soggy and his face and hands streaked from cinders. Apparently he'd ridden on a day coach all the way from Ohio without washing a single time.

Almost immediately, he was recognized as a hopeless fool. His Ohio accent, his big red ears, his eye-enlarging spectacles all helped. But the worst part was his conversation and beliefs. He had a strange way of speaking and the things he said were stranger. Simmons was religious: he'd come to The Academy to prepare for a chaplain's job. He anticipated war. This would be with England, however, not Germany.

"Think of it," he said. "The English make an alliance with Mexico. They've already got Canada and we'd be hemmed in."

Simmons addressed the first upperclassman he saw as "young fellow." This happened two or three minutes after his arrival. He came strolling in his mustard-colored suit through the main gate of Hemphill Barracks. In the most careless fashion he walked out upon the quadrangle and gazed up at the four tiers. An upperclassman ran toward him. Simmons started to walk off in the other direction.

"What are you doing on this quadrangle?" shouted the upperclassman.

"I beg your pardon?"

"Pop to!"

"Listen, young fellow. Kindly don't shout at me, I resent it."

"You resent it?"

"What's this place made of? Is that granite, or concrete?"

"Pop to! Heave her up there!"

That night at supper a thing happened which increased Simmons' reputation as a fool. He puked on the table.

[3]

His mess chief, a junior classman named Jocko de Paris, had been riding him throughout the meal. Finally Simmons complained of a sour stomach.

"Shut your filthy yap," said De Paris.

"Sir, I repeat I have a very sour stomach."

"Sewer stomach," said De Paris, imitating the Ohio accent. "Grind that dome in, mutt. Lay those juiceless ribs on the table and squat like a rock. I'm afraid I'm going to have to shear your ass for those insidious words."

Simmons braced.

"Listen here," said De Paris. "Make us a brace, will you? I'd appreciate seeing you throw some red out your nose, and you can do it if you try. Ducrow, bear up on that pile of guts; take my advice and brace, jerk."

Simmons then opened his mouth wide. A watery little hiccough came out and everyone at the table laughed. Then Simmons groaned and twisted his shoulders forward. His supper came pouring between his teeth, plopping and splashing over the table. There was a shocked silence. "Aaaagghhh!" said Simmons. He gave another heave and more food poured out. "Aaaaaaghh!" he said again. "My Christ."

The cadets at the table had meanwhile dodged out of the way. Jocko de Paris' tie had been splattered. He held this up and sniffed at it. "God Almighty. Filthy."

The accident gave Simmons his nickname. Sewer-belly. But this was later altered to Sow-belly. Sow-belly Simmons.

Robert Marquales was Simmons' roommate. The odor of urine hung in the air on the morning of the second day.

"Do you wet the bed?"

"No," said Simmons. He took up his drenched sheets and hung them out on the gallery rail to dry, flipping them and sending off clouds of odor.

Simmons' face was a serious disadvantage. He looked like a mule. A pale mule wearing spectacles. He had a long nose that was rounded off at the end in a remarkable way. His ears were huge and he could wiggle them. His lips were thin; he had the habit of going around with

[ 4 ]

his mouth open. This was bad because his teeth were always dirty. They were large teeth, the bottom row as big as the top; they slanted outward. Simmons' voice was thick and he usually spat forth flecks of saliva when talking. His body was emaciated; the bones stuck out all over him.

Everything about him was more or less distinctive. He had a distinctive love for his young sister, who'd died three years before. This love got him into trouble.

He had an enlarged, framed snapshot of the sister, taken when she was ten years old. It showed her standing in a white dress on the diving board of a swimming pool. Her face was nearly as ugly as Simmons'; she too looked like a mule. But she was smiling as he never did. She stood on the board with her hands poised as if about to dive into the pool.

Simmons had inscribed on the bottom of the picture: "Only three weeks before thy departure, Martha." He had the sentimental habit of kissing this picture. Word got around. Three or four days after Freshman Orientation Week began, Marquales, Bailey, and Leroy, who were all recruits, formed a plot. They stole the picture and kept it three hours, until Simmons said he meant to go talk to Colonel Evers about the matter.

The next afternoon Bailey took the picture again and put it into one of the toilet bowls in the latrine. This time Simmons actually started toward the office of the commandant. Bailey grabbed him, threw him down to the floor, and told him he was crazy.

Finally Marquales said, "Look in the latrine."

A few minutes later Simmons returned and went to Bailey and attempted to strike him. Bailey laughed and threw him down again. Then he got on Simmons' back and said, "Giddap, hossie." He then twisted Simmons' arm and asked, "Who's your boss?"

"You."

"Put a 'sir' on that."

"You, sir."

Simmons began to weep. He couldn't stop, once started, and he wept all afternoon wherever he went. During afternoon military drill

Harold Koble, cadet sergeant of the junior class, saw the tears on his face and told him to stop. It did no good. And Simmons made dozens of mistakes in the drilling. He often went in the opposite direction from that taken by his squad. When the command was "right oblique march" he would tear away to the left, banging into other men. Since he hadn't learned to keep in step he was always treading on the heels of the freshman in front of him and having his own heels trod upon by the fellow behind him.

He was drilled overtime with four or five others on the awkward squad. He returned to his room dripping with sweat and still weeping. His first discovery was that his smelly bed sheets were thrown upon the floor and decorated with the contents of a bottle of ink. His second discovery was that the picture of his sister was gone again.

He didn't get it back for a week this time. When he did, whoever stole it had taken the photograph out of the frame and done sketching on it. The child in the white dress had two breasts, a navel, and pubic hair from which a great penis emerged. Directly under "Only three weeks before thy departure, Martha" was scrawled in a crude hand the words, "X-ray eye takes a look at Sow-belly's Sister."

Simmons suspected fat Carlton Leroy. This time, however, he did nothing except clip out the face of the picture and put it into his wallet. A few days later Tim Bailey rose early one morning and stole the wallet from under Simmons' pillow. He drew a handlebar moustache on the picture and stealthily returned it. That afternoon Simmons burned the remains. He put a picture of his mother and father into the gold-rimmed frame.

Simmons had arrived at The Academy with three trunks. These were filled with many varieties of things—a chemistry set, stamp collection in nine albums, radio crystal with earphones, and a large number of books on the subject of religion. Simmons was forced to ship back to Ohio two filled trunks.

But so much remained he didn't have room for it, and he asked to borrow part of Robert Marquales' personal-possessions shelf. Marquales wasn't inclined to do him a favor. That night after taps Simmons prayed aloud for the first time.

"Oh my Father," came a dry whisper. "Soften Robbie's heart."

The next morning Marquales gave Simmons a part of the personal-possessions shelf.

"Maurice," he said. "You're a hypocrite to pray like that."

"I am?"

Simmons prayed aloud many times during the next two weeks.

There was trouble about the bed-wetting. Word finally reached Cadet Lieutenant George Cleer. One day during the noon meal he stopped by Simmons' table.

"Mister, I hear you wet the bed."

"Sir?"

"You better report to Colonel Girard after the meal. He'll tell you how to break the habit."

Simmons smiled. "What habit, sir?"

"Are you trying to be witty?"

Simmons dropped his eyes.

Jocko de Paris said, "Answer the question."

"All right," said Cleer. "We'll see if you can talk at attention. Pop to."

"Suck up those morbid guts, will you?"

"One moment, Jocko," said Cleer. "Now pay attention to me, Mr. Simmons. I order you, report to Colonel Girard after dinner. Then drive by my room on the first gallery and report to me. Understand?"

Simmons' arms were dangling loose, his chest touching the edge of the table. Sweat was beginning to form on his face. He stared straight ahead with half-closed eyes, directly over the rows of crowded tables in the mess hall. He moved his lips, but no words rose above the sound in the great room.

"What the hell's the matter with you?" asked De Paris.

"Sir, I can't talk while at attention."

"Just a minute, Jocko," said Cleer. "Mr. Simmons, you just talked while at attention. What do you want to say that's so difficult?"

[ 7 ]

"Who is Colonel Girard?"

"The Surgeon."

"Sir, why should I see the Surgeon?"

The other freshmen at the table laughed. Simmons joined in.

"Face front!" snapped Cleer. "You other Misters—what do you mean, laughing. Pop to. All of you smear those necks back while a fellow freshman is being questioned. What do you think you are, college boys? You are Academy men. You Misters sit up hard. Mr. Simmons, wrap that neck back."

"I can't talk, sir."

"I'm warning you to cut out the nonsense. Do you or don't you urinate in your bed?"

"Sir? I don't do anything like that."

De Paris interrupted, "You'll regret that morbid statement."

"You deny you wet the bed?" asked Cleer.

"Yes sir."

"Drive by my room after the meal," said Cleer. He walked away. Simmons asked meekly, "Can I rest now, Mr. de Paris?"

"Each word you pronounce is another laceration on your coccyx."

Simmons' eyes slewed over, liquid. Jocko stopped, hand holding a forkful of lima beans before his mouth. The lids of his blue eyes came together until they formed slits.

"I'm sorry," whispered Simmons. He faced front and went into brace.

"You'll be sorrier," said De Paris, with a modest smile.

Marquales was shining his shoes when Cleer and Simmons entered the room. The latter carried his bed linen.

"Rest," said Cleer to Marquales. "Are you Mr. Simmons' roommate?"

"Yes sir."

"Who are you?"

"Robert Marquales, sir."

"That's not the way to answer."

"Sir, this is Cadet Recruit Marquales, Robert."

[ 8 ]

"Okay. Do these sheets belong to Mr. Simmons?"

"Yes sir."

At that moment Peter Layne, cadet captain of Company Twelve, entered the room. Marquales and Simmons popped to attention. "Rest," said Layne. He ambled forward and sat down in one of the chairs by the study table.

"Mr. Simmons was just going to do some exercise," said Cleer.

"Fine."

"Return the sheets."

Simmons stepped outside the room.

"Nuts," said Cleer. "He beats me."

"Yeah?" said Layne, staring at Marquales. "Hey, Mister. What's your name?"

"Sir, this is Cadet Recruit Marquales, Robert."

Layne smiled. "Where'd you get those eyes?"

Marquales unfortunately had one brown eye and one blue eye.

"Don't know, sir."

Simmons returned from the gallery and was ordered to do deep-knee bends. He did about fifty, and that was all he could manage.

"Try push-ups," said Cleer.

"What, sir?" panted Simmons.

"Push-ups."

Simmons looked bewildered. Cleer got down and demonstrated a push-up. "See? Like this."

Simmons' gray Academy shirt was darkened with perspiration. His glasses were removed, and he breathed through his mouth in short gasps. Without the magnifying spectacles his eyes seemed tiny. At that moment he looked much like a tired old mule.

"Can I rest a minute, sir?" he said.

"No."

"I'm weary, sir."

"Rest tonight after taps when you're supposed to. You brought this on yourself."

Thirty minutes later Simmons lay motionless face downward on the floor.

[ 9 ]

"George, he's worn out."

"Get up."

Marquales helped Simmons to a chair.

"Want to change your attitude?"

Simmons nodded.

"You wet the bed, don't you?"

"Yes sir."

"All right. Now go report to Colonel Girard and ask him how to break the habit."

Simmons nodded.

"Don't nod at me," said Cleer.

"Yes sir," answered Simmons thickly.

Layne said, "Take a shower before you go."

"That's right," agreed Cleer. "Go take a shower."

When they were gone Simmons turned to Marquales and said, "Betraying rat!"

"What did I do?"

"You encouraged them!"

"Why, I was just sitting here."

"Sitting!" Flecks of invisible spit blew into Marquales' face.

Simmons didn't take the shower. He never bathed. It embarrassed him for other cadets to see him naked.

*2*  It seemed to Marquales that Layne found the disciplining of Simmons unpleasant.

Pete Layne was a senior of twenty-three from Knoxville. He was as popular with the cadets as with the authorities of The Academy. He was dark haired, handsome, six feet tall. He looked like a movie hero, despite an imperfection: crooked teeth. But Layne had many other virtues. He made superb marks in his classes. He wrote serious short stories for the school magazine, *Port Arms,* of which he was an editor. Furthermore, he'd been nearly expelled in his junior year because of trouble with women, and this gave him much glamour appeal with the corps.

A beautiful but wicked girl of a good Port George family missed one month. Then she missed another month. She went to a doctor and found out the truth, then rushed to General Draughton and named the man: Pete Layne.

But Layne immediately produced five cadets who swore they'd all layed the girl one night on Jamaica Shore.

There was a rumor Colonel Evers tried to persuade General Draughton to give the six cadets dishonorable discharges. But nothing ever came of it. The girl had an abortion and moved to Atlanta.

One night Major Pearson was playing solitaire in the guardroom of Hemphill Barracks when he thought he heard feminine laughter. He summoned the cadet Officer of the Day, detailed six orderlies, and instituted a search. But he found nothing. Then two weeks later General Draughton received the note:

Dear General:

A few days ago I was in your barracks with some of the gentlemanly cadets. It was in the room of a cadet named Layne. Do you permit such imorality? You ought to fire those kids. Perhaps ten of them got fresh. It was a vile experience.

Victim of Cadets

When confronted with the note Layne declared it to be the work of a practical joker. How could a woman get into Hemphill Bar-

[ 11 ]

racks? How could she have been hidden? How could she have ever got out? According to a cadet rumor the note came from a whore who hadn't been paid.

There was trouble about the incident. At the time Layne had cadet rank of first sergeant. He was expecting to be named cadet major of one of the three battalions for his senior year. But he finished that June as a private. During the summer the authorities weakened and finally elevated him to the rank of cadet captain of Company Twelve. So despite all the trouble Layne started his senior year as a high-ranking man, if not cadet major as he'd wished.

Sow-belly Simmons didn't like Layne. He told Marquales the mercy of Jehovah should be denied a man like him; immoral on-slaughter, the lust of carmine guilt, fickle smiles, and gay deception.

Marquales found life with Simmons difficult. There were many things about Simmons that made him hard to live with. The never-ending visits of upperclassmen, who were so strongly attracted, made it bad enough. But the worst thing was the prayers.

At night after taps Simmons would pray. Sometimes to himself, but more often in a hoarse whisper. Marquales dreaded this.

Simmons was plagued with insomnia. He rarely slept more than five hours each night. Unfortunately, he found it pure torture to re-main in his cot when awake. He told Marquales that in Ohio he used to potter with his chemistry set or work on his stamp collection. That wasn't possible at The Academy because it was required all lights be out at ten-thirty.

One night about an hour after the praying, Simmons started to tell himself a story. Marquales was awake and at once discovered that a story was much harder to endure than a prayer. This one seemed to be about a visit down below. Marquales tried to go to sleep, but the whispered drone was an insurmountable handicap.

"Well, well," said Simmons dreamily. "Take the elevator to the left, he said. Sure, I answered. Then I got in the car. There was a fiend driving it. He tried to bite me, but I held out my hand and said: Stop, I do not belong here, visitor from God. So he crouched

[ 12 ]

over the red-hot lever, snarling and snuttering, then he put over the door. Oh, well, it must have dropped a thousand miles, I suppose, then it began to get hot, the paint blistering and popping off the walls like a shower of flakes of snow, *hot* snow. I wasn't bothered, however. I didn't feel a thing; slight invisible asbestos suit He gave me, fit like a glove, marvelous invention, amazing, going over the eyes and mouth, even the hairs like an invisible film of protection.

"We reached the first level, where they kept some that'd been down a million years. They were due in another hundred thousand to start at the bottom once more and work their way up. According to how' much they suffered—agony meters, adjusted to the spinular system and worked by little batteries strapped on the naked backs. Very in‑genious! If they didn't suffer right they got detoured off on the up shift and had to go to one of the side levels for special treatment. My heart was moved when I saw them there. Oh, Lord, how unfortunate. How sad, how sad. They couldn't see what their sins would cost them. Such a sight moved me to great emotion, oh it was very great emotion. And my friends, of course, that is why I am working so less and less people will have to go to hell. I beseech of you all, do accept Christ as your Saviour. Join the fold. Does it hurt to do it? No. But it will hurt if you don't, oh how it will hurt. Am I asking too much? Really, can you say I'm asking too much? Oh, no, no, not too much."

Marquales interrupted, "What do you think you're doing?"

Simmons became silent.

"I never noticed you trying to save any souls."

Simmons didn't reply.

"Go to sleep!"

Five minutes later the dry whispering recommenced. Marquales decided to ignore it. He would think of other things.

It went on. At first Simmons' attitude was one of compassion, then it became vindictive. Soon he was whispering loudly about a series of hell-tortures. Victims were described as eaten by insects. They were perpetually cut to hamburger by huge gristling machines, while their severed heads looked on. They were molded back to their origi‑nal shape by the bloody hand of Satan, then given a reviving drink of acid, a highball of hell. Men disemboweled women, then fiends sewed them up with hot wires. Women disemboweled men, then fiends, and so on.

Finally Marquales said, "Shut up!"

"What in the world's the matter with you?" whispered Simmons.

Marquales arose and went across the dark room. "Shut up!" he said. "Stop whispering."

"I'm not whispering," said Simmons. "You must imagine it."

Marquales struck at the voice. His fist caught Simmons in the teeth. There was a gasp then long silence. One or two snores came from rooms down the gallery. Marquales felt blood running off his knuckles and he began to be afraid to stand by Simmons' cot. "My hand's bleeding," he said. "Loan me some of your iodine."

"You hit me," whispered Simmons.

Marquales felt his way to Simmons' press and fumbled on the personal-possessions shelf for iodine. He couldn't find the bottle among the jumble of things so he got a match. He had trouble holding the match still, but got the bottle of iodine. Then he wondered how Simmons looked and turned around, holding up the match. Sow-belly sat in bed, eyes wide open, teeth shining.

The sight startled Marquales so he dropped the match and went out of the room down the gallery to the latrine. He stayed ten minutes, then became angry and returned. He walked through the dark to his own press, got a flashlight, and spotted the bunk under the window. Simmons had his head beneath the covers. Marquales sighed and snapped off the flashlight. Thirty minutes later, as he was going to sleep, he heard the whisper again.

Several times a week Simmons awoke before reveille, which was at seven. Perhaps it was the sun that woke him; perhaps his clammy sheets. He would get up, dress, take his bed linen out to the gallery rail, then come back to the room and read one of his books.

When Simmons read he had the habit of making comments. He would say aloud, "True, true. Very good thought." Sometimes he spluttered, "How false a statement!" Occasionally something would impress him as funny. Then he gave an eerie, nervous, rasping noise with "overcome" coughs and gasps. It was as if he were trying to seem amused, but really was not.

The comments didn't always awaken Marquales. But the laughter did. He would look up, curse, and put his pillow over his head. Simmons never paid any attention to such interruptions.

During the first week Marquales found that other freshmen and upperclassmen were beginning to associate him with his roommate. To counteract this it was necessary for him to join in, stepping up his part in the jokes played on "the company crap-catcher."

It was the sergeant Jocko de Paris who found Simmons most interesting. At breakfast the day after Sow-belly puked on the table De Paris said, "Drive by my room with your brutal broom."

Simmons didn't do it. At lunch De Paris made him eat the entire meal at attention, and told him again to report "for a cutting."

That afternoon Marquales suggested to Simmons he'd better go to De Paris' room as ordered. Simmons didn't answer. A few minutes later De Paris came around, slamming back the door against the wall. He said, "Hello, Sow."

Simmons didn't reply.

Jocko smiled. "I said, Hello, Sow."

"Hello."

"Well, by God. I've at last found a nut that can talk. It's enough to upset a man's theory of life. Put a sir on that."

"Hello *sir*."

"Give me some information, Mr. Simmons. Were you born that way, or did you get dropped on your head?"

Simmons swallowed. "Sir, I beg pardon?"

"Grab your morbid ankles," said Jocko. "Hand me that broom, Mr. Marquales."

"No!" said Simmons.

"*What?*"

"Don't strike me, sir! I can't bear pain!"

"Gosh, you're in bad shape. How'd you happen to get that way?"

Simmons answered weakly, "It's my nervous system, sir. I'm very nervous."

"You are?"

"Yes sir. Doctors have said I was."

"Well, I suppose I'd better not cut your ass, then. I understand how a nervous system can act up on you, from the psychiatric point of view."

"*Thank* you, sir," said Simmons.

"However, you'll never get over this trouble, if you're pampered. Do you see what I mean? The idea is, if you have a weakness, fight against it."

"I don't pamper myself, sir," said Simmons.

"I believe you do."

"No, I don't, sir."

"Yes, in my opinion, you do."

"No sir, I really don't pamper myself at all. You see, my moth—"

"Grab those morbid ankles, you insidious brute!"

"Sir?"

"You heard me."

"Do you mean to strike me?"

"Do *I mean* to strike you? Brother, I'm going to hit you so hard your balls will explode. Grab those ankles."

Simmons' lip began to tremble. He pulled back his shoulders and said, "Very well, sir. Beat me if you wish."

De Paris tested the broom, swinging it back and forth in the air. He then poised it over Simmons' upturned rear. "Wait a minute," he said. "Get up."

"Sir?" whispered Simmons.

"Get up. Koble and McCarthy would probably enjoy having a talk with you. I heard them say they didn't think you put your all into a brace."

Jocko strolled out of the room.

"You're really going to get it," said Marquales.

Simmons didn't answer; he remained in a tight brace. A few minutes later De Paris returned with Harold Koble and Philip

[ 16 ]

McCarthy, sergeants and members of the junior class. Marquales came to attention beside Simmons.

"Pop to!" roared Koble. "Grind those necks back, you Misters. Come on, Mr. Simmons, stand up hard, you look like an old bat. Suck up the gut roll and grind that jaw. Stand up like red rock."

The three upperclassmen hurried to Simmons. All put their faces a few inches from his and bellowed simultaneously. The noise was approximate to that of starving lions battling over a kill. Simmons braced so hard he nearly fell over backwards. His lower face was creased in wrinkles from mouth to Adam's apple, his chest puffed to the point of explosion, his shoulder blades touching. Suddenly, his knees flew apart and he crumpled to the floor.

"My God," said McCarthy. "Has he got a weak heart?"

"No sir," said Marquales. "A weak brain."

They laughed in appreciation of the revealing jest and told Marquales he could get out of his shell.

"Watch an educational event," said De Paris. "I'm going to psychoanalyze him."

Marquales wanted to leave the room but was afraid. He went over to the window and tried to make himself unnoticeable. De Paris suddenly stooped over Simmons and made a grab for the freshman's groin. "Gotcha!" Simmons screamed and wriggled to one side. He jumped up and reassumed the brace where he had left off. They all howled with joy.

"You sure are deceptive," said Jocko. "We were fooled." He walked to Simmons, stopping a few feet in front of him. Then he struck a country match on his fingernail, inches from the freshman's nose. Simmons stared with popped eyes at the flame and made greater effort to brace, forcing tiny spasms in the muscle of his neck and shoulder. His trousers quivered in the region of the knees. De Paris slowly pulled out a cigaret, lit it, and blew smoke into the freshman's face. He reached forward and gently removed Simmons' spectacles. They all laughed because Simmons looked more ridiculous without his glasses. The room was quiet for about fifteen seconds. Then Jocko took a deep breath and bellowed, "Stand up, Mister!" Simmons started to shake all over. "BRACE!" yelled De Paris, his mouth in the freshman's ear. They all started to go over him. They did it simultaneously, then took turns. The din increased with in-direct relation to the degree which Simmons braced. It lasted for more than twenty minutes, until the upperclassmen were perspiring nearly as much as Simmons.

"Rest!" said Jocko suddenly. Simmons sagged, blinked in wonder. "It's time for you to be psychoanalyzed some more."

"Yes sir."

"Listen, Sow-belly. I want you to tell me a few things about your-self now we've tried unsuccessfully to brace you. Is that all right with you?"

"Yes sir."

"Okay. I'd like to know whether your mother's a virgin or not."

"What, sir?"

"Is your mother a virgin?"

"I don't know what you mean, sir."

"Mr. Simmons, you're really a mess for the psychiatrist. I ask out of scientific interest, and you sulk. What's the matter with you?"

"My mother is pure," said Simmons.

They laughed softly.

"My mother is pure!" said Simmons. "Don't talk about her!"

"Shut up, Mister," said Koble. "Why don't you tell us about that time you got siff from your nigger maid?"

"Harold!" said De Paris. "Not so vulgar, please, not so vulgar. Use the scientific terminology. Syphilis, not siff. That is actually quite morbid, Harold. Nevertheless now that the insidious question has been asked, do tell us, Mr. Simmons."

"Tell what, sir?"

"Oh, Christ, I'm getting tired of this. Listen, there's one more question. Is it true that you once tapped your sister?"

They chuckled—Koble and McCarthy in an uneasy manner.

"Sir, have you no respect for the dead?" asked Simmons.

Koble and McCarthy looked more uncomfortable, but they laughed when De Paris wailed in imitation, "Sir, have you no respect for the dead?"

"Alas, such sin," replied Simmons hoarsely.

"Alas, such sin," groaned De Paris.

"Sir, you ought to be ashamed in your very soul."

"You're getting too speedy," said De Paris. "Your brain works like a Bulova watch."

"There's nothing wrong with my brain, sir."

"Okay, you've been psychoanalyzed. Now let's carve some of the extra bone from your coccyx. Take hold of those ankles."

Simmons bent over and grabbed his shoe tops. De Paris took the broom from Koble, tested it back and forth with his wrists, and poised it. Then his arms swung back in a graceful arc, and his eyes half shut. The broom came down with a loud whacking noise. Dust clouded up from the trousers and Simmons grunted.

De Paris spelled out F-R-E-S-H-M-A-N. One blow for each letter. There was coagulated blood on Simmons' under-shorts when he took them off that night. Marquales caught a glimpse of Simmons' ass. The scrawny thing was covered with burst blood vessels.

Toward the end of the second week the days settled into a regular pattern of military drill, classes, inspections, bracing on the quadrangle, bracing before eating in the mess hall, study at night, trips to the canteen in the afternoon for coca-colas. Marquales decided that as difficult as it was, he'd adjusted to life with Simmons. Then one night he heard a scream, followed by the shouted words, "God, help, help, help! Help, help!" The shouting dissolved into a gargle. Marquales jumped out of bed and turned on the light, breaking regulations.

Marquales shook him for a long time. Simmons was in the corner under the washbasin, on all fours. He was moaning. When he woke up he was so frightened his body stiffened, and wouldn't move. A wet splotch appeared and grew over the bottom of his pajama bottoms. As the splotch grew larger Simmons began to choke. "Get up," said Marquales. "Please get up. Come on, Simmie."

By the time the cadet Officer of the Day arrived to see about the noise Sow-belly Simmons was back in bed. He hadn't bothered to change the pajamas.

The next day Marquales went to see Pete Layne and asked to be moved. He was put with two other freshmen: a boy of twenty named Les Wintermine, a boy of nineteen named Ben Hulitt.

# 3

"Mister, what's the matter with your eyes?" asked Koble.

"Nothing, sir." Marquales dropped the magazine he was trying to read. "My mother had brown ones, my father had blue. I happened to get an eye from each."

"Anybody else in your family like that?"

"I'm the only freak, sir."

Ben Hulitt said, "Robbie, I thought your older brother was born with three navels."

"No, two."

"Shut up. Somebody give me a cigaret."

Wintermine provided it, then lit one for himself.

"Did I give you permission to smoke?"

"Sure you did, Mr. Koble."

"For all the respect I get around here I might as well be a dog."

"Sir," said Hulitt. "Once you give a freshman an inch he'll give you six inches."

"Shut up," said Koble. "You talk too much. Always jabbering, every time I come in here."

"Yessir!" said Hulitt, saluting.

"Mr. Hulitt," said Koble. "You're as cute as the pecker on a baby jigg."

The three roommates laughed despite the fact they'd heard Jocko de Paris say it before. "You're the laziest polecat that I know," said Koble. "Do you spend your life laying on that cot in your drawers?"

"Sir, you saw me today sweating to death with the squad. I've lost ten pounds the last month. Ten pounds I can't afford."

"How much do you weigh?"

"One sixty-five."

"You have fat on you. I weigh one hundred eighty, but there's not an ounce on me." Koble smiled, waiting for a comment. He laughed hoarsely and remarked in an offhand manner, "I'm good natured or I'd cut your tails."

"Why would you do that?" asked Hulitt.

"You run crap on me every time I come in here."

"What time is it, Marquales?" asked Wintermine loudly. "Time for leave yet?"

"It's three."

Koble grinned and looked up at the ceiling in thought. His teeth were tiny and blue colored. There were little spaces between them. His legs were chubby, the upper part of his body long. He looked like an overgrown dwarf—a few cadets called him "Dopey," after the character in *Snow White and the Seven Dwarfs*. Koble liked that.

"Now, time'll pass," he said.

No one answered.

"Are you frosh going to enjoy your leave?"

Hulitt got up from his cot and put on a pair of Academy trousers, then carefully tucked his shirt-tail.

"I remember when I got my first leave when I was a freshman. I was so glad to get out of this hellhole I went out and drank a ton of beer."

Marquales picked up his magazine and Wintermine went and gazed out of the window at the parade field. Hulitt looked in the washbasin mirror and combed his hair. Koble squinted at each of them, then said, "In those days we didn't get out in any month. We waited six weeks."

"That's correct," said Jocko de Paris from the door. "We waited six insidious weeks."

The freshmen turned to look at De Paris, but none popped to attention. Jocko slouched into the room. "Well," he said. "You freshmen are still running crap. Mr. Wintermine, how are you."

"Fine, sir."

De Paris chuckled. "Give me a cigaret." Wintermine gave it and Hulitt struck the match. "One of these days you're going to fail to pop to when I walk in here and your fate will be settled."

"These freshmen aren't bad, Jocko," said Koble.

"What?"

"Of course they aren't military."

"Harold, I'm shocked. These freshmen aren't anything. Take a

[ 22 ]

look at Mr. Hulitt standing there. What are you doing, Mister? Primping up so you can tear it off this evening?"

"Combing my hair, sir."

"He's lost ten pounds," said Koble.

De Paris walked toward Hulitt. "Had some of that meat worked off you? How much do you weigh, about one seven five?"

Marquales, who weighed one hundred and thirty, read his magazine. Hulitt told De Paris his new weight of one hundred sixty-five. De Paris answered, "I've got you beat ten pounds." He then walked behind Hulitt, slipped his arms around him and started to squeeze the freshman's chest. Hulitt wriggled slightly, and De Paris squeezed harder, his tanned face going red.

"Come on," grunted Hulitt. "Turn me loose, sir."

"Make me."

"Okay." Hulitt's plump arms flew out and De Paris' hold was broken. Jocko stared, then patted Hulitt on the shoulder.

Koble said to Marquales, "Give me a cigaret."

De Paris strolled over toward the window, sighing. "I wish it was four," he said.

"So do I," said Wintermine.

"It's morbid the way you freshmen act so intimate. Don't you know I'm an upperclassman, Mr. Wintermine?"

"Yes sir."

"Then why don't you put sirs on your sentences?"

"Yes sir. But the other day you said freshman regulations were silly."

"I said they were silly?"

"You said you didn't care for them."

"Put a sir on that."

"Sir."

"I do care for them. Christ. Do I act as if I want them ignored?"

"All right, sir. But you were fighting with Hulitt and that's against regulations, sir."

"We weren't fighting," laughed Hulitt.

"Mr. Wintermine, you're starting to be cute?"

[ 23 ]

"Hulitt's strong, sir," said Wintermine nervously.

"What does that have to do with it?" De Paris stepped behind Wintermine and slipped his arms around him. "Break my hold." He squeezed.

"Come on," grumbled Koble. "Let's go get our mail."

"Just a minute," puffed Jocko. "Let Mr. Wintermine break this."

"I can't," said the freshman, giggling.

"Come on. Try and get free, I'm ready for you."

"No sir."

Koble called out, "Jocko, goddamn it!"

"Try and get loose!"

"Quit hugging that freshman. Do you love him or something?"

De Paris laughed and released Wintermine. He and Koble walked out of the room.

Wintermine went over and sat down on Hulitt's cot. "That scoundrel," he said.

"They mooch cigarets all the time," said Marquales. "I'd rather be braced by Cleer than have them around."

"They're all right," said Hulitt. "They aren't bad upperclassmen. Cleer, or Richardson, or most of those sophomore corporals would never act as friendly as they do most of the time."

"They aren't really friendly," said Marquales.

"Nothing ever suits you. And here in a few minutes we're about to get our first leave."

"It's an hour. Port George isn't much, anyhow, from what I can tell."

"You're a pessimist," said Hulitt.

Marquales didn't reply. Hulitt grinned and said, "That reminds me. Did you ever hear the Jewish joke about the girl who went to buy a stamp from the Pissmaster?"

"Let's go get our mail," said Wintermine.

As each freshman stepped out of the room onto the gallery floor he popped to attention, then marched directly forward to the gallery rail where he executed a square turn and headed toward the stairs at regular march step, chin back and chest up.

They reached the staircase and Hulitt snapped his arms to double-time position. He swiftly jogged down the steps. Marquales followed, then Wintermine. Cutting the first corner Marquales glanced up and saw Wintermine stooping over casually tying his shoe—an extreme insult to freshman regulations, which specified freshmen be constantly at attention in barracks unless in their rooms or the latrine.

Marquales then saw Larrence Corger standing a few feet away. Corger walked forward. Marquales pulled his chin back stiffly and strode past him in the freshman Frankenstein step. A split minute later he heard the senior's voice:

"Mister there! What are you doing?"

Marquales cut the next corner and tapped down more stairs, Hulitt in front of him. Outside the barracks they waited to see if Wintermine would follow. Ten minutes passed and other freshmen angled stiffly out of Hemphill Barracks. Finally Wintermine appeared, red and perspiring. He was more shocked than they were that Corger had let him go. "I was braced something terrible," he said.

They walked on across campus to the post office.


Larrence Corger was Cadet Colonel, highest ranking man at The Academy. It was said he had the energy, brains, and physical strength of five. He was perfectly military; neat, erect, reserved. At the annual hops, which he generally opened by a waltz with his fiancée, his glittering figure, complete with saber, red sash, and heavy rows of gold braid, overpowered the girls on the armory floor and most of the cadets as well. Corger had the reputation for being a man born to lead other men. He was the personal friend of General Draughton and often had tea with him.

Corger's face was odd, a dark bronze color the year around. But he had light blue eyes and yellow hair, which made him very handsome. However, his nose was so large it earned him his nickname, "Corger the Hawk."

Corger the Hawk was star and captain of The Academy boxing squad. A heavyweight, both his right and left hands were deadly. He was very fast for such a big man, and it was known he'd received two or three professional offers. Corger had a trick in fighting: he never struck what he called "middle" blows. His punches were either very soft or terribly powerful. For perhaps three or four rounds he would slap his man, then suddenly nail him with tremendous force. The idea was to conserve energy.

But he had many other abilities. He was an expert dash man on the track team; he once clocked 9.7 for one hundred yards. He was one of the commanders of the Senior Drill Platoon, which General Draughton called "the most capable small marching body to my knowledge." This drill platoon executed astonishing maneuvers between halves of The Academy football games. But Corger was also a contributing editor of the school magazine, *Port Arms*. Often he wrote editorials that were so good they were used as models of composition for the freshman English classes.

He possessed a set of Atlas Bar Bells. He was said to be able to lift great amounts of weight. Once at Jamaica Shore he picked up his fiancée and held her over his head with one hand—another cadet took a snapshot of this and mailed it to a strength magazine. To the horror of General Draughton (and Corger himself), on the following month newsstands all over the country showed a magazine cover of the Cadet Colonel of The Academy in bathing shorts holding a blonde in the air.

But Corger had his weaknesses. The principal one was his roommate, one of the few men in school who dared call him by his family name, "Laurie." This roommate was a strong liability. Roger Gatt was his name. Everyone except Corger called him "Black" Gatt—but not to his face.

No one understood why Larrence Corger roomed with Gatt. There was a rumor that Gatt paid part of Corger's tuition. Some cadets said the reason Corger liked Gatt was that he was sorry for him. Another explanation was that Gatt was the only person Corger could find who would be his sparring partner on the boxing team. Other cadets said the two men simply liked each other.

Gatt started school when Corger did, yet in the latter's senior year was only a sophomore. The big man took an assortment of junior, sophomore, and freshman courses, with first-year subjects predominating. He hoped some day to graduate. But it was expected when Corger himself finished the authorities would decline Gatt's enrollment the next year.

For he had failings more serious than an inability to pass courses. He had such a temper he was constantly being suspended from the football team, despite his ability as a tackle. His temper prevented him from being able to box at all—with anyone except his roommate. He drank and got into trouble in Port George. It was known Corger several times intervened in his favor and saved him from expulsion.

It was often said that Corger was all a cadet ought to be, and Gatt all a cadet ought not to be. Corger stood third in his class; Gatt was a poor student. Corger never went to any of the whore houses on Luck Street; Gatt lived in them on week ends. Corger had practically no money and was careful in spending what he had; Gatt was wealthy and spent money in a wild manner. Corger drank water; Gatt didn't. They were both twenty-four years old.

At the Guardroom the Amanuensis, an ugly young sophomore with a "crew" haircut, ordered Marquales, Winterminc, and Hulitt to pull their chins in—just to make certain they knew how, he said. They all knew how. "Okay, Misters," said the sophomore. "Drive on away. Get back in a sober condition before midnight."

As they went out the side door the Officer of the Day said, "Halt." They froze.

"Do you men have on garters?"

Each pulled up a trouser leg, exposing garters.

"Fooled you then, Colton," said the Amanuensis.

The senior addressed as Colton smiled and waved his hand in dismissal. "Carry on," he said in a husky voice. "And have a nice leave."

"Thank you, sir," said Hulitt. The O. D. beamed at him. Hulitt added, "We're going to take advantage of liberty."

"See that you do," came the pleasant, slightly hoarse reply. The O. D. then turned and picked up a clipboard, which he scanned in a preoccupied manner. Wintermine, Hulitt, and Marquales marched

[ 27 ]

across the room. At the door Marquales looked back and saw the Amanuensis picking with a knife at his fingernails. The senior peered at the clipboard, then his brown eyes rolled up and met the freshman's. Colton smiled. Then the roommates went on to Port George.

At eleven-fifteen they walked out of the movie house to the street. Hulitt stared at a large, tinted photo of Carole Lombard. "She didn't have much of a part."

"It wasn't bad," said Wintermine.

For a few minutes they stood around the front of the theater. Then they turned and slowly walked away. Marquales gazed at the street lamps of old Port George. "Look at those," he said. "They look like gaslights."

"This is a hell of a town," said Hulitt.

"But it's got its points," said Marquales superciliously.

"What points?"

"It's better than Atlanta."

"Who said anything about Atlanta? I've never even been there."

"Go there some time. It's a stinking place. They haven't even got any garbage collectors."

"Is that right?"

"Yes, but Atlanta has its points, too."

"*Five* points?" asked Wintermine, grinning.

"What's that?" said Hulitt.

"Where Peachtree Street branches out down there below Davison-Paxon's," said Marquales. "But I meant something else. The thing about Atlanta, other than the wonderful people that live there such as Vivien Leigh, is the fact that it's better than Macon. Now there's a rotten town. It doesn't have a plumbing system."

"I gather you don't like southern cities?" said Wintermine.

"No, I don't," said Marquales. "I like Chicago."

"Jocko de Paris is from Chicago."

"Don't blame Chicago. Besides, Jocko is really from *Atlanta,* which just goes to show you."

"Well, I think southern towns are much better," said Wintermine. "You don't get all that dirt and crampiness, people are friendly— what difference does it make about size? It's quality that counts."

"What's that down the street?" asked Hulitt.

A small crowd was gathered on a corner a block away.

"It's a fight," said Hulitt. "Let's go."

They ran, weaving through people who had just come out of the theater. The group on the corner was pressed in a circle around three gray figures in the uniform of The Academy. The crowd was shouting with laughter.

"What's going on?" panted Hulitt.

"They're drunk," called Wintermine.

As Marquales drew nearer to the circle he saw what it was. One cadet was standing up at rigid attention under a street lamp.

"Sow-belly Simmons," said Hulitt. "Jesus, look at him."

Simmons' cap was gone and his dark hair was tangled on his forehead. He was bracing. By his side was the jug-headed freshman Tim Bailey; a few feet from Bailey stood Carlton Leroy. Bailey was bracing Simmons at the top of his voice. Leroy was giggling.

Simmons stood in a violent brace, chin buried in his neck. His belly was a sucked-in vacant space and his thin chest was puffed up for all it was worth. He didn't seem to be breathing and had lost his glasses somewhere; his eyes were shut tight. He was grinning. From time to time he let out a wild giggle.

Passers-by took one look and burst into laughter. They continued to laugh as they listened to Tim Bailey, who was "spitting blood." "Stand up, you hunk of scum! Throw down red stuff out that numerous nose and suck up the pondrous gut! Stand up, boot ball!"

Simmons threw back his head and gave one of the wild laughs. Bailey yelled, "POP TO!" Simmons came out of the brace and began to do a tap dance on the sidewalk. Bailey shouted a stream of furious language, but Simmons flung his arms and legs about, mouth open, laughing.

"Pop to!" screamed Bailey in a drunken voice. "This ain't a dance floor! Pop to, boot ball, or I'll report you to the General!"

[ 29 ]

Several of the high-school girls in the audience called out, "Swing it, Cadet!"

Simmons responded with a shout and flung his arms in the air, striking his black Academy shoes upon the sidewalk. Suddenly his long body spun upside down and his head crashed against the concrete. The crowd gasped and there was a solemn murmur. Simmons rolled over several times then got to his knees. He sagged back in a heap, unconscious.

"Let's get out of here," said Marquales to Wintermine. "They'll blame us." He tugged at Hulitt's sleeve and pushed out through the people. Marquales heard shouts: "Call an ambulance!" He said to his roommates, "We'd better run."

They cut off Mall Avenue and headed down Quenton Lane, a dark residential street.

"The North Port George bus down Woodrow Wilson Avenue," panted Hulitt. "I had enough tonight."

A car down the block glared its headlights on them. Marquales said, "Wait. You'll see. They'd blame us for letting Bailey go on with that."

The car with the bright headlights coasted slowly toward them. They all stared. "That looks like Jocko's roadster," said Marquales.

"It is," answered Hulitt.

The car rolled on, then began to curve over to the wrong side of the street. About fifty yards from them it picked up speed and bumped over the curb. It came hobbling along, half on the sidewalk, headlights shining.

"Watch out!" said Wintermine. They ran up onto the lawn of the house on their right.

The car suddenly halted, and there was a shout from within. "Hey, boys!"

"Where's the driver?" asked Hulitt.

Marquales ran forward and threw open the car door. A gray form sagged out face downward to the lawn of the nearby house. They turned the body over and saw it did belong to Jocko de Paris.

"Look at the scoundrel!" said Wintermine in an awed voice.

**4** De Paris lay on the sidewalk, one arm twisted under his kidneys. They stared down at him.

"Let's go," said Wintermine.

"But we'll have to take him out to school," said Hulitt.

"He's none of our affair."

"We have to, though."

"No we don't. He can stay where he is."

"Les," said Hulitt. "I wouldn't leave a dog lying on the ground like that."

"Neither would I, but Jocko de Paris isn't as good as a dog."

Hulitt turned to Marquales. "Are you going to help me?"

"I'm leaving," said Wintermine. "You come on with me, Robbie, and if Ben wants to stay, all right."

"No," answered Marquales. "We might as well drive him out there."

"All right," said Wintermine. He began to walk away.

"Hey, Les, wait!"

"He'll come back," whispered Marquales.

"I don't see how anybody could leave a man on the ground."

The smell inside the car made Marquales ill. He turned to lower one of the windows. Through the rear-view pane he caught a glimpse of Wintermine's figure standing at the edge of light from a street lamp fifty yards away.

Hulitt said, "Jocko has the keys."

De Paris was sitting up on the sidewalk, eyes open.

"Give those keys here."

"No," answered De Paris thickly.

"Come on, be nice."

Jocko clawed at the sound of the voice and Hulitt grabbed his hand. There was a grunt and Hulitt said, "Hey, Robbie. Catch up."

Marquales caught the ring and started the roadster.

Hulitt wrestled with De Paris in an attempt to get him to his feet. "What's the idea?" asked Jocko. He spit on the sidewalk. "Get away."

Hulitt sighed, then stooped. "Listen here. This is Ben Hulitt and you know me. In the car is Marquales. You know him, too. Understand?"

"Yes sir."

"Who are we?"

"Yes sir."

Hulitt laughed.

"Ben, will you stop playing around?" said Marquales.

"This is the important part, Jocko. We want to help you and get you back to The Academy. Will you co-operate?"

"Yes sir."

"Get up."

Nothing happened, so Hulitt slipped his arms around Jocko's belly and hauled him to his feet.

De Paris sagged down.

"Come on!" said Hulitt.

Jocko giggled, spitting between his legs on the sidewalk.

Hulitt pulled him to his feet and started to carry him toward the open rear door. Jocko went limp, sagging once more to the sidewalk.

"Don't you know how to stand up?"

De Paris giggled and waved one arm. Marquales called, "Get up!"

De Paris pretended to weep. "Don't be mean. I'm drunk," he whined.

"You get in the car like a good guy," said Hulitt.

Jocko crawled into the roadster and Hulitt banged the door. In a sudden burst of energy De Paris passed through the car, opened the other door, and raced away down the street.

Marquales and Hulitt ran after him, shouting. Then Jocko reached Les Wintermine, whom he tried to embrace. Wintermine grabbed him by the shoulder and threw him down to the pavement.

"Les!"

"I was afraid you couldn't handle this, Ben," said Wintermine nervously. "Let's go ahead now and take him out there."

Jocko had cut his cheek. Hulitt pointed and said to Wintermine, "You ought to be ashamed. Look at that."

De Paris burst into more mock tears. "I am," he said. "I was a bastard for trying to get away. I'm no damn good."

Hulitt put his arm on Jocko's shoulder. "I didn't mean you."

"Pet him," said Wintermine. "That's right."

Marquales said, "It's a quarter to twelve."

De Paris continued to weep and Hulitt gave him a handkerchief. He put it to his nose and blew. Wintermine snatched away the handkerchief and threw it on the street. "Who gave you permission to do that?" he demanded.

Jocko crouched, turning his head. "I'm sick," he moaned. "I'll puke if you don't stop bothering me."

Wintermine pushed him into the car. "You rat!" De Paris slid down the car seat to the floor then tried to crawl out and escape on the other side.

"Catch him!" said Marquales.

Wintermine grabbed the neck of De Paris' blouse and pulled. "Hold still, I'll choke you."

"Don't hurt him," said Hulitt.

"Listen," groaned De Paris. "I realize I'm a bastard."

Marquales started the car and drove down Quenton Lane to Woodrow Wilson Avenue.

"Jocko ought to have some coffee before he goes in. He ought to be sobered up a little."

"Coffee?"

Hulitt pointed to a burger-wagon.

"Why of course," said Wintermine. "Let's manicure his nails, too."

Marquales pulled the roadster onto the burger-wagon parking lot.

Hulitt patted Jocko on the back and said, "Do you know where you are?"

"No."

"It's after twelve," said Marquales.

"Twelve?" De Paris sat down on the running board of the car and lit a cigaret. It slipped through his fingers. He tried to pick it up and lost his balance, falling off the running board to the ground.

"I can't even sit up," he groaned.

Hulitt said, "You've got to go through the Guardroom. Are you sober enough?"

"I'm so drunk I want to die," said Jocko.

"Maybe they'll shoot you tomorrow at dawn."

Wintermine said bitterly, "Stop laughing, Ben. It's not funny. We might be expelled for this."

"They won't kick us out."

"Why aren't you willing to listen to reason?"

De Paris had got up from the grass and was leaning against the car, retching.

"Let's leave him here," said Wintermine. "He's hopeless."

"Go ahead and leave," said Hulitt.

"Ben, you might disapprove of my attitude but I can't see any reason for helping him now. We're in trouble as it is. Can't you see every minute we spend trying to bring him to his senses makes it worse?"

"Why don't you go on alone?" interrupted Marquales.

"If I were you I wouldn't talk so big."

"What's Robbie done?" asked Hulitt.

"You think you are funny, don't you, Ben? That's all right with me. Go ahead and think so."

Marquales said, "Jocko's gone."

They all looked. De Paris was nowhere in sight.

"I'm reporting at the Guardroom," said Wintermine. He walked away into the moonlight.

Hulitt said, "We should have watched him. He's probably hiding behind a car. You go down that way, I'll go up here!" He ran off.

Marquales sat down on the running board. Far away he heard Hulitt calling, then there was another voice, sly and snuffling. Marquales dropped his head between his knees and looked upside down under the car. Stretched out comfortably and smoking a cigaret was De Paris.

"Look," he whispered.

"I see you, Jocko. Come on out."

"No."

"Come on out."

De Paris crawled from under the car and pulled himself up on the running board. He put his arm on Marquales' shoulder. "Give me another cigaret?"

"You've got one," said Marquales, wriggling him off.

"Act white, will you? Don't be that way."

"Hey Ben! Here he is."

A moment later Hulitt ran up, puffing.

"He was under the car."

"You're a fine fellow, I swow!"

"It's nearly twelve-thirty," said Marquales.

"The goddamn bastard treats me like a hound, coming up, grabbing me, shoving me over! Christ! What have I done to rate a god-blasted curve like that? You bunch of bullies."

"Jocko, sober up!"

"Go shit in your hat."

"Do you want me to bust you one on the jaw?"

"Hit me! Go ahead—do you think you can? I doubt it. You couldn't even *touch* me, much less hit me. Here it *is,* here it is, let's see you lay on it—by the god-blasted cock-ferglers you can't do a *thing!*"

"Shut up."

"I know what I'm doing. I know every second of this whole evening. I'm not drunk any more. If you want to get smart, then I dare you. Whatever you're up to, I can match it. If you don't believe me, by God, try and find out!"

They half carried De Paris from the parking lot to Hemphill Barracks.

"What are we going to do?" whispered Hulitt.

Marquales didn't reply.

"What can we tell the O. D.? We've got to have an excuse."

They then heard a noise and Wintermine stepped forward, tiptoeing. He whispered, "I thought it'd be better for us if we went in at the same time. What are we going to tell them?"

"Let's just tell them what happened," said Marquales. "More or less."

Outside the barred gate was a tiny bell with the sign: RING FOR GUARDROOM. Through the bars Marquales could see the interior of Hemphill Barracks with its moonlit quadrangle and gloomy tiers. The inner foyer was black. He raised his hand to straighten his Academy cap, then noticed a dark figure just inside the gate.

A cigaret end came up and glowed, showing the face of the O. D. Marquales stopped. Then the senior raised his arm and a gurgling sound came from behind the bars. The gurgling stopped and there was a deep sigh. Colton again raised the cigaret to his mouth and inhaled. For a second his face was half illumined by the cherry end. Suddenly the spot fell and he exclaimed, "Sir?"

A flashlight shone upon them. "Thank God," said Colton. "First I thought you were Lieutenant Suhlman." He snapped off the flashlight and there was the clinking sound of keys. A moment later the gate creaked and swung open.

"Hurry in quick," said Colton in a low voice. "Who's that with you?"

"Jocko de Paris, sir," said Wintermine.

"Please, not so loud! Hurry on to your rooms."

"You're not going to report us, sir?" asked Marquales.

"No. Don't mention it to a soul." Colton stared at Marquales. "Don't I know you? What's your name?"

"Robert Marquales, sir."

"Marquales, you and your friends keep this quiet."

The freshmen nodded.

"Be quiet going upstairs," whispered the O. D. "Especially by the senior officers' rooms. Make De Paris be mum. Now, Marquales, you come to see me tomorrow afternoon and tell me what this is all about. My name is Carroll Colton and I live on the bottom gallery and I'll be home around four."

[ 36 ]

Sow-belly Simmons and Tim Bailey were not at breakfast the following morning. Carlton Leroy, however, was there. After the meal Marquales stopped by his room and asked him what happened the night before.

Leroy was frightened; his face was a sick mud-color. His cheeks were generally the hue and shape of wax apples. He was a young man of nineteen with a sloping stomach and enormous butter-colored ass. There was something wrong with him; he had breasts, and undeveloped genitals.

"You and Bailey were ragging him on and I saw you," said Marquales. "Why not tell me the rest? I'm curious."

"No!" said Leroy. "You didn't see me ragging him."

"Whose idea was it to start the bracing?"

"Tim's idea."

"What happened when Simmons fell down?"

"Weren't you there?"

"I left, dope."

"Don't tell on me. I ask you, don't tell them."

"Why should I?"

"Sow-belly was lying there on the sidewalk," said Leroy rapidly. "What could I do? We got out in the crowd then an ambulance come up. When Sow-belly was laid on the stretcher he jumped off and started to sing. Then I heard a policeman tell him he was going to be sorry for doing that. So they put him in the ambulance and Tim and me had no idea what become of him until about 5 A.M. this morning.

"But they took him out to school and turned him over to Frune. Don't ask me, but he got out of the infirmary and came back to barracks. There must not have been anything wrong with him, but Tim and me thought he was dead until we saw him get up. Then this morning he came to our room at five and began to curse Tim. Tim slept. Simmons said he was praying, but he wasn't. And he meant to report Tim to General D.

"I got it in the moron's head he couldn't involve Carlton Leroy in this thing. At first he wanted me to get down and pray for forgiveness. Did you ever? But I wouldn't do it and I said, 'Look here, Sow-belly, come off that crap, you bastard! Keep your jaw shut or I'll beat your balls off.' He began to tremble. 'Carlton,' he says. 'I won't.'

"That's all I know and all I hope to know. If they ask me about it I don't know what they were talking about."

"I don't see why you had to take him out and make him drink."

"He wanted to do it."

"You're lying. He'd never do it unless somebody made him."

"The thing about Sow-belly is he's stupid. He hasn't got any sense, not that I think I'm brilliant."

"You had nothing to do with any of it."

"It was Tim Bailey, my boy. Tim Bailey did that stuff to him last evening, not me."

"You were innocent, I know."

"It's true so help me God. You know I wouldn't bother Simmons—why would I want to do that? Robbie, the truth is, I was hanging around."

"Why didn't Bailey wake up when you were talking to Simmons?"

"Why do you ask that?"

"I just wondered."

"Well, Tim was still drunk this morning at five, that's why. He had a lot more than me. He had more than Sow-belly, too. But Sow-belly got drunker."

"Why don't you call him by his name?"

"His name's Sow-belly as far as I'm concerned."

"Okay. Now if Simmons doesn't tell on you, then Bailey will."

"Oh, no Bailey won't."

"Where is he now?"

Leroy licked his lips, frowning.

"Why be mysterious?" asked Marquales. "I might tell on you my-self if you don't satisfy my curiosity."

"I'm telling you—the General's got him."

"Then you had hard luck. The General will cross-examine it out of him."

"What?"

"Just wait and see if Bailey doesn't tell them you were along."

"So your grandma says!"

Marquales took the blankets off his bed and folded them into a twenty-inch square. He folded the sheets in the same style and placed them on top of the blankets. The pillow he stuck upon the sheets, then put the entire stack on top of his press, adjusting it precisely to the edge. He slid the mattress of his bed into a slot at the foot of the press, then pushed the folded-down springs into their space under the mattress slot. He took a dirty rag he'd hidden behind the press, soaked it in water, and went over the wooden parts of the press. He gave the iron bars in the window a cleansing and made certain there was no rust on them.

He cleaned his fingernails, brushed his teeth, combed his hair, spent ten minutes shining his shoes; put on a new coat of polish and shined the shoes again, then put on a coat of higher grade finishing polish and shined them for the last time. He picked stray bits of lint off the blue stripes on his Academy trousers.

He put on the trousers, a white polo shirt, and his gray dress blouse. He zipped up the blouse tight to his neck and had Hulitt do him the favor of fastening the throat clips.

"Ten minutes before first call," said Wintermine. Hulitt and Wintermine were ready. Marquales snatched up his rifle and drove a few patches through it with the ramrod. He wiped the metal parts with an oily rag, then splashed rubbing alcohol over the oil and rubbed fiercely.

"Better not let anybody see you do that to that gun," said Wintermine.

"Ten demerits," said Hulitt.

Marquales put on more oil and cut it off with alcohol. Finally the gun was cleaned. In doing the job he'd soiled his white gloves. They were his last fresh ones so he borrowed an extra pair from Hulitt. Wriggling, he slipped into his crosswebbing. It got tangled and Hulitt helped him straighten it out. Marquales then attached the brass centerpiece and looked at it in the mirror. It badly needed shining. In a frenzy he snatched it from the crossed bands of webbing and scrubbed with a blitz cloth. The gloves were stained a black-green color on the fingertips.

At that moment the bugle blew first call. Marquales said, "Where's my waist belt?" His roommates were already halfway out the door on their way to the quadrangle.

He found the waist belt on top of Wintermine's press, then slipped it around the blouse, grabbed his rifle, hitched to port arms—then cursed and ran back for his cap. He gave the vizor a brush with his sleeve and pressed the cap square over his eyes. He hitched the rifle to port arms and marched on out of the room.

The two-minute steel blew as he took his place on the quadrangle. Upperclassmen strolled among the freshmen looking for flaws and making certain that all braced. From time to time Marquales heard an upperclassman shout: "Pull that neck back!" "Ram in that dumb dome!" He caught a glimpse of Jocko de Paris, who looked ill. Jocko walked by once, but said nothing.

Inspection began after orders from the cadet major. Marquales waited at attention. Ten minutes passed then R. C. Chester, Marquales' platoon sergeant, ordered softly: "P-toon . . . at ease."

Marquales slumped, then nervously ran his gloves over the rifle to pick up last-minute dust. The quadrangle echoed every few seconds with the sound of cadets bringing up their rifles to "inspection arms" —first the smack as the hand slaps the underside of the rifle, a thud as it grabs the butt, and a click as the bolts are thrown.

One of the several inspecting groups passed through the lines of the front platoon of Company Twelve. At that point Platoon Sergeant Chester called in a low voice, "P-toon . . . ten-chht."

The members of the inspecting group were: Major Roy Pearson, Commandant of Hemphill Barracks; Cadet Major Don Harris; Cadet Captain Peter Layne; Cadet First Sergeant Michaelson. They started down the line of the third platoon a few yards from Marquales' position. He felt his heart pounding with the usual anxiety. Finally they reached the cadet next to him. He heard that cadet snap his rifle to port and execute inspection arms with the click of the bolt.

Marquales tugged his gun clumsily upward, snatched at the mechanism, ducking down his head for the split-second demanded as the bolt is thrown. It was a snappier inspection arms than he'd thought he could do. Major Pearson reached out and plucked the rifle from his hands, turned it up and looked through the bore at the sky. The Major held the gun a few inches from his eyes, then murmured to Cadet Captain Layne. The stacking hook of Marquales' gun bore a flick of rust on its underside.

"Pull him."

"Yes sir."

"What's the trouble with those gloves?"

"Sir," said Marquales. "I got them dusty when cleaning my brass."

"You ought to know better than to wear gloves when cleaning your brass. And that brass could be better. Look at Cadet Layne's brass." Marquales stared: Layne's brass centerpiece gleamed like a jewel. "Pull him for brass and gloves. His vizor looks murky. Did you put vaseline on that vizor?"

"No sir."

"Pull him for that murky vizor." Major Pearson tossed back the gun to Marquales, who caught it and whipped it down in two snappy movements, cracking the toes of his right foot.

"Don't slam that gun like that!"

"Sir, it didn't hit the pavement, but my toe."

Major Pearson put his hands on his khaki hips. "What's this man's name?"

Layne replied, "Marquales, R., sir."

"I want him thoroughly pulled," said the Major. "Five demerits for general sloppiness. Marquales, don't come on this quadrangle again put together slovenly. Move on."

Room inspection followed personal inspection. Marquales received one demerit for the way his shirts were folded, two demerits for dust on press, one demerit for the condition of his spare shoes. Major Pearson did the inspecting.

"I believe I pulled you this morning on the quadrangle?"

"Yes sir."

"Improve, or you won't qualify here. Understand me?"

"Yes sir."

After inspection Marquales pulled the springs of his bed from under the press and tugged out his mattress from its slot. He took off his dress blouse and lay down and went to sleep. He'd received eleven demerits in all.

Hulitt awakened him a few minutes before time for dinner formation. He hurried into the gray-cotton Academy shirt. The first bugle blew a few seconds after he'd put the black tie around his neck.

On the quadrangle he was braced by Howard Knowleson, George Cleer, Harold Koble, and others. After ten minutes the bugle sounded last call and the upperclassmen took their places. The cadet major called the battalion to attention, the company captains reported, and shortly thereafter Company Eight swung around smartly out the rear gate of Hemphill Barracks, off on the three-hundred-yard march to the mess hall. Companies Nine, Ten, Eleven, and Twelve followed in succession.

It was seldom that Cleer, who at this time was Marquales' mess chief, ever felt it necessary to brace a freshman during the actual eating of a meal. He said that such a procedure possibly hurt the digestion. However, on this day he required all freshmen at his table to eat at attention. Passing the hour on the front four inches of his chair, Marquales wondered what was causing the action. By way of stealthy glances he saw that many freshmen at other tables were also bracing, particularly freshmen with seniors for mess chiefs.

At the end of the meal the corps was called to attention by Cadet Captain-Adjutant Starkson. There was a long silence, then the voice of Cadet Colonel Larrence Corger came over the mess-hall public address.

"Five minutes after termination of this meal there will be a special formation on each barracks quadrangle; company captains will march their men directly to the armory and there assemble them in military fashion. Dress uniform with sidearms will be worn."

Corger paused, then snapped, "Rest!"

Coming out of the mess hall Marquales heard one sophomore observe to another that the special formation meant a speech from General Draughton. Marquales went on to his room and put on his dress blouse again, throwing the gray shirt into a cubbyhole of his press. He slipped his hands into the dirty white gloves and strapped on his waist belt. He adjusted his cap and marched from the room. At the gallery rail he executed a square turn and passed on toward the stairs.

From one of the rooms he heard Carlton Leroy's whining voice. A moment later the door of the room flew open and Leroy walked out at attention. Marquales halted to avoid bumping into him.

Then jug-head Tim Bailey came out. He was not at attention and he didn't cut the corner. His cap was on the side of his head and there was a cigaret between his thick lips.

"What are you staring at?" he said to Marquales. "Do you think I give a horse-shit?" He spat onto the gallery floor, first removing the cigaret from his mouth.

*5* General A. L. Draughton let his eyes pass carefully over the assembled cadet corps. He stood with his long arms folded across the ribbons on his chest; his stance would have made most men look relaxed. He wore no hat, and the hair on his head, clipped short at the top, looked like an iron crown.

Behind General Draughton stood several of the U. S. Army officers stationed at The Academy. All were in brown dress uniform; most had their arms behind them at parade rest. They stood on the elevated rostrum ten feet over the level of the armory floor. The sixteen hundred men down below stood in a tight military rectangle.

The General said, "Gentlemen of the cadet corps." His voice was hoarse, yet deep and resounding, that of a practiced orator. He paused, glancing once more across the regiment, then folded his arms and began to speak.

"Gentlemen, on yesterday, the freshman class of this institution was permitted to visit the city of Port George. This was the first regularly scheduled general leave of our present academic year; however, no recommendations were given to those men. It had been assumed that they, as gentlemen and prospective officers of the United States Army, would instinctively comprehend the proper manner of comporting themselves in public, under the general view of those not connected with this institution—not connected other than to the accidental extent of being residents of the city of Port George and thus our civilian neighbors, as it were.

"I have no desire to fail to make myself perfectly clear, gentlemen, and I am not going to try to gloss over the ugly facts of this situation. Therefore, I inform you, if you are unaware of it, that the conduct of the freshman class on yesterday evening was far from being in accordance with what is to be demanded.

"It is by way of considerable personal humiliation that I issued the command ordering this formation. Gentlemen of the cadet corps, if indeed you deserve that appellation, I inform you in absolute terms that The Academy does not suffer the presence of those unequipped to behave in a proper manner.

[ 44 ]

"I will narrate to you specific instances of flagrant violation, yet let me first caution you to this effect—those of you who are boors will be weeded from us, we do not desire you. Certain of you men appear to reek with what I may take it upon myself to call the psychology of the enlisted man. And I fear you will not credit this institution in any sense. Nor will such dullards ever chance to serve as officers in the approaching world engagement, which would now seem to loom before our distraught, harried eye.

"If there is one sight that repels my deepest instincts it is that of an enlisted man wearing the bars of an officer. No, gentlemen, there is another sight which repels me more intensely, a sight that has had that power since I accepted my duties here several years ago. And that sight is the appearance of a graduate of this institution in lieutenant's uniform, provided that graduate is infused with the vulgar psychology and rude conscience one may expect from the less-favored enlisted man. The enlisted man, who however well he might serve his country in his appointed tasks, let no man deny, he is not an officer. And could never be an officer, except in the rarest of instances, for which specific provisions are made.

"Indeed, gentlemen, let me inform you of this—at present there are perhaps three or four respectable military institutions in this nation. These three or four, of which several are not at all what they might be, must, in conjunction with our regularly established officer school West Point, be called upon to provide our nation with officers for the coming engagement. The engagement with forces anathema to our conception of liberty and honor. How will that be possible? How can a mere handful of military institutions be expected to perform so immense a task?

"Do the authorities then see fit to scatter a number of R.O.T.C. units about the nation, R.O.T.C. units scarcely worthy of connection with the Army—do the authorities regard that as tantamount to solving the problem? I repeat, only this institution and several others are worthy of any appreciable military respect, excepting the example of West Point. Naturally the Point is far from being an R.O.T.C. unit in any sense. The attempt to hammer The Academy, as restricted

[ 45 ]

as I am by numerous stupidities, into as proud and glorious an institution as the Point has consumed my energies of the past years, as I am certain most of you know.

"You will pardon my introducing personal regard into this matter, yet I assure you we stand today on the brink of an abyss. Grant that we must turn for officers, as we did in the last world engagement, to material we would ordinarily consider well fit for kitchen or latrine duty. Grant that miserable fact and it is impossible not to foresee the perilousness of our time.

"The strength and power of an army, as every man knows but lacks the candor to put into words, does not lie in the untrained mass of its enlisted personnel, but rather in the caliber of its officers. It is the officer who holds his company under fire, the officer who makes the decisions, the officer who most often risks his life in battle, and the officer who is the brain of military conflict.

"Gentlemen, do not misunderstand me. Not for an instant do I fail to pay respect to the lesser personnel, whose bravery and labor are so necessary in the winning of an engagement. I merely point out to you, within the candid confines of these walls, a fact well known to every military man, as I earnestly trust many of you will someday prove yourselves to be. It is simply expressed by saying that the enlisted man is raw material. He is a mass of undisciplined nervous tissue, apt to scatter in all directions unless *you* are equipped to restrain him, unless you have the bearing, the intelligence, the power and the intrepidity of a true commander of men. He will look up to you, with beseeching eyes, for the guidance it shall be your duty to provide him. Without it, mark my words, he is worse than nothing. An uncontrolled mob, a confused civilian, albeit he may passionately desire the annihilation of the enemy.

"What I have said to you is so obvious that perhaps you might wonder I have exhausted time and effort for the purpose. Yet you will doubtless encounter, in published word, the newsreel, the addresses of our future military commanders, what must be analyzed as a romantic glossing bestowed upon the enlisted man. Which of course when taken in proportionate consideration is thoroughly due.

Truly there is no army without the enlisted personnel. I merely caution you—first, do not let yourselves be misled by such advices; second, take instant cognizance of the arduous and vital path that lies before you."

The General paused, scanning the sixteen hundred cadets. For the first time he took his arms from the folded position. He rubbed his hands together briskly then placed his tall body forward a few inches on the platform. With hands on hips he spoke again, almost shouting yet with unruffled dignity.

"What are you now? I speak particularly to the freshman class. Are you approaching your goal?

"No! It is not to be expected that you be anything other than a gathering of rude youth. However, this is to be expected, that you will take the steps necessary for the fashioning of yourselves into men. You have four years to do it, scant time enough. Harken to what I will say to you now with specific reference to the conduct of the freshman class last night.

"I have received reports to the effect that numerous cadets were observed marching four and five abreast on the sidewalks of Port George, roughly jostling the civilians encountered. Such a deed is not compatible with military courtesy and casts a hideous light upon the tradition of gentlemanliness consonant with the scores of years that this institution has graced the military annals of our nation.

"I have further been informed that a number of cadets, all of the freshman class, made mock of themselves and their uniform by striding through the streets of Port George in unreserved song. Yes, singing the athletic songs as well as other masculine lyrics of this institution. That is manifestly unpermissible. It is difficult to imagine a man possessed of normal intelligence doing such a thing.

"I have learned that several cadets made churlish advances toward some of the young ladies of Port George. I assure you that if I knew the names of these uncouth scoundrels I would personally escort them from this institution without parley. If there is one deed that revolts my conception of the cultured gentleman it is such a bestial affront to the virtue and emotion of womanhood. Should I ever again get word of such grossness a complete investigation of the entire cadet corps will at once be undertaken at my order and the churls guilty of such animality will forthwith be dismissed in dishonor.

"The general attitude of the freshmen on leave last night was such as not to give the citizens of Port George an accurate impression of The Academy. The Port George citizenry are familiar with this institution and respect it highly. I will not permit this view to bear correction because of the boorish misconduct of those new here. When you enter a business establishment, whether it be a stationery store or a restaurant, comport yourself as a gentleman, do not be flippant or loose tongued, suffer yourself to bear forth a manner of cool reserve. Remember this recommendation. It will not be repeated.

"I have one further thing to advise you, and it is with the deepest sense of personal humiliation that I do so. An utterly untoward incident occurred last night. An incident which far surpassed in extreme disgracefulness any other matter I have mentioned. As succinctly as possible, I will inform you of the event. Not I assure you because it gives me the slightest pleasure to do so, but because I feel it my obligation, placed as I am in the sometimes unrewarding capacity of administrator of this institution.

"A certain freshman last night took it upon himself to attack the self-regard of another freshman. He made of his classmate a donkey by constraining him to indulge in alcoholic beverages. This scoundrel succeeded in getting his victim entirely intoxicated. While in the grasp of abandonment to liquors he made of himself and his classmate a public spectacle. This freshman had the audacity to place himself on a busy sidewalk of Port George and there to call to attention his classmate; and there to revile that classmate, who was utterly helpless in the clutch of alcohol, an element strange to him. A large crowd witnessed this scene, in which were a number of Academy cadets. This disgraceful matter only ended with the collapse of the victimized individual.

"I will not dwell on the sordid ramifications of this incident, satisfied as I am to leave that to your imagination. I will say that much time will pass before this blot upon the school can be removed. The offending cadet, that is to say, the cadet who constrained his classmate to drink in excess—and actually against that classmate's will—is to be expelled summarily and in dishonor.

"After hearing the story of the exploited cadet I have decided to withhold final action in his case. This cadet will be put on trial for the next six weeks. At the end of that time, if it is the decision of the Regimental Cadet Committee, he will remain for a longer period and may hope eventually to redeem himself. This leniency, I suggest, is not to be a part of our future action in cases of this sort."

The General turned, muttered a few words to Colonel A. P. Evers, Commandant of Cadets. Colonel Evers nodded once, nodded again. Then he stepped forward on the rostrum. In a gravelish voice he said he agreed with all General Draughton had said, that he hoped the members of the cadet corps, and particularly the freshmen, to whom the speech was principally addressed, would profit by the General's speaking so frankly and at such great length.

Colonel Evers motioned with a scroll of brownish-white paper to Cadet Captain-Adjutant Starkson, who stood at the foot of the rostrum. Starkson mounted and seized the scroll of paper. He then snapped his black heels together and saluted. Colonel Evers returned the salute. Starkson then executed a precise about-face, unrolled the paper, and read very rapidly:

"*November —, 1940. The Academy. Port George. Special Order Number One. Subjects: Cadet Bailey, Timothy; Cadet Simmons, Maurice Maynall.*

"*Whereupon with the reading of Special Order Number One it becomes effective immediately that the enrollment of Cadet Bailey is obliterated from the records of The Academy. It will there be inscribed that by fault of grave misconduct serving to bring dishonor to The Academy Cadet Bailey is formally discharged in dishonor from this institution on the above date.*

"*It is here noted that in utter disregard for the precepts of gentlemanliness Cadet Bailey behaved publicly in such a manner as to forbid complete formal recounting of his action. In accordance with*

[ 49 ]

*customs relevant to such events no record will be retained of Cadet Bailey's registration.*

*"Cadet Simmons, Maurice Maynall. Whereupon with the reading of Special Order Number One it becomes effective immediately that the person of Cadet Simmons shall be denied conventional freedoms and courtesies of The Academy as are granted those of the cadet corps of his class and distinction. Inclusive: general leave on Friday and Saturday evenings, general leave on Sunday afternoons; permission to absent himself from any meals that occur on Friday, Saturday, or Sunday from which unrestricted cadets may be absent—namely, supper or third meal on Friday and Saturday, dinner or second meal on Sunday. This for a period to cover six weeks as of the above date at the end of which time further study of the deportment of Cadet Simmons will be made by the Regimental Cadet Committee.*

*"During this period Cadet Simmons will serve all tours of duty. Here stated: Wednesday afternoons, two services; Saturday afternoons, four services. These tours of duty will be marched in a military manner. Cadet Simmons will retire to his room on Friday and Saturday evenings and on Sunday afternoons and will confine himself under normal restrictions of the cadet under arrest.*

*"It is here recommended should Cadet Simmons fail in any respect to comply with both the letter and spirit of this order that another be issued expelling him for his share in the event which brought expulsion in dishonor of Cadet Bailey.*

*"Signed, Larrence E. Corger, Colonel of Cadets.*

*"Approved in full and signed, Colonel A. P. Evers, United States Army.*

*"Approved in full and signed, General A. L. Draughton, United States Army retired."*

**6** Robert Marquales hesitated, then pushed open the door without knocking. Inside were Carroll Colton and a wizened sophomore he had never seen. Nervous, as always upon entering an upperclassman's room, Marquales took two steps forward and popped into a brace.

The sophomore made a noise with his mouth as if to express disapproval. Colton genially said, "Rest." The sophomore murmured, "I'm weary of seeing freshmen assume that silly position." The two upperclassmen sat on Colton's bed. They had been talking excitedly when Marquales entered.

With eyes on Colton the sophomore asked Marquales, "Why didn't you knock?" He gave no time for an answer but snapped to the senior, "Now listen to me . . ." then he stopped, thought, and turned back to Marquales. He leveled monkey-like eyes at the freshman and gave him a candid stare. In a brittle but friendly voice he inquired, "Will you sit down and make yourself comfortable? We won't bite you."

"Thank you, sir."

"My name is Perrin McKee."

"Yes sir, Mr. McKee."

The sophomore turned back to Colton. "You don't understand **my** point, Carroll."

Marquales wondered who the sophomore might be; there was a pronounced tone of the river in his speech, which indicated that he was from Port George. McKee had a strange mannerism. He seemed to enjoy opening and shutting his eyes during conversation. This was meant to give profound weight to his remarks, but it impressed Marquales as foolish. Sometimes McKee would talk throughout several minutes with his eyelids drawn over the weak gray balls. Marquales sat down in a chair and began to try to understand the conversation.

In a moment he realized he was sitting on the discarded red sash he'd seen around Colton's waist the night before. That made him uncomfortable; he was afraid of wrinkling and crushing the satin material. At the same time he was annoyed with himself for not having noticed it. Cautiously, he started to pull it out, hoping neither of the upperclassmen would see him. But it stuck, seemed caught on the seat-caning. It was necessary for him to relax and let himself fall down on the sash.

He listened. McKee was talking. Colton's face was slightly red and he frequently interrupted, "No, Perrin. I didn't mean that."

McKee held up his hand for silence. "Just one moment, Carroll. I insist that your original remark was hopeless. It's equivalent to defining black as black to say simply the good man's the true man. Obviously. My point—the true man is true because he is operating at the summit of his potential; the good man good for the same reason. Aside from the fact your definition is nothing more than an identity equation it should also be pointed out abstract terms are meaningless unless attached in an experiential sense . . ."

"Now just a *minute!*" said Colton.

"Give me the pleasure of going into these inner meanings myself, will you? I think it was I who first objected to your remark. I think it was I who pointed out to you originally that such a statement could not stand on its own weight. I think it was you who vehemently refused to agree . . . at that time.

"This is what I'd like to say and I ask to be allowed a few minutes' grace to say it. First it must be recognized that human memory is the most perfect and powerful thing in the world, Carroll. And memory exists in two strata—sub-experiential and pre-experiential. Highly complex terms like these are perhaps best explained by anecdote or illustration. But first let me say it is the understanding of the connection between these two that makes the good man and/or the true man. That is to say, the man functioning on the most highly efficient level. It is toward this ideal we must strive if we are to justify our claim to have risen from the animal to the human."

Marquales listened to these remarks with his mouth open.

"First consider the sub-experiential stratum," continued McKee in his soft voice. "The most important components of the human individual are those least understood by him. Now the sub-experiential stratum I take to be those actual experiences whose significance is likely to be missed by us. By actual I mean those that occurred during the overt existence of the organism. Now you will understand what I mean in a moment.

"I have the perfect example of sub-experiential phenomena. Listen to this story. A cousin of mine once told me of a gruesome thing that happened to him. Although he himself had little comprehension of this shocking experience it was easy to gain knowledge from what he said.

"First, some vital statistics. He was the son of my mother's sister, who had married a man named Perrante, which gave her the euphonious married name of Martha Louise Perrin Perrante. Since the proud Perrin girls felt it necessary to keep the name of Perrin as alive as possible (my grandfather Alfred Perrin had no sons) all four of them have named their children Perrin by some twist or other. One aunt of mine went so far as to give her daughter, an only child, the name—Perrina. My own name of course is Perrin. Therefore my Aunt Martha was not able to name her son Perrin Perrante as she doubtless would have done, but she was forced to compromise and call him Philippe Perrin Perrante, Junior.

"That was absurd, by the way. His father's name was not Philippe Perrin Perrante but was Philippe Theodore Roosevelt Perrante. Yet I could never get anyone in my family to agree with me on the score of that 'Junior.' Would you believe it? Well, you might find it suggestive if I mention my family has been prominent in this town for too long a time. It might be more suggestive if I declare outright that the black rascals who haul catfish from the levee are their intellectual superiors, by and large."

McKee spoke the last few sentences with eyes open. He closed them, then opened them again and looked sharply at Marquales. "Are you in a hurry? Do you want to speak to Colton? You're not bored, are you? Can you wait until I get around to making this point about my cousin?"

"Yes," said Marquales.

"Thank you," answered McKee. "Phil was a prodigy. His intelligence was astounding, or at least very out of the ordinary. He skipped several grades and finished high school at the age of fifteen. However, despite his brain power he was a sickly person, rather like myself. He was however an extrovert, which is unusual for one so intelligent. In that respect he and I differed.

"Phil wanted to go to the University of Texas. His grandfather and great-grandfather attended The Academy, but he wanted to go to the University of Texas. I remember he used to joke about his reason for wanting to attend that barren hole, saying he once saw a cowboy movie and never recovered. Oh, he was a witty boy. He felt no compunction to get military training, you see. He even jested on that subject—despite the fact that even then it was evident a war was coming which would threaten the foundations of our culture.

"In many ways he was a moron, Phil. I say 'was' because he's dead now. An automobile cut short what had become the most mediocre of careers, with nothing to recommend it except an enormous popularity with his classmates at Texas and a vague interest in badminton. Do you know, that boy read with understanding the dialogues of Plato when he was nine years old? It was only the stupidity of his parents that kept him in our local high school so long. I might mention in regard to the accident that killed him that it was a woman who was his final defeat. A campus slut got him drunk the night it occurred.

"I said he was popular in school and he certainly was. Have either of you ever heard of the 'T' Club? Phil was invited to join the organization, thus gaining one of the greatest honors the University of Texas can bestow. Now listen, I am getting to the experience which with Phil was decidedly sub-experiential. First a brief preface, however.

"When he was ten the feeble-minded Negress who cooked for his family flew into a rage and sloshed a pail of boiling fat across his bare chest. He nearly died. During his delirium he screamed constantly, 'No, Marma! No!' The name of the moronic Negress. Phil's mother, my own gentle Aunt Martha (now of New Orleans), and his dandy little father were very solicitous, naturally. By virtue of endless skin grafts Phil was patched so there showed only three wavy

[ 54 ]

purple lines on his chest. However, it will be understood that within him the marks were deeper.

"Gentlemen, the scene is set. Do you know the initiation for the 'T' Club? It consists of one simple procedure: the willing victim is stripped to the waist and has a large 'T' branded on his chest with a white-hot iron.

"Phil spoke to me of his sensations as he waited in the gloomy attic where the initiations took place. He was third man. First came a young fellow whom he described as 'underweight and pink.' This lad lay down on the wooden rack built for the purpose, then waved away the hands of those who would help by pinning down his arms. With a smile the boy puffed up his chest. The brander pulled the red iron from the blow pile and without ado pressed it firmly onto the lad's breastbone, just between his nipples. The stench of burning flesh came up in a cloud, and the boy smiled.

"Next man in line was a huge football player. He didn't behave as well as the boy. His face was gray and his hairy knees were shaking. He lay down on the rack in the perspiration left by the boy, then he grinned and asked them to hold his arms and legs tight. Several of them grabbed him. But when he saw the iron in the brander's hand he let out a moan. The brand started down to his hairy chest and he stared with popped eyes, mouth opened wide as if to shout. Suddenly he begged for a drink of water, as the iron was about to touch. Naturally this request was better not honored; to prolong the business would have been cruel. The brander went ahead and pushed down the hot iron. The football player gave a great shriek, then fainted. Burned hair and flesh gave off the usual disgusting acrid smell. But my cousin, whose turn was next, felt very much improved.

"He was encouraged by the bad example of the football player. Yet when he got on the rack he shook so badly four men had to hold him. Thanks to a handkerchief he put in his mouth he didn't scream, but he did faint."

McKee stopped and examined his fingernails.

"What a brutal story!" said Carroll Colton. "You really love to talk about such inhuman, depraved things, don't you?"

"Me?" said the sophomore innocently. "I'm as gentle as a lamb."

Colton laughed. "A lamb with hydrophobia."

"I don't regard that as funny," said McKee, chuckling. "And you'd better not let any member of the famed 'T' Club of Texas University hear you describe the initiation as inhuman and depraved. I assure you they don't regard it in that light."

"You sadist," said Colton.

"Oh, stop the foolishness, Carroll. Everyone is a sadist. Now to continue. My stupid cousin Phil went on to tell me he regarded his experience under the branding iron as a valuable purging. He said it rid him of his old fear of being burned. A fear incurred to a pathological extent in his childhood. He said in effect: this is a human victory. What he failed to understand was that such an experience is more of a consolidation. It was the final dominance of a trait he never suspected in himself, despite his intelligence. It is the trait which leads man to argue he can justify himself by accepting, rather than giving. Phil had been made ready to believe by allowing himself to be hurt in the worst possible manner he was accomplishing something brave and meaningful. What an error."

McKee opened his eyes and squinted again at his fingernails, then glanced at Marquales and smiled. With a start the freshman realized he had his mouth open again. He blushed and closed it.

McKee continued: "Thus, Phil's experience was what I call subexperiential. It had significance he never realized. Now the first step toward becoming what we call the good or true man is to understand the existence of such sub-experiential phenomena. After that the task is to correlate these with the more involved, complex pre-experiential phenomena. It is toward this ideal, a brave one, that all thinking men must strive.

"One brief tale then I'll leave you. This will be cut short, if you permit. I can't hope to do more than suggest the intricacy of this subject."

Colton and Marquales waited for him to speak. He sat with eyes closed, head tossed slightly back. Thirty seconds passed in silence,

[ 56 ]

then a pained expression crossed the sophomore's gray face and his eyelids trembled and flew open. The enlarged pupils gradually contracted into small beady circles as light reached them again.

"My mother died at my birth," McKee said slowly. "An unhappy thing, no doubt, but to be expected if you know the racial composition of the Perrin family. Unadulterated Anglo-Saxon. Old English settlers. No other race considered worthy of them. The family thought it a disgrace for my Aunt Martha to marry Philippe Perrante, who was of French descent.

"At any rate it was unadulterated Anglo-Saxon. That white-skinned race of blue-eyed people, superior cousins of those the Chancellor of Germany calls Aryans. In such a town as Port George the Perrins were not able to mate with variational strains available in Great Britain thus the virility of the men and hardihood of the women was reduced. And, my mother died when I was born.

"I myself nearly died. There was no milk for me. As you might know, the milk of a cow is intended for the calf, not for the human infant. Science is not infallible; and I feel that here an error is perpetrated. I believe you'll discover that the child of true mental health is the child fed from the breast. My father takes the same view. It was he who rounded up my wet nurse."

McKee turned to Marquales and said softly, "I don't think I got your name."

"Robert Marquales, sir."

"A formal manner isn't necessary with either me or Colton, provided no other upperclassmen are present. Leave off the 'sirs' and address me as Perrin. And now pay attention, Robert. Do not tell anyone what I am about to say. Let the matter be between us, please. I am the one who must decide whether to mention this affair—and I always prefer not to do it if I feel unsympathetic."

McKee's wizened face then turned red. He murmured, "My wet nurse was a Negress. She was the most extreme type of that deplorable race. A blue-black color. With huge jet breasts overflowing with milk. She had the sullen, ugly face Negroes often have, particularly if they are of a blue-black shade. And she nursed me. I drank her milk. I drank deeply of the fluid squeezed from her clotted lymph glands, mixed with extracts of Negro blood and poured through the chest into countless funnels and minute tubes of the breast structure —and on up through the fatty, pulplike tissue and out the small orifices of her unwashed black nipple into my raw mouth and down inside my belly.

"I sucked her black tits for nineteen months. Daily, I kneaded that glistering carbon flesh in my fat little hands; daily I swallowed the thick yellow product of the Negress' body. I waxed strong, as any animal would on such attractive food!

"I thought I knew nothing of it. That is to say I thought I retained no memories of having been sustained by her. At the age of six I learned the fact, as I'll tell you, that the Negro woman once nourished me. But until a year ago, just after my twenty-first birthday, I thought my memories of the matter sprang from what I saw in my sixth year. That was not true. On the pre-experiential level I actually recall the entire suckling period. You see, gentlemen, it was only recently that I came to the final realization that there is yet another fundament in the structure of human personality. And this, which is clothed in the mysterious, is what I call pre-experiential memory. The pre-experiential memory, as you'll discover, is closely involved with race.

"When I was six I saw the Negress giving suck to a cousin of mine, whose mother wanted to preserve her bosoms. She thought more highly of the contour of her udders than the character of her daughter. That child has now, at the age of sixteen, been possessed intravaginally by several of our cadets.

"Gentlemen, the sight of that infant mashing its nose flat on the Negress' monstrous organ, sucking, sucking with those little pink jaws . . . it repelled me in the most horrible way imaginable. I wept. I lay on the floor and screamed. I kicked and shouted. When I was cajolingly informed that the black woman once performed the same service for me . . . the filthy thought I had once taken her nipple into my mouth plunged me into an illness of weeks.

"And, to cure me my father brought the Negress to my bedside and forced me to watch the little greedy cousin suck. I remember I would lie there in a state of breathlessness, eyes bulging from my head, perspiration rolling off my body. The beginning of my intellectuality was in those days."

McKee sighed and stood up. "That, gentlemen," he said. "That, there is my example of the workings of pre-experiential phenomena. I was a perfect subject for the demonstration of its power—sensitive, highly endowed mentally, and sickish. Furthermore, and most important, I was the child of a mother who died largely as a result of too intense a purification of the racial strain.

"I suppose you can get some idea of the interplay in my case of inborn racial opposites. But the matter is more profound and complex than I have time to explain in any complete fashion. In simplest terms what I call the pre-experiential stratum of human personality is to be found located in that which never happened to the individual himself. It is, rather, that which happened to his race. Tremendous scientific evidence supports my thesis. Though not caring to follow the dictates of the god science in all its perambulations I occasionally take the time to check on such matters. I prefer on the whole to rely on more basic truths than those science has yet been able to commandeer.

"Finally. In order for the individual to realize himself fully he must comprehend all hidden pre-experiential memories as well as sub-experiential. And then it is his task to perceive the relationship of the two. When he does that he will be the good man and the true man. He will be farthest divorced from animality."

Colton sighed and stood up. He asked, "Do you have to go, Perrin? Robert has come to tell me an interesting story—something about our old friend Jocko de Paris."

"Really?" inquired McKee.

"Yes, and also on a favorite subject, alcohol."

"Hmm."

Colton went on in a gay fashion, "Perrin, the freshman has made you such a good listener, having drunk your very words, I think you ought to stay and hear what he has to say."

"Robert," said McKee. "Did you understand what I was talking about?"

"No sir."

McKee laughed.

"But scientists say there's no difference in the races, sir."

"Yes, that sounds like the remark of a scientist. The scientist is always careful to miss what's sitting right under his nose."

"Well, I don't know myself, sir. But I like many Negroes better than a lot of white people I happen to meet now and then."

"Some of my best friends are niggers, too," said McKee slyly.

"Perrin, how about tonight?" asked Colton, smiling.

"No. Carroll, you understand perfectly about that. I have work to do. Perhaps next week." He faced Marquales and grinned. "However I agree that Robert has made a good, if sarcastic, listener. Some time he and I will have to get together and talk. Carroll, don't you think this fellow has the miserable glint of intelligence in his eyes? They sure are unusual eyes, anyhow—a very odd color scheme."

"Don't pick on him," said Colton. "I don't think he's naïve at all. And I endorse his remarks in defense of colored people. Negroes have a lot of charm."

"Who said he was naïve?" asked McKee, winking. "He's a sophisticate disguised to look no more than sweet seventeen."

Colton said, "Perrin, don't be so flippant."

McKee smiled and stepped to the door. "Good-by. See you gents later." He bowed in the sweeping manner of the Port Georgians, and finally made his exit. Colton sighed wearily.

The senior murmured to Marquales, "Can you keep a secret? Don't tell anyone." As he spoke he reached into his press between folded shirts and pulled out a half-filled bottle of brown fluid. "Want a sip?" Marquales shook his head then watched as the senior threw up the bottle and took several feverish swallows.

"Ah!" said Colton. "Remember, this is our secret. Now I want you to tell me how you had the ill luck to show up last night with Jocko de Paris. Do you realize if any other senior had been Officer of the Day you all would probably be sent along home with that freshman, Bailey? Jocko de Paris has nearly been expelled a dozen times; no one can understand how he stays in school. How did you happen to go out with him?"

"We didn't go out with him, sir," said Marquales. "We ran into him."

"Leave off those *sirs*."

"All right."

Marquales told the story of how he, Wintermine, and Hulitt had picked up Jocko and driven him home. He made several mistakes in the telling. Throughout the narrative he sat in the chair on Colton's sash. The senior laughed politely whenever Marquales made an effort to be witty.

It was not the interview Marquales expected the night before. The strange talk of McKee, Colton's daring drink of whiskey, the over-politeness . . . the freshman was uncomfortable. Then he mentioned having seen Simmons dancing on the street corner with Bailey and Leroy.

"That Simmons!" said Colton. "He acted like a madman last night. First he came in from the infirmary—that was around one—but we couldn't make any sense out of what he said. Later he came back and spoke in the strangest way to Lieutenant Suhlman. The things he said were ridiculous, in my opinion. Do you know him at all?"

"I was his roommate for two weeks."

"That *must* have been interesting. What's he like anyhow? I mean, what sort is he?"

"He's nervous and underweight."

"Do you know what he told me last night? He said alcohol was a discovery. Alcohol's in keeping with the word of God because it releases the human spirit." Colton let go a cascade of giggles. "But later he came back and he'd changed his mind. That was when he had his hangover. He was against alcohol at that point."

Marquales smiled.

"But that wasn't the last I got from him," said Colton. "He was here a few minutes before you came in."

"This afternoon?"

"Yes, he was around looking for me. He thought I was still Officer of the Day. Well, I told him I escaped the last hours of guard because of an exam. Then he actually accused me of being a liar. He wanted me to protect him from the other freshman, Bailey."

"Isn't Bailey gone?" asked Marquales.

"Of course he's gone," said Colton. "But Simmons said he was coming back."

"I thought Bailey left," said Marquales.

"He did, he left. He was put on the noon train out of Port George."

"What made Simmons come around?"

"He's mentally unstable, that's why. He has a persecution complex, and that Leroy freshman had been frightening him with wild tales. But Simmons is a very unusual type of person. You ought to have heard him last night. Or for that matter you ought to have heard him this afternoon. He was talking a blue streak, raving indescribably. The poor boy believed I was O. D., you know, and he invented a long account about how the Bailey freshman had done something—I don't know, parachuted out of an airplane, took a dock taxi back up to the Boat Club launching by means of a submarine, something wild, and was coming back to barracks to get him. Incredible how the human imagination runs away with itself. I had the hardest time calming him down."

"It sounds crazy," said Marquales.

"Oh, it was."

"Well," said Marquales hoarsely. "I've got to go report to awkward-squad drill."

"On Saturday?"

"Yes."

"That's cruel, they shouldn't do that to you on Saturday."

Colton arose and bade Marquales good-by with a friendly smile.

"Come back soon. Perrin monopolized the conversation this time the way he always does. But I want to have a talk with you."

"All right, I will," said Marquales.

There was no one in Simmons' room, so Marquales went on down to Bailey's. Leroy sat inside, a worried look on his face.

"Where's Tim?" asked Marquales.

"I don't know, I really don't. I haven't seen him."

"Where is he? After Simmons?"

"No! No, Robbie, he isn't. He's already out of Port George."

"You ought to be ashamed, you liar!" said Marquales. He turned and walked out of the room to the gallery. He meant to go speak to Pete Layne, but then he saw Bailey step out of the latrine door down the corridor. Marquales halted.

Bailey was dressed in a natty green suit, which was splashed with water, and smeared. There was an angry look on his face. He came up to Marquales, slapping at the wet coat.

"I got your old roommate," he said.

"All right, Tim, you'll be in trouble if you hurt Simmons."

"Kiss my ass."

Marquales circled and walked on down the gallery.

"I never miss!" called Bailey. "But he isn't hurt."

Marquales glanced inside the latrine, then entered. The floor was flooded with water from a stopped-up toilet in the right-hand corner, first of a row of ten. Marquales had noticed it that morning, and had been repulsed by the bowl of rank water floating with brown and gray turds.

Simmons lay exhausted in the right-hand corner on the floor. He stared up at Marquales. His glasses lay to one side with both lenses broken. A dark substance was smeared on his neck, hair, eyes, and mouth. Marquales turned to one side and vomited.

PART 2

*7* Sow-belly Simmons answered for sick call the morning after he was assaulted by Bailey. He had asthma.

A few days later Robert Marquales visited him at the Infirmary.

"Ah," said Simmons. "How are you? It isn't visiting hours, is it? What are you doing here?"

"Colonel Girard said I could come in."

"What of Miss Frune?"

"Who?"

"The Head Nurse. A true hellcat."

"Colonel Girard said it was all right."

"Well, I hope nevertheless she doesn't see you. There is no liking between Miss Frune and that cut-bones." He added, "This place is very unsanitary."

"What's the matter with it?"

Simmons was propped up on about six pillows. Around his bed had been arranged an elaborate system of canvas screens that sheltered or hid him from the others in the ward. At that moment, one of the cadets called out:

"Hey, Sow-belly! Quote some scripture."

Simmons indicated with a thin hand the direction whence came the jeering voice. "Robbie, that's what's the matter here."

There was a sudden hoarse scream from the doorway, reverberating through the large room.

"SHUT UP THAT HOLLERING! SHUT IT UP! SILENCE!"

Simmons jerked, gritting his teeth. "That's the Head Nurse," he whispered.

A big red hand reached over a canvas screen and yanked it backward, revealing a tall rawboned woman in white uniform. Her eyes were like two ratholes bored into her forehead just below the hairline; and she didn't seem to have a chin, although her nose was long enough and large enough to make her face seem balanced, if not normal.

"Cadet Simmons!" she said, not moving her bluish lips. "I've warned you often."

[ 67 ]

She passed her eyelashes back and forth several times over her eyes, obviously struggling to control herself.

"Cadet Simmons!" she said.

"Yes."

There was a giggle from out in the ward.

"SHUT UP!" yelled the Head Nurse.

"Yes," repeated Simmons.

"Cadet Simmons, I warn you. Get comical around here any more it'll be you and me and the General. He said to me, 'Miss Frune, if you have any more disruptions instigated by the cadets in the sick wards, inform me about it.' Those were his very words. And if things don't alter around here quick I will do just that. As much as I hate to bother the General. Let there be no more trouble from you, Cadet Simmons!"

"I have done nothing . . ." began Simmons.

"Shut that up!"

"He really didn't do anything," said Marquales in a low voice.

"Who are you and what are you doing in this ward? Who asked you for your opinion?"

"Just visiting, ma'am," he said, bowing.

She looked at him, bewildered, then rubbed the huge red nose with her rawboned hand, sniffing absently.

"Cadet Simmons," she said. "Any more of these rough disruptions and there will be a showdown."

"I'm a sick man. Very sick."

"You'll be sicker if you don't quit stirring up this ward. And, I mean it." She backed out of the enclosure and slammed shut the canvas screen. They waited. A few moments later her voice came from the doorway. "You're all *sick*! No more noise OR IT'S THE GENERAL! Do you want him to come over here?" The door slammed. From the fifteen or twenty beds came laughter.

"Ah," said Simmons. "A hellcat. A true hellcat."

"Do you feel bad?" asked Marquales.

"This asthma. It's terrible. And they're talking about an operation; it's gone into sinusitis now . . ."

There was a pause.

"I saw Carroll Colton the other day . . ."

"I am praying for him."

"He said for me to tell you he was sorry about making that mistake."

"What mistake?" asked Simmons nervously.

"In telling you Bailey had already gone."

"Let's not talk about such unpleasant matters. The only thing to do in the case of a spiritual liar is pray for him, however *old*-fashioned and humorous prayer is." Simmons glowered briefly at the canvas that divided him from the other cadets. Then he turned to Marquales and smiled, showing his yellow teeth back nearly to the molars. "Let's talk about the better aspect of life, by all means. How are all the fellows in the company?"

"All right. We drill all the time. Everybody's about the same."

"How was Chapel the other day?"

"All right, I guess. They had a preacher from Norfolk. He talked for over an hour."

"And what was his message?"

"I don't think he had any."

"He must have," frowned Simmons.

"I don't remember what he said now."

Simmons pitched forward his head, ran one thin hand through his hair. "Robbie. Are you going to be a low doubter all the time, or are you going to get over it?"

"Well, I think the guy talked about the Twenty-third and One Hundredth Psalms."

"Ah, you recall. Did he make any interesting remarks?"

"Not very."

"What was his main approach?"

"There isn't time," said Marquales. "Look, Simmons, are you going to tell the authorities about what Bailey did?"

"What do you mean?"

"Are you going to tell them how he treated you?"

"How he treated me?" said Simmons.

"You know."

"Where is Bailey now?"

"He's gone."

"Does that answer your query?"

"I guess so."

"Be sure that I pray for him to some extent, however."

Five minutes later Marquales departed, promising to fetch two of Simmons' books for him.

In mid-October, about two weeks after the visit to the Infirmary, Robert Marquales decided to take a fuller part in The Academy's social life by trying to join the staff of the school magazine, *Port Arms*. He spoke about it to his company commander, Peter Layne.

"Go see the managing editor," said Layne, who was the literary editor. "Tell him I said give you something."

Thomas Munro, the managing editor, promised Marquales special leave to visit Port George. There, he was to sell advertising space for the magazine.

A few days later Layne told Marquales that leave had been officially granted for a Thursday afternoon. Another freshman named William Poley would accompany him. Marquales had never heard of that cadet.

He subsequently boasted of the good luck to his roommates, and Les Wintermine objected: "Poley? You might as well not take the leave."

Ben Hulitt nodded.

"What's the matter with him?" asked Marquales.

"He's ugly," said Wintermine. "Too ugly to be looked at."

"Anyhow I'll get to town on a weekday."

"But what a price . . ."

Ben Hulitt said in a solemn voice, "Old Poley's having a hard time educating Lieutenant Nestor, isn't he, Les?"

"Sure. He thinks he knows more about those blue-ball ancient people than the teacher."

"I thought he was the teacher," said Hulitt. "Isn't he?"

"That Poley, and that other pal of old Mooch's here . . ."

Marquales turned aside.

"Talking to you, Mooch," said Wintermine.

"That's not my name," said Marquales.

"It fits you, somehow or other."

"Oh, be quiet, Les," said Hulitt. "Who did you mean a minute ago?"

"The sophomore in history class. McKee."

"Perrin McKee?" said Marquales. "Is he in freshman history?"

Hulitt asked, "He's the one that's always arguing with Lieutenant Nestor?"

"That's right. McKee and Poley. Two jawbone experts."

"What's McKee doing in freshman history?" asked Marquales.

"He claims Nestor doesn't like him, but the moron couldn't pass," said Wintermine. "That's what he's doing in there."

"Who's dumber?" asked Hulitt with a smile. "Poley, or McKee, or Lieutenant Nestor?"

"There's no telling," replied Wintermine.

On Wednesday afternoon Marquales received a visit from Pete Layne. When Layne entered he said affably, "Rest, rest. Don't brace so hard. Where are your roommates?"

"At chem lab, sir," said Marquales.

"Good. I wanted to have a talk with you. How do you like your roommates?"

"Why fine, sir."

"I wondered if you would mind going back with Mr. Simmons. He says he's lonesome up there in that room all by himself with only his asthma to keep him company, and if he doesn't get back in human society he's going to run amuck."

Marquales said, "But don't vampires go up to see him at night, sir?"

Layne answered, "I don't know, but you see my position, don't you? What would happen to this poor concrete building? Do we want it tore down?" He began to laugh, a long high giggle. "You've

[ 71 ]

got to watch Simmons! He's one in a million. Do we want mayhem?"

"No, sir," said Marquales, taking out a package of cigarets. Layne accepted one, tamped it on his knee, and said:

"Well, maybe he can endure a hermit life after all, if you say some vampires call on him at night."

"That's what I heard."

"Old Simmons seems to be getting along better now he's out of the clutches of Miss Frune. He walks his punishment tours all right. They might rescind his Special Order if he keeps it up. Did you see him the other day?"

"Yes, sir," said Marquales. He gave Layne a light.

"Wasn't he strutting?"

"Sir, I thought he was going to march a hole in the quadrangle."

"Mr. Marquales, I'm glad you have a sense of humor. That's one thing you need in life."

The freshman nodded.

"But to get off Simmons—what I came around here to talk to you about is the magazine."

"Yes, sir."

"How'd you happen to entertain the idea of working for *Port Arms*?"

"Sir, I like to draw . . ."

"You want to get in our art department? John Hornbuckle does practically everything. We haven't got much art to be done." He thought. "I figured you wanted editorial work from what you said. That's what the other freshman is after."

"I didn't believe there was much editorial work."

"There isn't," said Layne. "But less art work."

The freshman and the senior puffed self-consciously on their cigarets. Then Layne cleared his throat and asked, "How'd you ever happen to come to a place like The Academy, Mr. Marquales?"

"I don't know, sir. I often wonder."

"Didn't you consider any of the universities?"

"Yes, sir. I saw a couple last summer."

"Which?"

"Georgia and Duke."

"Is that so? And you turned them down for The Academy?"

"Yes, sir."

"Well, I can understand about Georgia. I wouldn't send a syphilitic zebra to that zoo. But what's wrong with Duke?"

"I thought about going there," said Marquales nervously.

"You should have gone to Duke instead of here," said Layne. He laughed. "It's a country club. I almost went to it. Then the last minute I signed over to be a jailbird at the Penitentiary of the South. Been behind bars ever since." He gestured toward the grillwork in the window. "No, seriously, Mr. Marquales. No freshman will ever believe it—I didn't when I was a freshman—but you'll get so you love this place, penitentiary or no penitentiary."

There was a pause. Then Layne glanced at his wrist watch. He said, "Oh, by the way, I meant to ask you. Have you got relatives in Knoxville? I knew some Marquales there."

"I don't think my family is kin to them," answered the freshman. "But I have some relatives named Warrenton that live in Knoxville."

"Warrenton," said Layne. He snapped his fingers. "Are you kin to Sue Warrenton?"

"Yes." Marquales did not remember having heard of her.

"That's quite a coincidence!"

"Oh, there're relatives all over the South," said the freshman, with a vague wave of the hand. "You know how it is."

"That's right. I can't ever keep up with mine. But old Sue Warrenton is a mighty nice girl. A sport. What do her folks do, anyhow? Run some kind of mill or other, don't they?"

Marquales thought and recalled that the Warrentons had something to do with selling material for houses. He told Layne.

"That's right," said the senior. "The Warrenton Builders' Supply Company. They once put a roof on our house."

Silence. Marquales stirred uncomfortably on the edge of the press. Layne leaned back in a weak-legged chair. He said slowly, "You know, once I went on a house party with Sue Warrenton. I was

[ 73 ]

about eighteen, and she was older. I got a little tight then after that Sue wouldn't give me other dates."

"Did you get very drunk?" blurted Marquales.

"They were all drinking," said Layne calmly. He dropped his cigaret to the floor and stepped on it. "The only thing was that I mixed my liquor. I wasn't tight as I was sick."

"Oh," said Marquales.

"Sometimes," Layne said, "women can drink better than men. That is, some men. Me, for instance. I could never drink to any extent and I'll admit it. I don't see the point, either. When a man gets drunk he doesn't care about anything, he could have Norma Shearer between the covers and she'd be the same as a worn-out whore. Or is that the way she'd be, drunk or sober either?" He gave the high giggle, then frowned and said quickly, "But don't misunderstand me about your cousin Sue. I don't mean she drank a lot; as a matter of fact she didn't. Only a reasonable amount—I've got nothing but good words for that little girl."

Layne once more looked at his wrist watch. "I've got to go."

Marquales stood up, thankful that the interview was ending.

"Oh," said Layne. "By the way, do you know this other freshman that wants to work on the mag? This boy going in with you tomorrow?"

"Poley? No, sir."

"Do you know anything about him? Where he's from? What kind of guy he is?"

"No, sir. I don't know him."

"Well," sighed Layne. "I guess I've got to have a talk with him."

At the door he paused. "Don't break your back selling ads."

The bus was practically empty when Marquales and William Poley boarded it.

"Aw," said Freshman Poley to the bus driver. "They can't keep *us* in that dern pen. We just walk out, weekday, week end, anything."

The driver gave them change, and asked, "But aren't you afraid the old General'll throw you in his Guardhouse?"

[ 74 ]

Marquales noticed an odd-looking, thin man sitting in the rear of the bus, just beyond the tidemark of the seats for Negroes.

Poley replied: "The General? We go up to him and tell him we're going to town whether he likes it or not. If he says anything we just bend him over and burn up his tail for him."

The driver opened his mouth and laughed harshly, starting the bus. Marquales secretly nudged Poley in the side. The freshman asked loudly, "What's the matter? What're you poking me for?" The driver stopped laughing; Marquales didn't answer. They took a seat near the front.

Poley asked again, still in a loud voice, "What were you poking me for?"

Hesitating, Marquales whispered, "That character in the back looks like a member of the faculty."

Poley turned and stared directly at the man. "Hasn't got on a faculty uniform," he said.

"Don't look at him!"

"He isn't on the faculty," said Poley, staring at the man. "I never saw him out there, either."

"Please. Turn around and shut up before we get in trouble."

"Okay, okay," whispered Poley. "Okay, chum."

A few moments later he began to talk about some girl he knew in Port George.

"Do you know the type anxious to get ahead in the world? I mean, the girl who reads society stories in the paper, but never saw society. Well, let me tell you; here's how it is. I know this girl, see, and right away she wants to know whether I have money. Why. Why? It *means* something to her. Now it doesn't mean anything to me. What do they make that money for in the mints in Washington except to be circulated? The circulation of the country's money is just like the circulation of human blood—cut off either one and you've got yourself a half-assed situation."

Marquales remembered having heard the same idea from one of his teachers: *"The circulation of specie is comparable to the circulation of the blood stream; should the blood stream of a human being*

*clot, death would follow; and should money cease to circulate human*
*life would be hindered, bringing economic death."*

"Once this girl," continued Poley, "realized both me and my
family are not minus cash, there was nothing she wanted to do more
than to go out and admire the bushes in Battery Square. Heh. She's
a little short girl, but stacked up like a goddamn brick sh——"

Poley's voice became louder and louder; he began to use incorrect
words to describe his adventures with the girl. People on the bus
looked angrily toward them, and the once-friendly bus driver turned
around and stared indignantly.

Then the skinny man, who had been sitting on the bus when they
boarded it, provided a distraction by leaving. On closer observation
they saw that the man carried a tin lunch box and smoked a salivary
homemade cigaret. He had a muddish skin.

"Jesus," laughed Poley. "You're mixing up niggers with the
faculty."

"He wasn't colored, was he?" said Marquales.

"I can recognize nigger blood a mile off," said Poley. "If there's
one thing I can do it's tell you whether a person has any nigger blood
or not. And that guy was a nigger."

Poley cleared his throat—"But for instance: there's all the difference
in the world between a guy with some Italian blood and some nigger
blood. You might think there isn't because some of them Italians
look pretty close to niggers; that's just like Hebrews that look like
niggers, too, in some little ways, you might say. You have to get so
you know them. How they look, the different ones, and know them
well. Then you'll never make any mistakes about it. You can tell at
a glance how to spot a nigger from any other kind of person. And
spot them right away.

"I was talking to my father one time about a guy in Valdosta, a
guy had a concession to go around to all the houses and sell subscriptions to magazines. Well, to a normal eye, the guy looked as
white as you or me and maybe whiter. He had blue eyes. Yellow
hair. And he dressed okay, not like a dirt-dobber, or the way a
nigger'll dress, but like a businessman—ornate. I started talking to

him now and then and he told me he knew of a kid across town that sold magazine subscriptions and won a bike. It was a balloon-tire type. Worth a lot of money. I got interested and thought I might look into it and see about selling some myself to get such a bike."

Poley stopped, coughed. "See, Marquales, I would have got one from the old man. But right then he was trying to get a hold of a laundry, and his cash was tied up. Later on he got that laundry and some more besides, believe me. But right then it was the depression, *you* know. My old man was watching his cash. Anyhow, all the money he can salt away isn't the point here, and I'm sure doesn't interest you any more than it does me. Because the point is we're talking about the fellow that sold those subscriptions and hoodwinked everybody. This is very interesting! If you listen you'll learn something.

"Imagine it!" sang out Poley. "Here he was, circulating around town, coming up on the front porches, chatting with the ladies in our neighborhood. And selling subscriptions all the time, talking about the weather and selling subscriptions; he was a smart son of a bitch and I'd never deny it—that guy was a smooth piece of silk.

"Like oil, that guy. I never heard such a smooth character when it came to conversation. 'I beg your pardon, moddom,' he'd say, then by God what'd come out of those pearly teeth would be the finest line of flingle you ever heard in your life, and the ladies around there would just sit and suck it up, smiling at him, blushing at his good looks, hee-heeing at his jokes, talking and laughing and now and then straightening out their hair and fluffing it up in the back of their head the way they'll do when something slick has took a good low-down hold of their thoughts . . . and Jesus Christ in Heaven above, you don't have any idea what all went on, and nobody else knows much more, but by God I'm damned if I didn't hear . . ."

Poley's voice throbbed: "Several of the women around the neighborhood invited him in the house and give him cocoa or lemonade. You know what that means, bud. A lot of those cocoa-givers turn out to be other kinds of givers. All the time—think of this sad fact for a minute—all the time the providers of the family were away hard at work earning the family living. With the thought that their homes were a sanctuary."

Poley hesitated. "Nevertheless," he said solemnly, "I might be mistaken insofar as the ladies of our neighborhood are concerned. I don't know, I would never say so about any of the ladies in our neighborhood, since they're all the most respectable people. Which is neither here nor there except that I want to keep the slate clean. That's the best policy . . ."

Poley looked out the window and saw a pretty Negro girl on the sidewalk. He rammed his elbow into Marquales' side.

"Eye that poon tang there," he said. "I could eat it with a knife and a fork. Where I come from we call that kind of stuff—*table pussy.*"

Poley gave Marquales another dig in the side with his horny elbow.

"Get this now, chum!" he said. "One day I started to talk to that guy I was telling you about. I remember how he took off his Panamaw hat and fanned himself with it like some Hollywood movie actor, and he started telling me how a smart fellow like myself would have no trouble selling subscriptions, and why didn't I go speak to Roberson down at the drugstore to see if I couldn't get a tryout. What that son of a bitch had up his silky sleeve I be dog if I know but I guess he figured he'd get something out of it, because otherwise I'd only be taking his business away.

"Anyhow I told Daddie about what I was thinking of doing. He says:

" 'That subscription fellow told you to do this? Well, don't.'

"And I says, 'Why?' I was mystified.

"And he says, 'Son, I suspect him to be a nigger.'

"Well, it never come to my mind that such a thing might be true, and I told Daddie he was wrong. 'Okay, Bill,' he says, and he offered to bet me a frawg he was."

"A what?" asked Marquales.

"A frawg. You know, on the arm."

"Frog on the arm?"

"That's right. So I took him up on it, and sure enough it turned

[ 78 ]

out the guy was a nigger and I got my arm frawged off. My old man don't hit no more than six inches, but just like Jack Dempsey he don't need much.

"That fellow was a nigger, and I'll tell you how Daddie got the secret out of him. Oh, cats, man, that was a hot afternoon around our house. It was boiling every which way. I remember Mom began to yell up from the basement, then she came tearing out on the porch where we were and started in on it for herself.

" 'Mr. Poley!' she says. 'Mr. Poley, please! That young gentleman's working his way through medical college!'

"Mom didn't know he was a nigger!" Poley laughed, whooping, and held weakly to his sides. "You should have seen her . . ." he paused, unable to continue, entirely unconcerned by Marquales' poker face. ". . . standing there, looking, not knowing what to think . . ."

It was necessary for Poley to take out a handkerchief and dry his eyes. He then got a grip on himself and continued:

"Marquales, here's the way it was. That afternoon this fellow came dandying up the walkway and stepped on our front porch, a stack of magazines under his arm.

" 'Sir,' said Daddie from the porch swing. 'I heard a fellow say you got nigger blood in you. Since you've come to my house again I want you to put me straight on this matter and tell me it isn't true.'

"This guy was standing on the front porch, smoking a Camel, dropping ashes down on our steps. When he heard Daddie's words he turned pale as a picket fence and said he never expected to listen to such a thing in his born days, that he was highly insulted; oh, he started up to talking, but he didn't get away with it long.

" 'You buttery son of a bitch!' shouts Daddie. 'I got you now, you're lying like a rug!'

"So he grabbed the guy, shook him back and forth and I threw that stack of magazines down into Mom's tulips, and my little old dawg came up and begun to bite at the nigger's ankles, tearing his silk socks all to hell and growling fit to kill, then Daddie slammed him back against the shutters, slamming him up hard and banging

[ 79 ]

the shit out of him, and he says, 'Look here, you goddamned black-assed hog-balled son-of-a-bitching bastard, don't you try and hand *me* any of that hocky about being a white man!' And he commenced to choke the goon, and hollered at him some more, and after awhile the nigger agreed he was a nigger, and Daddie give him an awful kick in his chops that carried him down the steps like he was a sack of meal with legs on it. I never did see my old man get so goddamned burned as he got at that nigger. The deceivah! Coming around with his fancy talk, his so-called good grammar, acting as if he were kin to the Stephenses, or the Richardsons."

Marquales started to answer. Then Poley said: "So Daddie gave me that frawg on the arm and I thought I heard the bone bust in two. Then he told me you had to keep your eye peeled for niggers all the time, and how it was that there were niggers up North that lived in white districts and had white wives and worked for white businesses and nobody up there knew they were niggers because nobody in the North could tell a nigger from an Italian, or any of those other New York types of people. Especially if there wasn't much blood from old Africa still in them."

Marquales said angrily, "My father would never have treated a colored man that way."

Poley threw back his head and looked down his nose at Marquales, laughing good-naturedly. "What kind of family you come from?"

"One that you never hear the word 'nigger'!" said Marquales.

"Well!" exclaimed Poley. "Man, you're talking about the black and the white. Don't you know what you're talking about? Why, a miss is as good as a mile and vice versa. Whoever said I'd hurt a good nigger, and what the crap do I care what your family says about the nigger's problem, whatever they say, and who are they that what they'd say would make any more difference than what the son of Alfred L. Poley would say? I ask you.

"I don't think nothing wrong about the nigger people, I'm all for their getting the best there is! The nigger is the white man's best friend. And I'm *for* him. But you come up and start talking about what your family says and what your family doesn't say . . . why in.

the name of Jesus Christ can't I say what I have to say and utter what I feel I ought to say, expressing my own opinion as I see the facts? Jesus Christ on the Cross!"

The bus stopped in the downtown section of Port George. Many of the passengers were looking at Marquales and Poley.

"Let's get off," whispered Marquales. He walked with lowered head to the rear exit, feeling the eyes upon him. He heard Poley stumbling along, then felt that freshman jostle clumsily against him; resentment boiled in Marquales and he pushed forward against a fat lady, escaping from his companion. Then, when he felt Poley bump up against him again he whirled around and stared into "Bill's" startled mud-brown eyes. "Stop it!" Poley was too surprised to ask, "What?" For the first time, as he stared at him, Marquales noticed that his eyes were askew: the right one pointed slightly upward. It gave him a philosophical, detached look.

Marquales about-faced and stepped out of the bus, yanking down the coattails of his Academy blouse.

**8** Poley followed Marquales from the hotel. On the street an autumn wind lifted red and yellow leaves toward them from Battery Square, which lay, with its rusted cannon and thick shrubbery, a few blocks ahead.

"I'm not used to it being this cold this time of year," said Poley.

"Well, the air's kind of wet," said Marquales. "From the river."

"This don't feel like no October weather to me."

"Don't feel like no October weather to me neither."

Poley faltered in his stride for a moment, then answered: "Fore long it'll be November."

"Shore will."

"Shut up," said Poley.

"What?"

"Nothing."

"You know," said Marquales lightly. "This shore don't feel like no October weather to me."

Poley exploded: "You're so smart!"

"Am I?"

"I told you not to try that place. I told you, yet you think you're so hot."

Marquales asked coolly, "To precisely what place do you refer?"

"What place . . ." spluttered Poley. "Why, that hotel! I told you not to waste our time going in there but like a fool you go busting in despite of what I said."

"They take advertising, don't they? Cadets' parents and friends come to town and get rooms, don't they?"

Poley inhaled, said, "Take it easy, chum."

"I'm taking it easy, chum. I'm selling ads."

Poley giggled at that remark, then patted Marquales on the shoulder in a placating manner. "Well, I really don't see why they send us both to town at the same time, do you? In all friendliness, how can they decide who's the best man that way?"

Marquales stopped on the sidewalk and glared at Poley. "What's selling this advertising got to do with the price of putty?"

Poley giggled again. "Why, it's the test."

"Little Red Romping Hood," muttered Marquales incoherently.

Poley smiled.

Marquales added in a nasty tone, "I don't see how a human brain could think up such dribble, 'It's a test.' The idea's beyond my poor mind, like a lot of yours are."

"What do you mean?" asked Poley with a gentle smile.

"I don't follow you!" shouted Marquales.

"Oh, well, I'll explain it to you then," said Poley. "Now look, here you got a school magazine, run by the school and by the cadets. Understand? Well, say, imagine there's cadets that want to try out to get on the magazine: you give them a test. It's simple. But wait, now, let's look at it this way. You're going to have an Academy career and I'm going to have an Academy career. We can't both go out for the same thing, can we? No, that wouldn't be possible. So here's the point. You go out on special leave to sell some advertising for the mag. I go out on special leave the same day. And with you alongside me, both of us doing the same thing! Get it? What's the point, I ask you?"

Marquales said: "I don't know."

"The point is there isn't any point. How can they know who's the best man sending us together like this? Why did they want to do that? Look, here's my plan. What we want—as good as your motives were buttonholing that clerk in the Wentworth Hotel—Munro said I was to get after those little delicatessens and flower shops down near the park. The hotels already have plenty of ads, and I figured the Wentworth wasn't ready to take more, having so much already. And though your motives were the best it was a waste of time to go in there.

"We'll take those delicatessens *and give them the works*. Now I'll take one and you take one and so on. Whoever gets the most ads is the best man. Okay? And we'll tell Munro who got the most ads. Okay?"

[ 83 ]

"Why not?" said Marquales.

"Great! Now you're talking. That's the way to co-operate! Okay, now that I got that settled I'm going to give you some advice about how to handle the Hebrews that run these delicatessens; there's no reason I shouldn't try and boost your sales as well as mine. Hell, the most important thing is that we should both sell a lot. But first, did you ever know a Yid personally?"

Marquales nodded.

"Well, then, of course you realize they are chinchy."

"What?"

"About money."

"Are they really?" asked Marquales. "Is that so?"

Poley whacked Marquales on the shoulder. "Man," he said. "Oh now, *man*! I heard you the first time but repeat it again."

On the tower the clock of the old Battery Square Fort struck two o'clock. Poley looked at his wrist watch. "The damn thing's slow," he said.

Marquales walked along, listening to the talk of his companion, becoming more and more annoyed.

". . . but there's ways of fooling them just as there's ways of fooling everybody. They think they're the smartest in the world, but as Abraham Lincoln said, with regard to people who think they are smarter than the next, 'You can fool part of the people part of the time but you can't fool the whole people the whole time.' Amen to that, brother. I never heard a truer saying, and don't let anybody try and tell you Lincoln wasn't a great President. I never have let anybody around me say anything against Lincoln.

"A few days ago a couple of upperclassmen had me in a brace and one of them, a Yankee, said, 'Look here, Mr. Poley. Who was the greatest, Robert E. Lee or Abraham Lincoln?'

"So I says, 'Abe Lincoln.'

"I didn't even put a 'sir' on it. Well, another of them was from Louisiana, and he raises up his head and says, 'What's that?'

"So I says, 'Sir, as great a man as Lee was, I have to admit Lincoln was greatest.'

[ 84 ]

"It got me in trouble with the Southerners at my table, and I prac tically braced myself to death. They kept saying I was a traitor to the South, that I didn't deserve to be born there. But I had to stick by the truth.

"Let's get back to the Yids. Here's the point. When you're trying to sell something to a Hebrew there's only one thing to do and that's make him think he's stealing something from you. Then he'll buy it. But not otherwise. Hell and high water couldn't make a Hebrew turn loose a nickel unless he needed his hand to pick up a dime and likely as not he'd try and swaller the nickel first.

"Now I'm going to tell you what I think about the ideas of a Hebrew, the way I started out. When you . . ."

"Look, Poley," interrupted Marquales. "I don't need you to tell me anything. Quit lecturing."

"What? Well, that's a fine attitude, by God that's slapping down the hand of a friend—do you think I'm doing this for my own good? I'm just trying to help you."

"But I don't need any of your help," said Marquales. "I do not want your advice."

Poley became silent; his cockeyes looked down at the sidewalk. Marquales noticed that the freshman's shoulders were sagging.

Les Wintermine had said of Poley, "too ugly to be looked at." That was not quite accurate, although Poley's physical appearance was undoubtedly a disadvantage. His face was sharp boned, nearly like an American Indian's. His unbrushed teeth bucked out past his lips, and his high cheekbones looked peculiar under white, "tow-headed" hair, tufts of which lay upon the tops of his ears. Poley's ears alone were enough to give him a deformed appearance. They were extremely large, and of an orange color. Finally, he had many blackheads on his forehead, spread in random clusters above the crossed eyes. Marquales shuddered from what he felt to be absolute physical revulsion, and broke the silence by asking:

"Would you like a co-cola?"

His companion brightened at once. They stopped in a drugstore and took seats on stools at the counter of the soda fountain. Poley insisted the drink-man put no ice into the glasses. "You get more coke that way." The coca-cola was watery, Marquales thought, with the extra soda.

When they got up to pay, Marquales at first tried to take the checks, then realized he had exactly twelve cents left from his allowance. "My father doesn't seem to realize the depression's over," he said uncomfortably.

"Here, chum," answered Poley, taking a large roll of dollar bills from his pocket. "My old man can set us up this time."

Marquales started to shake his head.

"Do you need a loan?" whispered Poley, paying the checks. "Go ahead. I'll never miss it."

"All right," said Marquales, taking two dollars, the exact sum of his weekly allowance. "I'll pay you back tomorrow when I get my money." He put the bills into the watch pocket of his trousers, followed Poley out to the street.

"Haven't you got a wallet?" asked Poley.

"Yes."

"You ought to put the money in there, then."

"It'll be all right where it is."

They walked on.


Poley said, "You come in with me this first time, and watch how I do it."

"Thanks."

"Then you take the next one on your own. Okay?"

Marquales didn't answer. Poley hesitated, then as they walked into the delicatessen he whispered, "Wish me luck."

A gray-haired man was behind the tall counter. Poley marched up to him. "Sir . . ." he began.

The man glanced at him, then called: "Tommy."

"Sir . . ." said Poley again.

A fat boy came from the rear of the store. About his waist was a dirty, cream-colored apron.

[ 86 ]

Poley cleared his throat. "I'd like . . ." he said slowly, in the manner of an orator.

"The boy'll wait on you," said the man.

"I'd like . . . to talk to you about a matter involving your business, sir," said Poley. The boy, who was about fifteen years of age, stood gaping.

"What?" asked the man.

"It's this," said Poley. "You're a businessman and I know you want to build up your business. Have you ever heard of the school magazine of The Academy?"

"No," said the man.

"Well, a friend of mine said to me . . . the other day, that he came into this establishment and bought some of your fancy imported Norwegian sardines. I'm sure numerous other cadets would like to know where they can be gotten. So, I thought you might be interested in taking an ad in our magazine, and getting many other cadets down here."

"I don't handle Norwegian sardines, son. And I can't take any ad for your paper. You run along now."

"Just wait a minute," said Poley.

"Look, I'm busy," said the man.

"May I have an explanation of that?" asked Poley desperately.

"I don't do any advertising; the business isn't large enough."

"Well. Don't you want it to get any larger? Isn't that the idea?"

Marquales said, "Let's go."

"Don't you want it to get any larger?" demanded Poley again, ignoring Marquales.

The boy in the apron began to giggle. The man smiled.

"Now look, mister," said Poley. "We're going to get ads from *all* you delicatessens in this part of town. Every one is going to give an ad that hasn't already."

"Poley," said Marquales.

"And several have already taken space. Now these ads don't cost much, because they will pay ten times what they cost. They have a value—and that value is money. Do you know there's a huge market at The Academy, and I'll tell you frankly, mister, the ones that don't take ads will be out in the cold looking in wondering what the score is. They'll be put on the magazine's blackball list. And no cadet would ever come around."

"I'm not interested in an ad," said the man.

"Well, I'm surprised to hear that! Of course, there are some cadets out at school who wouldn't be. There are those that would shrug their shoulder and ask hopelessly, 'What do you expect . . . from a Jew?' "

The gray-haired man rolled his eyes up toward the ceiling.

"But I'd never say that myself," added Poley quickly. "Because I disagree with the idea that a Jew is tight with money. I happen to know from experience that a Jew is generous with money. *Very* much so."

Silence.

"You know," said Poley. "There's an awful lot of good will to be gained from taking this little ad I'm offering you on a friendly basis. You won't get yourself blackballed, and there won't be any misunderstandings anywhere along the line."

"Poley," said Marquales anxiously. "He doesn't want an ad. Let's go."

"*Will you shut up?*" whispered Poley angrily. "Mister," he pleaded. "It'd be mighty simple for you to take a little space in the magazine. And I guarantee you the entire cadet corps would appreciate it."

"Tommy," said the man to his clerk. "I'm going back to the stock room to see about the order with Johnson."

"Hey!" said Poley. "I'm not through talking. Don't you want to extend the courtesy to listen at what I have to tell you? Hey!"

The man turned. "Go right ahead and talk to Tommy," he said.

"Come on," said Marquales, as the man disappeared into the back part of the store. "Let's go."

The kid Tommy broke into laughter. He shook his head, laughed so hard it became necessary for him to blow his nose. He reached into his coat for a rag, and Marquales then noticed, with surprise, that the boy wore on his vest-sweater the emblem of Willard High

School, Port George's seat of advanced learning for the Negro race. The boy, who seemed to be white, was a mulatto. Marquales observed the poll of unmistakable Negroid hair, jet and kinky, saw that the boy's nostrils were too flared to belong to a representative of the White.

"He leaves me in here to talk to this character," said Poley, enraged, trembling.

"Go on," said the boy, impudently placing his hands on his fat hips. "Tell me some more of that sale talk."

Poley took a step forward. "Look here, greasy guts," he snarled out of the side of his mouth. "There's guys that can buy and sell a hung-up halfbreed like you and never know they did more than let a poot." He took another step forward. "So swaller your hairy tongue or it'll get cut right out you!"

The boy stepped behind the counter. "Tell me some more of that hot sale talk," he said.

Poley ignored him, turned to go. At that moment the proprietor called from somewhere in the rear: "Tommy. Have those kids gone out yet?"

Poley whirled, glancing from the clerk to the sound of the voice. "Come on," he said to Marquales in a low voice. "Let's get out of this Yid dump."

At the door they heard the man again, "Tommy!"

Poley faced toward the rear, then suddenly shouted: "There'll be no cadets in this Yid dump any more!"

Quickly, Marquales walked out. Poley banged shut the screen door. On the sidewalk, he said: "Well, I guess you ruined that sale, buddy."

"It didn't seem to me to be much of a sale to ruin," said Marquales.

"Why did you keep pulling at me? A man would think you didn't *want* that bastard to buy an ad."

"Well, well, well," said Marquales in a gleeful voice. "That's one try for you, Poley, and you get *zero* on it. One time up to bat, and Babe Ruth whiffs."

Poley was green with rage. "It doesn't count," he choked. "Or it shouldn't. I swear to God how can a man make a sale with you standing there yapping, 'Let's go, Poley, let's go, Poley! He don't want it, Poley, come *on*, Poley'!? Jesus in heaven, but you sure do have a vulgar streak in you!"

"Let's get down to the next store," said Marquales. "It's only three o'clock and I'm just dying to sell *more* ads!"

"You know, I don't think you want to sell any ads this afternoon. And by God I'm half a mind to tell Munro and Layne how you caused me to miss that one back there."

"Listen," said Marquales. "I don't care what you tell Munro or Layne, and I doubt if they'd pay any attention to you anyhow. But the truth is that man wouldn't have bought an ad from you whether I'd been there or not."

"Well, when we get to the next store, I'm going to go in with you and I'm going to say: 'Come on, he don't want it! Let's go, it's hopeless!' And we'll see how you do."

"No," said Marquales. "I want to go in by myself."

"In that case," said Poley, "we won't count this last store as an attempt. You can't put it on the record. And that's final!"

"All right," answered Marquales.

"I'm glad that's settled. No point in arguing. And all I've got to say is, here you see what a tough job it is to sell something to a Hebrew. Brother, they just hold onto their money until it storms. But by God the next one I run into isn't going to get away with such stuff! I'm going to give him a real sales talk."

"And he'll get mad, hit you on the head, and have to bury you in the basement under the pickle barrels."

"I'm not joking."

"Neither am I."

"Oh, piss," said Poley. "Whoever heard of a Yid having the nerve to get cute with a white man?"

At the next delicatessen Marquales entered alone, leaving his companion against a telephone pole on the opposite corner. There was

[ 90 ]

no one inside the store. He started to call out, then he noticed the door in the rear was open. He saw a part of the back yard.

The sooner the better, he thought. A moment later he was across the yard, over the small fence, through an alley, and racing like a gray shadow down Pinkney Street.

Three blocks away, he cut back onto Mall Avenue. Stealthily, he slipped across the sidewalk and ducked behind a parked car. Then he looked: Poley was still leaning against the telephone pole. Marquales stooped over to tie his shoe, and when he looked again, Poley had disappeared. Five minutes passed.

Then suddenly, as Marquales watched, the door of the delicatessen flew open and Poley came tearing out. A short, plump man in a white apron had one hand on the seat of his trousers, one hand wrapped into his collar. Poley seemed to vibrate all over; Marquales realized that the man was giving him a violent shaking. Poley's gray Academy cap shot off his head and rolled down the sidewalk, then the man shoved him forward a short distance, drew back his foot and delivered a terrible kick square to the freshman's rear.

The last that Marquales saw—before he turned and hurried away in the opposite direction—was Poley sprawled on the sidewalk, beginning to sit up, and the short man walking back to the store.

# 9

Marquales looked across the yellow Mississippi. The east bank was a pale spine of land. He saw an old steamboat a thousand yards away, rolling down mid-channel. Below the bench on which he stood, the muddy water was hitting the rocks at the foot of the river wall.

There he saw a dead fish caught in a pocket of boulders. A few yards away, two birds were skimming over the waves, then water suddenly tumbled upon the fish, burying him in cold foam. The two birds circled on toward Port George Park.

He caught a glimpse of tiny feet hoisted beneath the tail of one —then the sky was filled with blood cells, in the shape of small circles. He lowered his head, experimentally rubbed his eyes, watching figures blaze before him, going brighter as he ground harder with his knuckles. In a moment he stopped, took a mirror from his pocket. He looked into his brown eye, into his blue eye, saw himself twice reflected in the black pupils.

A car passed behind him, tires hissing on the asphalt. A short blast from a horn. He turned, saw a station wagon go by. It was driven by a girl who grinned over her shoulder. He put the mirror in his pocket.

In a moment the car was beyond the edge of the park, beyond the River View Hotel, beyond the drive and on past the "Water-front Row." Undoubtedly, the girl, who thought it funny for an Academy cadet to stand on a bench and stare into a lady's mirror, lived in one of the homes along the drive.

He sat down on the bench and decided to risk a cigaret. Several cars rolled past. Each time, he held the cigaret behind him. Then he tossed it over the wall into the water and stared across the drive at the trees of Port George Park.

On one of the park benches an old man sat reading a newspaper. Marquales watched him get up and wander away, kicking at his shoe as if there were a pebble in it. Marquales took off his own shoes and looked: a few grains of pink sand fell out. He put on the shoes again, first pulling up tightly his damp socks.

He got up and walked across the drive to the park. He stood for awhile looking at a squirrel. Then he sat on a bench.

It was nearly four o'clock. The squirrel was chasing a friend. Poley, doubtless, was still selling ads. There wouldn't be time for a movie, but he could go see Luck Street. He got up.

A number of people were in the center of the park, gathered around the animal cages. The cages were under the same roof; that of a small, flat structure, a remainder of long ago when Port George Park was the town's amusement center. There was then no River View Drive, no River View Hotel, no mansions: there was only the river itself. And the nice homes were all farther uptown, on Cheney Street.

An old lion was still there, and a leopard. The lion was asleep, his mouth half open; the leopard sat stupefied in a corner: lion- and leopard-dung were moldering on the floors of both cages. There had been two wolves and a bear but they died, and their cells were empty. One cage was filled with birds, another had raccoons; there were three separate cages of monkeys.

Most of the people were in front of the first monkey cage, in which small brown monkeys played on the limbs of an old tree stuck in the concrete floor. Marquales walked on to the chimpanzee cage. It was a small box containing a single ape. A red-faced man in a derby stood staring into the cage, and Marquales took a place by his side. The man had a cigar between two fingers of his right hand. On one of those fingers was a diamond ring.

They looked at the ape, who looked at them.

"Ugly fellow, isn't he?" said the man in a rumbling voice.

"He sure is," answered Marquales.

The man took off his derby and began to rub it with his coat sleeve. He had a full head of gray hair. "But according to the standards of an ape—who knows?—he might be beautiful, or handsome."

"I guess so."

"Oh, yes. These apes train well, too. A chimpanzee."

The man flicked ash to the sidewalk, and gently inserted the well-modeled brown tube between his lips. He puffed meditatively, sucking on the cigar in a way that wiggled his gray moustache.

The man said to Marquales: "I saw a remarkable show one time. They had these apes roller skating all around a stage, and one of them wore formal dress. Remarkable. I should have brought my niece over here to see this one here."

In the cage the chimpanzee yawned, stared at one of his hairy, bethumbed feet. He picked at the fur on his ankle, caught something that he popped into his mouth. He yawned, turned his puddly eyes toward the ceiling, blinked solemnly, yawned again.

"Doesn't he look stupid?" asked the gray-haired man, extracting the cigar to speak.

The chimpanzee closed his eyes. Marquales smiled, started to move away.

"Ssst," said the man. "Sssst! Look here, monk."

The ape opened his eyes and looked at the man, who began to wave his cigar back and forth. "Do a trick for me and this lad, monk."

The man had a northern accent: Marquales decided he was a tourist.

As they waited the chimpanzee turned, walked across the cage, walked back, turned again, walked back. Suddenly he leaped up, grabbed the limb of the tree in the cell, pulled himself rapidly hand over hand until he was just beneath the roof. Grinning, he urinated down in a long splattery yellow stream to the floor.

"Mpf!" said the man, drawing back his arm and hurling the cigar at the monkey. The missile sailed between the bars and struck the opposite wall, showering sparks. Dangling by his arm the ape swung from side to side, grinning.

"You're lucky," said the man to the ape. To Marquales he said confidentially, "That's the trouble with bringing children to a zoo; you never know what one of those animals might be about."

"Yes, sir," said Marquales.

"Glad my niece stayed at the hotel," said the man, as he walked away, chewing at the end of another cigar. So a tourist, thought Marquales.

[94]

Before the large monkey cage a child was throwing handfuls of popcorn through the bars. Another child was holding onto the skirts of its Negro nurse, weeping, looking at the monkeys, who fought for the popcorn. One old lady stood by, yanking at a string attached to a poodle. Marquales edged by them.

He passed through the park, cut down Morton Place until he reached Pinkney Street. He walked up that thoroughfare for a few blocks. Afraid he might run into Poley he crossed to Maringo Street, the borderline of the colored district. Ten minutes later he reached the projecting street sign that said in small letters: "Maringo Street," and in large, "LUCK STREET." Some joker had climbed the lamp post and slightly altered the "L."

Marquales was reminded of verses about Luck Street he had once heard from fat Carlton Leroy.

The street was only two blocks long. One side was occupied entirely by Negro house-apartments, large homes that had been mansions when the street had a different character. The houses on the other side were of the same kind, but for the most part were in better repair.

Far down the block two white women were sitting on a front porch. One read a magazine; the other seemed to be whittling on a stick. From that distance Marquales couldn't tell whether they were good looking or not. But the house they belonged to needed a coat of paint.

Then there came from one of the houses on the "white side" a short, dapper figure, with a bamboo cane. It wore gray suede gloves, gold-rimmed spectacles, spats, had a handkerchief peering from one sleeve. Marquales watched in fascination as the figure approached, and was startled when it spoke to him:

"Good afternoon there, young fellow."

Marquales did not reply. The man, a pale mulatto, had scarlet touches of lipstick on his mouth, and his mellow eyes were shaded by long false lashes. There was powder on his cheeks, the glisten of cold cream on his eyelids. At each step he threw his shoulders forward

[ 95 ]

with an odd spasm, and shook his skinny gray-trousered hips from side to side.

How nauseating, thought Marquales as he watched the figure disappear down Maringo Street. He looked again at the two women on the distant porch—confused.

Marquales reported in the Guardroom of Hemphill Barracks at ten past five. From the Amanuensis he learned that Poley had not returned.

He hastened to the Administration Building and walked up the stairs to the *Port Arms* office. At first he thought no one was there, then he heard a laugh he knew came from Thomas Munro, the managing editor. He knocked, and entered.

Tom Munro, Pete Layne, and a junior named Albert Wilson were inside.

"Sit down," said Wilson to him.

Layne and Munro were reading a typed manuscript; Wilson watched them. At first, Marquales did not remember Wilson's name, or where he'd seen him; then he recalled the fact that this cadet was one of Jocko de Paris' close friends. Wilson had known Jocko in Atlanta, and had visited the De Parises when they moved to Chicago: both the Wilson and De Paris families had winter homes in St. Petersburg, Florida. Albert Wilson's father was a famous Atlanta lawyer, recently appointed to a job in Washington, D. C.

The two seniors read on. Layne began to laugh, and shook his head. "It's not half bad, Albert," he observed.

Marquales sat nervously in the straight chair by the door; it was possible that they expected him to sell ads despite Layne's advice that he not break his back in the attempt. He watched Munro pass the last page to Layne, saw him smile at Wilson.

"Congratulations, Albert," said Munro.

Wilson grinned; they waited while Layne read the last page. Then Wilson said, "Pretty good?"

Layne nodded his head in agreement.

"Albert old man," said Munro. "She likes you. That's all there is to it."

Layne said, "I don't know why."

"Neither does Wilson," said Munro.

"No," said Wilson. "Not much."

"It must be some kind of manhood."

"What?"

"Virile manhood. You know."

"A little runt like Albert?"

"Runt," said Wilson. "Who's a runt?"

"Oh, it isn't size," said Layne. "Nor good looks. Being six feet tall, that is, tall, dark, and handsome, is likely to be as much of a liability as it is an asset. It puts them on their guard. What really counts is . . . personality, the sense of humor, and getting the best of them. That's the story, gentlemen."

Wilson's face was without expression. He said to Layne, "If you are being funny—ha, ha, ha."

"Oh, I'm not joking," said Layne quickly. "I mean it, Albert. Hell, don't be so sensitive. I'm paying you a compliment, fellow."

"There're women who hate good-looking men."

"Don't I know it?" laughed Layne. "No, seriously, I meant all that I said, Albert."

Marquales sat back in the shadow, and fidgeted in his chair. He wondered when Poley would arrive, listened for the sound of steps in the hall outside.

"Well," said Munro. "That girl ought to go to Hollywood."

"She couldn't make the grade out there," blushed Wilson. "No tits."

"I mean, to write love scenes," explained Munro.

"Tom," said Layne. "If they put something like that letter in a picture show the movie morons would get out of hand."

"They're out of hand already," said Munro.

"No. They're *in* hand," grinned Wilson, moving his fist.

They laughed: Munro extended his arms for silence. "Ginger," he said in a hoarse whisper. "Ohhhh, Ginger. Wherefore art you?"

"Ooooo," said Wilson, falsetto.

"Ginger!"

Layne interrupted: "How could anybody like that painted blonde? Jean Harlow, now, brother—but Ginger Rogers, never. Make it that Harlow."

"Shhh," whispered Munro. "We're movie morons. HEY, JEAN! ARE YOU THERE, GAL?"

"I'm here, Mergenthwaite," answered Wilson in a piping voice. "Let me have Moby Dick."

"You'll get Moby Dick!" growled Munro. "You'll get Moby Dick than you ever got, you old bat!"

"You boys quit," said Layne. "Jean Harlow's dead."

"But what a slab of backside," said Wilson.

"For maggots."

Laughter continued three or four minutes, then Munro said:

"Albert, that girl of yours types a dirty typewriter, and I'd never deny it. But she's no better than one I once knew. Some of the letters I used to get from that girl, I swear to God.

"You know, a long time ago I thought girls weren't evil minded. I know that sounds awful dumb, but I really thought women were different in that respect. Then when I got some of these masterpieces from this old girl I decided by comparison men were pure as spring water. And about twice as cold.

"I'll never forget when my father got his hands on one of her letters. I never went through such hell. I thought he was going to give me a whipping, I really did, and I was nineteen at the time. It was a disillusion to the old boy. He believed I still had my cherry. And the only way I could stop him from writing to the girl's father was by telling him that if he did I'd have to quit school and marry her, and that it'd be hell to be married to a girl who'd make you scared to go into the bedroom at night because you'd never know which one of your friends you'd find in the bed. Pop cut off my allowance for six goddamn months."

"How'd you get by all that time?" asked Layne.

"I didn't."

[ 98 ]

"The same thing happened to me once," said Layne. "Just about the same thing. I was around seventeen years old, and one night I went out with some little old girl, I don't remember who, but anyhow the next morning when Dad went to the garage and got in the car he found a rubber draped over the steering wheel. I'll be damn, to this day I don't know how that thing got there.

"But I remember selling my clothes to our cook, after the allowance was cut off. Shirts at ten cents each. Do you know I wasn't supposed to get any more money for a year? Then I pawned my watch; and I actually pawned the old watch chain that belonged to great-grandfather. Then Mother found out about it and raised tumultuous hell getting it out of this pawnshop. And she started slipping me a little money. She didn't know what the hell was going on, and it still tickles me to think about the arguments she and Dad used to have about why he cut off my allowance."

"It's funny," interposed Munro. "I'm always amused when I think about how my father was so indignant just because I got myself a piece of tail. Why, he's worse than I am, if the truth were known. At least, I don't buy it: or only now and then. I'll never forget that time he went to St. Louis and brought me back a silk bathrobe. He said it was new, but he'd worn it once or twice, he claimed, when some business acquaintances came to see him at night. They must have been the kind of business acquaintances that wear brassieres and panties because there were a couple of used rubbers rolled up in a nasty handkerchief in the bathrobe pocket.

"That damn old horny goat, going around the country screwing business acquaintances. Then cutting off my allowance when I salvage a piece of free pussy. It's a hell of a note. Isn't it?"

"Sir," said Marquales suddenly. They all looked at him.

"Where'd he come from?" said Wilson. "Sitting over there quiet as a mouse."

Layne said, "Mr. Marquales just wanted to be polite."

"Well good for him, then," said Wilson.

"Hi, Mr. Marquales," said Layne. "How'd the ads go? Did you sell any, or did you go to a movie?"

"I didn't have any luck with the ads, sir," said Marquales. "Nobody wanted any, I'm afraid."

"Poor General Draughton—disappointed again," said Munro.

"Oh he doesn't care about that fucking budget, but he's really going to get on our necks if we don't dig up another Editorial With A Message," said Layne.

"I guess we ought to get Corger to write one," said Munro.

Wilson remarked slyly: "But he's too busy running the school." They laughed, and Wilson added, "I don't go for any of that military crap."

There was a pause. Then Munro said, "Naturally: And what private ever did?"

"I could have got rank if I wanted to kiss Evers' ass."

"Colonel Evers didn't keep you down—Jim and me blackballed you," said Munro.

"I wouldn't be shocked if that was the truth."

"Well, vengeance might be yours some day. If we all get in the regular army to go shoot off Hitler's cods then these cadet buttons won't mean anything. You might outrank Munro and me."

"If I do, it'll be too bad, bud."

"We realize that. It's a chance we have to take."

Marquales interrupted again: "Sir, I wanted to speak to you about Poley . . ."

"Oh," smiled Layne. "Isn't he a card?"

"Yes, sir, he is . . ."

"How is it you're not with him now, Mister?" asked Munro. "Didn't you two go to town together?"

"Yes, sir," said Marquales. "That's what I wanted to tell you. We went together, but I ducked him after awhile."

"What did you want to duck him for? Was he trying too hard to sell ads?" asked Munro sarcastically.

"I just don't like him," answered Marquales.

"That's putting it straight," said Munro. "Now and then I like a freshman who comes out and says something, instead of this eternal dreary chicken shit. I like you, mister. What the hell's your name, anyhow—and have you got insurance?"

They all laughed.

"Let me do this freshman a favor!" said Wilson. "Say, Mister Freshman, may I offer you a cigaret? Please accept. A light, Mister Freshman, sir?"

Marquales took the cigaret, said, "Thanks."

"What's his name, anyhow?" said Munro to Layne.

"His name's Marquales," said Layne. "He's kin to an old friend of mine, a Knoxville beauty."

"Well, Mr. Marquales," said Munro. "From what I've seen of this Poley boy I don't blame you. Where is he, anyhow?"

"I guess he'll be in soon, sir," said Marquales. "It's five-thirty."

"What's today?" asked Layne. "Thursday? We've got a meeting tomorrow night, haven't we. How would you like to come along, Mr. Marquales? Nobody will beat your tail."

"We don't want any freshmen this early in the year," said Munro.

"Oh, why not? We've got to scout around, or we are going to get short stick again this year. How'd you like to come, Mr. Marquales, and meet some of the men?"

"But what is it, sir?" asked Marquales.

"The Hair-of-the-Hound Club," said Munro. "Upstairs in Neddie's Grill, down Mall Avenue. If you come be there before nine and don't you get drunk. Freshman can't. They're liable to be sassy."

"Yes, sir," said Marquales.

Wilson said, "And don't go blabbing around."

"Oh, no, sir."

Wilson looked steadily at him. "By the way," he said. "Are you the freshman that rescued Jocko?"

"Yes, sir."

"He's hell when he's drinking, isn't he?"

"He was so drunk that night he didn't do much, sir."

"What's all this about?" asked Munro.

Layne said: "Mr. Marquales and his roommates lugged Jocko in one night."

"Somebody's always lugging him in," said Munro. "One of these days they'll kick him out of this school."

"He never could hold his liquor."

"Considering the amount he drinks he holds it better than anybody I know," said Wilson.

"He'll get the knife from Evers some day."

"Evers, hell. Somebody'll probably beat him to pieces in one of those honky-tonks," said Layne.

"I've never known Jocko to be whipped," said Wilson. "And Colonel Evers wouldn't kick him out, he knows his father."

"The General, then."

"That old lanky bastard wouldn't either. He thinks Jocko's an angel, and he and Jocko's old man are B. H. B's."

"The Dreadnaught could change his mind."

"Not him. He hasn't changed his mind in thirty years."

"Well he ought to. The one he's got is worn out."

Munro stood up. "My teeth are drowned," he said. "Has Willy closed up the can yet?"

"No, it's open," answered Layne, glancing at his watch.

Munro walked across the room to the hall door—just as his hand started to touch the knob it suddenly drew back, and William Poley rushed through the door, breathing hard. Munro dodged to one side, but Poley nevertheless clumsily bumped into him. The freshman didn't pause—he marched on across the room toward Layne, who was sitting with his feet on one of the desks.

# 10

"Hey," said Munro.

Poley turned; he saw Marquales. *"There* you are!"

"Hey!" shouted Munro.

Poley looked blankly at the senior. "Sir?"

"Oh, skip it," said Munro, walking away.

"Who's this bat-in-the-belfry?" asked Wilson.

"I am William S. Poley, sir."

"Well, close your trap, William S. Poley."

"Sir?"

"Leave him alone, Albert," said Layne. "Quit imitating Jocko."

*"Bullshitsky!"* Wilson held up his right middle finger.

Poley stepped forward: he came to attention.

"Hi, Mr. Poley," said Layne with a wave of the hand. "How are tricks?"

Poley relaxed, glanced coolly toward Wilson. *"Thank* you, Mr. Layne. For letting me speak."

"Listen to this mutt," said Wilson.

"Sirr?"

"Prrrt!" said Wilson with his tongue and lips.

"Well, Mr. Layne," said Poley with a shrug. "Here's my report. I had a big afternoon, made a lot of contacts, saw a lot of people, talked the mag up . . ."

Albert Wilson burst into a long sustained laugh.

For several seconds the freshman stood immobile, then he shook himself, squared his shoulders, and continued: "Well, sir, I had a big afternoon, as I was attempting to tell you. A big afternoon!" Poley thrust out his hand—in it were three trembling slips of paper.

"What's this?" asked Layne.

"Receipts, sir! For sold ads!"

Layne murmured, "That's fine, Mr. Poley."

"Thank you, sir."

"The General will be grateful."

"Will he, sir?"

"Of course."

"That makes me glad, sir."

[ 103 ]

"You've done well."

Then Poley said in a different voice, "Sir, I have a matter to settle with that freshman setting over there. May I speak to him freely?"

"Listen to the bird," said Wilson.

Poley stared up and down the junior. "Sir?"

"Don't 'sir' me another time like that or I'll chop off your ass," said Wilson.

"Er, go ahead and ask Marquales whatever you want," smiled Layne. "Don't mind Albert; he's only talking."

Poley stepped toward Marquales. "Just where did you go?"

"Down on the farm to call some hawgs," answered Marquales.

Wilson and Layne laughed.

Poley said, "Marquales—don't go getting smart or I'll let you have it."

"Jesus," remarked Wilson. "A real rough type."

"Take it easy, Mr. Poley," said Layne, smiling.

Poley ignored the upperclassmen. "I saw you, Marquales," he said, narrowing his eyes, twisting his lower lip. "I saw you running off down that street. Now what deal did you have on with that Yid?"

"Me?"

"Don't play dumb, you bastard!"

Marquales stood up.

Poley hunched over, backed away several steps. "Don't look at me in that tone of voice," he said, "or I'll stomp your guts out you."

"Jesus," said Wilson, laughing.

"All right, all right!" said Layne. "You freshmen shut up. Shut your mouths."

Poley said, "Come on Mar—"

"Shut up!"

"You're saved, Marquales," said Poley.

"Did I tell you to shut up?"

"Mr. Layne, you just saved Marquales . . ."

"I always was lucky," said Marquales, sitting down.

Layne said, "You'd better go now, Mr. Poley."

"Sir?"

"Go on up to barracks."

Poley stared.

"You can't act like that in this office. Go on up to barracks. This is a magazine office, not a poolroom. In this place we edit a publication, we don't hold open house—it's not like coming to town on Saturday from the farm—you can't talk like that, even if you were an upperclassman, but you're a *freshman*."

"Sir," said Poley, choking. "May I ask a question?"

"What?"

"I request that that son-of-a-bitch put on the gloves with me."

"For Christ's sake," said Wilson. "This guy gives me a pain. Grab him and beat the hell out of him, Marquales."

"Wait a minute!" said Layne. "Mr. Poley, you march yourself right out of here: I'll give you three seconds! Get!"

Poley mumbled, "I'll fight him any time. Marquales, don't make the error of thinking I'm scared of you, I'll lay you out . . ."

"Get on away from here!" said Layne, half smiling.

"But sir, don't I get an assignment?"

"A *what*?"

"An assignment . . . a job of writing something."

"For the magazine?"

"Yes, sir."

"Jesus," said Wilson. "A pinhead."

"You go on now, Mr. Poley," said Layne.

"Very well then, sir," said the freshman. "I worked hard this afternoon, sir. More hard than he did . . ."

Marquales thought Poley was going to cry. Then Poley turned and marched to the door, opened it, and bumped heavily into Tom Munro, who was just returning from the washroom.

"Hey, you!" said Munro.

Poley walked on.

Munro asked, "What's going on—a freshman revolution?"

"Oh, it was nothing much," said Layne. "That Mr. Poley just started to kick up his heels, and raise his voice in anger."

"Who at?"

"Mr. Marquales here."

"These freshmen are getting out of hand. Especially the hicks. I swear they are."

"Lord, I'm hungry," said Layne, yawning. "I hope we don't have those meat balls tonight."

"What's the matter with them?" asked Wilson. "They have to do something with those old inner tubes, don't they?"

Munro said, "Every time I eat one of those meat balls it reminds me of that story about the fellow found a human knuckle in his hamburger, and complained. The guy said, 'It's fresh. Isn't it?'"

"Ugh," said Layne.

"No, it actually did happen—of course when the fellow found it nobody made any joke. Turned out that one of the guys at the meat packers had caught his hand in the machine. They didn't want to throw out all the meat."

"My appetite," said Layne weakly. "Where'd you hear such a repulsive lie?"

"In one of the bean wagons downtown. But it's true."

"I doubt that seriously."

"The hell. I don't doubt it for a minute."

"The sanitary laws forbid that kind of thing."

"Sanitary laws, hell. When you eat hamburger you never know what it is. You think it's low-grade beef, but everybody knows it might be horse meat."

"Why you could get sent to the penitentiary for that," said Layne.

"Look," said Munro. "De Paris was telling me the other day about the Chicago slaughter barns. From what he said about them I'm surprised the whole country doesn't die of it."

"Don't tell me they mix horse meat with beef."

"I wouldn't be surprised what they'd do."

"Look, let's change the subject. I know they're going to have that hamburger tonight, and this conversation is making me sick."

"Pete, I don't know how you got through your freshman year."

"I don't either. There was a fellow here then that would make any of the present upperclassmen look like angels. A big guy named

Mack Hagan. You knew him, didn't you, Tom? He used to talk about the nastiest things when I was trying to eat. I finally got off his mess, thank God. I was about to starve. I just couldn't eat when he started to talk about that stuff."

"Hagan?" said Munro. "Hell, I spent the whole spring term on his mess. Me and a freshman named Carter were the only first-year men at the table.

"The food was worse then than it is now. Jesus, it was monotonous. Pete, you remember. That goddamn spaghetti. I've never seen spaghetti like that anywhere. You could take a strand of it and hang yourself."

"I don't recall this Hagan bird," said Wilson.

"He was a senior; graduated the year before you got here," said Layne.

"Well, I remember him all right," said Munro. "I'll never forget him."

Layne said, "He was the lad that stuck Bob Carter's nose into the electric light socket, wasn't he?"

"Yes, that was Hagan, all right. A true-blue bastard."

"Did you see him do it?" asked Wilson.

"No, Hornbuckle did. He was rooming with Carter then. Used to tell me how Carter carried on—you can't blame him."

"Who was this Carter?" asked Wilson nonchalantly.

"He didn't come back after his freshman year. Didn't have the money."

"I don't know that I'd talk against him if he didn't come back if he did have the money."

"Sir," said Marquales from his post near the doorway. They all turned toward him. "Wasn't the fellow hurt?"

"Well," chuckled Munro. "Carter claimed he couldn't smell shit for two weeks—and there was sure an awful blister on his beak."

"You know," said Layne quietly. "They ought to kick an upper-classman out of school who'd treat a freshman that way."

"No. They ought to just do the same thing to him," said Munro

Albert Wilson said, "This Carter must have been dropped on his head or something."

"What do you mean?"

"I mean to let a guy pull one like that on you."

"It was this way," said Munro, scratching under his arm. "Hornbuckle told me Hagan didn't like Carter because Carter wouldn't loan him some money one time. In the first place, poor old Carter didn't have any money to loan. It was all he could do to get enough money from his folks to buy his uniforms—and they were second-hand, at that. They were nice people, his family, but the depression must have been too much for them.

"Anyhow, one afternoon Hagan came around to see Hornbuckle and Carter and he started to cut ass. After awhile he left Hornbuckle alone and latched on to Carter. Well, he cut it, and he cut it, and he kept on cutting it. He splintered their broom, sent Hornbuckle next door for another one. Finally, Carter started to boohoo. He commenced to beg Hagan to stop it. So Hagan laughed and said he guessed he would stop all right, but not until he spelled out the word C-R-Y B-A-B-Y on Carter's tail. That meant eight more licks counting the period at the end, so the freshman began to slobber like hell, just begging up a storm, saying it'd kill him, he couldn't endure another knock from that broom, and on like that.

"So then Hagan asked him how he'd like it if there wasn't any more ass-cutting for a whole month. Naturally, Carter was hot for that idea. So it happened that Hagan talked him into the socket deal—partly by that promise to leave him alone for a month, and also partly by arguing that if Carter would just put on his overshoes it wouldn't amount to more than a tickle. Hagan said he wanted Carter to do it because he'd made a bet with a girl that he could make a freshman go through such a thing—I guess he invented that stuff, because as far as I remember Mack Hagan never saw any girls unless they were Luck Street whores."

"The bastard would never talk me into it," laughed Wilson.

"Maybe if you knew how Hagan could lay on with a broom you wouldn't say that. The man could almost knock you out by jarring your backbone. I mean it, and I know. He used to blister me three times every Friday, just as regular as the calendar. Now, as much as I looked forward to getting general leave on Friday night, I used to hate to see the day roll around. I'd dread it all week. Those Friday afternoons—man, they were hell."

"I wouldn't put up with it," said Wilson. "A little ass-cutting now and then isn't bad, or at the end of the year, when you're recognized. But that regular stuff—no, sir. I'd have done something."

"What?" interrupted Layne.

"Yes, what?" asked Munro. "Hagan was a high-ranking senior."

"Put a board in my pants if nothing else."

"Listen," said Munro. "You think that's funny, but one week I made up my mind I didn't want to get whacked the same old way. So before Hagan came around I put on about six pairs of undershorts. I was smart, I was going to fox him.

"Well, kids, he hit me once, and he started to frown. Then he gave it another lick, and he said—'Mister, that don't ring right!'

"I knew the game was up, so without waiting to be told I took off my pants. He was laughing like hell. I went ahead and took off all those undershorts. Then he told me to get over the press—he used to say, 'Get in the old position, honey.' Well I got in it, with my bare ass poking up in the atmosphere. I felt like my day had come, and I remember thinking—'Will I live through this? Will I look back on this and laugh about it?'

"Hagan stationed himself halfway across the room, like he was in a batter's box, and says, 'Here I come!' Then with a hop, skip, and a leap he came running across the room, and I just had time to grit the hell out of my teeth before I heard that broom singing through the air. Then there was that goddamned thud that doesn't even seem to be connected with you. At the same time there was a funny sound, like a pistol being shot, then all at once, a good second after she landed, I felt the broom, and my poor ass went numb like a cake of ice, then it shifted to a hunk of red-hot charcoal, and about that time something popped the ceiling up above and came down and conked me on the head—it was half of the broom. He'd broke the thing clean as a whistle, and sent half of it flying up to the ceiling. Now there are those that claim a lick that breaks a broom automatically doesn't hurt you as much, but so help me I never saw it in that light . . ."

Wilson said, "I haven't got much respect for a freshman that lets an upperclassman run over him that way. Not that I blame you, Tom. But as for me, if he'd come up and started cutting my tail that way, or started some electric socket business, why hell, I'd tell him that if he didn't stop it I'd kill him. And I would, too, by God. I'd lay for him in town some night, get myself a piece of plumber's pipe, and I'd knock out his brains."

"Oh, bullshit. You wouldn't do anything like that, Albert," said Munro. "And if you made such a remark to Hagan—oh, brother, it would be too bad, you'd never recover from what he'd do."

"I *guarantee* you that NO MAN would ever put MY snout in an electric socket. I'd kill him first. Or he'd kill me."

"All this killing stuff," laughed Pete Layne.

"I mean it," said Wilson. "I'm not kidding. I don't care what the consequences would be . . ."

"Well, look," said Munro. "If you'd been such a poor shrimp as Bob Carter I doubt if you'd have the nerve to do a damn thing. What could he do? Hagan was a big strong guy."

"A girl could swing a lead pipe hard enough to fix him up."

"But she might not have the nerve . . ."

"Then she ought to have her snout put in a socket."

They all began to laugh uproariously.

After a few moments Layne said solemnly, "Well, all I've got to say is it certainly was a mean trick for Hagan to pull, and they ought to have kicked him out of school for such a thing."

"Oh, it was plenty mean all right," agreed Munro. "The very *thought* of it makes me shiver. Christ! What an awful thing! I'll never forget when Hornbuckle told me about it. You know, up till then I really didn't realize there were mean guys like Mack Hagan in the world.

[ 110 ]

"Hornbuckle said Carter took the socket himself, unscrewed the bulb, and got his snout in place, with Hagan holding the other end of the wire. Then Carter closed his eyes and hunched over in a knot, waiting. So Hagan says, 'Here we go,' and plugged the cord in the wall. Christ! The sparks scattered all to hell over Carter's lap, and the poor guy began to shake and go, 'Muuuuu, Muuuu.' Old Hagan stood there awhile, then he slipped out the cord and walked away like he'd just left one of Colonel Whitlow's tea parties."

"Hell, man. In those days we lived a hard life, and I don't mean maybe. Mr. Marquales, you don't know how lucky you are they don't grow them like Hagan around here now. The upperclassmen in those days were so goddamned mean that they ate gunpowder."

"Oh," said Layne. "They'll be talking like that about us in a few years. They always glamourize the past."

"What I wouldn't have done to Hagan if . . ." said Wilson.

"Wait a few years," said Layne to Munro. "Why Mr. Marquales and his crowd of freshmen will be sitting around telling about how awful *we* were, what a fiend *I* am, and so forth." He began to giggle.

"You might be right," said Munro. "I mean about how when a thing is finished it gets glorified in your imagination. I remember in my freshman year how everybody used to talk about a guy named Phelps—he was supposed to be quite a son of a bitch."

"He couldn't have been much worse than this Hagan bird," said Wilson.

"He was supposed to be. Hagan himself used to talk about what a bastard Phelps was."

Layne said, "Wasn't it Phelps who dragged that sissy freshman down to Luck Street?"

"Yes."

"What do you mean, dragged him down to Luck Street?" asked Wilson.

"He took him down there and made him lay one of the whores."

"What's wrong with that?"

"But this one was a nigger whore."

[ 111 ]

"Well, I don't mind a slab of poon tang every now and then," said Wilson brightly.

"But he told the freshman that the whore had siff. Besides, you have to keep in mind that this kid wasn't any whore-hopper like you, Albert. He'd never had a piece of tail."

"Well, one does have to lose one's innocence some time or other."

"That's true enough."

"And anyhow, I'd sure rather go through *that* torture . . ."

Marquales gave a nervous giggle, and they looked at him.

". . . than get next to an electric socket."

"I guess you got a point there," said Munro. "But don't have the wrong idea about Hagan, now. He had his good side, just like everybody else.

"I remember at the end of the year, when all the upperclassmen were touring around the galleries with brooms beating hell out of the freshmen recognizing them as sophomores—well, old Hagan came in my room, and God almighty I practically let out a groan when I saw him, because my tail was like a rainbow already.

"So he told me to get over the press, and I did. I waited, and waited, and at last I heard a laugh and Hagan says,

" 'Get up from there, Munro you goddamned son of a bitch, you, and shake my hand.'

"So I asked him didn't he mean to cut my tail, and he said he guessed he'd already about beat it off. Then I grabbed his hand and shook the hell out of it and he said, 'You call me Mack.'

"From then on until the end of the year, about three or four days, we were good friends. Of course, during the other nine months it was the other way around."

They laughed.

"I'd never have shaken his hand," said Wilson.

"If you didn't he could still have considered you a freshman, not a sophomore, and could have made your last few days unjoyful."

"Well," said Wilson. "Oh, crap on the whole thing."

Layne got up and stretched. "Mmm," he said. "Gosh, are they going to let us starve to death? When's that bugle popping off? I'm hungry."

William Poley appeared in the *Port Arms* office several days later with an essay entitled, "A Freshman On The Academy."

The opening sentence: "Many freshmen come from all parts of the U.S.A. to this grand school—albeit they are mostly from that arena of the country known fondly as 'Dixie.'"

Munro kept "A Freshman On The Academy" for a few days and showed it to other cadets. He returned it to Poley with the mark, "F."

Because Poley's handwriting was illegible he had laboriously printed the essay: it was about five thousand words long, and covered thirty-seven pages.

Poley then joined the Georgia Club. At first he thought it similar to one of the illegal cadet clubs; he pictured drinking parties, beer barrels, camaraderie, good times, rented beach cabins.

When he discovered that the Georgia Club did little more than have its picture taken for the school annual he joined the Boat Club and at the same time tried to place himself in the Cadet Choir.

Unfortunately, at the first rehearsal of the choir Poley told a dirty joke that was overheard by Miss Scotter, the choir mistress.

It was too cold to sail when he joined the Boat Club; therefore activities consisted of occasional meetings in which sailing trips were projected for the following April. At his first meeting with the members of the club Poley arose and made a ten-minute speech. In no uncertain terms he berated the members for idleness. "Let us have action!" he said. "Why not a bunch of parties and things?"

Thus was born the Poley Cold-weather Action Committee—Chairman, Cadet William S. Poley. The first project of the Committee was a party, a gala event called:

THE POLEY COLD-WEATHER ACTION COMMITTEE CLAMBAKE.

Poley, in his capacity of chairman, was asked to dip clams from the Boat Club anchorage. The freshman spent several dollars for clam equipment, then he took his position in a dinghy by the dock pilings and began to dip. At first, many Boat Club members stood on the docks and cheered him on, gave advice, praised him, said he was giving the organization new life, etc. Then they left, because it was an unusually cold day and had begun to drizzle.

A long time later one tenderhearted member traveled the half-mile out the catwalk to the dock and told the chairman the truth.

Poley said, "I was actually trying for catfish."

To the members of the Boat Club he was known as the "Baked Clam." Other cadets—nonmembers of the Boat Club—spoke of him as "The Pride of the Boat Club." The story of how Poley "dipped for clams" in the Mississippi was widely related. Other cadets called him "Mr. Moe." He understood that "Moe" was an abbreviation of "moron": his constant rejoinder—"No white man eats sea food."

Late in November an accident sent Poley back to Valdosta, out of The Academy life forever.

One night he went on leave to Port George, alone, and saw a movie at the Port George Theater. He sat high in the balcony and fell asleep, not awakening until nearly two o'clock in the morning. The theater was black and silent.

He went creeping down the stairs, reached the mezzanine. There he saw light: the manager's office. The door was partly open; inside, on a leather divan, the manager was caressing a half-naked usherette.

Poley stared from the doorway, blinking. At that moment, unfortunately, the manager tried to pull off the usherette's panties, and she protested, sitting up—and let out a horrible shriek as she saw Poley standing in the door. He at once bolted away into the darkness.

Pausing to switch on the lights, the manager gave chase. He ran after Poley throughout the theater—up one flight of stairs to the balcony, and down another, back and forth in the mezzanine, between the rows of seats in the orchestra. Poley was finally trapped in a toilet stall of the men's lounge.

He wouldn't come out. The manager got a mop and swung it back and forth under the partition trying to hit his ankles. Poley stood on the toilet seat. The manager tried to reach him over the partition but Poley snatched away the mop. He said he wasn't doing anything, and the manager answered: "Come out, then." After a few moments the lounge door slammed, and Poley crept out of the stall. The door leading to the theater was locked, but he succeeded in crawling out a small window and dropping to the alleyway below.

Meanwhile, the manager called the police. And the police, in turn, called The Academy, to discover whether any cadets, or cadet uniforms, were missing.

Poley was afraid to return to school. At three o'clock in the morning he sent a telegram to the Hemphill Barracks Guardroom. The telegram stated that he was taking the 1.00 A.M. bus out of town. He said he'd called Valdosta and learned his mother was dying. The telegram arrived one hour after the police call.

The cadet Officer of the Day awakened Major Roy Pearson and told him the details, pointing out the strange fact that Poley's telegram stated he was taking the one o'clock bus, yet was sent at five past three. Then, most suspicious circumstance of all, there was the attempted robbery of the theater at two o'clock.

Major Pearson first called the residence of Alfred L. Poley in Valdosta, Georgia. Mrs. Poley herself answered the phone.

Major Pearson then rang up the police for a description of the theater marauder.

The next afternoon about twelve hours later Poley walked into the Guardroom of Hemphill Barracks.

He said he had ridden the bus to a town two hundred miles from Port George. There, unable to control himself, he called his family long distance to see if his mother were still alive. When he learned she was in good health, he immediately took another bus back to Port George.

"It was a practical joker!" he said to Major Pearson. "Some wise guy sent that telegram."

Major Pearson asked him how he had received "that telegram." Poley said he got it from the telegraph office in Port George. Why? How did he know it was there? Every Friday night, said Poley, he stopped by the telegraph office in case there might be something for him. But hadn't he said in his telegram to the Guardroom he had not got a telegram but had called long distance to his home and had then learned by telephone, *not* a practical-joker telegram, that his mother was ill? "No," said Poley, sobbing—"Western Union screwed things up."

Major Pearson said the manager of the theater was thinking of hauling him into court and that the manager's wife had almost suffered a nervous breakdown at the thought of her husband fighting off a thief alone. The Major added that were it in his hands he would prosecute to the full extent of criminal law.

Poley continued to insist that he had not tried to steal anything, and that he had simply gone to sleep in the theater. Finally, he mentioned the half-clothed usherette. That ended the interview with Major Pearson.

Poley was then examined by the Regimental Cadet Committee. Cadet Colonel Larrence Corger recommended expulsion on three counts:

1. Unauthorized absence.

2. Lying.

3. Suspicion of theft.

The final sentence of Corger's report stated that he and the other members of the Regimental Cadet Committee felt that Cadet Poley was not of the material from which an Academy man might be built.

That night at nine o'clock General A. L. Draughton examined Poley.

The General wrote a message to Colonel A. P. Evers advising that severest action be taken against the culprit.

At ten o'clock Poley was escorted by cadet orderlies to the train station in Port George. The orderlies bought his ticket for him and saw him upon the train: he was finished. His baggage followed two days later, after it was first inspected for stolen goods.

*11* Friday didn't start well; it began with a nightmare that terrified Marquales very much.

He woke up an hour before reveille, trembling violently. An acid phlegm covered his throat. After a moment he reached under his cot where he kept cigarets at night—his match lighted up Hulitt and Wintermine on their cots across the room.

He had dreamed, with utmost vividness, that a Persian cat was on his chest. The cat had its claws anchored in Marquales' abdomen and breastbone. Making a horrible slobbering sound, the cat was devouring, crunching and ripping with his teeth, the soft glands in Marquales' throat. It had moonstone eyes, from which fell blistering moonstone drops upon the lower part of Marquales' face. The cat also had a hooked nose, like a human being.

The meat balls Layne mentioned in the *Port Arms* office the day before—they were undoubtedly responsible. Marquales condemned himself: he had eaten three.

He smoked the cigaret until it stung his finger, then lit another off the end and stared at the wall, watching the room turn to grimy pink as the sun came up. Wintermine murmured in his sleep. Hulitt was snoring mildly.

The acid taste in Marquales' throat began to come into his mouth. He became so uncomfortable he got out of the cot and took a dose of bicarbonate of soda. Then he lay there, and thought about his life at The Academy.

For breakfast there was regular Friday oatmeal. It had a burned, sulphurous stink he attempted to hide with sugar and canned milk. It sickened him to swallow the mixture, so he pushed his bowl aside and drank three cups of black coffee. Then the heartburn returned.

He wanted more cigarets, another dose of soda. The others at the table were eating piles of grits, scrambled egg, sausage patties. When the upperclassmen sat back in their chairs and indulged their privilege of after-breakfast cigarets he decided to beg Cleer's permission for latrine leave. Then the corps was called to attention by Cadet Captain-Adjutant Starkson. Marquales coiled into a brace.

During the next fifteen minutes on the edge of his chair he sat immobile, neck wrinkled like corduroy, eyes front. He listened to Starkson read a long order-memorandum about the Armory floor.

Throughout the morning Marquales could taste the burned oatmeal. Between classes he hurried to the latrine for a smoke. There was never time to finish a cigaret. It was his habit to duck an unfinished end, brushing away the fire on the tip and sticking the half-consumed stub back into the pack.

During the second class, about nine-thirty, Marquales heard an ambulance enter the school grounds, siren wailing. At ten, when he reported to the latrine for a cigaret, he learned the ambulance had come for two cadets he knew: the senior, Carroll Colton, and the sophomore, Perrin McKee. Colton and McKee had fallen down a flight of stairs in Hemphill Barracks. The sophomore had suffered a severe heart attack, had broken his leg in the fall. Colton was injured—but Marquales did not discover more details at that time.

When the last morning bugle blew he gathered up his textbooks and joined the stream of cadets leaving the Academic Building. He ran down the macadamized driveway toward Hemphill Barracks in order to get a cigaret before two-minute steel.

In his room he quickly shined his shoes, brushed his clothes, tucked his shirttail in the manner prescribed, carefully dusted the top of his cap. He blew down the bore of his rifle, rubbed the steel parts on his shirt sleeve; a faint trace of oil came off on the sleeve, but he didn't worry about that because it wouldn't show. He put on the bulky cartridge belt, stuck his hands into a pair of white gloves, and adjusted his tie.

He had time for the cigaret. As he smoked he took out the five or six ducks accumulated during morning classes and transferred them from the pack to a small tin box that stank of tobacco tar and nicotine: his store-place for half-smoked ones. When he could afford it he smoked fresh cigarets. Then when his money was gone he turned to the ducks.

Noon drill was hard, tiring. Cadet Captain Layne marched Company Twelve to the parade field and for ten minutes called the

[ 118 ]

manual-of-arms. Then Cadet Lieutenant George Cleer put the company through half an hour of close order. Cleer commanded rapidly, often allowing only four counts between words of execution. This cut the platoons very sharply, giving the men hardly time to think before pivots. Cleer pulled the customary tricks: after a flurry of flank and rear commands he screamed for right oblique, then suddenly, the order of halt. Men who did not remember to halt in the original line of march were reprimanded. Not many were caught.

Marquales, however, made one terrible mistake that morning, a mistake that threw him entirely out of his platoon. He was marching on the outside right column, and cut to right flank for a command of left.

Cleer unfortunately was Marquales' regular Mess Chief, and at lunch he inquired:

"What's your right, Mister?"

Marquales held up his right hand.

"What's your left?"

The freshman held aloft his left hand.

Cleer said, "Keep them straight from now on." Then he added, "You should have learned by this time that when you are asked a question by an upperclassman you do not answer by the means of sign language. Is that correct?"

"Yes, sir," said Marquales.

"Very well, then. To impress this upon you suppose you do me the favor of telling us: *What Time Is It?*"

Marquales took a deep breath, said, "Sir, I am dee—"

"Come to attention when you comply with a freshman regulation."

Marquales slid to the edge of his chair, lifted his chest to the table, and pulled back his chin.

Cleer said: "What number freshman regulation covers the answer to *What Time Is It, Mister?*"

"Freshman Regulation Number Twenty, sir."

"Proceed."

Marquales took another deep breath, then unfalteringly answered: "Sir, I am deeply mortified and burned by a fire of unhallowed shame that the situation is such that the tremulous tintinnabulations that temper the time-telling tones of the untercentenaricalistical tickies and tockies of my tinny timepiece have rendered it errant, sir; however, to estimate as nearly as possible to that divine computation of our relative position with the stars given us by the United States of America Army astronomers through bafflingly ingenious mechanisms far beyond my mental power I can guess it is now fourteen minutes, thirty-seven seconds, nineteen ticks, and eight tocks past 1.00 P. M., sir."

"All right," answered Cleer.

It was late October but still considered warm enough for the "icebox luncheon." The icebox luncheon was potato salad covered with gobs of mayonnaise in which tiny puddles of peanut oil gathered, like little golden eyes. There was also bologna, goose liver, sweet pickles, and iced tea. Afterward, servings of tapioca pudding on enameled tin plates. Cadets seldom bothered to eat this pudding. They called it "frozen snot."

When Marquales returned to his room after lunch he was surprised by a note for him on the study table. It was on violet stationery, which bore at the top the block letters: T H E  A C A D E M Y. Under that was the emblem of two glistening sabers crossed over the trunk of an oak tree. At the far-right upper corner: *Carroll Colton,* in tiny thin print. A message was awkwardly scrawled:

MR. ROBBIE MARQUALES:

A SICK FELLOW WONDERS WHEN YOU ARE GOING TO COME TO SEE HIM. HOW ABOUT AFTER LUNCH? WILL YOU?

C. C.

Marquales wondered how he had got out of the hospital.

It was nearly two o'clock. In five minutes he was due in chemistry lab, which would last until four. Then he would have half an hour to prepare for the regular Friday parade. His dress uniform was at the tailor shop being pressed and he'd have to go over and get it. His brass centerpiece was so badly scratched that he would have to go to the Administration Supply Room and sign a requisition for another. His webbing was soiled and would have to be changed. He needed a shave. His shoes were not properly shined. All his white gloves were dirty.

He went down the concrete stairs to the bottom gallery, and around the corner to Colton's room. He entered without knocking. Colton lay on a cot in an old-fashioned union suit; his right arm in a sling, his face badly swollen and discolored by a severe bruise.

"Come on in," said the senior in a weak, friendly voice. "Excuse me if I resemble Frankenstein's monstah."

"I thought they took you to the hospital," said Marquales in astonishment.

"I was at the Infirmary for awhile, here in school. Just talked my way out of there about an hour ago. But is it that bad? I suppose I'll have to take your word, I couldn't bear to look again in the mirror. Not that I'm under the delusion I'm another Jimmy Stewart." Colton spoke with a whimsical smile, and talked through his teeth. His unbruised lips looked more cherubic than ever, despite the livid mark on the upper right half of his face. "I simply took a bad fall," he said matter-of-factly, "and banged myself up a bit. Didn't you hear all about it? Perrin was hurt, too. They took him to a Port George hospital. Did you not hear?"

"I heard a little," said Marquales.

"Come, sit down, and I'll tell you how it was. Come," said Colton, pulling a blanket over his legs, which were plump, puffy in the yellow underwear. Marquales picked up the senior's trousers from a chair and hung them on a coat hanger in the clothes press. Then he sat down, about ten feet from the cot.

"Will you light me a cigaret?" asked Colton.

Marquales held out a package of Philip Morris. The senior murmured, "No, you light it for me, please."

Marquales fumbled a cigaret between his lips. He lit it, then passed it over. Colton held it clumsily in his left hand, smiling. Then he didn't smile, and said: "So you heard about Perrin."

Marquales said: "You and he fell down the steps . . ."

[ 121 ]

"You want the sad details," replied Colton weakly. "Know how weak Perrin's heart is? Very weak. For a long time he didn't go to school anywhere—even high school. He was taught by a tutor. Then it got better, so what did Perrin do. He ran away. Lord knows where he went. But he didn't take care of himself, and now his heart is weak again. He should never have enrolled at The Academy. Ah, they told him last year, but he wouldn't listen."

Marquales asked: "Is he in R.O.T.C.?"

"No. He is not. He would never be. Ah, but anyhow, to give you the sad facts of this morning; everyone is always curious about unpleasant things, have you ever noticed that? Get something grisly and they will just hover around—like buzzards! Which proves they are grisly, themselves. You should have seen those cadets this morning, all hovering around, just staring with popeyes, their old tongues hanging out, enjoying the sight of Perrin's face—and seeing me there with a broken wrist, and half unconscious. Oh, sometimes I wonder if human nature is good! Such mobbery! Why couldn't they at least have decent sympathy? But no, they must make such remarks as, 'Boy, he looks like he's croaked.' And such delay in getting assistance."

"How did it happen?" said Marquales.

"Did you not hear? Perrin had a heart attack just as we started to walk down the stairs from the top gallery. I tried to catch him, and instead I lost my balance and the next thing I knew came this horrid crash against my head . . ."

"That's thirteen steps," said Marquales.

"Fifteen, on the top gallery," answered Colton with a sad smile. "Far enough for me to fracture my wrist and get this blow on the face. But Perrin broke his leg—and was bruised all over."

"Did he break it bad?"

"I actually couldn't say," answered Colton in a whispery voice. "The fellows didn't know about the leg at first. You see, Perrin's heart attack was much more dramatic: he changed to a ghastly color, and his throat was rattling so we thought he was dying, or dead.

"Poor Perrin! These people don't understand what he's gone through all his life. The poor boy . . . I don't care what he does, I will always have a place for him. I mean, he is one person I do regard as a real friend . . ."

At that moment they heard the bugle for two o'clock class echoing across the quadrangle outside the door. Marquales arose. "I've got to go," he said.

"Oh, yes," said Colton. He coughed, then spoke in a firmer voice: "That message I sent you—Robbie, I want you to do me a favor. You say you have a class this afternoon?"

"Chemistry lab."

"On Fridays?"

"Yes."

"I didn't know they had two-hour classes before parade."

A glassy smile had appeared on Colton's face, little dimples were on either side of his mouth.

"There aren't many," said Marquales. He shifted from one foot to the other, looked nervously toward the door.

"Sit down," said Colton. "You won't be late."

Marquales sat down.

Colton said, grinning in the glassy manner, "Well, now, just a minute. Listen, this is serious, I fear. You see, I'm in considerable pain. I don't show it but my wrist hurts, and so does my head. This blow on the face ruins my spirits much worse than it does my good looks!

"They had me in the Infirmary with that old goat nurse, but I made them let me come over here. You know it only happened four or five hours ago. I mean the accident. The truth is I ought to be in a real hospital after the fall I took. Colonel Girard thinks the cadets, of course, are no better than vermin . . ."

Marquales arose.

". . . and so does Miss Frune, too!" said Colton. "Listen! I feel terrible—you've got to do me a good turn to make up for my shocking experience this morning!"

"I *have* to go," said Marquales, edging toward the door.

"One moment!" said Colton in a high, loud voice. He still wore the glassy smile. "Old man," his voice sank. "I feel terrible."

[ 123 ]

"Yes, I know," said Marquales.

"All right," laughed Colton. "I'm completely bored. Bored to an infinity, and what I would enjoy is a sort of bottle of something right now."

Marquales stared at him dumbly.

"Well," said Colton carelessly. "Would you go to town and get it for me?"

"But I have a class," protested the freshman. "They'd expel me in a minute . . ."

"Well, old fellow, you undoubtedly wouldn't be caught if you used your noodle."

"But I have this class, it isn't just the liquor part . . ."

"Very well, old man."

"I'm sorry."

"That's all right. *Truly.*"

After a moment Marquales said, "Doesn't Major Pearson . . ."

Colton interrupted, "I keep it in a hole under the radiator. And I very very rarely have a swallow here."

For a few seconds Marquales stared into the senior's large brown eyes, which were surrounded by little smiling crowfeet.

"Now you'd better trot along or you'll be late to that class," said the senior.

"I really have the class. I really do."

"Of *course* you do," said Colton. "G'bye now."

"No parade!" sang Hulitt, dancing about the room.

"We could put on our tow sacks and have it," said Wintermine.

"How I love that moist stuff," said Hulitt. "Especially on Friday afternoon . . ."

The voice of the Amanuensis came over the barracks public address system: "*Attention. General Leave will begin in five minutes. Repeat. General Leave will begin in five minutes. That is all.*"

"That's enough!" said Hulitt. He gave Marquales a whack on the shoulder. "Am I right?"

"Watch out," said Marquales, who was writing with pen and ink on a slip of paper.

"But am I right?"

"Sure, it's enough."

"What are you doing, Mooch?" asked Wintermine curiously.

Marquales didn't answer.

"What are you doing?"

"My name isn't Mooch."

"Oh, no?"

"No."

"Mooch Marquales: that goes together perfect."

"We can't all be sons of billionaires."

"Well, I do try to smoke my own cigarets."

"Nobody else ever does."

"We'll see if I ever donate any more to you—Mooch."

"First see if you get asked."

Hulitt interrupted: "What are you writing, Robbie?"

"This is a thing I want you to sign," said Marquales. "It says, 'We testify Robert Marquales goes to lab Friday afternoon.'"

"Okay," said Hulitt. "Give it here. I'll do it for the flag."

Wintermine asked, "What's it about—Mooch?"

Marquales was silent.

"Come on, what's it about?" repeated Wintermine.

Marquales answered, "I just want to prove something."

"How do we know you go to lab?" asked Wintermine. "You say you go, but what's your word worth?"

"It's worth more than your signature."

"Then what do you want my signature for?" laughed Wintermine.

"To see if you know how to write."

"Okay," said Wintermine, signing the slip. "Now we'll find out can you read."

Hulitt murmured, "Looks like Les got the last word."

Marquales took the paper and stuck it into the pocket of his canvas raincoat.

"That tow sack isn't right, if you want to know," said Wintermine.

"I don't," said Marquales. He nevertheless carefully tucked the raincoat, as prescribed, folding the excess canvas neatly under the cloth belt.

"Where are you going, Robbie?" asked Hulitt.

"Downstairs."

"Not only can't he read," said Wintermine. "He's mysterious, too."

Marquales stopped suddenly, took out the slip of paper, and saw underneath Hulitt's signature the words: *Kiss My Butt.* He walked over to Wintermine and said, "Would you write your other name—nobody knows this one."

Hulitt let go a wild horse laugh. After a moment Wintermine chuckled slightly. Marquales watched him slowly scratch out the three words and write *Lester Wintermine.* "I take a lot from you," he said.

Marquales moistened his lips to reply, then he thought better of it, and left the room with a good-natured smile.

*"Entrez,"* said the voice behind Colton's door.

Marquales entered. Colton was still on the cot, but had the blanket pulled up to his neck. The freshman stood at attention, waiting for the senior to speak. Colton didn't even open his eyes. Finally Marquales said, "May I rest, sir?"

"Why *certainement,*" said Colton, eyes shut.

Marquales walked to the side of the cot and said, "Sir, I wanted to tell you I wouldn't have gone to town for you because I don't want to be expelled. *But,* I had a class . . ."

Colton looked up, said softly, "Who said you did not?"

"I thought maybe you didn't believe me." He held forth the slip of paper signed by Hulitt and Wintermine. Colton pulled his left arm from under the blanket and took the slip. He read it, dimples of amusement pimpling his cheeks.

"Really," he said. "This is so silly and sophomoric. You're naïve enough to think I'm a big bad wolf? What gave you the idea I didn't believe you?" He chuckled. "This testimonial is pompous."

"I thought I'd show you," said Marquales nervously.

"Listen," answered Colton. "Perhaps I was a little cool to you, out of disappointment. That's understandable, isn't it? I'm just another human being you know, with frailties and faults. But Lord, I didn't mean anything by it. Not at all. And, now, you come here to visit me and go through that 'popping to' affair at the door. Ah, my. My, my."

"Well . . ." said Marquales feebly.

"Now what are you going to do with yourself tonight in all this pouring rain?" asked Colton, dismissing the trouble cheerily. "Are you heading for town just the same—an evening of ribaldry?"

Marquales hesitated to mention his engagement with the Hair-of-the-Hound Club. He said he expected to go to a movie.

"Don't pick up Jocko de Paris later," said Colton, laughing. "This time you might not get through the Guardroom. I'm not O. D. now, you know, and my time won't come again for a few months, thank the Lord. I really hate that job of O. D."

Marquales told a lie. "I don't think I'll see Jocko tonight."

"Well, you watch out for him," said Colton, wagging a fat finger. "He's a mean-hearted boy, I'm afraid. He lacks human sympathy. A superior mind, though, which makes it so much more a shame."

"Jocko?"

"Oh, yes. Really very shrewd, but let's talk about something else; he's a sore point with me for personal reasons. Haven't you made pals with any of the little Port George girls? I hear there're some lovely ones at that nice finishing school on the Drive."

"St. Anne's?"

"Uh-hum. That's it."

"I don't know any girls. None at St. Anne's. Not even a waitress in a bar downtown. I've been a lone wolf so far."

"Well! You express yourself in a quaint enough fa—"

Colton suddenly hiccoughed very loudly. "Sorry," he murmured. Then he laughed, patted the blanket over his stomach. "I guess you found me out," he said. "Do I appear to have accomplished this?" He pulled forth a bottle of liquor—it was two-thirds empty.

Marquales smiled. "How did you get it?"

"Rather easily," said Colton. "Well, now that you've discovered my little secret I might as well have a swallow. Would you care for one?"

"No, thank you."

"'So primly from her scented bath, trips the maiden down the path.' You're just like Perrin. The remarklance is resemable!

"Oh by the way—his stepmother called and left a message at the Guardroom that they've taken him from the hospital to his house in Port George. That must mean he isn't as badly hurt as we thought."

"That's good," said Marquales.

"Yes, poor Perrin. I still can't quite realize he's had this accident. Some people seem invulnerable to such things. Yet it's strange *Perrin* would be like that. He's really so vulnerable in most ways. Or am I making sense? I guess I'm more leery-weery than I thought I was."

"Does McKee have a stepmother?" asked Marquales.

"He certainly does. How Mr. McKee ever married her . . . of course . . . but then you can't tell by the surface, strange things, *strange* things!" Colton made a long groaning sound. ". . . so sorry for these *pore* old Southern families, it's a shame. Just a pathetic shame. Why does it have to be that way? They're so unhappy when they haven't got any money any more. The wasted, faded grandeur of that old Cheney Street barn. Well, that's life. No use bothering about what's gone, because when it's gone, it is gone. Pardon me— now out of memory, as Perrin would say, for all the dear, dead gallants who now are mere chalky fragments beneathhhhh the soil—to them, and to everybody including you . . ."

Colton stuck the end of the pint between his lips and tossed back his head. He seemed to be still smiling. Marquales watched in wonderment as the senior's neck throbbed steadily and the brown fluid became lower and lower in the bottle. Finally the whiskey disappeared; for a second or two Colton held the bottle to his mouth, eyes shut tightly. Then he took it away, made a smacking inhalation, licked his lips. "That's that," said he hoarsely.

Marquales laughed.

"Brrrrehh!" shuddered the senior. "That would jolt a horse. Well, where were we? I was telling you about Perrin—were we getting close to him spiritually, is that what we were doing? We're nice, aren't we?" He giggled, wiped some of the brown liquor from his chin. "Well, maybe we shouldn't spoof something that other people feel so emotional about. There's no profit in being unkind: if there is anything I loathe it is an unkind person.

"You ask me seriously about Perrin. Well, I'll tell you. Just to warn you, old man. Perrin is deceptive. That is the thing about the young genius. The good Lord endowed him with too much brains. You *never* know what he's up to. But that keeps him from being dull. I never get bored with Perrin. Heaven forbid—or Heaven not for-bid?

"By the way, he seemed impressed with you that afternoon he talked with you about his ideas. That afternoon the Simmons boy had that horrid experience."

"Yes," said Marquales.

"Perrin told me he liked you." Colton's voice began to drag. "He said you might have the ability to learn. It sounds pompoid but you have to expect that from Perrin. Did he ever go around to see you? I was just wondering."

"No."

"He never did?"

"No."

"Well, Perrin is deceptive. He never did stop by, even for a little chat?"

"No," said Marquales. "I haven't seen him."

"Is that so? Well, it's too bad you won't get a chance. He's really a brilliant boy, if you can overlook some of his flaws. You must come to see *me,* though, even if Perrin won't be here any more."

"All right," said Marquales. "I will."

Colton lay back on the pillow and closed his eyes. "It's hot in here," he sighed. "Would you open the window for me?"

"Sure."

Then Colton murmured something that sounded like, "Thanks, darling."

[ 129 ]

Marquales said, "What was that?"

The senior's eyes struggled open. They were swimming red, bewildered, the pupils enlarged into dim holes, as if not focussed upon anything. His pale face took on color—"Hmm?" he said. "I feel delirious. I guess I am. That last one was suicide. You open the window for me, will you?"

Marquales got up from the chair and crossed the room to the window. He opened it wide. Then he glanced down and saw a large envelope on the study table. Scrawled across it were the words: "*Carroll—Want to read my masterpiece to handsome Jocko de P.?*"

"What's this?" asked Marquales curiously.

"Hmm?" said Colton.

Marquales picked up the envelope and took it over to the cot. Colton stared at it groggily, then said, "Oh. Now you better give that to me. Did you look at it?"

Marquales felt a heavy weakness drag through his legs, up his spine as he answered casually, "No. Is it a big secret?"

"Don't apologize. It's nothing but a letter Perrin wrote to someone. Someone he'd never, never dare show it to. He gave it to me a week ago to read. Just to torment me! Upset me!"

"I'm sorry," said Marquales.

"You're so apologetic," said Colton. He sank back upon the pillow and closed his eyes. "Did you open the window? This rain makes things humid. And those radiators."

Marquales answered, "I think I'd better go." He slanted his eyes toward the bulky envelope in Colton's left hand.

"All right. I do feel sleepy. Thanks for stopping by." He opened his eyes and gazed blindly toward Marquales, smiling. "Don't worry about it. Maybe sometime you can read the letter. You'd be fascinated by it, I guess. Perrin is so clever that sometimes I wonder if he really feels anything the way a decent fellow would. Is he satisfied with anything, or does he chase pretty rainbows to flatter himself? He's broke his leg now . . ." Colton stopped talking, closed his eyes. His mouth opened slightly.

Marquales asked: "Why didn't Perrin send the letter to the person he wrote it to?"

"What?" said Colton.

Marquales repeated the question.

"Because he never meant to," whispered Colton. "I know him like a book. He can't hurt my feelings."

The senior's eyes closed for the last time, and the letter dropped from his hand. He immediately began to snore noisily.

Marquales tiptoed across the room, took the envelope from the floor, read the inscription again: *"Carroll—Want to read my master-piece to handsome Jocko de P.?"*

The freshman quietly slid off his raincoat, settled down in a chair by the study table. He listened for a few minutes to the loud snoring from the cot. Then he read Perrin McKee's letter to Jocko de Paris.

# 12

My dear Mr. Pharaoh:

I have been wanting to write you a letter for a long time. Imagine my pleasant sensations now that I'm able.

Perhaps you wonder why I call you Pharaoh. Here is the answer. I learned yesterday afternoon about your secret, your *dark* secret, and last night I dreamed that I saw you by the shores of the Nile. You held a young female child by the hand; and your face was ennobled considerably by that spade-like beard of the Egyptian King.

Suffice to say, it amuses me to call you Pharaoh.

And now, get ready. Here we go:

1. Is it true that late this summer you contracted an ailment from a young Chicago lady?

2. Did you, on or about September 3rd, rob an Academy professor's daughter of her precious innocence?

3. Would you like for it to be known that you and your "Juliet" have received stealthy treatments for your affliction by a Port George doctor?

If these questions answer themselves, my dear "Romeo," then I advise you to follow this letter carefully. And do not let my tone annoy you; fine fellow, fine Pharaoh—I am an admirer of yours. I have always been, and please don't forget that, however critical I might seem from time to time.

I think that this admiration is more than a mere "searching for the not-to-be-had." I decidedly feel that you would never have cut sparks off the flint of my soul were you not perhaps more available than you seem. For I do not practice self-attack. Many months I have observed you, paid you silent tribute—this cannot be without foundation. Yes, despite your filthy ways—your depravity—I feel confident you are unaware of your real being—and that you now exist in a spiritual vacuum. This is often true of violent people. In general, it can be said that the organism in extreme motion is dissatisfied with itself. The volcano is smoking, Mr. Pharaoh of the Nile! And how much boiling lava is waiting underneath to rise? I may say it is my humble wish to give you a healthy eruption.

A quick parable, now.

Many years ago there was an animal. For various sad reasons it could not see itself. The animal wondered—what am I? Bird? Deer? Buffalo? Finally the animal became so confused it lost its good opinion of itself. And, it made up its mind: I am a sheep. It took to the fields and ate grass. This gave it stomach ache. It became terribly starved. So it associated with vultures and munched carrion. Thus the animal died! Because it was a LION, and LIONS cannot live on maggots and filth.

That—was a parable. Not a fable. It might have come directly out of the Old Testament. Perhaps it did. Have you read the Old Testament recently?

Well I know you are curious about how I discovered your secret. Probably you won't pay any attention to my remarks until I dissolve that curiosity and assure you that you are in no great danger of being expelled. You aren't. I learned about your private affairs by accident. Here's how it was.

The man you've been seeing happens to be my family physician. I went to visit him yesterday afternoon and noticed on his desk a paper that bore your name. When he left the room I looked at it. It was a typewritten report marked *Very Confidential.*

Well, at any rate—I was glad to see that now although the girl is yet *positive* you are *negative.* How lucky!

But weren't you told that alcohol upon it is like oxygen to flame? I must say, isn't it peculiar, how things operate. Here we have this young girl, undoubtedly terrified out of her adolescent senses. Undoubtedly doing everything the doctor tells her. Undoubtedly praying at night that she will get over this horror and join decent clean society again. On the other side of the door we have you, drinking little water but a lot of whiskey and beer, most probably continuing to mire yourself with other local femininity. Yet you pass through it like a breeze, shedding gonococci like an old coat!

Now I would like to borrow some of your time and tell you what happened to a certain cadet last year. His fate might interest you.

We won't be coy about his name. You, we know as Pharaoh, but this young man was Cadet James Gow, of Charlotte, North Carolina. He was at The Academy for only seven months, quitting in April of his freshman year.

Long ago, when Port George was a distinguished city instead of a run-down wharf dump, the gentlemen used to have a word that would fit James Gow perfectly. When one of these men, who now molder in our "quaint" graveyards, felt some person to be a coward he would remark coldly:

"Sir, you are a poltroon."

If he were correct, the matter would be finished. And, socially, so would the poltroon. Otherwise, the sound of silk flicking against the offender's face, and at an early date the deadly shot cutting the air until one should be hit, and fall.

In a sense James Gow may be called a poltroon. He certainly received the slap from the glove, and he chose ignominiously to refuse to accept. After that no mercy was wasted on him, with the result that he was forced to leave The Academy. I hear he got a position last summer with the Coca-Cola Company.

During the past year, I myself was a freshman. Therefore, despite the fact that I was then older than most upperclassmen, I had to find my friends among the recruits. I don't complain of this. It is understood that the military life will necessarily make certain demands upon individual existence. Merging of military destiny with personal destiny is a long-lived process, but of course an extremely necessary one if we are to achieve obvious spiritual and national goals.

One of my freshman friends was James Gow. I met him about the time of Thanksgiving last year. By the spring I knew him well, if not intimately. And, I was interested in the boy. He seemed unusual.

I suppose his father's family may be considered good. There are Gows in Port George, as perhaps you are aware. I know very little about his mother's people, except that his maternal grandfather was a kind of rag picker, or peddler, I believe, who made a success out of whatever it was he did.

In all likelihood James profited from this blend: the father was apparently declined, choleric, irrational, low in intelligence. He was unable to maintain the family after 1931. This task was shouldered by a lonesome bachelor known as "Cousin Bob," a thirtyish, bald-headed relative of James' mother. Cousin Bob had some kind of mill, a toy factory, I think, and he was well-to-do, very successful financially.

James had one sister, named Louise, who was several years older than himself. In the summer of 1931 she was attacked by infantile paralysis, which permanently deformed her right arm, in a pitiful manner. Louise, judging from her pictures, was a pretty, sad-faced thing who resembled Lillian Gish. People often spoke of this resemblance (especially James) and always commented, with an undying banal wonder, that the initials of the two girls were the same.

At any rate, in the same week that she became ill, catastrophe breathed its malodorous breath into the already reeling household. Old man Gow's business failed miserably. Mrs. Gow had a nervous breakdown. The bank called the mortgage on the house. The cook and butler (who had not been paid for several months) threatened to quit. Then Cousin Bob moved in: he arranged for the sister to be taken care of, paid many bills, settled with the bank, sent Mrs. Gow to a sanitarium for a rest, and pacified the Negro servants.

He remained with them. The following year he had the house done over to his taste, including a new wing for his own rooms. The attic was cleaned out and a billiard table installed there; also a miniature bowling alley for the children. At first old man Gow was humiliated by it all, but as the months went by and Cousin Bob continued to pay the bills, he became more friendly. Three years passed before Mr. Gow brought home any money. He finally got a job as an insurance salesman—he who had once been so important! Yet the miserable fifty dollars he made each week entitled him to wrangle with Cousin Bob, talk behind his back, depreciate him. They somehow never seemed to get along well. However, it was Cousin Bob who sent Louise to Vassar, and James to The Academy.

Pharaoh, I'm sure you must wonder what James Gow has in common with you. My answer must be—nothing directly, but indirectly, a great deal. You will soon discover what I mean by that.

Well, in the summer months, just before James began his career at The Academy, a sad thing happened. It began when Louise, the sister, commenced to behave in an abnormal manner.

She either wouldn't talk at all or she talked a great deal; she often had a hangdog expression, and developed a peculiar reserve toward the members of her family, especially her mother and father. One afternoon Cousin Bob came home early from his streamlined factory and found her reading the poetry of Edna St. Vincent Millay. Thereafter, nearly every night at dinner, he would ask her in his jovial way if a certain pimple-faced beau of hers had been calling. She would always deny having seen this lad, but in a strangely emphatic manner. At that time Louise was twenty years old. The poor girl's right arm was about two-thirds the size of the left.

Well, one night in August, James was up late reading a novel. At two o'clock he became weary and put out his bed lamp. Just as he was falling asleep he distinctly heard his sister say from her bedroom next door—*"Please don't hurt me."*

It woke him up. He propped himself on an elbow and listened for a few minutes. Then, he decided that he had been having a dream, and lay himself down again.

He was almost asleep when he made up his mind that it was hot in the room. He got up to push his window farther open. Then he heard a strange sound coming from his sister's room. He stuck his head out and listened.

At once he crawled out upon the garage roof that ran past both the bedrooms. He crept along to his sister's window. Alas, he should have returned to bed; but you see, he suspected that some person had used the convenient garage roof in much the same way as he himself.

Crouched under the open window he listened—caught the sound of furious rustling bed sheets, sighings, and again, that slow, steady squeaking of the telltale bedsprings. Then, in an unnatural whisper, his sister's voice—*"Don't. Don't."*

James raised to his full height and stared into the room. Two naked bodies were tied in a sweating knot on his sister's bed. He caught a glimpse of moonlight reflected off the top of a bald dome—and he exclaimed aloud in horror! There, Cousin Bob! The fat scallawag leapt off the bed and ran groaning out of the room. Sister Louise was too terrified even to cover herself with the sheet. James crawled miserably back down the roof to his own room.

It seems that the sister begged him not to tell. She offered no excuse for herself.

When James asked her why she did it she replied, "He insisted all the time."

When he asked her if she wanted to do it she replied, "No."

When he asked her if she enjoyed herself she replied, "How can you think that of me?"

And when he asked her if she ever intended to do it again she answered him, "No, brother. Never again."

So the depraved coward said nothing to his father or mother. He even failed to speak to the Cousin Bob. And when the time came, he allowed the scoundrel to send him to The Academy: he accepted the bribe of a man of no decency. James Gow acted as a poltroon, I'm sure you'll agree.

However, I must say it was not precisely this streak of cowardice that I had in mind originally. No, I was thinking of something else. For my friend James Gow soon faced another problem after having confessed that sordid, lewd tale to me.

I will now tell you that Jimmy Gow was the sort of male who exists wretchedly upon the edge of a knife. A blade that slices through his soul, cutting him into separate parts, because he is unable to forge himself into that metal harder than any knife. This self-torture, which we see very often, is always regrettable. But many times it can be corrected: it was my hope to do this service for James Gow. I spoke with him at great length, and if I may say so, rather well. For my trouble, precisely what did I gain?

The poltroon threatened to attack me! I can see his peaked, whitened face before me now, scowling and yelling out its stream of vulgarity, superstition, fear. He who had been my friend, he who had smoked my cigarets, drank my beer, profited from my conversation—turned upon me like a viper, ignored the wisdom I had laid before him, forgot it instantly!, and dared mouth his asinine threats . . .

I had no choice but to enter into a brief correspondence with his father. Two letters were sufficient. It was then the time of Vassar's spring holiday. The sister, Louise, was home. Old man Gow, convinced by me, watched them closely, and one night caught Cousin Bob in the act. Naturally, that led to a family reorganization: on the basis of fifty dollars per week income, with no more streamlined factory hanging around the house.

I was sorry for James's moral failure, sorry to see him leave The Academy. I was sorry to hear about his job washing Coca-Cola bottles.

And now I feel confident that you are ready to listen to what I am so hopeful of explaining to you. We arrive at last to the point where we may accomplish something directly, as far as you and I personally are concerned. Read very carefully, Mr. Pharaoh, these next few pages.

First, let us look at existence on the globe today. What can we immediately say about it? Everywhere there is unrest. Correct? In Europe, what? The scattered howlings of weak-minded idiots, who would like war but lack the courage for it; who desire true upheaval, but have no real ideas about what it may be. In China? India? Strife, bloody anxieties, trouble, fear, warped minds.

Such is the situation today. On all sides we feel the tension. Now for a moment allow me to speak in terms of the far past, and the far future.

You have undoubtedly heard something of the biological history of man? I'll assume that you are familiar with the conjectures of the better-known anthropologists. From them a certain amount of valuable information can be gleaned. For quite a long time in my life I studied Darwin, Huxley, Wallace, and others. I do not regret this

[ 138 ]

time, however much I might disagree with these men in some respects. They have hewn down many of the trees of ignorance, and if they have left a forest behind them we can shrug and say, it would have been larger but for them, and proceed ourselves to take up the axe of enlightenment. Allow me to make several points immediately.

First, we cannot assume, as the biologists do, that the creature who descended from the trees and became *homo sapiens* is nothing but an extremely complicated animal.

Second, we cannot assume that *homo sapiens* is any more the end of a line than was jibbering *Australopithecus*.

Now do you think, to look more deeply yet, that the first *ape*like *man* felt himself to be merely a step along the way? No. He naturally would conclude he was the end product—if he concluded anything at all. Ah, the illustrious Peking cannibal—the Java monstrosity—the gorilla-fanged Piltdowner—the Neanderthalian imbecile! Can't you hear each of them—"I'm it. There couldn't be anything superior to this magnificent thing that I recognize as MYSELF."

May I ask you, what does *homo sapiens* think?

But is it likely that (however profound is the distinction that sets him apart from those others) he is himself *not* to be succeeded?

I am unable to put into "scientific" terms that which sets modern man apart from these ancestors. Yet there is a titanic difference, as any moron can notice. Do not tell me that it is simply a matter of intellect. The Cro-Magnon *homo sapiens* possessed a larger brainpan than any of the present-day varieties, yet what did he make of it? A few pictures and hatchets. Certainly not much in comparison with our own accomplishments. No, the Cro-Magnon lacked somewhere. I feel that he surely lacked an essential human ingredient, precisely what I can't say, but something.

And I feel, in turn, that modern man, when compared with the man of the future, will lack just as definitely. This future creation will be as superior to William Shakespeare as that fellow was to the Neanderthalian. The term, *humanity,* will become one of abuse, not praise. It will be said of some aberrant person in the future, "He acts as if he were human."

[ 139 ]

Now, what thing has been true of all prehistoric branches of man? (I think it fairly certain that only *homo sapiens* has exhibited within himself a certain tendency, which I will discuss soon. I speak here of the relatively latter-day *homo sapiens*.) I feel that that which has characterized, for the most portion, all the flowerings of prehistoric man has been a biological-social systematism, which did not contain a frame of reference toward the great emotive split which we recognize as having smelted the greatest of the ancient civilizations: the Greek. Thus, the ape-fanged Piltdown female, the Neanderthalian female, the Cro-Magnon female were all duly honored—to whatever extent a slobbering seizure by the hair can be so regarded. It was with the appearance of *homo sapiens* proper that we first perceive the biological-social mutation of man that I happen to regard as the yet-undelivered pregnancy which will birth our successor some day.

Let us look at my theory of the turmoil of the modern world. I may be mistaken. I realize a large part of my theory bases itself on mere conjecture, which of course is *never* right, as any dog-leg scientist can glibly tell you. But, nevertheless, I will be brave, and say that it seems clear that this great world tension, this never ending struggle and strife, is the result not of superficial social-economic disorders (why are *they* caused?), but rather of some other more profound and tremendous development. You may be sure that man's situation is today terrible. Yet you may be equally sure that this fact is rich with meaning. It is simply a matter of discovering this meaning, and one holds the key that will unlock the ponderous door to the garden hitherto denied hard-pressed mankind.

What else could this meaning be than a festering, long-due change in the nature of man himself?

What, heretofore, has been the fate of those who made Greek history magnificent? Let me suggest that now, in the most casual manner, modern technology has introduced a method of artificial propagation that, I think, will have the most enormous effect on future life. (Have you noticed? the most interested persons in this discovery, this technique, have been a lot of cattle breeders.) In the past, the man not tolerant of woman has by definition been doomed to be the last of his line unless he overpowers his repugnance which in most cases is not possible. Can you sense the struggle? Can you feel it, almost hear it, filling the ether with its cries for release? Think of it: these men have been appearing and reappearing for many centuries now. They have ever met with persecution, the brand, the knife, the whinnying superior airs of "moral" idiots, who themselves exist like beasts. And these men have not merely been attacked, but almost without exception they have died without passing on the power of their mutation. Despite this fact, so strong is the mysterious propulsion which creates them they continue to appear! Through the centuries, they have come, and come again, and I tell you, they will continue to do so. They cannot be stopped by all the *homo sapiens* heathens in the world.

For now the bit of technique that permits indirect propagation will make it possible for these men to become more and more numerous. (Let us not ignore the purport of the female: she will continue to shoulder the necessary biological operations. Her demise in the future will be entirely with regard to social-cultural manifestations.) These men need not die so rapidly nor struggle in such fashion, once they succeed in reaching for this weapon. And they will bring into the race a new blood, a virile, new man, and the present-day depravity, the limiting of growth, the oppression will all cease, to permit those who arc born with the power, but die never knowing it, to live fully, to develop according to their tremendous capacities, and to people the earth like mountainous spore explosions with their own kind.

You have no comprehension of the difficulty with which I have come to originate this theory, my friend. There have been placed in my path a multitude of distractions. A side of my nature has yearned for the old, the gone, the disappeared. I have sought, in utmost personal misery, to equate my nature, and my being, with that rich world of the immediate past. It was with terrible heartache that I came finally to realize that the old world, the splendid existence of man here in our South before the days of debasement, was an artificial thing. When one is personally involved with the history of a race, it is difficult, from the subjective point of view, to accept a revolutionary

[ 141 ]

concept. One wishes somehow to fit that which one has respected as a child into that which one knows to be true as an adult: such an integration is mad, and impossible.

I have renounced, intellectually, the shards of the old world. The old world is dead and gone. It was not meant to be. And we must be steadfast, and look for a new world, a world of really much greater dimensions, a world not of adolescence, but of potent, surging, undeniable maturity.

But forgive my enthusiasm. I tend to forget that I am writing to someone encountering these complex ideas for the first time. They are so much a part of my spiritual life that I overlook the fact that to another they may not be self-evident.

Now I have several words of advice to give you. Perhaps as yet you do not share my enthusiasm for these ideas. However, in time, I hope that you will. For although you are probably unaware of it, you have the manner which belies your actions; the manner and hidden attitudes of those of most import to the future.

I have propounded a term which will be, I hope, of some value toward attaining the understanding of the self that will be necessary if the new man is to achieve full and widespread growth. This term embraces a complicated theory of human behavior which I will not go into just now. Remind me, however, to speak to you about *pre-experientialism*. There is also a complementary theory that attends to the more direct problems of self-realization. This I characterize by the word, *sub-experientialism*.

Briefly, the latter deals with that which is REAL, that which is ACTUAL, in terms of one's personal history. And, specifically, it emphasizes the exploration and investigation of those ACTUAL experiences which are not within the sphere of awareness. To vulgarize the concept, one might say that it is applied by "taking a memory shower."

This is what you must do. Look deeply into your past, search for the hidden memories, the unknown experiences. And, understand their significance. Now I am aware of the fact that no one voluntarily undergoes such a difficult thing. For that reason I have planned matters so that you will not be doing it on a voluntary basis. Between you and me, Mr. Pharaoh, things will proceed apace of my own initiative.

You will forgive this.

But if I waited for you to make the decisions in all probability you would not pick up yourself from the mud at our feet. You'd remain there, victim of the modern world.

I take matters into my own hands. A direct attack can be made on your past life by not paying heed to your inhibitions. Instead, we will plunge intrepidly into the real, and the actual. For that purpose, pay attention to the following:

You will receive this letter on September 26th. On the following Friday night you will meet me in a small private room of Number 86 Luck Street. It is in the basement of the house. The bell will be marked: *Mr. Pharaoh.* Tell no one about this letter. Bring it with you on Friday night. If you have not appeared by eight o'clock a note will be sent by special delivery to the father of the girl you carelessly infected on September 3rd.

A final word. Do not be afraid, I am gentle with virgins.

Sincerely,

YOUR FRIEND

PART 3

# 13

Robert Marquales was escorted to the private room of the Hair-of-the-Hound Club by the manager and owner of the restaurant, a fat fellow named Neddie. Twenty or twenty-five cadets were there, seated about a long rectangular table. It was hot and most of the cadets were in their undershirts.

Munro introduced Marquales to the company.

"Now boys," said the fat man, smiling. "Put on your shirts."

They paid no attention.

"Say there," said the man. "Next thing you'll have your britches off and will scare this young girl here." He patted a middle-aged waitress on the fanny as she went by balancing a tray of ale.

Several of the cadets looked up and laughed briefly. One of them, until stopped, slowly patted the waitress as she unloaded.

"Hey, boys. Put on your shirts," said the restaurateur.

Finally one of the cadets said, "It's hot in here, Neddie."

"Then open a window."

"And ask for pneumonia?" said the cadet.

Layne leaned across Marquales and whispered, "Watch this, Tom." Then he called out, "Felix! Felix! Where's our steak?"

There were cries of "Felix!"

Layne giggled as the man wagged a fat finger and said, "Steaks when you get your shirts on, boys."

"Felix!" said Layne loudly. "We'll stomp the plaster out the ceiling downstairs! Felix!" He began to bang his feet on the floor. Others joined him.

"Felix!"

Said the restaurateur, "Well—keep your shirts *off!*" There was laughter from all sides; the stamping ceased at once. The man rolled his eyes and moaned, "Boys! Boys! No more, now. That's enough."

Layne was convulsed. "Oh, Tom! He'll do it every time, won't he? Old Neddie is one guy I'm going to miss when I finally leave The Academy!"

The fat man opened the door that led to the back stairs and remarked, again wagging his finger, "You keep your shirts . . . *off!*"

Marquales asked Munro, "Was that fat man born that way?"

Munro was not at all amused. "Neddie was kidding," he said.

"But who's Felix?"

"Neddie is. When we get mad at him, or want our steaks, we call him Felix. Because he doesn't like it."

"He likes Neddie," said Layne, "and hates Felix."

"What's his real name?" asked Marquales. He spoke in such a low voice the question had to be repeated.

"Felix," answered Munro coldly.

Layne chuckled. "For ten years Neddie has been trying to do two things: get us to stop calling him Felix, and get us not to sit up here in our undershirts. Oh he's a grand guy, a wonderful guy; the best friend you'll ever have."

"Why don't you take off your shirt, Mr. Marquales?" asked Munro.

"Do I have to, sir?"

"You don't have to do anything, but breathe."

"Well, I'll leave my shirt on, then," said Marquales.

The air in the room was fuzzy with cigaret smoke and heat. Damp raincoats had been piled upon a sofa near the door; caps hung like blue fruit on the antlers of a deer, whose stuffed head slanted off one wall.

Marquales didn't even remove his blouse, much less the shirt underneath. This was due in part to a strange desire to annoy Layne and Munro. His main concern, however, was for Perrin McKee's letter, which was folded into the pocket of his blouse. He did not want that letter to fall into wrong hands.

He loosened his collar and lit a cigaret, trying to look as if he felt at home. Cold water began to run down his sides; his eyelids burned. He had a sick headache from reading McKee's letter.

"Have a beer, freshman," said a cadet across the table. "Go on and enjoy yourself."

It was an unusual room the Hair-of-the-Hound Club had selected. The ceiling, painted a bright red, was low, just overhead, and had been decorated with hundreds of gilded Coca-Cola bottle tops. The walls were muraled with semi-naked houris. Their charms had faded long ago. Scrawled over the dancing figures were names, mottoes, addresses, pencil sketches of sex organs, telephone numbers, comments about various girls of the town, signatures of past members of the Hair-of-the-Hound. Marquales saw written on the wall just by his seat the words:

"*Men:*

*I finally crawled Mary Jane Cummings last night. She mee-owed like a kitty.*

*Sgnd, Lyle Montgomery,*
*April 10, 1933."*

Under that was,

"*Only a cad tells. B. L. Drummond, Oct. 3, 1935."*

But above,

"*I had Mary Jane last year in her own bathtub ten times. Ben Wallace, April 12, 1933."*

And penciled in large block letters to one side, the single word: "*Bullshit."*

Marquales noticed that the dates written by the names went back as far as 1931. He leaned on his elbows and stared along the table. Two tiny windows were at the far end of the room. Both were closed tight, hidden by silver curtains. On the rug of the floor below the windows lay a mess of cigaret stubs, bottles, overshoes, burned matches, bread crumbs. The table dominated the room. Very long and low, it was covered by a white cloth upon which sat baskets of Italian bread, dozens of dirty glasses, whiskey bottles, gin bottles, soda bottles, Coca-Cola bottles, ginger-ale bottles, wine bottles, beer bottles, ash trays, jugs of steak sauce, tiny salt-and-pepper pots, ice bowls filled with floating hunks of country butter. In front of each cadet was a large wooden steak platter, with accompanying bone-handled knife and fork. From somewhere in a wall a radio played yowling "swing," which behind the surf-roar of talk was a *bad* noise; monotonous pipings from the clarinet of Benny Goodman. Or, riffs by Harry James. They both seemed to be there.

Marquales smoked intently, staring at his cigaret as though interested in it. He was sorry that he had come. He knew only Munro, Layne, and Albert Wilson of all those present. After the brief introduction—"Fellow Hounds! This is a willing freshman named Marquales"—he had been ignored by almost everyone, even Layne and Munro, who, he thought, now seemed to regret having asked him to attend.

And the steak cost a dollar and twenty-five cents, a sum that would practically strip him of his week's allowance. The beer was twenty cents a bottle; he knew it was expected that he drink three or four bottles.

He sat in the chair, wedged between Munro and Layne. The conversation in the room was loud and energetic—it seemed to Marquales that no one was having a good time, however.

Munro leaned across him and asked Layne, "Where is everybody?"

Marquales looked: about three-fourths of the table seats were occupied. Several cadets were playing with a pair of dice at the single card table at the other end of the room.

"Nearly everybody's here," answered Layne. "By the way, I think Jocko is bringing a visitor tonight."

"Who?"

"Jocko de Paris."

"I know, I mean who's Jocko bringing."

"Roger Gatt."

Munro said, "Who?"

"Can't you hear? Gatt. Black Gatt, the coed's dream."

"That guy? Jocko knows better than to bring a nut here."

"What did you say?" A smile appeared on Layne's handsome face. "I can't understand you."

"Jocko knows better!" said Munro.

"What say?" The senior cupped a hand over his ear. Marquales followed the direction of Pete Layne's eyes, and saw, standing in the doorway, De Paris.

Munro shouted, "Jocko hasn't the guts to bring that Gatt bastard!"

For an instant conversation died through the room—in the interval, De Paris, whipping off his blouse, said: "Meet Mr. Gatt, gentle-men."

Behind him lurked a huge figure.

"Jocko!" sang out Albert Wilson across the room, rising from his seat. "How's it there, boy?"

"Hello, Junior," said De Paris. "Come in, Roge."

Then Roger Gatt stepped in. "Hi," he said, holding up one big hand. For a moment all eyes were on him. Imitating Jocko, he swiftly took off his raincoat and blouse. He rolled them into a mass the size of a basketball and threw them upon the sofa in the corner. He stood there, a bewildered look on his face. Jocko tapped him on his hairy shoulder and said, "That's stripping her down, Roge. Come along and have a drink of something."

"All right, Jock," said Gatt. "Beer."

"BEER FOR MR. GATT!"

Albert Wilson called, "Hey, Jocko . . ." He beckoned De Paris.

"See you later, Junior," called De Paris. "Roge and I will sit up here with our pals, Layne and Munro."

De Paris and Roger Gatt took seats directly across the table.

"Well, I'll declare," said Jocko. "Little Sir Galahad."

"Hello," answered Marquales.

"How's tricks, Jocko?" asked Munro.

Gatt said, "I'm drinking beer tonight. Nothing but beer. No whis-key, and no gin. Just beer."

"Good for you," said Layne.

"What," said Gatt.

"I mean, beer's a good thing to drink."

"Oh."

Jocko said, "Tom. Weren't you saying something as we entered?"

"Saying something?"

"That's right."

"Me saying something?"

"Yes, you, Tom."

"I didn't say anything."

"Tom, I believe you made a reference toward my friend, Roge."

Gatt looked up. "What?"

"I didn't say anything," murmured Munro.

"He didn't, Jocko," said Layne.

"Excuse me for making the error," said De Paris. "But I actually thought I heard you employ the term, 'that Gatt bastard.' Please ex—"

"What," said Roger Gatt.

"Listen," said Munro, smiling. "Nobody said anything about you, Roger. Sit down, now, and let me buy you a drink. Quit trying to stir up trouble, Jocko."

"Me? Trying to stir up trouble?"

Gatt was half out of his chair. Conversation about the room had stopped.

"Come on, Roger," said Munro. "Have a drink on me, fellow."

"I'm drinking beer tonight. You spell that B-E-E-R."

Jocko bellowed, "What the hell! I said a minute ago: Beer for Mr. Gatt! And you spell that B-E-E-R, for your information!"

Munro arose. He took a small gray dunce cap out of his pocket and put it upon his head. "Fellow Hounds . . ." He began to bang on the table with a bottle. Gradually the room became quiet. "All right, fellow Hounds," said Munro. "It's time we had one or two of the old songs . . ."

There was lackadaisical applause, several boos.

". . . a couple of the old songs to get an appetite for the steaks Neddie will get up here some time tonight, we hope."

"Felix!" yelled a cadet.

"That's right," said Munro uneasily. "Now let's sing up an appetite."

"I second the motion of the chairman," said Layne.

"Now," said Munro. "What's the ticket?"

One cadet called, " 'The Hair of the Hound.' "

"To hell with that," said another. "Let's sing 'The Kaptain Kops the Kid.' " Robert Marquales did not know it, but moved his lips as if singing.

Well, once there was a salty dog
Who sailed the ocean deep.
But old Kap he were a faulty dog;
His ship she stunk with sheep.

Ohhhhh . . .
Baa! Baa! Baa! *But!*
Baa! Baa! Baa! *But!*
He didn't walk the decks with a hard-on.

Amongst the rumps of rare fat wool
A kid was heard to say:
"Mah Nanny, Ah so scare that you'll
Sho catch dat Kap today!"

Ohhhhh . . .
Baa! Baa! Baa! *But!*
Baa! Baa! Baa! *But!*
He didn't walk the decks with a hard-on.

There were twelve or fifteen other verses. Marquales "sang" on;
his head began to swim, and he noticed that Roger Gatt was staring
at him in a peculiar manner.

At ten minutes of eight the steaks were served. Three Negro waiters
appeared and hurriedly forked them onto the wooden platters from
steam trays, which contained depressions for gravy and French fried
potatoes. Neddie stood in the door, caressing his stomach with folded
hands. He beamed: "Are they thick? Or are they thick?"

Hump-shouldered, the cadets began to carve the red-interiored
meat with their bone-handle knives, shoving large squares of it into
their mouths. The clatter of the eating implements blended with
smacking of lips and sobbed grunts of approval.

A fluff of paraffin fat lay in blood on Marquales' platter. It bordered
like a necklace the lean, which was seared and blackened. He sliced;
beneath the crust was scarlet blood. In the time eating the pound or
so of beef he drank two cold bottles of beer.

[ 153 ]

Halfway through he heard Roger Gatt say to Jocko: "Who's that funny-eyed kid there?"

"A wealthy freshman," answered De Paris.

Gatt stroked his blue-black chin. Marquales, listening, stared down at the meat on his platter.

"Is the freshman a mascot or something?"

"Sure," said Jocko. "You know it."

Later in the meal Gatt went to the washroom. Jocko then fixed Marquales with his eyes and said, "After the announcements you go to that green card table there. I'll do you a favor."

"Yes, sir," said the freshman.

Munro heard De Paris' remark. He said, annoyed, "Leave the kid alone, will you? He's not here to get messed up with you and your goddamn visitor."

The corners of Jocko's mouth lifted and he said, "Tom, shut your mouth or I'll kick the shit out of you."

Munro started.

"Mr. Marquales, I'm doing you a favor," said De Paris. "Ignore that tit-sucker."

"All right!" said Munro, throwing down his fork. He stared, narrow eyed.

"Go on," said Jocko.

"One of these days somebody might call that bluff."

De Paris returned the stare, rock faced. "It won't be Tom Munro, you dirty bastard."

"Don't be overconfident," said the senior in a low voice. He had turned white.

"I don't *like* you, Tom," said Jocko. "I never have liked you. Just looking at your face is enough to make me puke. The reason is you're a yellow tit-sucker. If you open your mouth again, I'll be all over you before you get it closed."

Munro did not reply; he began to eat his steak. De Paris looked at him for a few more seconds, then turned to Marquales and smiled. "Just keep quiet when the time comes. Then follow my lead and we'll cob brother Black Gatt."

The freshman nodded.

Gatt came heavily up the stairs from the washroom, tromping loud as if to announce his return. He swung back the door and walked into the room, head about two inches beneath the ceiling. Waving both hands in an awkward manner he said, "Hello, Jock. Hi, everybody." Gatt had a tenor voice that came out through his nose.

He had eaten one steak and now began to eat another.

A few minutes later Albert Wilson got up from the end of the table and came to Jocko. "Are we getting a game?"

"At that green table, Junior. You go and reserve it for us."

"Who's in?"

"Me, you, Mr. Marquales, and Roge."

"What are we going to do?" asked Gatt. "Gamble?"

"In a manner of speaking," said Jocko.

Gatt burst into a thunderous laugh that quieted conversation in the room for a moment.

"Junior," said De Paris to Wilson. "You go and reserve the table."

"Sure thing," said Wilson. He looked curiously from Gatt to De Paris. Then he went over and sat alone at the table, adjusting his pint of rye before him under the cone of light from the "poolroom" lamp.

Soon thereafter Tom Munro stood up. "All right, fellow Hounds." He tapped with his knife on a glass. Cadets leaned back on the hind legs of their cane chairs, misty-eyed from heat, liquor, talk, steaks. They smoked, or picked their teeth with matches, or drank more beers and whiskies.

Munro crowned himself with the small gray cap. "Okay, fellows. Meeting in session. What we want to discuss tonight is the football game with the University. There aren't but two weeks left to get our plans set. At the meeting before last I appointed Ralph Jackson chairman of our committee for the game this year. I hope he's figured out a good stunt. We'll hear from him in a minute.

"But before I call on Ralph the Hair-of-the-Hound is glad to have tonight as visitor that mighty lineman of the team, tackle Roger Gatt. He's here breaking bread and taking salt with Jocko de Paris—a Hound from the beginning."

There were several chuckles. Jocko smiled, and Gatt, who had risen, craned his neck staring up and down the table. The tiny blue eyes in his face looked like melting ice; bleary, bewildered.

"Roger," said Munro. "I would ask three cheers for you, fellow. But Neddie says people downstairs in the regular restaurant don't like us to—they think the ceiling's coming down. But the thought's there, though."

Gatt slowly looked around the smoke-filled room, his greased black hair brushing the golden bottle tops on the ceiling. He said, "Don't worry, bud. We're going to beat the University."

There was scattered applause. Gatt seated himself and began to drink a glass of beer. Munro pointed down the table: a thin senior stood up and said:

"Thanks, Tom. Most, most of you don't know what we have in mind this year. Now last year we didn't do a damn thing. Then, then the Bunghole Buddies come along with that stuffed bobcat.

"Now, we tried to steal it, but they got it locked up somewhere down in the damn Registrar's office, and Frazer Williams and Colonel Hart are like this . . ." He held up two pink digits, one crossed on the other. "They can keep their goddamn bobcat, because with the idea we got the other day it won't be any skin off our ass. The inspiration of a famous member—well, he wants to tell you about it himself. Jocko?"

De Paris stood up, a hand on one hip. "Here's the idea, fellows. Downtown in an old costume shop there's a masquerade bobcat suit for rent. Considering thirty of us in the club the charges would only be about twenty cents apiece. I'd cover the deposit myself. I've asked Phil Harper and the other cheer leaders if it'd be okay for me to get down in front of the stadium with them—dressed in this bobcat suit —and help out with some cheers. They all say it's great. What do you think?"

There was applause.

Jocko said: "The whole thing is kind of corny. But the novelty of it will catch attention. There are going to be newsreel cameramen at the game, probably because of the Senior Drill Platoon between halves as much as anything. I think they'd take a couple of shots of me jumping around in that bobcat suit. That ought to get the credit away from all the other gangs, the Bunghole Buddies included: their stuffed bobcat would make no impression at all. How does the idea strike you?"

In the midst of applause Albert Wilson stepped forward a few paces from the green card table. He said, "I'll cover half of the deposit, Jocko."

"Thanks a lot," said De Paris in a shy manner. Then he leaned out across the white table, placing his hands on either side of his steak platter. "All right, fellows. Before I give the floor back to Tom Munro, I think we'd all like to get some inside dope on the condition of the team. And there is a man here tonight who can give us that information. This is one of the reasons I invited him to have steaks with us, aside from the fact that I knew we'd all enjoy his company very much . . ."

Several cadets cleared their throats nervously; all looked at De Paris with solemn eyes.

"I am talking about Roger Gatt," said Jocko slowly. "Roger B. Gatt. He is one of the *greatest* football linemen in the South. No, I will go farther than that: he is *the* greatest. This man . . . is no doubt one of the giants of modern football. And why is this? I ask you . . . why?" Jocko raised his fist and thumped it down to the table. "Brain! Brain!"

Silence.

"Most football players are stupid!" shouted Jocko. "But it is Roger Gatt's intelligence that makes him the tackle he is."

Pause.

"Roger, have you anything to tell us about the prospects of the team as you see them?"

Gatt arose slowly from his chair: the thirty cadets, many of whom had their mouths open, were darting their eyes back and forth between the two men. Then Gatt smiled, and his head fell over. He stared down at his big folded hands and muttered, "Aw, Jock, you lay it on too thick."

De Paris solemnly replied, "No, Roge. Not at all."

"I just try and get my head in their guts when I can."

"But you also prognosticate the play, don't you, Roge?"

Gatt laughed loudly. He said, "What the reff doesn't see doesn't bother the reff."

"Roge," said Jocko earnestly. "I hope two weeks from now you prognosticate the hell out of those University bastards."

Gatt smiled self-consciously—again his head fell over in limp embarrassment.

Several cadets laughed.

"What's funny?" snapped Jocko. "Don't you know modesty when you see it?"

The room became silent. De Paris glared for a moment then turned to Gatt and clapped him on the shoulder. "Well, Roge, before you step out of the spotlight there's one cretinous thing I want you to tell us, if you will."

"All right," said Gatt, craning his neck toward the cadets who had laughed.

"Roge, do you think we will beat the University?"

Gatt said, "Don't worry, Jock. We're going to beat the University."

"*Thanks,* Roge."

With a pale smile Jocko bowed to Tom Munro. Munro nervously declared the formalities of the meeting finished.


On Marquales' right was Jocko de Paris. On his left, Roger Gatt. Facing him, Albert Wilson. The lampshade of green glass gave their skins a sick color.

Marquales still wore his Academy blouse despite the heat in the room. He had unzipped it, exposing the sweat-drenched shirt underneath, and had ruffled up his brown hair. Yet his companions were in their undershirts; Gatt had even rolled his trousers up from his hairy black calves over his knees. The freshman felt an urge to remove his own blouse and shirt: once Jocko de Paris asked him to do it, and he had said nervously he thought he'd better keep on his clothes.

Jocko was dealing; rapid flipping motions that sent the cards sliding face down over the green felt.

"We'll start it light?" asked Wilson. He tossed a quarter onto the table.

"Light," said Gatt. "Ante up, guys! Ante up."

"That's correct," said Jocko quietly. "NEDDIE! Come here, YOU FAT HOG!"

A few minutes later, Marquales, swallowing painfully, saw the waitress place a gleaming tray of coins on the table. Jocko gave her thirty dollars.

"I'm bankman," he said.

"We don't need all that silver," said Wilson.

Marquales had less than three dollars.

"We're going to play until time to go to barracks," said Gatt, staring at his cards.

Marquales asked for three dollars worth of change. Gatt looked at him strangely. Then the freshman remembered he didn't have even three dollars.

"Make that two in quarters," he said to De Paris.

Gatt began to laugh, slowly.

"I didn't bring much with me," apologized the freshman.

Gatt bellowed. He nudged Marquales in the ribs, nearly knocking him out of the chair.

Marquales caught a glance from De Paris; "S . . . F . . ." went Jocko's lips. The freshman said, "Only seventy-five bucks."

"That'll hold," smiled Jocko.

Gatt laughed again, this time more loudly. "It'll hold!" he said, and put one of his hairy fingers deep into the freshman's ribs.

"Ouch!" said Marquales, shuddering.

Gatt then laughed so hard his ice-cube eyes began to melt tears of hilarity. "You guys have a funny mascot," he said.

The game progressed. After losing four hands Marquales had thirteen cents. He said in a feeble voice: "I'm supposed to go see someone at eight-thirty. What time is it?"

They all looked at him. "Who?" asked De Paris.

[ 159 ]

"A friend, just a friend."

"Gal?"

"No, not a girl. A friend."

"Well, who?"

The freshman selected—"Perrin McKee"—and regretted his choice at once. They all leaned forward.

"What are you doing around that guy?" asked Wilson quietly.

"Nothing," said Marquales.

"Is that so?" said Wilson.

"McKee broke his leg today."

"So I heard."

"Yes! And I promised I'd go see him."

"You couldn't get in a hospital," interrupted De Paris. "Not at this hour."

"What I don't understand," mused Wilson, "is how you could promise McKee you'd visit him, considering the fact that he was unconscious when he left here this morning. Or so I heard."

"What is this all about?" said Gatt.

"I didn't promise McKee," said the freshman. "Colton."

"*Carroll* Colton?" asked Jocko.

"That guy?" said Wilson. He shook his head. "Mister, you travel in funny company."

"Well, McKee called Colton, that is, McKee's stepmother called him, at the Guardroom . . . and Colton asked me to visit McKee tonight and try to cheer him up."

"This is boring," said Gatt. "Deal the cards."

"They took him home, he's not at the hospital; and I think I really ought to go now," said the freshman. Something brushed his knee.

"The game ends when we have to go to barracks," said Gatt.

"But I'd hate to disappoint him!" said Marquales.

"I'd hate to disappoint him, too," said Gatt. He bellowed with laughter.

"Let's play," said Wilson, eying Marquales.

"Well, I suppose I'll go now," said the freshman, pushing back his chair.

"Ante up, guys. Ante up," said Gatt.

A sharp pain skyrocketed through Marquales' leg as Jocko kicked him on the shin. Again, something brushed against his knee. It was crispy, and he looked down, palming a ten dollar bill.

"Change," he sighed, placing the money on the table.

But the ten dollars lasted a short time. The bets grew larger, Roger Gatt taking nearly every pot. Marquales was sweating profusely; he began to speak again of going to visit his friend, Perrin McKee. He got another kick on the shin, and another crisp bill. Gatt continued to win.

Jocko said, in a thoughtful voice, "Luck? What *is* luck? My Lord, nobody knows. But it looks to me like Roge has all the luck around here. Oh, brother, what insidious cards the man draws. Isn't it amazing how peculiar luck is?"

Wilson said, "There's no such thing as luck; the law of averages works it out so—" He winced, gritting his teeth.

"Were you *always* lucky, Roge?" asked De Paris.

"Yes. I was."

"Some people are born that way," grinned Wilson eagerly.

"What," said Gatt, turning.

"I say, some people are luckier than other people."

"How do you mean that, bud."

"Roger, all I meant was that you have beautiful luck."

"I play poker," said Gatt. "You spell that P-O-K-A, in case you want to know."

"Sure you do," said Wilson. "And you were born with the gift of luck."

"He plays poker!" said De Paris. "In case you don't know, Junior, that is spelled P-O-K-A. And luck has nothing to do with anything."

"Sure," said Wilson.

"That settles it," said De Paris.

Silence. Jocko flipped out five cards to each of the players.

"But I always was lucky," said Gatt. "Few people have my luck."

They stared at him. "It looks like you can't lose," said De Paris softly.

"I can lose," said Gatt.

They gathered up their hands.

"It really doesn't look as if you can be beat, Roge," said Jocko.

Marquales felt something brush his right knee. This time, it was five cards that he palmed—three aces and a pair of queens.

# 14

"Don't talk so much. I can't think," said Gatt.

"Everybody close his trap and play poker," said De Paris. "Deal them cards, Junior."

"Wait a minute. Hold the deal, bud," said Gatt. He began to count his money, wetting his thumb every bill or two; twice he stopped and started over again. Wilson nervously shuffled the deck while they waited.

"How do you stand, Roge?" asked De Paris.

"Give me a pencil, Jock."

Marquales moistened his lips and stared about the room. The overhead lights were off and nearly half of the members of the Hair-of-the-Hound Club had departed. The remaining ones were grouped over a dice game at the end of the long table.

"I'm out thirty dollars," announced Gatt, sticking De Paris' pencil behind his ear.

"That's too bad," said Wilson, starting to deal. "But the night is still young, Roger. You have two hours to get it back."

"Two and a half," said De Paris. "It's only nine-thirty."

"Hey," said Gatt to Wilson. "Wait a minute and let me think."

They waited. Wilson said, "Where's that waitress? And what's happened to this place?"

"Looks like she's deserted us," said De Paris. "And a lot of the fellows have gone, too. Maybe they don't like our company."

"Oh, no?" said Gatt. He arose and walked to the door. He shouted down the stairs, "Waitress! Beer!"

"Watch it, Jocko," whispered Wilson. "Watch it."

"Shut up," said De Paris.

The waitress appeared with more beer and a check totaling twelve dollars.

"Neddie says he wants you to please pay as you go along," she said.

De Paris answered, "Tell him to go shoot himself."

Gatt poured a bottle of beer down the edge of his glass. "You bring some more in ten minutes."

The waitress left, and soon thereafter Neddie appeared in the doorway. He ambled toward them, smiling at Jocko.

"Hello, boys," he said.

"Hello," answered Gatt.

"You boys wouldn't mind paying as you go along, would you?"

Jocko motioned toward the cadets playing dice at the other end of the room. "Are they paying as they go along?"

"But you're drinking a lot and you might forget," said Neddie.

"We won't forget," said De Paris.

"I'd appreciate it if you'd pay as you go along."

"Have I ever ducked a check up here?"

"Oh, no."

"Well, don't worry."

"Oh, I'm not worrying."

Gatt looked at the fat restaurateur, craning his neck around to see. Neddie said, smiling, "I notice you've got your britches rolled up."

'What," said Gatt.

"I see you have your trousers rolled up you there."

"How do you mean that, bud."

Jocko said, "Neddie's just admiring your legs, Roge."

The fat man looked curiously at Gatt's hairy calves. "They sure do need a shave," he said.

"What," said Gatt. "What."

Neddie walked away, now and then turning and looking back over his shoulder.

Gatt said, "Who was he?"

"The manager," said Jocko. "He hasn't got any sense."

Neddie stood in the door, talking with the waitress, now and then glancing back toward the table. After a moment he backed out of the room and she came forward, smiling.

"Anything you boys want?"

"Bring Mr. Gatt more beer," said Jocko. "And take this check and go sit on it."

The waitress smiled, then said, "Neddie has a stomach-ache tonight, hon'." She was looking at Gatt. "He didn't mean anything."

Gatt said, "Tell him to cut down his weight then he'll never get anything wrong with his stomach. I'm an athlete and I know."

"Okay, I'll tell him," she said.

They watched her undulate to the door.

"Too bad she's such an old hag, Roge," said Jocko. "She seemed hot for you."

"Yeah?" said Gatt.

Marquales meanwhile was counting the money he had won. It totaled forty-five dollars. This was the equivalent of his allowance for twenty-two and one-half weeks. The money had been taken mostly from Gatt, by means of brazen cheating. At regular intervals De Paris slipped the freshman extra cards.

"You know," said Jocko, "speaking of Neddie, he acts very much as if he was a homo." He looked reflectively at Marquales. "By the way, you know what your pal McKee is, don't you?"

Marquales turned red, and answered, "Yes."

"Now and then I used to think that McKee was giving me 'come hither' looks," said Albert Wilson. "He and his buddy, Colton—his true beloved sweetheart. That's another friend of yours, isn't it, Mr. Marquales?"

"No," said the freshman.

"What is McKee?" asked Gatt.

"A natural-born fergler," answered De Paris.

Wilson said, "What are you doing around those guys, Mister?"

"Nothing," said the freshman.

"Can you understand how they act that way? I can't. The way they act is beyond me."

"How is that, beyond you?" said Gatt, bewildered.

"Can *you* understand that stuff, Mr. Marquales?" asked Wilson.

"It's like this," said Jocko suddenly. "Take a woman ninety days gone. Slice open her belly and what would you see? You'd see a goddamn thing known as a foetus. It would decidedly not be human. And, you'd never be able to tell if it was a male or a female. A foetus looks more like a snail than anything else in the world."

Gatt said, "How do you know, Jock?"

[ 165 ]

De Paris paused. Then he said, "Roge, I'll tell you something that I've never told a single person before. All of you keep this secret, or there'll be no telling what will happen. If it got out, Port George would be absolutely crazy with the news . . .

"On second thought maybe I'd better not tell you."

"Go on, Jock, go on."

"Well—"

"Go on, Jock," said Gatt. His mouth hung open.

"No, Roge, old man. I'd be an absolute cad."

There was a long pause. De Paris sipped thoughtfully from his glass of whiskey then said, "Junior, in the case of guys like McKee and Colton, something went wrong with them when they were foetuses. They got their wires crossed. You see, it's all in the brain. They have the brain of a woman but the body of a man."

Gatt said, "What was that you were going to tell us a minute ago?"

"Roger, he would be breaking his word," said Wilson with a simper.

Gatt said, "Jock, won't you tell us?"

"Roge, old man . . . I just can't tell you that. Not now, anyhow. You see, Roge, I gave my word."

"All right then, Jock. You gave your word."

There was another pause, then Wilson asked, "Jocko, why aren't there women like that, too?"

"Don't be dumb, Junior, there are."

"Oh, hell."

"You know these women that won't lay? That's what's wrong with them."

Wilson laughed. "I never heard of women that won't lay."

"They might lay. But they don't like it."

"But that's disgusting, and besides, I never heard of any women that don't like it."

"Are you trying to argue with me? I'm telling you the way it is; if you don't approve of it, then write Jesus Christ a post card and criticize him, but shut your mouth around me."

"You don't need to get mad, Jocko," said Wilson meekly.

"The trouble with you is simple, Junior. You can't think."

Gatt said, "Hey, mascot. Are you and McKee sweethearts?"

"No, sir, I don't even know him well, I—"

"Roge, this freshman is all right. I can tell when a man is all right, and Marquales is all right."

"You know, I'll tell you something, Jock," said Gatt. "Those guys pay for it. Isn't that funny?"

De Paris answered, "They're morons, Roge. That's their trouble."

"I think they're in*sane*," said Wilson.

"One of them came up to me once," said Gatt.

"They're absolutely in*sane*."

"This one smiled at me. He said to get in the car. I gave him a look, and he came up and grabbed hold of my arm. Get in the car, he whispered. What for, bud, I wanted to know. So he said something you'd expect, real nasty, and I hit him. It knocked him down on the running board, and he was clinging there. You know what he said then!"

No one answered.

"Do you know what he said then."

"What?" asked Jocko.

"He said, 'Don't you beat me, dear, I'll give ten bucks!' He'll give me ten bucks, dear! You should have heard me *laughing*. I was laughing so much I nearly died. I just lay there and laughed. I laughed so much I nearly died. He says, 'I'll give you ten bucks, dear, don't beat me!' Did I laugh! First of all, I laughed because he was crying—I don't mean crying, I mean boohooing. Well, he was boohooing because he got himself knocked down and his mouth shot up, but how is that? . . ."

Gatt paused, opened his melty blue eyes very wide.

". . . When he never knew what hit him? Ohhh, haw-haw-haw!"

The cadets at the other end of the room looked up from their dice game. Wilson, De Paris, Marquales all laughed hard. Gatt roared on for about three minutes, shaking the table with his knees.

[ 167 ]

Jocko finally said, wiping away an imaginary tear, "Roge, I never heard anything so funny in my life."

"Neither did I," said Gatt, starting to laugh again.

Marquales ran his hands over his face, then wiped them on his sides.

"And then the guy said to me, 'I'll give you ten bucks, dear!' It struck me as the funniest thing in the world because he said, 'dear.' That's what you say to a woman, if you like her. You don't talk that way to a man. I laughed and laughed."

Wilson asked, "What finally happened between you and this guy?"

Gatt looked at him. "How do you mean that, bud." The grin faded.

Wilson smiled frantically, "Did you beat him up or something?"

Gatt began to chew at his left thumbnail. After a long time he said slowly, "You know, the thing that got me was that the guy wanted to pay ten bucks. I never heard of anything as funny."

"It really was a scream," said De Paris wearily.

"What," said Gatt. "What, Jock."

De Paris asked, "Tell me, Roge, was this guy a big, strong fellow?"

"Which guy, Jock?"

"The guy that wanted to pay you ten bucks."

"Oh, him." Gatt stopped, and again chewed on his thumbnail. "What about him?"

De Paris leaned over. "Was he a small, puny fellow?"

"Oh, no," said Gatt. "He was a big, strong guy."

"Did you fight him?" asked De Paris solemnly.

"Me? Fight him? I never fight anybody. I just sock them and then there never is any fight to be fought."

"Did you have to hit this guy more than once?"

"No. Not but once."

"But he was able to talk after you hit him?"

"Hell, no. He couldn't open his mouth."

"Didn't he say he wanted to pay you ten bucks?"

"Yeah, he said that."

"Well. You must not have hit him very hard."

"Oh, I didn't sock him hard. He was just a little puny guy so I cracked him with the flat of my hand."

There was a pause. Wilson was tying his shoe: noises came from him, snuffling sounds. Gatt craned his neck toward him.

Marquales said in a hoarse voice, "Well, I really think I ought to go visit Perrin McKee. No matter what he is, he broke his leg today."

Gatt said, "What are you doing under that table?"

"Tying my shoe," said Wilson. He sat up, red faced.

"Is your shoe funny?" asked Gatt.

"Say, Roge!" said De Paris. "Won't you have a drink of this fine bourbon?" He held up a half-emptied quart.

"Nope, Jock. I promised Laurie I wouldn't touch anything but beer tonight when I told him I was going out with you."

"You don't let Corger run your life, do you?"

"He's the Cadet Colonel," said Gatt.

"But do you let him tell you what to do?"

"Nobody tells Roger B. Gatt what to do. But Laurie and I room together, and always have. Here's what I said to him this afternoon: 'Laurie, I will drink only beer tonight.' And he answered me: 'Good for you, Bob.' "

"Does he call you by that nickname?" asked Wilson.

"The Academy Bobcats is the reason for that name," said Gatt. "Laurie calls me Bob when he's feeling good. I'd beat the piss out of anybody else that called me that. It goes with *Bob Gatt*. Just like you say *bobcat*. And the Bobcats are the football team. But I don't like to be called by name of any animal. Unless it's Laurie."

"I don't blame you," said Jocko.

"Do you know what some of those cadets used to call me behind my back?"

"What?" asked De Paris eagerly.

"They used to call me Black Gatt. That goes with black cat. You say *Black Gatt* quick then it sounds like *black cat*."

"Isn't that a hell of a note? What in the world made them give you a nickname like that?"

"They never gave me the nickname in the first place. I used to get called that in Birmingham."

"Well, I'll declare," said Jocko.

"That's Birmingham, Alabama," said Gatt. "That's where I'm from."

"A lovely city," said Jocko.

"It's better than here. You can always find something to do, there." Gatt yawned and stood up. "Hold everything, I'm going to take a leak."

They watched him tromp out of the room.

"Shut up!" said Jocko to Wilson. "I know what I'm doing. He doesn't know he's alive, and he's crawling with money. When he goes out of here by God he won't have a dime."

"He's going to catch on if you don't quit riding him," moaned Wilson.

"You just handle that deck faster!"

Wilson nodded; De Paris shifted a pair of angry blue eyes upon Marquales. "What's the matter with you? Get that green look off your face, what are you sweating about?"

"Nothing," said the freshman.

"Cut out talking about going to visit McKee. Gatt'll take a poke at you in a minute; he thinks you're trying to dodge."

"All right," said the freshman.

Wilson said, "Jocko. Corger knows where he is . . ."

"So what? You worry about cleaning out that deck. You have the deal, keep it. If Gatt wins it buy it back: offer him five bucks, he'll bite, just don't bid the fucking deal, he doesn't want it, he can't hand out five cards. But don't leave those floating aces in here, get them out as fast as I feed them to Marquales. Let Gatt draw five and he'll catch on, he's not that dumb."

At that moment the waitress brought two more bottles of beer. Silently they watched her place it before Gatt's vacant chair. When she left Marquales said, "Mr. de Paris . . ."

"My name is Jocko."

"Jocko. If I win all Gatt's money, what will he do?"

[ 170 ]

"He won't do anything. What could he do?"

Wilson said, "Why don't you try and get him to drink some liquor?"

"Haven't you seen me sit here and coax a keg of beer down his throat?"

"I mean, liquor."

"Junior, you dope. Didn't you hear me ask him a minute ago? He won't touch it.

"That goddamn Corger! How I hate that dirty son of a bitch! Corger this, Corger that. 'Laurie!' Dear old 'Laurie!' 'Laurie' my balls! *'Laurie!'* That morbid son of a bitch, I could cut his throat, the bastard."

"He's so military," said Wilson.

"Military—paaauuhh!" snarled De Paris. "It's not just that. He's a corn-fed son of a bitch beneath that goddamned pleated uniform and behind those goddamn boxing gloves. He's just as stupid and snotty as the day is long, the bastard. To hell with him. Change the subject."

"I wish I was out of here," said Marquales, trying to be funny.

De Paris said, "Don't be yellow like the rest of them."

Marquales was unable to look him in the eye. "Don't be yellow," repeated De Paris angrily. "It isn't worth it."

"What do you want to tease Gatt for?" blurted the freshman.

"Why . . ." Jocko hesitated, then said, "I hate the son of a bitch. One look at him makes me want to puke. He's a no-good crazy bastard, he and Corger both. One of these days I'm going to get them."

"Well, you'll do it, all right," said Wilson. "If you say you will."

"Okay, talk about something else. I hear him."

Silence. Then Gatt's feet on the stairs.

"Do you know Perrin McKee very well, Jocko?" asked Wilson.

"No."

"He's a peculiar person," said Marquales nervously.

"So I'd imagine, just to look at him," said De Paris.

"What would you say is peculiar about him?" asked Wilson.

The question was put to Marquales, but Jocko replied, "The shape of his mouth."

Albert Wilson leaned forward. "What did you want to see him for, Mister?"

Marquales answered, "Well, he pulled a funny trick."

"*What* funny trick?"

Gatt threw open the door.

"McKee's no friend of mine," said Marquales. "I told you he pulled a funny trick."

"What did he do?" asked Wilson.

"He wrote a threatening letter," said the freshman.

"Who?" said Gatt, coming forward.

"I've only seen McKee once or twice. He's no friend of mine. But he tried to pull a trick."

"What the hell are you stuttering about?" asked Jocko. "Nobody accused you of anything, or if they did," he glanced toward Wilson, "they're a dope."

"But what's the trick?" asked Wilson. "I'm curious."

"So am I," said Gatt.

"It wasn't anything," said Marquales carelessly. "I was only talking."

"Well talk on," said Wilson. "I'm curious how that McKee could play a trick on anybody."

Marquales swallowed.

"What was it?" asked Wilson.

Marquales said, "He found out about something and wrote a person he'd inform if they didn't meet him in a room on Luck Street."

De Paris laughed.

"It was about a girl."

"Naturally," said Jocko, smiling. "What surprises me is that the little runt would have the nerve. Who was his victim?"

"Me."

"Obviously it was you," replied De Paris, irritated. "But who was the piece? I might look it up."

Marquales sighed. He felt Gatt standing over him. Across the table

[ 172 ]

Albert Wilson had leaned forward, staring. De Paris' hands were folded under his sharp chin: waiting with a smile.

"Hi," said Gatt. "I'm back."

De Paris said politely, "Hello, Roge. Sit down."

Marquales spoke in a low voice to Wilson, "McKee found out something about a girl."

"Who?" said Wilson.

"Well, I . . ."

"What girl?" asked Wilson. "Answer up, we're curious."

"Who?" said Gatt. "What girl?"

"I can't say," answered the freshman in a whisper.

"That's right," laughed De Paris. "Don't be a cad. What difference does it make, anyhow? Maybe next time you'll use a rubber."

The freshman blushed, took out a handkerchief to wipe the perspiration from his eyes.

"Pull off your coat," said Jocko.

The freshman shook his head blindly.

"I don't blame you for wanting to get after McKee," said De Paris sympathetically. "I'd want to get after him myself."

Marquales shrugged.

"Somebody ought to kick McKee in the ass," said Wilson.

"How did McKee threaten you?" asked Jocko.

"I don't remember exactly. He said he'll tell General Draughton about the girl. He said I had to meet him in that room. Then before I could do anything, this morning he fell down the stairs and broke his leg."

"Saved you having to do it," said Jocko. He laughed harshly. "The ugly little runt—why this damn McKee has more in him than I'd have thought."

Marquales shrugged.

"Why don't you go around there and stuff a towel in his mouth?"

"But this poker game is keeping—"

"The game doesn't break up for two hours yet," said Gatt.

"On with it!" said De Paris. "We've wasted enough time in aimless chatter! Shuffle the fucking cards, Junior."

[ 173 ]

"Shuffle the cards!" said Gatt. "Shuffle the cards!"

With a sick feeling Marquales sank down in his chair. He watched the cards flip from Wilson's hands and go sliding across the table. He rubbed his own hands on his trousers, drying the palms. He felt Roger Gatt's eyes upon him.

Wilson laughed and said, "Some of us ought to go ride McKee on a rail—to protect this freshman here." Marquales looked up: there was a suspicious sneer on Wilson's face.

"Ante up," said Gatt. "I'm down. I'm down thirty dollars. You guys have got yourselves a lucky mascot."

"You'll probably win it back, Roge," said De Paris. "You're very lucky yourself."

"Yeah," said Gatt.

15 Hulitt was whistling the tune of an old air. "Mr. Marquales," nagged Wintermine. "May I ask if you are going to get up sometime before inspection? Or did the unendurable ordeal of eating breakfast exhaust your princely carriage? Say something. Don't just lie there on your rear. **Are you** going to get up?"

"Listen to this," said Hulitt. He leaned forward and sang:

> *I dream of Jeanie with the light brown hair,*
> *Borne like a vapor on the summer air;*
> *I see her tripping where the bright streams play,*
> *Happy as the daisies that dance on her way.*
>
> *Many were the wild notes her merry voice would pour,*
> *Many were the blithe birds that warbled them o'er;*
> *Oh! I dream of Jeanie with the light brown hair,*
> *Floating like a vapor, on the soft summer air.*
>
> *I long for Jeanie with the day-dawn smile,*
> *Radiant in gladness, warm with winning guile;*
> *I hear her melodies, like joys gone by,*
> *Sighing round my heart o'er the fond hopes that die:—*
>
> *Sighing like the night wind and sobbing like the rain,—*
> *Wailing for the lost one that comes not again:*
> *Oh! I long for Jeanie, and my heart bows low,*
> *Never more to find her where the bright waters flow.*

"That's lovely," said Wintermine. "But we *are* late this A.M."

"Okay," said Hulitt, shrugging.

Wintermine said, "I should be smart enough, dumb as I am, **to** know that Marquales has to be spoken to by his title. One hath **to** address him as Crown Prince; otherwise he won't answer one."

Hulitt belched humorously.

"Oh, Crown Prince," said Wintermine. "Is your highness enjoying his rest?"

Hulitt let go four belches and said, "I thought you were the Crown Prince here."

"No," said Wintermine. "I'm a mere serf."

Marquales rolled on the cot, turning his back to them. He felt a chemical stink in his nose; and reflected on the possibility that he might be smelling his own beery breath.

"Of course I'm room orderly this week," nagged Wintermine. "Of course I'd get demerits if the floor wasn't swept. Of course, it is hard to sweep when a cot is parked in the middle of the floor. These are just some incidental thoughts nobody has to listen to."

Marquales sighed in disgust.

"And naturally these thoughts do not make the slightest difference to the Crown Prince. Why should he care if his roommate gets pulled? It is nothing to him. Oh, no; it's none of his business at all. Sure, he can just lie there on his rear taking it easy waiting till the last minute. Then, perhaps, he will get his bed out of the way, if he feels like it.

"Of course, it'd be too late to sweep, then. But what if a mere room orderly does get pulled, gets demerits, gets put down on the slate? What possible difference does it make? Who is this guy Wintermine that royalty should bother about him? Just look at our royalty there. You'd never think the royalty heard me. It's as if I don't exist. I guess that's the result of my being below him. He's the Crown Prince and why should he listen to a mere serf? That's all I am, of course. Just a serf. Just a moron serf—who studies. Have you ever heard of anything more stupid than to study? It's serfy!

"Now I never asked to be born as a serf, but, ha-ha-ha, obviously I was. Some of us are born to be the Crown Prince and lie on our rears half the morning. And, some of us are born to be an unimportant serf! But am I complaining?"

"Yes," said Hulitt.

Marquales laughed into his pillow.

"Listen to the Crown Prince laugh! Ben: could it be possible he stoops to laugh in the presence of common dirt like us serfs?"

"Count me out," said Hulitt. "I'm a Republican."

[ 176 ]

"You're nothing. Absolutely nothing. Because the Crown Prince is above you. He's so far beyond you he doesn't know you exist."

"How long is it until inspection, Ben?"

"An hour and a half, Robbie."

"Terrible rush, isn't it?"

"An hour and a half isn't too long for what's got to be done!" said Wintermine. "Do you think I want demerits? Do you think I *want* them?"

"I don't know," said Marquales. "If they've got any judgment they don't want you."

"What I'd like to know is if you're going to get up or not, never mind the wit. Are you going to get up or are you going to lie on your rear—"

"That word is ass," said Marquales. "What kind of Sunday school did you go to?"

"There he is making dirty cracks about religion again! A fine thing. It shows his character. What's more, it shows what a wonderful family he must come from. I'm getting sick and tired of these irreligious remarks!"

"Don't look at me," said Hulitt. "I didn't do it."

"Well, don't try and act as if he were merely joking. I know him backwards and forwards."

"Were you joking, Robbie?" asked Hulitt.

"Wait a minute," said Wintermine. "Listen, Marquales. No arguments, just answer my question. Do you have any faith whatever?"

"Faith in what?" said Marquales.

"Do you think you made yourself? Or do you think God made you?"

"My family did," said Marquales.

Wintermine said in a low voice, "More vulgarity."

"That wasn't vulgar," said Marquales.

"I wonder," said Wintermine. "If it wasn't, what was it?"

"Just a statement of fact."

"Explain that."

"I don't feel like it."

[ 177 ]

"What kind of family did you come from that could let you grow up and talk the way you do?"

"A big family."

Wintermine leaned forward. "Did your family believe in God?"

"Yes."

"Then why don't you?"

"Do you really want to know?"

"Yes. I'm curious."

"Okay, then," said Marquales. "I'll tell you all about it."

"No nonsense now."

"Oh, no. I'm going to tell you all about it. Well, first of all, like I told you, I come from a big family. That was the main fault of it. It was too big. My mother and father had a peculiar resemblance to Brer Rabbit. I had fourteen sisters and fourteen brothers!"

"I do not wish to hear any more nonsense," said Wintermine.

"Let him tell it," said Hulitt, smiling.

"Brer Mother and Brer Father were both religious," said Marquales pensively. "They . . ." he turned his head to one side, choked briefly, then tipped the edge of his sheet gently under one eye. "I'm okay now. It's all right, really. That was a long time ago. I can talk about it.

"One day they . . . they all piled into the Model A to go to church."

"All thirty of them?" said Hulitt.

"No one got out of going to church in my family," said Marquales. "Everybody went. I was just five years old then, but I went, too."

"Where did you sit?" asked Hulitt. "On the roof?"

"No, I lay across the hood in front of the windshield. There were so many in the car my father couldn't see to drive anyhow."

"So funny," said Wintermine.

"Go on," said Hulitt.

"Well, we got in the Model A that time to go to church, and we arrived to the railroad track—I mean, we arrived *upon* the railroad track . . ."

[ 178 ]

"He doesn't even know how to tell his fool joke," said Wintermine under his breath.

"Of course we lived on the wrong side of the railroad track, next door to a family strangely enough named Wintermine. Anyhow the Model A got upon the railroad track, and stalled dead.

"My father began to pray to God because a train was thirty yards away, highballing down the track. It got twenty yards away and my mother chimed in. It got ten yards away and all fourteen of my brothers and all fourteen of my sisters began to pray. When it was one yard away they started, the whole bunch of them, to sing 'Nearer My God To Thee,' and right then I jumped off of that hood.

"Well, they had the funerals in four counties."

"Just what have you proved?" burst Wintermine.

"I was just explaining how I came to be against God. My family didn't deserve to be scattered that way."

After awhile Wintermine said, "I wouldn't laugh, Ben. There's nothing funny about spitting in the face of our Creator. It is not modern; it is just as bad as it was a hundred years ago. Besides, that is a stupid, foolish story of the kind a child would make up and think cute."

"What a way to talk to an orphan!" said Marquales.

"Well, I'll talk to you in another way, oh Crown Prince. When are you going to get out of my way? Are you going to lie there on your rear all morning? Do you realize who's inspecting barracks? Or does it make any difference to you? Tell me, I want to know. I'm the most curious serf you ever heard of. I'm highly curious!"

Marquales groggily put his feet on the floor. "You're curious, all right," he said.

"Are you insulting me?"

"Oh, no. I'm agreeing with you."

"You think you're smart, don't you?"

"No. Ohhhh, no!" said Marquales, imitating Wintermine's voice. "I'm just a serf, that's all I am, just a mere serfy serf."

Wintermine started to speak, then mumbled an unintelligible word.

[ 179 ]

Marquales ignored it and stood up, rubbing his temples gingerly. He winced, shut his eyes tight.

"A hangover?" asked Hulitt casually, looking out of the side of his eye at Wintermine.

"Yes. I drank too much beer last night."

"Not only is he smart," said Wintermine. "But he can drink more beer than ordinary people who are foolish enough to believe in God. And of course he has a worse hangover than we could ever have, naturally."

Marquales yawned.

"Look at him," said Wintermine. "He doesn't care what one of his inferiors says. He's so smart! When I say something he just yawns, and is veddy veddy bored by it all."

Marquales took the blankets off his cot, folded them to the proper size, then folded the sheets. He laid the stack on the top of his press, and shoved the mattress into its slot. He then broke down the cot frame and stowed it away beneath the mattress.

Hulitt asked, "Where'd you go last night?"

"To a meeting. A stag."

"One of the clubs?"

"Yes."

"Which one? What kind of stag?"

"Nothing much. I can't talk about it."

"We won't tell."

"They made me take an oath not to talk."

"Why can't you tell us?" asked Wintermine. "We're your roommates."

"Well, Les, if you were my nephews I couldn't dare say anything. You know how these clubs are: they'll murder anyone that talks about them."

"Why he actually sounded polite, and to dirt like me!" said Wintermine.

Marquales said, "Sometimes I think that inferiority complex of yours is the real thing."

"You've got an inferiority complex! That's why you act so—"

"I've got one," interrupted Hulitt. "An inferiority complex. That is, I had one until I grew out of it. Listen and I'll tell you a sad but exciting duplication. One haunted morning . . . I was born."

"How amazing," said Wintermine.

"Well, wait. This is the truth. One morning I was born. The doctor held me up and shook me. Then he reported a fact to the nurse. She reported it to the old mammy, who was standing by with a pail of boiling water—to drown me in if it turned out I had two heads like my uncle and grandfather. When the old mammy heard the news from the nurse she ran and told my father. He was outside in the hall hoping I was normal. He was nervous so he was eating the rug. When he heard the old mammy he began to eat the old mammy."

"Ha, ha," said Wintermine dryly.

"What did the old mammy say to him?" asked Marquales.

"Do you really want to know?"

"Yup, yup, yup!" said Marquales, moron voiced.

"She told my father about my inferiority complex. That's what the doctor noticed when he held me up. There the inferiority complex was, right between my legs."

Marquales and Wintermine laughed.

"I know you'll want to hear what happened next," said Hulitt, wrinkling his brow. "That's a matter of scientific terminology, however. Just the same, though, since I like you fellows, I'll try and remember exactly what it was that happened next. Wait a second."

Hulitt frowned thoughtfully for a few moments, rubbing his round chin with two fingers. Then he said solemnly: "First of all the doctor gave me a needle of haba daba the left ninnin and a medical cat shake, quick some folly below this and that, afterwards the remainder of the completion and the itch. Suddenly, the tiny wrinkled abradism, so carmanistic and belotic, showed signs of pluverisma, thank God, and I was saved."

Wintermine had a peculiar laugh—it was a steady fluid sound like a metronome clacking under water. The laugh never seemed to get up as far as his eyes.

"And," said Hulitt. "I've still got a complex, but it isn't inferior."

"Ult, ult, ult," said Wintermine to the disgust of Marquales.

"Oh, I imagine . . . 'bout six inches," said Hulitt solemnly.

"Ult, ult," remarked Wintermine. Then, shaking his head, he asked: "Ben, old boy, are you trying to make me laugh myself to death? You know, if the world started to come to an end you would be joking."

Marquales gritted his teeth.

"Ben," said Wintermine. "I daresay if you end up sitting on a hot coal after Judgment you will still be making jokes."

Marquales said, "Les, you'll be squatting there studying chemistry."

Wintermine's smile blinked away. He declared, "It's better to study chemistry and learn something than to spend your life talking like a fool! No offense to you, Ben."

Marquales said, "There was more information in what Ben said to us a minute ago than anything I ever heard out of you."

"All right!" shouted Wintermine. "You're not man enough to talk like that."

"What do you mean—man enough?"

"You're not large enough!"

"What's size got to do with it?"

"Plenty!"

"Wait," said Hulitt. "Don't argue on my account."

"My objection is to the insulting remarks Marquales continues to make at me. One of these days I'm going to get mad. I don't want to, because I don't like the idea of hurting him. But one of these days if he keeps riding me I'm going to get mad."

"Who's riding you?" asked Marquales.

"You are!"

"I just defend myself."

"I'm warning you, Marquales. Watch your step!"

There was a long silence, then Marquales said, "That's all I ever try to do—watch my step."

"You'd better calm down," said Wintermine. "And now, if you

don't mind, I think I'll get to work on the room instead of . . . instead of wasting my time in this ridiculous conversation."

"Yowsah."

"Then you give me your permission?" asked Wintermine.

"Yowsah, I give it to you."

There were ten minutes Marquales spent cleaning the rifle. Thereafter he went to work on his uniform. He brushed it thoroughly from top to bottom, then paid particular attention to his cap, glossing the vizor until it shone. A few minutes later, in new underwear, he stepped to the washbasin in the corner of the room and began to comb his hair. Wintermine came forward with a razor and tube of shaving cream; Marquales looked unconcernedly ahead at his own dim reflection in the dollar-nineteen mirror. There was a sigh. Marquales combed his hair gently, began to hum the melody of "Jeanie With the Light Brown Hair."

"Would you stop monopolizing the mirror all morning?" asked Wintermine.

"Now who's making insulting remarks? I just got here."

"I have to shave. I'm already late cleaning up the room because you wouldn't get up from bed."

"You're not late. There's plenty of time and you knew that when you were pestering me."

"I'll pester you!" shouted Wintermine. He violently pushed Marquales away from the basin. "Maybe you'll get some sense."

"What's the big idea?" said Marquales.

"I told you to get away."

"I was at the mirror before you were."

"You were monopolizing it."

"I was not. I'd just gotten there."

"I bought the mirror anyhow. Me and Ben."

"You did not. We all bought it together. I paid one third."

"Like hell! You were *supposed* to, but somehow it just never entered your mind to come across with the money. Ben and I bought the mirror and you never gave a dime."

"I gave you the money before you ever bought it."

"That's a dirty lie."

"And that's another."

"You rat! Don't call me a liar or I'll jump all over you."

"Go ahead and jump. I paid the money, and if you say I didn't you're telling a lie. A dirty lie."

Wintermine leaned forward, fists up and his face cold pale; Marquales backed away several steps. "Wait a minute, Les," said Hulitt. "He paid you the money. Jump on somebody your own size."

"What?"

"I said he paid you the money. And you heard me."

The look on Wintermine's face changed to humiliation. For a few seconds he stood uncertainly between Marquales and Hulitt. Then he faced Hulitt. "Are you sure?" he said, angrily.

"I'm damn sure," answered Hulitt. "I remember when he gave it to you."

"Well all right then," said Wintermine. "In that case I was wrong. It was my mistake. Go on, Robbie, the mirror's yours. Help yourself."

"I'm through," said Marquales. He crossed the room on numb legs. "Go right ahead and take advantage of the prize you won."

"No hard feelings?"

"No," said Marquales bitterly. Ben Hulitt then gave him a wink. Did I pay for that mirror? thought Marquales.

A few minutes before first call for inspection Albert Wilson walked into the room. Hulitt and Wintermine popped to attention.

"Well, Mister?" said Wilson to Marquales. "Are you a privileged character? We're in barracks now. Do you think you're exempt from regulations just because I see you in town and don't make you brace then? Pull your bloody neck back! Stand up hard!"

"Sir, may I offer an explanation?" asked Marquales, his neck in wrinkles.

"Go ahead."

"I thought you'd feel like Jocko about freshman regulations, considering the fact you're a good friend of his."

"Does Jocko let you freshmen stay low when he comes in here?"

"Yes, sir," said Marquales.

"Well I'm not Jocko. But you can rest anyhow."

They relaxed, and Hulitt said with a smile, "So you're a good friend of Mr. de Paris, sir? I thought I knew all his friends." Hulitt rubbed his tail, laughing.

"The next time I come in here," said Wilson hoarsely, "you freshmen leap to like a rock and don't waste any time about it. Also, don't ask questions of an upperclassman without permission."

Wilson was in dress uniform. He carried his Remington under an arm; snowy gloves were pushed behind the brass centerpiece on his chest; his black leather cartridge box flopped over the small of his back; and his cap was down square upon his eyes, which were bloodshot. He said:

"You two freshmen go to the latrine. Shit or something, I want to talk to this man."

Hulitt and Wintermine at once departed, popping to attention as they went out the door to the gallery.

"Slice those corners square," called Wilson.

Through the door Marquales saw his roommates cut the ninety-degree angle and head down the gallery.

"What are those guys like?" asked Wilson.

"Sir?"

"The plump one looks suspicious."

"Suspicious?"

"I mean he has a funny mouth."

"Hulitt, sir?"

"I don't know his goddamn name. The heavy one."

"There's nothing like that about Hulitt, sir."

Wilson's face was fresh shaven but ashy. He looked sick. "You had hard luck with him, eh?" he asked hoarsely.

"I don't know what you mean, sir."

"I mean if you move a goddamned rock you'll find one crawling cut."

"Sir?"

"Don't sir me like that."

"No, sir."

"It seems to me that a lot of your friends and roommates look as if they have their lunch downtown."

"Sir, I swear none of my friends are like that."

"And what about McKee and Colton?"

"Sir, they're not my friends."

"All right, all right!" said Wilson impatiently. He swallowed several times. "We'll worry about that later. Right now there's plenty else."

Marquales waited. Finally Wilson said, "Jocko wants you to come by his room after inspection. You'll get your share of the money then. Everything that's coming to you."

"Yes, sir."

"Meanwhile, if you see Corger—I mean, if he sees you—don't say anything about the game last night. Nothing. Just sit there and tell him nothing. You never saw Gatt, you don't know what happened to Gatt in any poker game, whether he lost or won, and so forth. In short, you tell Corger nothing, in case he stops you."

"Yes, sir," answered Marquales, wondering, as he watched Wilson stride out of the room, how he could manage to say nothing to Larrence E. Corger, Cadet Colonel.

*16* The cadets stood on the quadrangle of Hemphill Barracks, lined in perfect formation, rifles hoisted to present arms. Gaunt General Draughton peered under his brown Army cap across the air: he seemed taller than in the Armory. Slowly, his arm flowed to a careless, but precise, salute.

The Cadet Major said, "Order . . ."

At the word "Arms!" the rifles fell and the sabers of the senior officers whipped in the sunlight, making bright arcs to twenty padded shoulders. There was a long ringing silence.

"Members of the Second Battalion," said General Draughton in a deep voice. "I have a short message for you this morning. Your close attention, please."

Finally the General said, "I wish to inform you that The Academy is to be inspected by a Reviewing Board sent from Washington, D. C. This will occur two weeks from today. As some of you have learned in the past, it is the responsibility of this Reviewing Board to estab- lish—for the convenience of the Department of War—ratings of the numerous military institutions throughout the nation. That is to say: those institutions operating under the auspices of the Army or the R.O.T.C."

The General hesitated. "Gentlemen, there is no need for me to im- press upon the Second Battalion the importance of this visit. All of you certainly realize that the officers who will inspect your ranks will determine the status of The Academy with the Department of War. These officers will leave Port George with two possible atti- tudes. First, they will be satisfied that they have again been able to bestow upon The Academy the highest possible rating. Second, they will leave in another state of mind. I am sure that these officers would be sorry if it became their duty to take away this institution's rating of *Excellent:* a rating that has been enjoyed by The Academy since first such rankings were made.

"Gentlemen. It will be your task to see to it that the officers of the Reviewing Board are favorably impressed. The matter is in your hands and nothing that I or Colonel Evers or any of the members of the military staff can do will separate that fact from its connection with the objective view of what we actually face two weeks from today. You have now been members of this institution, all of you, first-year men included, for a considerable space of time. I speak to you not as mere recruits. Rather, as somewhat seasoned and experienced men—whose neatness, alertness, and military courtesy are developed past a beginning and approach a finished product.

"On week after next, gentlemen, you will not fail to ready yourself with the usual industry and skill for Saturday Formal Inspection.

"One matter. I have been advised by Major Pearson that the standing of Hemphill Barracks in co-relation to South Barracks and North Barracks is rather favorable, on the whole, particularly with regard to the condition of the rooms. It now appears that the demerit graph of room penalties indicates appreciable superiority on the side of Hemphill Barracks. May I say that I am fond of this barracks: it was standing firm when I arrived at this my final post some years ago. I hope it will be standing firm when I depart—which, I trust, will not be in the immediate future."

The General smiled, looking back and forth across the Battalion.

"I also hope, gentlemen—aside from the delicate issue of my state of preservation—that you will continue and even improve upon your record of care, discipline, effort. Above all, may I add, do not allow yourselves to lapse on the particular occasion of week after next, at which time we will be under the critical eye of Washington, D. C. What avails the gem to cast its crystal sparkle in an undiscovered cave?"

The General paused briefly, then said, "*If* your shoes are polished excellently, that fact will be observed by the Reviewing Board. *If* they are not, that too will be observed by the Reviewing Board.

"In short: we will be served as we serve.

"The task is ours. I do not doubt its outcome.

"If you are asked questions by any member of the Reviewing Board—then answer them as you think I myself would answer.

"The Reviewing Board, you may be confident, will be impartial. In short: we may expect from the Reviewing Board a severe but objective examination. You may very well realize that subconsciously. That is to say: I am certain that you are aware of the import of this event.

"I do not for a moment doubt its outcome. The Academy will win its usual mark of *Excellent*. No other possibility exists."

The General paused—and smiled again; he smiled, folded his arms, and put one foot out in front of the other one.

"I'm going to tell you something. You will be glad to hear this, I'm sure. Gentlemen, despite my frequent pronunciamentos and sharp criticisms of you, I have a confession I think it fitting I now make. Therefore . . ."

For a moment the General lost his voice; but his smile did not alter.

"Let me say to you under this sunny Southern sky that I am deeply proud of you. Deeply proud. My heart swells beneath this khaki when I see what you have accomplished in these short months. Continue your pace, gentlemen, and you will maintain this pride forever. Continue to grow and to develop yourself according to our ideals. I predict that the day will come, regardless of what the renegades and cowards of our time say and print in their newspapers, the day will come when my present sense of accomplishment insofar as you are concerned will dwindle into nothing by comparison. Your role in history awaits you! Never drop the standard, men! NEVER!"

Silence. The standard waved aloft in the grip of the color sergeant. After several sighs the General pulled himself together and said in a matter-of-fact yet ingratiating voice:

"Gentlemen, have your uniforms freshly pressed for week after next. Attend to the matter as soon as possible following this week end. Be particularly careful about brushing the lint from the roof of your cap. I saw you from the vantage point of the second gallery a few moments ago when you were forming. I happened to notice several caps that held lint. Also, you might purchase from the Canteen a new strip of blitz cloth: your brass must be like fire. Brilliant brass speaks for itself. Be cautious about not forgetting to put on silk garters. What is underneath is important, too, and never forget that.

[ 189 ]

Be sure the garters are black. And, pure white webbing, of course, is absolutely necessary . . . however, I do not need to tell you these details. You know them, and I'm sure you realize what is wanted.

"Perfection. Nothing less than that. Perfection. Each man must present himself in a manner that will leave no doubt in the mind of the Reviewing Board.

"All cadet officers, commissioned and noncommissioned, will make extreme effort to bring out the battalion at its best.

"One further detail about the relative positions of the three battalions. I have spoken to Cadet Colonel Corger about the condition of the battalions as he sees it. This particular fact relates to the Second Battalion:

"Cadet Corger feels that the First Battalion has on the whole been more attentive to the care of its short arms than either this battalion or the Third. I intend to speak in the future to the members of the Third Battalion. Let me advise you now to devote more effort to the proper care of your rifles, cartridge belts, bayonets. These items are important —to say the least. Nothing disturbs a military mind more than to see rust about the bore of an expensive gun. This is not only untidy, but grossly destructive to Army property. And it is thoroughly inexcusable."

General Draughton smiled.

"Today, in my inspection, I hope to discover that Cadet Colonel Corger has erred in the matter of your attention to your short arms. However, I may say that it is very seldom that Cadet Corger has made any such error."

The General stopped smiling.

"Gentlemen, I will expect the Second Battalion to be a credit to The Academy week after next."

Colonel Evers stepped forward, exchanged salutes with the General, and said in a voice that was thin, reedlike:

"I hope that you men will profit from the General's remarks to you this morning. As for me, I would like merely to express my trust in your good faith, certain that you are aware of the necessity to rise to the occasion. Therefore, on week after next carry out your duty."

[ 190 ]

Cadet Captain-Adjutant Starkson stepped forward, saluted with his saber, and about-faced to the corps. His red sash rose, subsided gently to his hip. He gave the order to prepare for inspection.

Due to the visit of the General, inspection lasted two and one-half hours: an equal division of time spent on the quadrangle in personal inspection, and later, in the rooms for room inspection.

Much of personal inspection was passed at the position of attention; but the rain of the day before had disappeared and a bright autumn sun warmed the battalion.

Many cadets were reprimanded in Company Twelve—Robert Marquales' Company—during personal inspection. But Marquales himself passed. He was even commended by the General for the appearance of the vizor of his cap, which he had polished with machine oil and spit.


"Gates, I can't take it any more," said Jocko, moaning. "It wasn't as if I was out drinking last night, but this morning, my *God*."

"You look all right," said Wilson.

"Look? It's how you feel that counts. I wonder how much I had. It couldn't have been much. Did I drink any more than a third of a pint?"

"I don't know what you drank," said Wilson glumly. "All I know is that as soon as that damn card game started *I* quit drinking."

"Well, to hell with you, then. Did I have as much as one-sixth of a pint, Marquales?"

"I thought you had an even pint," said the freshman, smiling.

"Well, I didn't. Yet this morning I have a hangover. And a bad one, too. My head's full of scrap iron."

"Jocko," said Wilson.

"What?"

"Corger gave me a very funny look this morning."

"You told me that once. Are you trying to be boring?"

"I'm worried."

"I'm not," said Jocko.

Wilson put his chin in his hand and stared down at the floor.

"Hey, Marquales," said De Paris. "Put that stuff in your pockie."

The freshman had been holding the money, thirty dollars, twisting and turning it in his hand.

"Yes, sir," he said, wadding the bills into his right rear pocket.

"Jocko," said Wilson. "I think we ought to give Gatt back his money before we get in trouble with Corger."

"You told me that once, too," said De Paris. "You're both acting like chicken-shits. We win a batch of money—you're afraid to take it. And what are you afraid of? A big cretin. A big cretin who hasn't got enough sense to go to the toilet." De Paris laughed. "Corger does it for him."

"It's Corger I'm worried about," said Wilson.

"Junior, when are you going to learn the facts of life?"

The door of the room was then flung open; Marquales saw, on either side of the vacant space, two rigid orderlies. The space was filled in by the gaunt form of General A. L. Draughton.

"Attention!" called De Paris sharply.

The three cadets leapt to their feet.

"At ease," murmured the General. He walked slowly into the room, gazing reflectively at the walls. "Cadet Starkson."

Starkson stood in the door, head slightly to one side.

"Give me that inspection clip board, then wait outside."

Marquales found it difficult to breathe. He had never seen the General at such an intimate distance: the Chief Executive of The Academy looked older. There were deep lines sunk into the tan forehead; the neck skin was dry and in loose folds. Marquales was especially shocked to see in General Draughton's mouth false teeth of a slightly gray shade. A white-white mustache, perfectly cropped, was under the large nose; a wide path of tan skin divided the mustache into equal segments.

Returning Marquales' stare, the General asked, "What is this freshman doing in here?"

"Visiting, sir," said De Paris.

"His name?"

"Robert Marquales, sir."

"He may be excused."

Marquales turned stiffly to go. "Wait!" said the General. "Perhaps it might be informative for him to remain and hear what I have to say to two members of the Junior Class."

"Yes, sir," said the freshman.

"Your name again?" asked the General.

"Cadet Marquales, Robert, sir."

"Very well. Cadet Marquales, I hope you profit from what I say to Cadets Koble and De Paris."

"Sir," said De Paris. "Cadet Koble isn't here just now. This cadet is Junior Classman Albert Wilson, sir."

"Cadet Wilson? And where is Cadet Koble?"

"Sir, on week-end leave."

"Week-end leave?"

"Sir, his father is ill. It was cleared through Colonel Evers."

"Then you alone were responsible for the condition of this room this morning?"

"Yes, sir," said De Paris.

"Cadet Wilson, I take it that you also are visiting?"

"Yes, sir," said Wilson hoarsely.

"Very well," murmured the General. "At least, Cadet de Paris is here. And, if he was responsible wholly for this room, then he is the only man necessary for me to see."

"Shall I go, sir?" croaked Wilson.

"You might also just as well hear what I have to say."

"Yes, sir."

The General sighed, turned, walked to the window, and touched his lemon-colored gloves to the bars. He held up a finger to the three cadets. Then he walked to the rifle rack, touched the wood with his gloves, and held up another finger, turning it from side to side.

"*Room Number 394,*" read the General from the clip board. "*Occupants, De Paris, J., Koble, H. Room orderly of the week, Koble, H.*

"*Dirt and rust on window latticework. Filth accumulated along woodwork of rifle rack. Lint on spare uniforms. Bed linen folded carelessly, not flush to top of press. Lavatory: stained. Floor: unswept.*

*Clothes hung in improper order in clothes-hanger section of press; buttons of shirts hanging in clothes-hanger section not fastened. Alternate shoes of both occupants of room improperly shined; laces untied on black extra shoes belonging to Cadet de Paris. Shelves of press belonging to Cadet de Paris in great disorder. Shirts folded very irregularly, underwear cast in hidden pile to rear of second shelf, soiled pajamas unfolded, hidden on bottom shelf under uneven stack of towels. Personal possessions shelf in extreme indescribable disarray.*

"This," said General Draughton, "is what I found upon inspecting this room forty minutes ago, gentlemen."

There was a long silence. Then the General said slowly, "Cadet de Paris. I have never inspected a room in worse disorder than this one. It is as if pigs live here. Not human beings, but grunting, filthy PIGS. Do you hear me, sir?"

"General Draughton, I am not a pig, sir."

"Then kindly do not live like one."

"Sir, I was ill when I awoke this morning."

"Cadet de Paris, such a cowardly dodge does not impress me in the slightest," said the General calmly.

Jocko answered, "I'm sorry if you consider me a liar, sir."

"I am equally sorry, Cadet de Paris, that you find it necessary to be one."

"General Draughton, I give you my word of honor as an Academy Cadet that this morning I nearly fainted on two occasions."

"You maintain that?"

"I do, sir."

"Then will you kindly account for this odd malady?"

"There's nothing odd about it, sir. I've been ill for the past two days. The trouble began with the meat balls served to the defenseless corps Thursday night in cadet mess."

General Draughton's face turned dark, then white, making the lines much deeper. He said slowly, "Are you daring to speak impertinently to me?"

"Sir, I meant no impertinence," said De Paris lightly. "I assure you of that."

[ 194 ]

There was a long silence. Finally the General asked, "Do you maintain that the condition of this room is the result of illness on your part?"

"Of course I do, sir."

"I would appreciate it if you would state in so many words just what it was that you found wrong with the meat cakes served to the corps on Thursday night."

"I hesitate to answer, sir, for fear you will think me impertinent."

"Speak up," said the General slowly. "Answer my question as your conscience decrees. This won't be the last that I will ask you."

De Paris paused for a moment, then seemed to give a slight shrug. He said evenly, flashing his white teeth, "General Draughton—the meat balls in question of debate contained a high percentage of indigestible gristle. They were cooked, if such a word may be used, in some variety of rancid frying oil and were severely burned . . ."

"I think that will be sufficient," said the General, eyes glittering. "Now another question: have you reported on sick call, sir?"

Jocko faltered. He stared sidewise at the General, opened his mouth to speak, then closed it.

"Kindly answer my question, please. We will follow through this surprising fiasco."

"No, sir," said Jocko finally. "I did not go on sick call."

"And now my final question." The General leaned forward. "Why not?"

"I didn't want to act like a weakling. Everybody had to eat that hamburger, after all."

"Thank you," said the General. He smiled broadly. Then his smile began to come to a narrow point, until, though his false teeth were smiling, his eyes were lifeless. After several moments he cleared his throat and spoke:

"Cadet de Paris! I fear that you have forced me to speak to you in a way that I had hoped would not be necessary.

"Cadets Marquales and Wilson, listen to what I will say, in order that you might learn once and for all a basic principle of The Academy. I ask you not to keep what you will hear to yourself. Pass it on to your classmates.

"Cadet de Paris. You may consider yourself at this moment on the point of expulsion. I have not as yet made up my mind, but in a few minutes you might no longer be a part of this institution."

"Sir, I—"

"Silence!" said the General.

"Yessir," murmured Jocko.

"I want you all to hear me say this. Perhaps it is already known, but now you will hear it from me.

"Mr. Roy de Paris, the father of Cadet de Paris, has been, and is, one of the better friends of The Academy. At a time of dark need, Mr. Roy de Paris intervened in important circles for the purpose of securing for this institution necessary governmental funds. Mr. Roy de Paris, and several others, including Mr. de Paris' friend, Mr. Patrick Webster, did much to help me in my task here. I and The Academy owe Mr. Roy de Paris a debt of profound gratitude.

"However, if anyone thinks, for one moment, that these facts will allow Cadet de Paris an iota of special privilege at this institution, he is profoundly mistaken. I am sure that Mr. Roy de Paris, an old Army man himself, would be the last to disapprove of this statement.

"Cadet de Paris. When you enrolled at this school three years ago I expected much of you. And until recently I continued to expect much of you. However, during this term your attitude has been unfortunate. I have had reports from both Major Pearson and Colonel Evers that your behavior has been what we may expect of a coarse vice-steeped ape, not an Academy man.

"This morning when I inspected this room I was shocked. I observed the filth on all sides, the amazing sloppiness—and I decided then that I would return after completing room inspection of the remainder of the barracks. I decided to report to you what has been set against this room on the clip board of the Captain-Adjutant. My intention was to reprimand you most severely and to penalize you and your roommate twenty-five demerits. However, that decision has been qualified by the news that you alone were responsible for this room, since your roommate is out of barracks for the week end. It has also been qualified by your astonishing impertinence to me a moment ago.

"I will now permit you three minutes to tell me why I should not expel you at once."

The General pulled back the sleeve of his Army coat and examined his wrist watch. De Paris sighed deeply, bewildered. Finally the General said:

"You have two and one-half minutes."

Jocko's lower lip twitched, then he cleared his throat and said, "Sir, I want to continue my studies here and to enter the ranks of the regular Army upon graduation, if possible."

Silence. More time passed. Wilson and Marquales were as white and shaken as De Paris.

"You have two minutes."

"Sir," said Jocko. "You wouldn't expel me on a moment's notice like this, would you, sir?"

There was no reply.

"General Draughton," said Jocko feverishly. He paused, then spoke rapidly, words jumbling on top of each other. "I admit that I had a bad attitude a moment ago. Sir, I should not have spoken to you like that. It was impertinent of me although I swear I didn't mean it to sound that way—it was just a matter of expressing myself carelessly and without thinking about how it would sound. I am sorry, sir. I apologize to you. I apologize to these cadets, Mr. Wilson and Mr. Marquales, for having embarrassed them. Sir, I regret my behavior. Sir, I am sorry to say that you are correct about my attitude this fall. I have not behaved properly. I am very sorry about that, sir, and if you will give me another chance I pledge that I will never again act in such a way as to throw discredit on The Academy, any discredit whatever."

Silence.

"You have perhaps a minute remaining," said the General indifferently.

Jocko moistened his lips and said, "Sir, let me tell you that the reason for my bad attitude this fall has been the difficulty of my studies. Also, sir, let me point out that I have been having trouble with my eyes and have just been fitted to a pair of reading glasses which I hope will stop the bad headaches I've been getting. Sir, this isn't just an excuse! Colonel Girard has handled the matter. He will back me up if you ask him.

"And sir, please let me say that I realize the room was in very bad order. I am terribly sorry about that and offer no excuse at all. I simply neglected my duty and admit it, sir. There is no excuse for my letting the room be found by you in such condition. I deserve the severest punishment for that, sir . . . but I beg of you not to expel me. I beg of you to at least pause for a few days and give me the opportunity to prove to you that I . . ."

"Your time is exhausted," said the General dryly.

Silence. Tears were in the corners of Jocko's eyes. His lower lip trembled. Wilson and Marquales stood at attention, despite the fact that "at ease" had been given them.

"Sir," said Jocko in a broken voice. "Not because of my father but because of my own career, I ask that you don't expel me. It has been my ambition all my life to join the Army and get into the Air Corps, if there should be a war. Sir, I ask that you give me one more chance to prove myself."

After a long pause the General cleared his throat in a thoughtful manner. Then he said, "I do not know what I am going to do. However, in any case, I assure you, and I assure all of these gentlemen, that my decision will have nothing whatever to do with your father, and you err even to mention him. The Academy will not stoop to favoritism. Never! And he who thinks that The Academy will soil its honor in that way is doomed to bitter disillusion. We play no favorites here!"

"Sir . . ." said Jocko.

"I think the best thing you can do now is keep your mouth sealed," said the General. "Now you other cadets. I believe I owe you something of an apology. I had not thought to subject you to this fiasco. However, I hope that what you have heard will make a strong imprint. The Academy does not show favoritism of any kind. No military institution worthy of the name shows favoritism. The man of value will rise to command by himself or he will not rise at all. The man incapable of progress will remain at the foot.

"Now Cadet de Paris. I believe that at present I am not in the proper objective mood to consider your case. I intend to wait for one week before making up my mind. It may be that then I will expel you, or merely give you a special penalty.

"This much is certain. You will lose your rank. That we might as well take care of now. You are hereby reduced to the status of Junior Private and will remove from your uniforms all sergeant bars you now wear.

"Cadet de Paris, you will report at my office one week from this minute. Make arrangements for your possible expulsion, meanwhile."

The General turned and walked out of the room, his face calm and detached. The two orderlies, both freshmen, glanced in for a moment, wide eyed, then closed the door. Wilson, Marquales, De Paris stared blankly at one another.

"Well, what do you know?" said Wilson softly.

*17* "I'm telling you, he doesn't dare go too far," said De Paris between his teeth. "That goddamned old . . . let him come around here and chew his yap at me. By God, the fucking day hasn't been seen that he can get the best of Jocko de Paris! So let him," Jocko's voice became a whisper. "So let him. Just let him. But beyond that certain point—he can't go, and won't go. By God, he knows that. He knows he can't kick me out of here."

De Paris got up from the press, crossed to the window. He spit onto the bars. He spit again. Then he spit once more, furiously, his face blanched with anger. "That for his spirit of cleanliness! I'll clean those fucking windows—like hell! They can drop out of the fucking building first!"

"Jocko," said Wilson. "Somebody's going to hear you."

"And who!" shouted De Paris. "That old bastard? So what? He just bluffed me, that's all. I don't care if he's still standing outside the door. That bastard! Do you want me to tell you what he is?"

Jocko walked forward, stooped, half-shut his eyes, and, chopping out the words, shouted in a hoarse voice:

"He's a goddamned syphilitic long-John son-of-a-bitching boot-baller bastard, father of a long line of hair-teethed little jobbers covered with crabs! By God, *the old turd*! Filthy slobbery bastard! Christ, I could blow out his brains, blow out his maggoty brains! SMASH HIS PUTRID GUTS! SMASH HIS GUTS! KICK HIS GUTS AND LIVER! BEAT HIS GUTS OUT!"

"Jocko," said Wilson, laughing nervously.

De Paris sat and gritted his teeth, shutting his eyes and shaking his head blindly back and forth. His face was the color of milk.

"Take it easy, Jocko," said Wilson in a gentle voice.

After a long time De Paris relaxed, and said in a much calmer voice, "You know, I was really surprised to hear him turn against me like that. So surprised that I ate dirt. Did you hear me? I ate dirt and apologized to that bastard. That's how surprised I was when he pulled that stuff about expelling me. The bastard—I'll never forget how he made me eat dirt. By God, I'll never forget that. Not that it makes a damn. I didn't mean a word of it.

"If I hadn't said anything at all, do you think he would have kicked me out? No. He would not. He just wanted me to crawl—what a sucker I was, what a sucker! *Jesus! I fell for it!*

"But I still don't understand why he turned against me that way. What have I done that I didn't always do? What got into him, turning against me?

"You know, ever since I first laid eyes on that old bastard I haven't liked him and he hasn't liked me. I'll never forget that time I got in an argument with him about Paddy Webster. Well, the General was all for Webster because Paddy was helping him in Washington. But I was against the bastard. Against Paddy, that is. I remember it like a book. It was one night in Chicago when the old skunk came out to the house for dinner. This was right during the time when Paddy was helping him in Washington, along with my old man. I told the General I thought Paddy was all right, but was unfortunately insane. Well, what did the General say? Did he have the guts to talk to me like he did a minute ago? No, he smiled that sickening smile of his and said, 'My boy, I think you're a bit impetuous. But sometimes an impetuous young man makes a splendid officer, when seasoned correctly.' Have you ever heard such stuff? And the way he talked to me a minute ago! Heh. He had a different tone that night in Chicago. Yes, sir, you can bet you ass on that! He was slobbering at the mouth for new barracks: and here they are, South and North Barracks! Millions of bucks, by God, and who got him in with Paddy? Who, for Christ's sake? My old man. My old man. Who got it for him? Paddy and my old man! Why that skunk—*Jesus* Christ."

De Paris sat down weakly in a chair.

"That old bastard would never dare expel me," he said.

"No, I don't think he would," agreed Wilson.

Jocko scratched his chin for a few moments, then smiled amiably at Marquales. "Kid, when you lugged me back to barracks that night you did yourself a big favor. That put me on your side. See? And when you've got me on your side, nothing can happen to you at The

Academy. Neither me nor any of my friends will ever get the boot from General A. L. Draughton." De Paris turned to Wilson. "And you bellyache about Gatt and Corger."

"Oh, no, I don't," said Wilson.

Jocko thought for a minute. Then he asked, "Did you know, last year Gatt beat up a sailor, and the Port George Naval Command almost talked the General into kicking him out? Well, what saved Gatt? Naturally, Corger. But what can Corger do, if Gatt loses money in a poker game? Poker's against the rules. The Hair-of-the-Hound Club is against rules. Gatt was there. He'd be just as guilty as we were. And how could it ever be proved we cheated in that game? It couldn't. So don't tell me Corger can do us any harm."

"Well, maybe not on account of the poker game," said Wilson.

"Don't tell me Corger's behind this," said Jocko. "The General could never act that fast. He's been plotting this business this morning—I know that old bastard like a book. He's had this up his sleeve for at least a week. Well, I'm not worried. If he meant to kick me out he would have done it this morning. That much is obvious. He's just trying to scare me now. I'm through being scared by that son of a bitch. Let him try it again."

"Jocko," said Wilson. "I don't think he'd dare do anything to you."

"He certainly wouldn't. If I got kicked out it would mean two things right away. First, my old man wouldn't be behind the General any more. Second, Paddy Webster wouldn't be behind the General any more. Those two facts would mean that Washington wouldn't be behind the General any more! And if Washington wasn't behind the General, then where the hell would the new barracks and the new administration building come from? Hell, there's nothing in the South but Nehi signs on barns! Oh, that old bastard hasn't got all he wants yet, he's greedy." De Paris threw back his head and laughed.

"Who is Paddy Webster?" asked Marquales curiously.

"A bastard politicking son of a bitch. He interferes with everything. I hate his guts and always have, but he likes me."

"Is he a Congressman?"

"This whole thing gets me," said De Paris dreamily, hand on his chin.

"Or is he a Senator?" asked Marquales.

"Well, to hell with the whole thing," said De Paris wearily. "To hell with every bit of it. I'm not going to let it bother me, I'm going to forget it. Nothing that I said to him makes any difference. I didn't mean a word of it."

For a long time De Paris sat slumped over in the chair. Then he looked up and said cheerfully, in an entirely different voice:

"Let's make some plans for tonight. Are you doing anything, Marquales?"

"No," said the freshman nervously.

"Well, Junior wants us to go around and bother McKee."

"Why do that?" said Marquales carelessly. "Say, are they really going to build another barracks here? Do they expect that many—"

"You're changing the subject," smiled Albert Wilson. "That's very clever, by God."

De Paris smiled. "Kid, I swear it looks as if Junior thinks you're a pansy. But don't let that bother you—Junior thinks everybody is a pansy."

Wilson said, "Never mind that, Jocko."

"Marquales, if you're not doing anything else, come by the room around four. I've got to get the taste of this morning out of my mouth. We'll jump in my car, go out to the beach maybe, have some dinner, a couple of good shots of bourbon or something, then if we feel like it, we'll go see this guy. Okay?"

"Sure," said Marquales. "Only I don't think they'd let us in to see him at his house. But I don't care."

Wilson laughed, staring at Marquales. "You seem sort of upset," he said.

"Oh, leave the kid alone, Junior."

Ignoring Wilson, Marquales said in a bored manner, "Jocko, your father must be pretty important to hobnob with Senators—God, that's more than my father does. Congressmen are his limit."

"Yah," said Wilson.

[ 203 ]

"My old man is just a country boy who made good," said De Paris, smiling. "He was born on a red-dirt farm right outside Atlanta."

"So your father pals around with Congressmen, eh?" said Wilson. "You're very modest. Who do you pal around with?"

"I told you to leave him alone!" said De Paris.

"I'm only kidding," said Wilson.

"And what's all this stuff about Senators? Did I tell you anything about my old man and Senators?"

"Yes, wasn't that other guy—"

"You mean Webster? Paddy Webster? Listen, if he was in the Senate you might as well dynamite the U.S.A. and let the Atlantic Ocean take over. He's nuts, and everybody knows he's nuts. I never told you he was in the Senate."

"Well."

"Furthermore, he happens to be a first-class bastard, although he likes me. He's a pompous old bastard all right."

De Paris paused for a moment, then said thoughtfully, "It just goes to show you how many morons there are running around loose. On the one hand we have this nutty bastard Draughton running the best military school in the South. Whatever he himself is, the school is damn good. Then on the other hand, despite the fact that Webster himself is both a bastard and a nut, there he is, running the best newspaper in Chicago, and no doubt about it. This is a peculiar world, if you ask me. The nuts get ahead."

After lunch, Marquales hurried to the Canteen. He went to the rear and stepped into a telephone booth.

Information gave him four McKee numbers. He called the first. He asked to speak to Perrin and there was a click. He called the second number. A voice said, "We are not interested." The receiver banged down. Marquales sighed, shook his head, called the third number. It was more rewarding. A man answered the telephone and said that Perrin McKee didn't live there. He lived with his stepmother on Cheney Street. Under the name of Clarissa Bellemond.

Marquales spoke again to Information and got another number. This time a Negro woman answered the phone.

The conversation didn't last very long.

"Who do you want?"

"Perrin."

"Perrin's in bed. He broke his hip."

"I thought it was his leg."

"He can't be jabbering to any of you on the phone."

"But I have an important message for him."

There was silence, then, "Wait a minute."

The woman returned and said wearily, "I'll write it down."

"Tell him that his letter to Jocko has been found." Marquales hesitated. "Tell him Jocko thinks he wrote the letter to Marquales. M-A-R-Q-U-A-L-E-S. And tell him Jocko and Marquales are coming tonight."

"Nobody can come here," said the woman.

"And Wilson, too," said Marquales.

"I told you nobody can come here."

"Give him the message, that doesn't make any difference."

"I won't. What do you mean, boy? Stay away. Nobody can come here; Perrin's sick."

"Well, you please give him the message, just the same."

"He's sick. Who are you?"

"That doesn't matter. Just please give him the message."

"I'm going to hang up."

"Will you be sure and tell—"

There was a click.


Marquales stood at the canteen counter and ordered a milk shake. Suddenly a soft mass bumped into him. He turned and stared into the face of Carlton Leroy.

"Hey, Robbie. How's my boy?"

"Go away, Carlton."

"How's your health, Robbie? I never see you these days. Why

don't you come up sometime? I'm all by myself now Tim isn't here any more."

Then Marquales had an idea. "Let's go to a booth," he said. "I want to ask you to do me a favor."

"I'll take care of your order," said Leroy. Quickly, he spoke to the soda boy. A minute later he followed Marquales to the booth, bearing in his fat hands two glasses of Coca-Cola.

"What became of my milk shake?"

"Robbie! Did you order a milk shake?"

"Never mind. Listen, Carlton. I want you to do me a favor."

"Anything you want. Anything."

"Do you know Jocko de Paris?"

"Oh, yes. I know him."

"Will you give Jocko a note for me?"

"A note? What kind of note, Robbie, old man?"

"A note saying I'll meet him somewhere downtown tonight."

"But you see, Robbie, my policy is never to go seeking upperclassmen. I'll tell you the reason I got for that. The reason is if you seek them they're liable to seek you. It's my policy, old man, but I'd be glad to do anything for you. You're a true friend. A real true-blue pal. Robbie," Leroy seemed to choke, "I know how you saved me."

Marquales felt ill. Leroy stank from the need of a bath; his fat, pig-like face was still covered with blackheads and infected pimples. An image of fat Carlton in the shower—brought back the memory of his enormous buttery hips, and the memory of those folds of belly that loomed over his disgusting abnormality.

"I didn't save you," Marquales said angrily. "You cretin!"

"Now, Robbie," said Leroy. "Don't call my folks names!"

"Cretin means feeble minded," explained Marquales. "And overweight, too. That is, big."

"Does it? Well, I'll declare."

"Yah!" said Marquales scornfully. "So you can drop that stuff about my saving you. I didn't save you."

"Oh, yes you did. You prevented me from being expelled out of The Academy. I know you did. Don't try and be modest and deny

it. Because I know you did. I appreciate that, Robbie. I am very grateful to you and anything you ever want me to do no matter what it is
I'll do it."

"All right, then," said Marquales.

"Do you know that in South America there's a tribe of natives that
have a thing known as a blood brotherhood? Do you know what they
do? When one of them saves another one's life, then they become
blood brothers. They each pierce a little blood from their wrist and
then they rub their hands together good and hard so the blood of
one goes in the cut of the other. Then they're blood brothers! That's
what they do in South America, and it sounds like a doggone good
way of showing your friendship for a true friend."

"All right, cut out the bullshit, Leroy!" said Marquales.

"Why Robbie, I mean it."

"Listen, will you give De Paris this note, or won't you?"

"You're so modest, Robbie. That's what I like about you most of
all. Here you go save me from being kicked out of school. Then
don't even take the credit for it."

"If I had saved you, which I didn't—other than to keep my mouth
shut—there wouldn't be much credit about it."

"You've got such a good sense of humor, too. That's another thing
I evaluate about Robbie Marquales, Esk. Now you take a guy like
Sowbelly Simmons.

"Hey! You know! He's stuck on me! He thinks I'm great, the
jerk. He's always coming in the room, talking to me about 'that good
old-timey religion,' yeeaaa Lawd! Yeeeeaaaaa Lawd! He never had
any thoughts in his head. Isn't it amazing how dumb Simmons is?
The thing about him that always bores me is he has none of your
sense of humor. He's solemn all the time and it gets so dull around
him. Hell, I wish he'd stay away from me. But he won't."

"Simmons kept you from being expelled," said Marquales.

"Yes, he did. Yes, sir. I'm very grateful, too. He really did a noble
thing to forgive me. I mean that seriously, Robbie; even though I
may joke once in awhile about Maurice, he is a good lad. And very
religious. It was truly Christian of him to forgive me.

"But of course Tim Bailey did it. I never wanted to get him drunk And it was Tim Bailey that rubbed that crap on him, not Carlton Leroy. I'd never do an inhuman bestially thing like that. But the important point is that *in the first place* I never had anything to do with it, I just happened to be along with Tim Bailey. That was all."

"Sure," said Marquales. "I heard that story."

"It's true, Robbie! It's true, so help me God! I always was friendly to Maurice. Even if he is dumb as a post and twice as religious. He reminds me of a snake-handling preacher, if I may make bold to say so."

Marquales laughed, muttered sarcastically, ". . . 'make bold'!"

"But you know about him and religion, don't you?" continued Leroy. "Poor Robbie. You must have had a hard time rooming with someone as boring about his religion as that. Religion is a matter between one person and God; every man is his own church. But Simmons! He thinks he's a cathedral! Well, they couldn't get me in there with him for five hundred bucks. I'll room alone all year before I'd get in a cage with that guy. No, sir! None of that 'good old-timey religion' for Mr. Carlton Leroy!"

"Listen. Now shut up and listen. I want you to do me a favor. Will you do it?"

"Sure, Robbie! Anything for you. What?"

"Will you give Jocko a note?"

"Robbie, if it was just anybody else in school. Oh, that Jocko swings a low-down broom. Believe me."

"I promise Jocko won't do anything. All you have to do is hand him this note."

"What note?"

"The one I'll write. Give me a pencil."

"Robbie, I've only got my pen with me. But I'll go buy a pencil. I'll buy one especially for you."

"Sit down, sit down. Give me the pen."

"My pen? You're welcome to anything of mine that I possess."

Marquales accepted an instrument that seemed to be made of solid gold. Inscribed on the side of it was the legend: *From Myrtle to*

*Bubber with oodles of love.* The engraving covered most of the surface of the pen.

"How much did this thing cost?" asked Marquales.

"Nothing," said Leroy. "Myrtle gave it to me."

Marquales sneered.

"Myrtle is my mother," said Leroy politely.

"I know she's your mother," said Marquales in a disgusted voice.

"That pen's made out of gold," said Leroy. "Myrtle paid a pack for it."

"A pack of what?" asked Marquales. "Chewing gum?"

"No, a pack of money."

"Jesus," said Marquales. "A real cretin." He picked up a menu and wrote on the back.

"I have a big appetite," said Leroy. "That's why I'm so big."

Marquales finished the note. It read:

*Jocko: I have to go see someone this afternoon, a femme. Sorry. But will meet you at McKee's house nine o'clock sharp. We shall razz that lizard in good style, I hope. Yours—R. Marquales.*

"Now, Carlton, you give this to Jocko. Don't just slide it under his door or anything. Give it to him personally."

"Robbie, I will do it."

"Are you sure?"

"Robbie, I have said I will do it. I will."

"You'd better," said Marquales.

"Are you coming up to see me soon?" asked Leroy.

"You mean to your room?"

"Yes."

"Well, Leroy, I'll do that," said Marquales.

"Robbie, I'll be very glad to see you. And remember what I told you about South America."

"What?"

"Blood brotherhood."

"Oh, cat-shit!" said Marquales, getting up.

Twenty minutes later he stepped out of a bus in the center of Port George. He stood on the sidewalk for a short while, watching the civilians go by. Then he went to a movie.

*18*  Marquales stood in the center of Raggedyville on
South Karraway Street.

Ten or twelve years before, a rich man from
New Orleans appeared in Port George. He bought
four blocks of the colored district and announced
a plan to build low-cost, low-rental apartment
houses—for Negroes. It was suspected that he himself was a Negro.
His name was Daniel King Armstrong. The failure of his project
left a waste land in lower Port George. Once blasted away, the de-
crepit shacks were not replaced; the decay of real estate values kept
the blocks empty, devastated. Bootleggers were said to have stills hidden there, and it was sometimes used by Academy cadets as parking
space in which to date girls.

South Karraway in darkness, darkness and thistles, detoured
Eighteenth, deepening at Twentieth. The little path was superior to
the regular sidewalks; they were cracked by weeds and could hardly
be distinguished from the dump heaps on the vacant lots. Yet, calling
the path a street seemed to be someone's idea of humor. An ancient
sign stood to one side, its flaking letters barely legible in the moonlight. It read:

This is
SOUTH KARRAWAY ST.

Not far from there was another sign, much larger. This one sagged
on rotten boards, leaning forward over an old satchel on the ground.

Colored Peoples
Live SOUTH and sing your KARRAWAY
In the coming decent apartments to be created by
KING VENTURES, INC.
(Daniel K. Armstrong, agent)

It was nearly eight o'clock. Marquales walked through the light
that slanted across the vacant lots from the half moon, leaving the
path. He went for a short distance under the ugly oak trees on
Twentieth, reached Twenty-first, then came to the arc light at the
corner of Cheney Street—and saw the McKee mansion.

[ 210 ]

An elaborate wrought-iron fence trailed along the sidewalk, separating the house from the outside world. Marquales stood, gathering nerve. It was a gloomy scene: the darkened building, the row of yard elms, the jungle lawn. In the midst of the weeds he saw a metal deer, with antlers bent down defensively. At first he thought it was a watchdog. Sighing, he pushed through the iron gate and slowly went up the walkway.

"What do you want?" said a voice, as he stepped upon the porch.

Startled, he turned and saw two men sitting a few feet away in rocking chairs. It was dark, and he couldn't make out their faces, but the voice was that of Perrin McKee.

"Perrin?" he asked.

There was a choking sound from the smaller of the two men. The other stood and said, "It's chilly out here, Bob. We'd better go back in the house."

"No," answered the little man. "I like this porch. It has sentimental associations."

The other beckoned. "Come on. We ought to go inside now."

They walked forward into the dim light that came through the front door. Marquales bowed, smiling.

The little man said quietly, "I am Perrin's father. Will you come in with us. There's something you ought to know about my son, if you are his friend, I think."

Marquales followed. In the hallway he saw that the small man looked remarkably like Perrin McKee. There was the same wrinkled face and warped shoulders. There was even the same habit of blinking the eyes, although the father's were not gray, but a pale timid blue. The color of the hair made another difference: the father's was dry white.

The large man nudged Marquales in the side and whispered, "Humor him."

"What?" asked the freshman.

Mr. McKee said, "I'm afraid the house isn't very tidy tonight. We'll go into the parlor."

"Sir," said Marquales nervously. "I don't know Perrin very well, but I thought I'd stop by tonight—there's something I wanted to tell him. My name is Robert Marquales."

"Robert, he is dead," said Mr. McKee.

Marquales stopped. Blinking, Mr. McKee said in a gentle voice, "Perrin died shortly past seven o'clock."

"He did, sir?"

"Yes. Less than an hour ago. I'm afraid you came at a bad time—but maybe you didn't after all. I don't know. But come into the parlor for a few moments, I'd like to talk to you about him."

"Sir, I'm awfully sorry," said Marquales, embarrassed and frightened.

"Robert—were you a close friend of Perry's? I mean, did you know him well?"

The freshman gravely shook his head. Then the tall man, who loomed over little Mr. McKee, reached out and patted Marquales on the shoulder. "Come in for a little while," he said kindly. "If you will."

Mr. McKee murmured, "This is Dr. Charles, our family physician."

"How do you do," said Marquales hoarsely.

The doctor nodded.

"Excuse me," said Perrin's father. He walked into the black parlor.

The doctor said quietly, "Don't stay long. Just help out a little while until I can get him back to The Manor. He's upset, poor old fellow."

"Of course, sir," said Marquales.

The doctor leaned over and gave a slow wink. The light flared on in the parlor; and, shocked, confused, Marquales followed him into the room.

Mr. McKee motioned him to a ragged velvet chair. He had pulled another close by. The doctor strolled across the room and sat down in a straight chair by the fireplace; he immediately began to tamp a briar pipe with yellowish tobacco. Marquales hesitated then sat down in the velvet chair. Mr. McKee, who seemed to be waiting for him to sit, at once slid forward into the other chair. He rested his veined blue eyes upon the freshman, and thoughtfully washed his hands in midair, with a delicate motion.

"Tell me, Robert," he said. "Was Perry well adjusted at college this year?"

"Yes sir."

"Was he happy and well liked?"

"Oh, say, lad!" called the doctor. "Bring me a match."

Surprised at the imperious tone, Marquales got up and went to the fireplace. "Psst," said the doctor frowning. "I said humor him."

Marquales returned, sat in his chair. Perspiration was running like insects down his body. He held his knees close together, bearing a grieved look on his face.

"Death," said Mr. McKee, staring at the ceiling from lidless eyes. "How outré it is. How outré."

The doctor said, "All right, Bob."

"No, not so soon," said Mr. McKee. He closed his eyes, began to tug at a watch chain that dangled over his thin belly. He smiled and said, "Outré. Outré."

Marquales replied nervously, "You were asking me about Perrin, sir. His last few months at school. And he was very happy, I'm sure."

Mr. McKee looked sternly at the freshman. He said, "I wish you would attempt to describe for me how Perry was during the last few days."

Marquales moistened his lips, staring back and forth between the two men. The tall one was puffing at his pipe, trying to make it draw properly.

"What were his last few days like?" demanded Mr. McKee. "I wish to learn the facts of my boy's life for the past few months at the college he loved so much."

Involuntarily Marquales pushed back into his chair, getting as far away as possible.

"Robert," said Mr. McKee suddenly. "I tell you, that boy had genius. He was endowed with as brilliant a mind as you'd ever encounter. Listen. He began to talk when he was four months old. Have you ever heard of anything so unusual? I don't mean simply to mangle out such words as mama or papa but rather to construct full sentences somewhat in the manner of, say, an ordinary ten-year-old. At the age of four months. You think I exaggerate, don't you. You think that my grief has probably made me unreasonable. No, Dr. Charles will support me in this—however much he might want to get a sleeping draught in me and put me to bed. I think I'm bearing up pretty well. After all, there's been enough shock in my life for this to be nothing new. Perrin's mother died an hour after he was born; my choice of a second wife was a tragedy; my aunt, and my own father, died a violent death. There have been many shocks; it is nothing new to me. One learns to bear under them.

"No. I am not exaggerating Perry's mental power. It was very considerable. If only he hadn't been so conceited about it, which tended to spoil the pleasure. Yet probably that was my fault, or his stepmother's. I don't know. She was always *there*. Of all things that might be said about her, pro and con, she was forever *there*.

"You know, I understand that the modern authorities believe the real index of intelligence is mathematical ability. They say that's much more important than any sheer sensitivity, as far as pure intelligence goes. Perry certainly had an astonishing gift for figures, didn't he, Dr. Charles?"

"He was a bright kid," said the doctor.

"I think perhaps the word 'bright' isn't the proper one here. Our Negro cook could be called bright—because when she perspires her skin glitters. However, I don't think she could be called intelligent, much less a genius. As a matter of fact she is literally an imbecile. But she is loyal—please don't misunderstand me, or think I tend to underrate her worth.

"About Perry's knack with figures, though. Listen to this, Robert, it's very interesting.

"When that boy was twelve years old I could say to him something like this: 'Five by nine, divided by eight, multiplied by seven-fifteenth of ninety-one, multiplied by two plus ten plus twelve, divided by seventy-three, divided by two, subtracted from six thousand four hundred and fifty-four and one-fifth, subtracted from minus five, substracted from seven, subtracted from minus fifteen, multiplied by eighty-three, divided by six, and multiplied by one hundred and seventeen.'

"He would pause for about five seconds then give me the answer. You see, I'd have worked out the problem beforehand, on paper. I believe it's pretty obvious anyone capable of such brain tricks as that is a genius of first class.

"And he was an eager boy, too! Very anxious to make something of himself. He desired to become a soldier; a tactician. However, I shouldn't burden you with all these reflections—it's really unfair to you . . ."

Marquales smiled unhappily.

"I shouldn't do it," said Mr. McKee. "I realize that, but at a time like this it is very hard."

Marquales shook his head. Then, embarrassed, he nodded.

"The bad thing, of course, is the difficulty of accepting such a sudden blow as this," said Mr. McKee thoughtfully. "You can realize, as young as you are, how that is, I'm sure. Perry . . . was in perfect health. Dr. Charles here often laughed about the boy's dark predictions—Perry was forever saying he had a bad heart; it was a trick heart. No flaw could be discovered by skillful medical examination, but the hidden flaw (that somehow the boy was aware of) waited, then suddenly made itself known. It made itself known by killing the lad."

"Bob," said the doctor.

Mr. McKee smiled sadly, blinked. Washing his hands, he said, "This afternoon about four o'clock Perry told his stepmother he'd seen someone come into his room and stand by the bed with a hypodermic syringe. Of course she laughed. The boy had been suffering during the past few days because of his accident at school, and no doubt she scored off the apparition to suffering.

"Of course, pain *can* cause such disruption in the mind. And that is particularly true when one is concerned with genius. I know often in my life I have had troubles of that kind. I once broke my wrist, a mere fracture, and badly bruised my forehead in a fall down a flight of stairs. I suffered intensely; however, I could 'ambulate' as they say in hospitals. Yet would you believe it?—I saw a very grim thing that day. I recall it was a monster of—"

"Bob," said the doctor wearily.

"This afternoon Perry spoke earnestly to his mother, I mean his stepmother, describing the man with the hypodermic syringe. He declared the fellow came out of the wall. Perry was of course in bed; he had been asleep. He looked up, saw the wall seem to open, then the chap came out, grinning, bearing aloft the needle. The lad told his mother how he struggled to escape—but it was impossible. Slowly the apparition approached, then down came the syringe, stiff in a rubber-gloved hand, cutting into the exact center of his right nipple. Stung as if white hot. The figure leaned over (imagine how terrified the lad was), blew a cloud of steaming breath into the face, bared a row of filmy tusks—then laughed. Yes. Laughed. Very softly of course. But it was a blood-stopping malignant thing with the mouth open a space of two inches between the rows of loose yellow teeth; the black tongue up in a hump and throbbing from the laughter; the eyes of milky balls black in the center standing forth in a red hairy face."

The doctor sighed, bored. He began to knock the ashes out of his pipe, dropping them carelessly onto the unswept rug.

"Then the revolting nightmare was gone," said Mr. McKee in his placid voice. "And Perry's thigh began to ache. A tiny blue bump appeared there, at the point which the needle entered, and this was most sensitive to the touch. The ache spread through his legs until they shook as with the ague. It seemed, he said, that the marrow of the bones of his legs was changed to brine. At that point he called his stepmother and told her the story and showed her the bump on his thigh. After that it became very much worse.

"At five-thirty the ache reached his heart. He lay in bed and listened to it beat. Something was wrong. There seemed to be a kind of whistling, straining sound to every other thump or so and he had a dull, hard pain in his side. He could feel the skin over his heart move slightly with each pulsation. Now the skin was most sensitive to the touch. Meanwhile that blue bump on his thigh had changed to vulgar red. It burned. Fierce pains began to stitch through his groin."

"Now," said the doctor. "Now, Bob, old man, get a grip on yourself. This boy doesn't want to hear about it."

Mr. McKee said, blinking his eyes, "That dead child was my son. He was my son, my only child. I loved him. His death . . . I don't know what to make of it. I ask myself if I am responsible because I brought him as his father into the world. No. I say: Oh, Lord, what kind of world have you created in your seven days and your seven nights? A poor child born of his father must suffer like this? What doth it avail thee, oh Lord?"

Marquales said, "I think I'd better go now."

"Don't leave. You haven't told me yet what I asked you."

"Sir, he was very happy in the last few months he spent at The Academy."

"But that boy would never have made a soldier," said Mr. McKee. "It takes a *man* to make a soldier! Not merely a so-called genius. I used to tell him that, I'd say, 'Boy, you'll never make a soldier! You can't beat the odds!' I laugh when I think of it. By God, I laugh.

"The soldier has a rare quality, Robert. He has courage. He is brave. The soldier is not a poltroon. He is not a poltroon."

Mr. McKee paused, then asked, "Are you familiar with that word? It is one that was used in the old days, when Port George was a queen city, not a dilapidated wharf dump. It is a word of racial basis. It is kin to the New Orleans expression, *quadroon*. It's strange, how words have lives and relatives of their own. Take the word, *goon*. And another, *coon*. And the Negritic word for sing, *croon*. Then if you'll pardon me, the expression, *poon tang*, meaning the winy essence of the Negro female. And as you know, a Negro never says a girl is ruined, she is *rooned*. They sing, *toons*, not tunes."

"You missed one," said the doctor, smiling.

"What?"

"Think of it."

"Well, of course the stem of all these words is *moon*."

"*Loon*," said the doctor.

"Yes," laughed Mr. McKee. "I see what you mean. But that word comes from something entirely different. It can hardly be considered a moon-stem word at all."

"Well where did the word *moon* come from?"

"That was derived from the entirely different word, June."

"Why?"

"Why? Dr. Charles, I am certainly no semanticist, but sometimes I do believe you suffer from acute word blindness. Actually, I suppose the word derived from the fact that the moon is especially visible during the sixth month of the year. That's all."

"Listen, why don't we go upstairs now, if we're going?" asked the doctor persuasively. "You know, we really ought to get back soon, and under the circumstances—"

"Poltroon is the most interesting of all the moon-stem words I mentioned, in my opinion," said Mr. McKee. "The young blades of the town, many years ago, considered the expression a vital part of their vocabulary. When one of them felt another to be a coward he would draw himself up and hiss through his teeth, 'Sirrah, you are a poltroon!'

"And if he were correct that would be the end of the matter. However, were he mistaken, there would be a swift flick! and against his face the glove would fall.

"There's one thing. You rarely find both courage and genius in one human shell. It is not strong enough to contain both those volatile ingredients. One or the other will eat its way out, and carry the victim away. And victim is the proper word. How dangerous it is to be supremely intelligent.

"Of course there are exceptions. When I was five years old my father, who disapproved of my puny physique to an intense degree, told me that I was mentally unfit. Whenever my little eccentricities have happened to dismay someone I merely tell them that they are not the first to make such an objection to me, that my father did it when I was five years old! Ah, but father was a grand old man! Fierce, mustachoid, brimming with energy and nervous raciality, enormous physically, a great speaker, narrator, drinker; how he laughed at this comedy called human life, and how little effect its slings and arrows had on his leathersome hide. A grand old man!"

The doctor interrupted again, "Bob, I think we ought to go upstairs now, if we're going."

"Why do you continue to call me 'Bob'?" asked Mr. McKee. "You know I am repelled by that name."

"What had you rather me say?"

"My name, if you want to be so darn familiar, is Robert. Like Robert here."

The doctor chuckled. "Let's go upstairs."

"Wait," said Mr. McKee, smiling. He stood up, held out his hand to Marquales. "You must come up for a moment. I want you to see how Perry looks."

"Maybe the boy should run along now. You've had a long talk with him and nobody's interrupted."

Mr. McKee's face became serious. "Robert, would you mind—would you do it as a special favor to me? I realize you've been subjected to an arduous experience tonight—but I really would appreciate most deeply . . ."

There was a pause.

"I want him to come up," said Mr. McKee. "He was an old friend of Perry's, and I really feel the need for him to come up with us."

The doctor slanted his head upward. They walked out of the parlor to the bare hall. Mr. McKee led them up the stairs. Near the top the doctor patted Marquales on the back and whispered, "We'll leave."

They came to a door at the front of the hall. Mr. McKee stopped. For a long time he stood there, face about six inches from the paneled door, washing his hands.

He said, "I don't want to go in."

"All right," smiled the doctor.

"He's too sarcastic. Who taught him all he knows? His father. But would he admit that fact? Such conceit the world has never seen since its inception."

"Well, we'll go, then. You can ride on the rear seat with Billy and as soon as we get back to The Manor you can have a pot of cocoa."

Mr. McKee rapidly shook his head. "Not that flea-covered mutt," he said.

"Well, in the front seat with me, then."

Mr. McKee sighed profoundly and shook his head as if he were dizzy. He said, "Robert. You go in."

"That's right," said the doctor patiently. "Just remember, though, that you came all the way up here—and for the second time, not the first—and wouldn't go in. Remember that, and don't complain the minute we get away."

"No," said Mr. McKee.

'It'll be a long time."

"Let's do it my way," whispered Mr. McKee. "Have Robert go in. Then we'll follow in a minute."

The doctor nodded. Marquales walked forward. Mr. McKee smiled triumphantly and said, "Robert, you realize that my boy, whom I love, is not feeling healthy now?"

"Yes, sir."

"Go in, then."

"All right, sir."

Mr. McKee giggled without opening his mouth.

"Go on in, lad," said the doctor. "And my thanks." He leaned over to open the door.

"Wait," said Mr. McKee. "I'll do it." He opened the door, turning the knob silently, mouth hanging apart from the effort. The door six inches wide, he gestured histrionically and the freshman stepped forward. A moment later Marquales was in the room. He felt the door drawn shut behind him, then, listening intently, he heard the sound of Mr. McKee and the doctor going off down the hall. Then their feet were on the stairs. Mr. McKee was talking excitedly, but in the dark room his voice was only a dull murmur.

# 19

It was dark. Marquales struck a match and saw that the room had no furnishings of any kind. Cobwebs hung down from the cracked ceiling. He stood for a moment then turned back and opened the door. No one was in the hall, but he heard Mr. McKee and the doctor going out the front door of the house.

He walked angrily down the staircase. At the rear of the ground floor he heard a small noise. A door there showed light. He walked to it, knocked loudly; a moment later it swung open. He stared at a long, thin woman in middle age; she had a harelip, which had been very crudely repaired, leaving stitched scars over and in her upper lip.

"Yeth?"

"I'd like to see Perrin."

"What do you want to see him for? How'd you get in the house?"

"I want to talk to him," he replied.

"He has a broken leg."

"I know that."

"Is all you want to do talk?"

"Yes, yes," said Marquales. "May I come in, please?"

"Come on in here in the parlor and have a glass of beer with me, and talk to me for awhile. I'm his mother."

He followed her into what was apparently her bedroom. By the unlighted fireplace was a bucket filled with chipped ice and bottles of beer.

"Is Perrin busy?" asked Marquales.

"Yeth. He has company. You know, I don't think I ever saw you around here. We never met, did we?"

"No."

"Well I'm Perrin's mother—Clarissa."


"I'll call you Bob," she said. "That's Mr. McKee, Perrin's father's name. I'll never forget that name. Woe is the day I first heard it and got myself out of a nice place into this damn house. They're all a bunch of broke has-beens. Little old Bob McKee, whipping his team

[ 221 ]

of bays around the town in high style—but look at the old thing now, withered like last year, and right out of his head, poor man.

"But, Bob, they're people of traditions: the McKees. I remember when the old man was alive. Old man McKee. They used to call him Georgia cracker because he and his pa bought eight hundred niggers in Georgia when the States were going down, because they thought Lee'd win. Little did they know, but they were gentlemen. Old man McKee's pa, Perrin's grandfather, owned four separate plantations, and on one of them they never done a thing but grow magnolias and water lilies. Bob, I could tell you about that family all night, since you ask me. I could tell you about those men and how they used to have their favorite nigger gals on the plantations, their favorite creole gals in the sporting houses. And old man McKee used to get his share, too. He was the rootinest old fellow I ever saw, and I saw some real rooters back in those days. But am I making you bashful, now, telling you these things?"

"No," said Marquales.

"Well, old man McKee was a character. You know, there's a long snake in these parts that the niggers call the coach-whipper snake. Now they used to call old man McKee, Perrin's grandfather, nothing but that. He was the Coach Whipper. That's what they used to call him behind his back. To his face, of course, it was General McKee. He wasn't any General, though. He was only a Colonel. They used to call him 'Marsh Hen McKee.' The Yankees called him that, and they meant it to be making fun of him being a Master of the slaves, that is, you know, 'Old Marshter.' And also they called him 'Marsh Hen McKee' because he used to hide with his men in the swamps, and the Yankees never could catch him there.

"Well, plenty of people think he was the greatest military man of the War Between the States, with Lee excepted, but Lord, the day I married that son of his. Don't tell me he fathered that runt because I know better. A Yankee must have done it. Mrs. McKee was just like the old man, and when he was away in those swamps who knows what the old girl didn't do. In my opinion old man McKee could never have fathered that runt. And look at *his* boy, little Perrin. My

God, what a son I got from Bob McKee. What a no-good he turned out to be."

Marquales said, "This General you talked about was Perrin's grandfather?"

"Yes, sir, he was. Quite a difference, isn't there?"

"And his son was born about the time of the Civil War?"

"Yes. In my opinion, a Yankee fathered him."

"Then that would make Perrin's father nearly eighty years old, wouldn't it?"

She stopped, rubbed her face. "Well, now, *no*. I got it wrong. He's closer to fifty." Suddenly her eyes lighted up. "The General was Perrin's grandfather. No, no, no! I mean, his *great* grandfather! That's what he was. That's right." She laughed. Because of her harelip it was difficult to understand much that she said.

"Then a Yankee wasn't the father of Perrin," said Marquales.

"Nobody ever said he was! Little Bob McKee was the father of Perrin—and that's a fact, because I'm his mother, and I know."

Marquales laughed. "I meant to say, a Yankee wasn't the father of Perrin's father."

"No. But, on the other hand, he might have been, anyway. Let's see. Old Bob was born about 1890. Wasn't there a war on somewhere then? If it was, then old man McKee was a Colonel in it. The war with Spain? I don't know. But I do know for a fact that Bob McKee is the father of Perrin."

"Well," said Marquales. "You're sort of tight, I think, and I've got to see him before nine o'clock. Would you tell me where his room is, or take me there?"

"You're *my* guest," she said. "Isn't his mother as good to talk to as he is?"

"Now look, you know you're not his mother. Come on and admit it—you're the cook."

"Me a cook?" she smiled. "Do I look like a nigger?"

"How about telling me where his room is?"

"Do I look like a nigger?" she said, smiling archly.

"You're really drunk," said Marquales.

"Well, I'll sober up if you keep on being so mean to me."

"Who's being mean?"

"You are."

"All I want is for you to tell me where his room is."

"Why don't you stay here with me? Don't you want a bottle of beer?"

"I have to see him."

"Oh, let it go! What could you want to see him for? He's no good for a boy like you."

Marquales sighed impatiently.

"Here you are bein' mean," she said coyly. "And me doing my best to make you comfortable, entertain you, get to know you. Then as we begin to make one another's acquaintance you up and want to leave."

"I've got to go," he said.

"How do you know but what I'd be friendly if you were friendly?"

Marquales looked at her stringy gray hair, her wrinkled thin face, the red scar of the sewed harelip. She seemed to be about fifty-five years old.

"What do you mean, friendly?" he asked.

"A couple of beers and some nice conversation."

"Well, you've had a couple of beers and we've had a lot of nice conversation."

She asked, "Are you mad because I said I was Perrin's mother? I was just fooling; I tell everybody that, because it makes him mad, and he and me don't get on well. I just want to see if I can fool people."

"Where's Perrin's room?" he asked, standing.

"I never get a chance to talk to anybody any more," she said in a mournful voice. "And me that loves to talk." The words were very mangled, as always, by her harelip. Marquales laughed, and said again, "Where's his room?"

"You can't see him. He's asleep now."

"I'll find it myself," said Marquales, walking toward the door.

"It's upstairs at the end of the hall," she said wearily.

"Thanks."

"Maybe you'll come back by here when you get through seeing him?" she asked hopefully.

Marquales entered without knocking. It was a large room with a high ceiling. In one corner stood a bedstead draped with curtains. A fireplace was lighted by several popping logs, and in front of this sat Carroll Colton, his plaster-casted arm hanging down out of the sling. His eyes were open, but vacant. He dozed.

For a long time Marquales stood and looked at the room. Finally he walked forward and put his hand on Colton's shoulder. The senior moaned, "Perry's napping." His eyes came to a focus, suddenly narrowed. "What are you doing here?" he said thickly.

Perrin McKee's voice came from the curtained bed, "Who is that?" No one replied.

"Who is that?" said McKee. "Father? Dr. Charles?"

"They've gone," said Colton nervously.

Marquales said, "It's me."

"Me?"

The curtains flipped back and Perrin McKee's face peered out. He stared blankly at Marquales; then, the freshman smiled. McKee colored slightly. He said, "Carroll, will you come over here and draw the curtain?"

McKee sat braced against four pillows. His broken leg stretched out thick and white in a cast, suspended by crisscross wires hooked to the posts of the bedstead. Smiling, he gestured Marquales to a seat at the fireplace and said, "This is an honor. But I suspected you might come sooner or later."

"Did you get my message?"

"No. You called? That wasn't necessary."

Colton hurried forward. "Perry, it is important I talk with you alone."

"Why, don't be rude," said McKee.

"I must talk with you privately. It is vital."

McKee frowned. "Can't you see we have a visitor? Don't be impolite."

"Perry—"

"Shut up!" said McKee shrilly.

[ 225 ]

Colton turned away with a martyred look on his face. He said, "Very well."

McKee smiled at the freshman. "Don't let Carroll annoy you," he said, his voice pulsing hoarsely. "After all, Carroll is to be seen and not heard—and who wants to look at him?"

Colton said, "Perrin, stop that. I won't endure it."

"But I'm only teasing you."

Colton asked dramatically, "You don't realize who your real friends are?"

"Carroll, until a moment ago I thought you were not just a real friend, but, as far as The Academy is concerned, an only friend. I thought you were the single person who cared if I nearly killed my-self on those stairs—"

"Do you know Jocko de Paris?" interrupted Marquales.

McKee stared thoughtfully at him and said, "What a peculiar question."

"I just wondered. Do you know him?"

McKee laughed, wriggling in the bed. "Do you think he's interesting?"

"Sure," said Marquales, smiling.

"Well I wish I could offer more, then. But I haven't had the pleasure of meeting De Paris. By the way, isn't your first name Willie?"

"Robert."

"Bobbie, they call you?"

"Robbie—but I don't like it."

"Why?"

"It has a sissie sound to it."

"R-robbie," said McKee, rolling the *r*. "Excuse me for forgetting it; I won't do that again." He smiled, showing his crooked teeth. "I was about to try to give you a compliment, R-robbie. I wanted to tell you that as far as Jocko de Paris is concerned I admire your taste.

"You know, sometimes, although the most estimable people are not *always* distant, it seems the finest article has an unreasonable price tag. We have to leave it on the counter—in the clutches of some

[ 226 ]

salesgirl." He grinned. "I like that. *In the clutches of some salesgirl.*

"Oh, I could tell you a bit about your De Paris, even if I never actually met him. Maybe I will, if you ask me nicely."

"Perrin," said Colton. "I resent this, and think it unwise."

"You resent everything," said McKee excitedly, chuckling. "You leapt from your mother's womb with resentment toward the liquefactious sack that had been your home! The physician leaned over to examine you and you tee-tee'd in his face to express your resentment! In short your life is an accumulation of resentment. However, is that our fault?"

Marquales laughed.

"Don't laugh," said Colton. "He's not funny. He's only seeing how vulgar he can be."

"I'll laugh if I want to."

"Good for you," said McKee.

"We'll see who gets the last word," said Colton. "I smell dead fishes in the garret."

"Be quiet, now," said McKee.

"Colton, did you call me a dead fish?" asked Marquales.

"I just said there's the odor of a fish market in the air."

"What do you mean by that?"

Colton said, "Perrin, I want to talk to you *alone* about something of the *utmost* importance."

McKee folded his arms over his thin nightgowned chest.

"I insist," said Colton. "I insist because it's for your own welfare that I ask it."

McKee looked up and fixed his eyes upon the senior. "You insist," he said. Unblinking, his eyes were like dusty gray glass lying in the head of a stuffed animal.

"Oh, Perrin."

"Try and control yourself. You're acting like a wife."

"Well," said Colton, looking away.

"If I die before my time, this journal will have to make me immortal," said McKee, tattooing the notebook with the fingers of his

[ 227 ]

right hand. "There's quite a bit in here about De Paris, but I'll only read you two entries. A great deal of the material wouldn't be appropriate at this stage I think. But these two entries you will find of some interest, perhaps.

"Now this first one, made almost exactly one year ago, needs a brief—"

"Perrin," interrupted Colton. "I refuse to listen."

"You don't have to."

"This is despicable."

"Why don't you go downstairs and talk to Clarissa awhile?"

Colton got up, stamped his foot, and walked to the bathroom, his hips wagging. The door slammed.

"He's at peace," said McKee.

Marquales smiled.

"I'm very sick of him," said McKee.

The sound of a flushing toilet came through the closed bathroom door.

"He's such a characterless sort of fellow," said McKee. "Well, however, about De Paris."

Marquales watched the sophomore adjust the notebook on his lap, saw him peering through the gold-rimmed glasses, which made his eyes seem smaller.

"Last fall I was of course a freshman," he said. "Just like you. Naturally I was older, but I nevertheless faced the same rigorous restrictions and was at the mercy of any upperclassman. I think perhaps that had something to do with my making this first entry, which has a naïve air about it that is embarrassing.

"It was a cold day in early November that I made this particular entry. You ought to know that at that time I had no friends in The Academy. I was much by myself and very lonely. My roommate was a stupid person; a wrestler, an expert in 'holds.' I had gotten into bad arguments with my teachers. At about this time the arguments more or less reached a climax. As you know, the instructors at this institution are very uneducated. My history teacher was worse than any— he was aware of three historical facts: one, Jesus Christ died in the electric chair; two, Columbus seduced the Virgin Islands; three, Franklin Delano Roosevelt has an extra penis hidden under his left arm that he uses on Congress. This teacher knew nothing else. And I used to tell him so. To this day the man hates me; I believe it was about this time last year, however, that I got into my first serious argument with him. At any rate, maybe you can imagine my mood when I wrote this."

McKee cleared his throat, pushed his head into the notebook, and read:

Today an odd thing happened to me. I'm not sure just what it was but I am certain it is important enough to record in these pages. The experience consists of thinking for five minutes that I had fallen in love at first sight. Or did I think it longer than that?

I was walking down the Drive admiring the gulls and wondering if I would ever finish this freshman year. I passed into Port George Park. I took a side path in the general direction of the cages. Then, I saw a small crowd gathered about two men. They were fighting. I hurried forward, and got very close.

One was a sailor. The other, an Academy cadet. The sailor was much larger. I'd never seen the cadet. He was tall, slim, and remarkably angry. As he beat the sailor with his fists, dodging and leaping about, he cursed in a ferocious manner. Blood was on the sailor's face; he seemed entirely unable to hit the cadet, who, as I said, was giving him a licking.

It didn't last very long. Soon after I got there the sailor slipped to his knees, and the cadet struck him four or five sharp blows in the face. The big man went to his hands and knees.

Another cadet came forward and patted the victor on the back. He told him that it was a pretty fight. The first cadet put his hands on his hips in a saucy manner and said to the crowd: *This is what happens when a deck washer makes an insidious remark to an Academy man.*

They walked away—the smaller one patting him on the back. The sailor then got to his feet and complained that his opponent was a trained prize fighter. He then happened to notice me—and to avoid trouble I hurried away, aware he had no liking for the uniform of The Academy.

I have been wondering about this business of love at first sight. Of course it sounds foolish. But isn't it true that the shape of a face or the look of an eye can do more to determine love than the deepest spiritual compatibility? Isn't it true that the man who loves is not rational? Well, it seems very possible to me that one can make the error of falling into love at first sight. I believe *the correct person* can make a mark that is unremovable.

Five minutes after leaving the scene of the fight I traced over these same thoughts. I stopped, under a magnolia tree, and repeated to myself: love is a myth. For a moment it was as if I had never seen him at all; yet despite all that I tell myself I now wonder.

"Well," said McKee after a moment. "That is the first entry."

"But who did you fall in love with?" asked Marquales.

McKee said gently, "Don't you know?"

"The cadet who won the fight?"

"Yes."

"Who was the cadet?"

"You know that, too. But let me read the second entry before you comment on the first."

"All right," said the freshman. "I'll hear this one, then I'll comment on the first; I'll comment on both of them."

Turning the pages of the notebook, McKee glanced up for a moment. Marquales smiled. "Yes," said McKee.

"Now I think this second part will be self-explanatory. It was written five months later. I hope that you find it interesting despite the spring fever that got in it."

He read:

I had seen them swimming some distance from shore, playing about a rubber raft in the sunshine. I wondered who they were—both were handsome. I lay on the sand in my old bathing suit, toes in the sand.

ldly I wondered, I reflected. Perhaps I can condense some of these thoughts, idle that they were.

First, the comparison between myself and them. Me, the eternal me. My advantages are not in evidence, on the beach. I felt every inch of myself, mirrored back to me as from a giant reflector. Then I conjured up a scene in which he sat with the girl in a dark bamboo-walled room, her golden head in his lap, native music from somewhere, lemonades or iced whiskies sitting near-by, mosquito netting in place . . .

My thoughts were cut short as I recognized them. It was Jocko de Paris and a girl that I had seen about the campus grounds. Her father is a teacher at school. She looked well in a bathing suit, as the Great Expression of Our Times puts it. A blonde with tan skin and blue eyes. She is sixteen, I know, but this morning she seemed twenty-two or three. Perfect features, milky teeth, on the whole boyish looking, but with large ugly bosom and squashy hips—she wore a tan two-piece bathing suit; her navel was so small it looked like a raisin in a burned cookie. It didn't occur to me that he by some chance wasn't sleeping with her. Romantic characters like Jocko de Paris nowadays do not become famous poetic celibates. This, be it known, is the Age of the Condom. Oh, he has her, I know. Her name, incidentally, is Olive. What a thing! Olive.

De Paris was clad in a pair of purple swimming shorts made of expensive gabardine. His brown limbs were covered with sun-tan oil. He was smiling, laughing, shaking his head like a puppy. His body was tanned like rich leather, beautifully—and the oil made him look the perfect athlete. The muscles were built into him in a subtle way; not obtrusive like a weight lifter but smooth and powerful like a champion swimmer. His hair was wet from the water and the sun made it curl just a bit over his forehead, which is very high and intelligent. The light-brown color of the hair had been changed to a darker shade from being wet, and there was on the top of his head a patch of hair that had been bleached by old Sol. This touch of creamy hair, this tiny wet streak of pure gold, gave his entire head and face a look of absolute beauty; the gentle smile in his violet eyes showed what his heart is really like, beneath his cold wall of sensitive reserve, which, God willing, I will someday break down. He wore beige sandal-slippers and held a jewel-studded gold wrist watch between two fingers. There was an unlighted cigaret in his mouth. Although it didn't interfere with his smiling and talking it provided the only discordant note. That pale white cylinder stuck between those lips was the signification, you might say, of this machine-geared Age of the Condom.

I propped on my elbow to watch them. They walked slowly, the girl clinging to his arm, leaning her wet body against his at every opportunity. I stared at them frankly. About ten feet from me they stopped and he tried to light his cigaret. Perhaps his lighter was out of juice, or perhaps the wind prevented it from catching—at any rate, he kept flicking it, flicking it, and it did nothing but throw pale little flint sparks onto his brown hand. After a moment he began to scowl.

Meanwhile I was trying to get up the nerve to say something to him. I'd seen him many times at school, but I really had no hope of his ever having seen or noticed me. After all, I am a freshman, he a lordly sophomore. The difference between two of the three parts of the kingdom of God. Nevertheless, I was determined to say something, so just as he began to scowl I called, "Hello." He looked up. "How's the water?" I said, in a hopeless voice. I was petrified with anxiety, overcome by my own boldness.

He looked at me. Those blue eyes came from the lighter and scowled into mine. Then he laughed to the girl. He said, "You can't beat The Academy. Our freshmen follow us around just to be of service."

Dragging the sandal-slippers he walked up to me and said, "Give me a light, Mister."

But I didn't have a match. And if I had had one I don't know whether there would have been enough strength in my hand to hold it to him. All I could do was repeat to myself: *He knows me. He knows me. He knows who I am.* The words sang within me.

And now, as I pen these lines, they sing again—and four others sing with them. I am in love.

[ 232 ]

# 20

McKee sighed, smiling. Then he shut the note-book and tossed it aside as if it were of no conse-quence. "I was very romantic last spring," he said. "Now I'll comment on those little entries," said Marquales.

After a pause, McKee answered, "If you enjoyed it—maybe I'll read you some more some time. There's quite a bit else in this journal of mine—all very rough, but interesting, I think."

"I'd be fascinated to hear it!" said Marquales.

McKee said nervously, "Would you call Carroll out of the toilet, please?"

"That's where he belongs," said Marquales. "Why not let him stay there?"

"I don't want to hurt his feelings too much."

"I heard him flush himself," said Marquales.

"Would you call him, please?"

Marquales went to the bathroom door and knocked. There was no reply. He threw it open: no one was there. He saw that a door lead-ing to the next room had been opened, and he walked to it, looking in-side. The adjoining room was dusty and without furniture; light entered it from the hall door. Marquales recognized the room to which he had been led by Mr. McKee. He returned through the bathroom to Perrin McKee.

"Colton slipped out the other door."

McKee didn't answer.

Marquales said pleasantly, "Well, have you got all through telling me about yourself and Jocko?"

"Didn't you want to hear about him?" asked McKee, puzzled.

"I loved it."

"Listen, Robbie," said McKee. "I believe I know what you're think-ing. Well, please believe me—Jocko de Paris now means nothing to me. I've gotten over that and am perfectly free."

Marquales put his hands on his hips.

"Don't worry about Carroll, either," said McKee quietly. "He's nothing—just a piece, that is all."

[ 233 ]

"I'm going to puke," said Marquales. "It was funny for awhile. Now, I've had enough of that hot gas."

"What?"

"You make me sick."

"Just a moment. Let's try to analyze that state—"

"You've had your fun," said Marquales. "Now shut up."

McKee stared, bewildered.

"There are several things I want to tell you," said the freshman. "First, you are the most repulsive person I ever knew. It makes me ill to set eyes on that ape face of yours. Second, do you really think I came up here to play with you? What a sap you are, if you do.

"You say you're free. Who cares whether you're free or locked in a bughouse? You're crazy, just like your father. Furthermore, you happen to be unusually stupid. Do you want to know why?"

"No," said McKee.

"Because you have such a large opinion of yourself. But unfortunately there's nothing to base such an opinion on—but hot air. You've got verbal diarrhea, with these journals, notes, speeches, and things. Now I've been waiting for a long time to tell you this—and it really gives me pleasure to do it."

McKee laughed.

"And I hate to add," said Marquales. "That your high opinion of yourself is mainly about a weakness. You are proud of being a pervert. There's something wrong with your brain, and healthy people would never have anything to do with you."

McKee pretended to throw something from his nose with two fingers. He said, "How healthy are you?"

Marquales said angrily, "You're disgusting; you and all like you."

"Thanks for explaining it to me."

"There're a lot of things I could explain to you," said the freshman. "I could explain to you that women aren't disgusting, that they have good and bad qualities just like men."

"Brilliant," said McKee.

"As a matter of fact, women are often superior."

"Is that so?"

"Any decent woman is superior to you."

"*What* kind of woman?"

"You're hopeless," said Marquales. "You ought to be put out of your misery."

"But what have I done to deserve this particular misery?"

"You're depraved."

McKee laughed. "Don't stop. Go ahead, this is very enlightening to a man suffering from verbal diarrhea."

Marquales said, "I'm afraid you're completely warped."

"I'm not actually bored," answered McKee. "I really am interested in these probing observations of yours. Please continue."

There was a long silence. They stared at each other; two pairs of hatred-filled eyes. McKee was pale, and Marquales felt the skin on his own face tingling.

"Say something!" barked McKee. "I'm offering you two good ears."

"Do you know what person you remind me of?" asked the freshman.

McKee said, "Mae West?"

"You remind me of William Poley. Do you know him? I understand you're both in the same history class, both flunking it. That's the history class you failed last year, but no doubt that was the teacher's fault. The guy probably doesn't know his ass from Mammoth Cave. He must not have realized he had an amazing mathematical genius in his class. How much is five times seven times two and a half divided by eleventy-nine? According to your father that would be a snap for you. What's the answer? Huh? You don't know? The answer is TIE THAT BULL OUT THE DOOR."

McKee flushed angrily.

"Poley is your twin," smiled Marquales. "You and he are as much alike as two pills. When I hear you talk I always think of him. Because you both jabber like a streak and what you say makes just as much sense. That is, you're just as ignorant and conceited a runt as Poley is. You even *look* like him. Cross those eyes of yours and you'd be exactly like him."

"I'm getting tired of this now," said McKee. "In a moment I'm going to call Sarah Ann and have her ask you out of the house."

"How would you like it if I came over there and gave your neck a good twist?"

"Just a moment," said McKee. "Listen, please, to just a little hot air. What right you have to this scene, I do not know. I believe you came here of your own free will? And *uninvited,* at that. As I remember you entered this room with not so much as a knock at the door. And no sooner had you laid your undefiled eyes upon me than you simpered. Yes, you simpered, grinned, and coaxed me to read to you from my private journal. And then you throw this stupid, boring abuse on me.

"What are you trying to do? May I ask that? You certainly must have realized early in the evening, if indeed you didn't know it all the time, that I am that dismal, depraved, unhealthy, and all-the-rest-of-it thing—a practicing homosexual. And not a repressed one, like yourself, I may add."

Marquales was speechless with indignation.

"Now I am older than you, and not merely in years. There is a great deal that I understand that is beyond you. For although you seem intelligent you are young. You are inexperienced. Do you actually know anything about the women you think so highly of? I dare say you've never seen a nude female—as for me, I had experiences at the age of ten that would rot your little prostate. What I could tell you about the fair sex, you pathetic, trapped fool! But I'm afraid I haven't the time and energy to try to set you right about many things that confuse you now. You see, I broke my leg just the other day and had a severe heart attack at that time. Therefore I think you'd better leave, now."

"Are you finished?" said Marquales.

"Let's not have any silly rhetorical questions, you insolent clown—just get up and leave."

"I'm not sitting down," said Marquales. "Your tongue seems to be flapping. Now listen, I came up here to tell you one thing, and I will hereby tell you, if you don't mind."

McKee waited, an impatient smile on his face.

"I've read that filthy letter," said the freshman.

"What letter is that?" asked McKee nervously.

"That disgusting thing you wrote Jocko."

McKee paled, turning his head to one side. He kept his gray eyes on Marquales.

"Now let's see if you'll laugh," said the freshman. "Jocko also read it, *and he's coming after you!*"

McKee's face turned milky white. He slipped down into the bed, sliding from the pillows. The wires holding his leg gave a squeak as the cast was elevated a few inches.

"Jocko's read it!" repeated Marquales, leaning forward. The smile on McKee's face had changed to a paralyzed grin. Nearly every tooth in his head was visible and his eyes were shining with fear—his head lay twisted to one side which made him stare at Marquales from an angle.

"You'd better cringe," said the freshman in a cruel voice.

At that time the door of the room opened and a large Negro woman walked forward. "Perrin," she said. "Mr. Colton's down in the kitchen drinking up all Miss Clarissa's beer." She stared at Marquales.

"Sarah Ann," said McKee faintly.

Examining Marquales with swollen eyes the woman said, "Mr. Colton told me there was a boy up here bothering you." Marquales saw that she had a Coca-Cola bottle clutched in her hand.

"Sarah Ann!" said McKee hoarsely. "Go downstairs and lock the door!"

She waddled toward Marquales.

"Go downstairs!" screeched McKee. "It's somebody else—don't bother about him!"

"Who's this boy?" she asked. "What's he doing to you?"

"Lock the front door," said McKee.

As she left the room he began to cry. He wept like a child, turning his face from Marquales, who suddenly felt sorry for him.

"You asked for it. It does me good to see you shaking in your boots. However, I came up here to do you a favor. And I called this afternoon to warn you. I talked to that colored woman but she didn't give you the message. You deserved to have your leg pulled and I led you on. You're crazy when you say I'm like you. I don't happen to be out of my head yet. The reason you think that is because you're so conceited you think everybody is like you. That idea of yours about the homos inheriting the earth shows how conceited you are. When that happens horse-shit will be dropping out of the sky because horses will have wings."

McKee was weeping. The tears ran out of his shut eyes, down his cheeks, dropping onto the flannel nightshirt over his thin chest. Now and then a sob came from him. "Hell," he said. "Why did Carroll do it?"

"He was drunk," said Marquales.

"I never meant for him to read it. The note was just made up for fun, and I didn't intend half of it when I wrote it. I was just trying to express a mood. What must he think of me? Oh, Jocko! Jocko!"

"Listen," said Marquales. "De Paris never read the letter at all."

McKee's teary eyes sprang open. "What?"

"Jocko hasn't read the letter. He's not even aware you ever wrote anything to him. So don't worry. He thinks you wrote a letter to me. But he doesn't know any more than that."

McKee closed his eyes tightly. He asked, "Then he's not coming here at all?"

"I was drinking last night," explained Marquales. "I started to talk, then it slipped out I had gotten a crazy note. I don't even know why I said it—I guess your letter was on my mind. Albert Wilson was there and he kept hammering at me until I had to say something, so I said it was you. I never thought anything would come of it. But because of Wilson's nagging Jocko decided to come by here tonight."

"So he's coming," said McKee.

"Yes. That is, he was going to be here at nine. To rag you for writing me a dirty letter. No more, just rag you. However, it's twenty after nine now, and I don't think he's going to get around at all, if you want my opinion."

"To think of it," said McKee. "Meeting him under such circum-

[ 238 ]

stances as this. I'd rather never meet him at all. I'd rather be dead."

"Maybe the woman will keep him out."

McKee answered, "Suppose she hurt him."

The door opened. Carroll Colton walked into the room.

"If she hurts him," said McKee, "I'll have her jailed."

"What's happened?" asked Colton. "Sarah Ann's running wild all over downstairs with a pop bottle."

"This freshman stole the essay I loaned you. The one called 'Pharaoh.'"

Colton wheeled toward Marquales, "I thought he did!"

"Why didn't you tell me?" asked McKee, his voice stronger.

"I meant to," said Colton.

"You meant to. You're a poltroon if there ever was."

Marquales said, "You'd better tell that crazy colored woman not to hurt Jocko if he comes here."

"Jocko?" asked Colton. "Here?"

"I'll jail her if she does!" said McKee. "I'll see her in the damn Kangaroo Court, and she can sit six weeks washing jailhouse linen!"

Colton said, "She was running around downstairs looking for your father's gun."

McKee licked his lips, then said, "The gun was pawned long ago."

"Listen," said Marquales. "It won't do any good to have the poor woman put in jail after she already does it."

"Be quiet," said McKee. "I'm trying to think."

"After all, she's doing it to protect you," said Marquales.

"There is no problem about this at all," said McKee. "If De Paris comes he won't be able to get in the front door. It'll be locked. In the meantime, Carroll, you go snap my bedroom lock there."

However, just then the bedroom door opened, and the thin beer-drinking woman with the gray hair entered, holding the knob behind her. "Hello, boys," she said. "And how's the invalid tonight?"

"Clarissa," said McKee coldly. "Please don't disturb us. I have visitors here."

"Oh, Lord, yeth! The house is full of company tonight for a change. And, surprise! Here's another one out in the hall. . . ."

[ 239 ]

McKee's eyelids quivered and fell shut.

". . . now where is he?" She walked back to the door, stuck her head into the hall. "Oh, Mr. de Paris? Hey, come down this way, honey—here we are!"

McKee pulled a pillow over his face, and the suspending wires again squeaked as they rocked his broken leg up and down.

"Hey ho hi," sang a feeble voice that did not belong to Jocko de Paris. Albert Wilson tumbled through the door, half falling into the room. They waited. Wilson stood with an empty smile on his face.

"Where's Jocko?" said Marquales.

McKee dragged the pillow from his face and stared across the room.

"Here!" said Wilson, saluting with one hand and banging his chest with the other. "I'm going to get myself a hunk." He stumbled across the floor, hair in his eyes, blouse open. "Where can a man sit?" He dropped backward in the direction of a stool by the fireplace, but missed it and jarred down to the brick hearth. "Christ!" he exclaimed. "Trying to crucify me in the ass, the bastards."

"Where's Jocko?" repeated Marquales.

"I've taken over the reins," smiled Wilson. "Poor old Jockie isn't up to standards. All he does nowadays is talk."

"I'll declare," said the harelipped woman. "He doesn't even know who he is. Just look at him setting there on the floor. It beats me the way these nice cadets go on. Who would think to see those pretty boys parading down that field all spick and span that they'd get themselves mucked up like this? It's just as if they were a bunch of niggers out Saturday night drinking white lightning."

"Can it, grandma," said Wilson, getting to his hands and knees.

"Isn't he cute? You should have seen him downstairs. He drank two of my beers without stopping for breath. Then he chewed up a cigaret and swallowed it. Lord, he got my hair all mussed, too." She touched the hair delicately with the tips of her fingers.

Marquales saw that there was lipstick smeared on Wilson's face.

And the harelipped woman's mouth was also smirched—rouge circled her scarred lips like grape jam.

"Hey," said Wilson, looking at Marquales.

"Hello, Mr. Wilson."

"Call me Al, pal."

"Hello, Al."

"Psst! Do you want a piece of pussy?"

"No."

"Are you abnormal?"

"Listen, is Jocko with you?"

"Jocko passed out."

"Where is he?"

Wilson leaned toward Marquales, a finger pressed over his mouth. "Shist!" he said, spraying saliva.

"What?"

"Shist! Shhhist!" sprayed Wilson. Then he whispered loudly, "You see that old grandma over there? Well, she's burning."

There was silence.

"She's not my speed," whispered Wilson, smiling. "I don't want the damn stuff. You can have it, kid."

"Well, I never!" said the woman. "You nasty child!"

McKee groaned from the bed.

"Hell," said Wilson. "I'm not so hard up I have to screw a harelipped hag. I can pick the tender tulips and don't doubt it."

"You dirty intoxicated boy!" said the woman. "What a nerve you have to think I would even so much as *glance* at you. You probably don't know what a woman is like, except from dirty drawings in privies!"

"Listen at her!" said Wilson. He shook with mirth.

"Don't talk to me," she said. "You're intoxicated."

"Grandma *you're* intoxicated. Not me."

"You don't even know who you are. The idea, making up a crazy name like that, and saying it's yours."

Wilson said thickly, "You're an old croker sack full of bugs."

"I am *Mrs. Robert E. McKee.* You ought to be put in prison for saying such vulgar things in this house."

"Grandma, if you had as many sticking out of you as you've had sticking in you, you'd look like a porcupine."

"Well, I never," said the woman.

McKee suddenly shouted, "Sarah Ann!"

"I want a drink of water," said Wilson. "I'm sick." He staggered toward the bathroom.

"That boy's out of his head," said the harelipped woman, touching at her gray hair. "I'm sorry for him—if his poor mother saw him now she'd probably weep from very shame. Such vulgarity."

"How do you turn on this faucet?" called Wilson from the bathroom.

"Up above," said Colton. "The lever's up above."

There was a pause, then Wilson said, "I don't understand this fucker. How do you turn it on?"

Colton hurried forward. "I'll show you."

McKee was looking toward the hall door, the frozen grin on his face.

"What's the matter with you, Perrin?" asked the woman, staring curiously at his face. "Still think you're better than the girl your father married?"

Wilson came a moment later out of the bathroom, leaning on Colton. He saw McKee in the bed. "Why, there lies the petunia!" he exclaimed.

"Dear, don't bother him," said Colton.

Wilson turned slowly, looked at Colton's face. He ran his eyes down to his own shoulder, where the senior's hand lay. "Don't try that with me!" he yelled.

"I'm not doing anything," said Colton, snatching away his hand.

"You're not?" asked Wilson. There was a splattering sound as he gave Colton a slap in the mouth.

"Awr, aw," said Colton, his face wrinkling. He began to weep, his underlip twisted downward.

"Let that be a lesson," said Wilson, rumbling. "Where's a towel, I'm going to stuff it down your mouth."

McKee called in a piercing voice, "Sarah Ann! Sarah Ann!"

"A pansy is on the level of an ape," said Wilson, staring philosophically at McKee.

"You're right, honey," said the thin woman.

Colton stood in a corner weeping hoarsely.

"Sarah Ann!" screamed McKee.

"Shut up that hollering, Mr. Pansy," said Wilson. "I'll throttle you." He moved chuckling toward the bed.

Sarah Ann appeared in the hall door, panting. "Perrin, honey?" she said.

"Watch out," said Marquales. He grabbed Wilson's sleeve, pointing toward the door.

"Just a nigger," said Wilson. He leaned over, scowled, and pinched McKee's left nipple, keeping it tightly between his thumb and hand. McKee curled like a burned spider, gasping. "What have I got?" laughed Wilson. "What have I got here?" His teeth gritted as he pinched more severely. "Say it. Say *titty*!" McKee groaned deeply; the leg in the sling creaked up and down. "Titty," he whispered.

Suddenly there was a yell, and Marquales saw the big fat Negro woman come rushing across the floor, her eyes white with rage, her Coca-Cola bottle lifted. There was a dull sound as it struck Wilson on the forehead. He staggered backward, and threw up his arms.

"God you!" shouted the Negro woman. She struck again. Wilson dropped stunned to the floor.

The harelipped Clarissa hurried forward and kicked the Negro woman in the leg. "You black nigger!" she said. "The police'll get you, you black nigger! Out of here! Leave my guests alone!"

"You all right, Perry?" asked Sarah Ann.

He didn't reply. His eyes were closed, his right hand lay over the spot Wilson had pinched.

"Nobody's hurting your precious little Perrin!" said the thin woman, pushing her toward the door. Stumbling, Sarah Ann allowed herself to be shoved gradually out of the room. The hare-lipped woman quickly shut the door and snapped the bolt. "A fine thing!" she said, turning back toward Wilson, who had got to his feet.

"Christ!" he said. "The bastard tried to kill me." He rubbed his head, holding his fingers before his eyes to see if there was blood.

"Honey, you have a hard head," said the harelipped woman. "It didn't even get cut. She'll be put in jail for it, just the same, if *I* have anything to say about it."

"I'm sick," said Wilson, moving toward the bathroom.

There was a soft knock on the door.

"Go downstairs to the kitchen!" yelled Clarissa.

They heard Wilson vomiting.

Weeping, Colton said to Marquales, "Look at what you've caused."

A few seconds later Wilson peered out of the bathroom. His face was green; a knot had risen on his forehead.

"Where is the nigger?" he said cautiously.

No one replied.

"All right. That's a hell of a note. I come up to this place on a visit and a crazy nigger tries to murder me. Where is the guy? I'll cut him down into steaks."

"This is what we get for having a feeble-minded nigger in the house," said the harelipped woman. "I've said that a thousand times, but would he listen to me?"

McKee began to tremble in the bed; tears again rolled down his face. "Carroll," he said.

"Help! He's having a heart attack!" said Colton.

"He's putting on," said the woman. "I know him."

Wilson swayed. "Christ," he murmured. He sat on a couch near the windows, raising a cloud of dust. He lay there, an arm flung over his face. "I'm going to pass out," he said.

"You'll be all right," said the woman. "Hold your stomach back." She went over to him.

McKee began to sob loudly, pulling the pillow over his skewered face. Colton ran to the bed and patted him on the arm. There was at once a noisy banging on the door.

"Open up!" called Sarah Ann. "I hear my child crying!"

Colton pulled away the pillow and tenderly kissed McKee on the forehead. "Don't cry," he said.

The banging became louder. "Shut up!" yelled the harelipped woman. She sat down on the couch by Wilson.

"Carroll," said McKee weakly. "Don't ever desert me."

"I won't, darling," said Colton. He put his cheek against McKee's and kissed him. "I'll never leave you."

Marquales stood in the center of the floor. There was a sound like a beating sledge in his brain. Each blow of the thing dimmed his vision, until the room turned full of whirling light; the fireplace, the lamp by the couch, and the reading light over McKee's bed. He rubbed his eyes. Then he looked up and saw the harelipped woman sitting on the couch by Wilson. McKee and Colton were cheek to cheek, both weeping like children. Marquales swayed; it occurred to him that he was about to faint.

"No," said Albert Wilson. The woman was squatting like a toad. Marquales closed his eyes.

A moment later there was a grunt; when he looked up Wilson had thrown the woman to the floor. He saw the junior slap her roughly in the face. She did nothing; just sat there.

Wilson got up, stood swaying. "Let's get out of here."

They walked through the bathroom and to the door of the dark adjoining room. From there Marquales saw the Negro woman standing in front of McKee's room thirty feet down the corridor, banging on the panels with her Coca-Coca bottle. He whispered to Wilson, "Come on." They crept into the hall and went down the stairs.

"That filthy old hag," said Wilson, leaning heavily on Marquales.

They passed out of the house, down the porch steps, and past the metal deer in the yard. Marquales pushed open the gate. Then he saw, parked a few feet away and lighted up by the corner arc light, the lemon-colored sport roadster. They hurried to it, Wilson stumbling, his arm about Marquales' shoulder. The freshman threw open the car door. Lying on the front seat in a pool of vomit was Jocko de Paris.

"Hey," said Jocko. "Where've you been, boys?"

Marquales drove them to a burger wagon and gave them coffee. They both vomited, then he gave them more coffee. By eleven-thirty they were almost sober. De Paris talked very much about General Draughton. He also talked about Larrence Corger and Roger Gatt. He said that he believed Gatt and Corger to be responsible for the General's attitude. And, he vowed that someday he was going to take a horrible revenge.

At five minutes to twelve they passed successfully through the Guardroom of Hemphill Barracks.

PART *4*

PART 4

21    When Jocko de Paris didn't appear for breakfast formation Sunday morning an orderly was sent to check about the absence. The orderly found De Paris on the floor of his room rolled tightly in a blanket, his cot capsized, clothing strewn everywhere, a can of foot powder sprinkled over the radiator, window sill, and floor. De Paris at first refused to get up; he said he was sleepy.

The orderly, the Amanuensis, and the Junior O.G. helped him to the school hospital. Miss Rebecca Frune, chief nurse, took his temperature. She put him to bed with an ice pack on his stomach and said he had acute food poisoning. Jocko remained in the infirmary from Sunday until Saturday morning.

Robert Marquales didn't take advantage of leave Sunday afternoon. When Chapel service was finished he went to his room and studied his chemistry book. At one o'clock he went to the mess hall for Sunday dinner.

This was usually broiled chicken—a famous dish at The Academy. The chicken was sometimes served half cooked; therefore cadets called it "the blistered animal." However, on that Sunday another specialty known as *le ros bif* was presented. Cadets called it "dog meat." There was a story that once the dietician overheard a cadet use the term. She went to the General and asked if he were going to permit a cadet to say such a thing. The story had several endings; all variations came to be known as "dog meat jokes." The General would always be described as very indignant when he heard what the dietician had to say: he would splutter, fume, and rush to the kitchens to sample the meat. According to one version he would then say "Grrrr." According to another he gnawed at his tunic with his false teeth as if after a flea. According to another, after tasting the meat, General Draughton told the dietician it was superb and that the cadet would be called to order. Then, as he went out the door he got down on all fours and hurried over to a fireplug, lifting one leg. There were numerous other variations.

[ 249 ]

After dinner Marquales returned to his room and sat down again to the chemistry. He wrote in his notebook:

### THINGS TO LEARN

*1. All the symbols of the elements, such as: O oxygen, Pb lead, Ag silver, etc. etc.*

*2. All the atomic weights of the elements correct to one decimal point, such as: gold 197.2, oxygen 16.0, phosphorus 30.9, etc. etc.*

*3. All the atomic numbers of the elements, such as nitrogen 7, helium 2, zinc 30, etc. etc.*

*4. The difference between an element and a substance. A substance is a mixture of elements? Check textbook definition. Do this, Marquales.*

*5. How to balance equations. The laws of the various scientists. The definition of chemistry. The means of conducting an experiment. The way to prove water and air both contain oxygen, for example. The physical properties of the most important elements. The chemical properties (?) of these elements. Definitions of solids, gases, and liquids.*

Marquales faced a chemistry examination on Monday and he knew almost nothing about chemistry. He didn't learn very much that afternoon. He found he could remember some of the things, but it always occurred to him he couldn't possibly learn all he had to learn; therefore, why study any of it. By the time Ben Hulitt and Les Wintermine came in at three, Marquales was sunk in reflections about his life before he had come to The Academy.

Hulitt brought from Port George three sex-life magazines. Scientific journals circulated on newsstands to break down the widespread public ignorance of sex. One was called *Marital Technique,* another, *Sexual Union,* another, *Sexism: The Biology of Mating.* Marquales and Hulitt and Wintermine read them for several hours.

After supper the roommates sat around picking their teeth and talking over the gossip's tale that General Draughton once knocked up the pretty young wife of an Academy instructor, thus being forced to discharge the man. They then discussed the story told about Colonel Evers: that he had once been seen masturbating in the Chapel. They concluded that this was probable, in view of the Colonel's wife. That led to a discussion of the strange Chinese curio supposedly a dear possession of Miss Frune, chief nurse.

Call-to-quarters blew and Marquales again took up his chemistry book. He stared at it for awhile, then decided to read another of the articles on sex. He read one in the form of a double story. First a visualization of the man with marital hygiene on his wedding night. He was taken into the hotel, past the clerk, up the elevator, in the room, out of his clothes into pajamas, between the covers. At that point he had a hygienic, tactful conversation with his bride.

The second part of the story was a visualization of the man without marital hygiene. He got to the hotel, exchanged a lecherous remark about double beds with a clerk, winked lewdly at the elevator boy, rubbed his hands gleefully when in the room, stepped into a closet and put on his pajamas so fast he tore them, raced out into the room, leapt into bed. Then he had an unhygienic, untactful conversation with his bride—so much so that she burst into tears and ran to the bathroom, locking the door and refusing to come out. At the end of the second part was an italicized note mentioning the subscription rate of the magazine: one dollar.

A fuck for a buck, thought Marquales, laughing.

Then he read another piece, an article called: "On the Forbidden Subject of the Hymen: Its Structure." There was an asterisk by the word "hymen." A footnote stated in tiny print, "This is the scientific term for what is commonly called the *maidenhead*." Marquales read the article carefully but found it too dry.

Then he read another one. "Is There an Ideal Size for the Phallus?" An asterisk explained the object up for consideration. The author, a woman doctor by the name of Barbara Fleming Watsen, concluded in her article—"No."

By that time Marquales was sleepy. He again picked up his chemistry book and tried to memorize a few atomic weights. The words melted into rivulets of smeared print. After awhile he got into a discussion with Hulitt about venereal disease.

They were talking about syphilitic spots when Wintermine interrupted to describe an odd disease known as the blue balls.

"You catch it from colored women," he said. "Your cods turn blue and dissolve."

Hulitt objected, saying his had been the color of robin's eggs for years, but hard as rocks. Marquales maintained firmly there was no such disease, and that he who thought there was suffered from the superstitions of an obsolete boob. Wintermine finally admitted he was mistaken, but qualified himself by saying one of his closest friends suffered from the disease. The roommates then talked more about syphilis. Hulitt got up and mimicked the gait of locomotor ataxia, clutching his genitals and lolling his tongue.

Suddenly the conversation shifted to a discussion of cadet military rank and how to be appointed to it.

"Neatness," said Wintermine.

"A.K.'ing," said Marquales.

They argued for about ten minutes. Then Hulitt, who was more or less trying to write a theme, settled it by saying, "Good grades." Marquales and Wintermine took the hint. The former again picked up his chemistry book.

A short time later when he tried to read one more article in *Sexual Union* he found he couldn't follow the line of thought. He would become stranded halfway through a sentence then would feel his brain singing, his eyelids sliding together, as he began to fall asleep.

—Conjunctual, conjunctual he said to himself.

He sat in the chair, elbows on the table, half dreaming. Finally at nine-thirty the bugle sounded the end of Sunday-night study period. It was then permissible to set up beds. Marquales quickly hauled his mattress and springs out of their hiding places, took his bed linen from the top of his press, and assembled it all, tucking the covers tightly in sack fashion. He threw off his clothes and put on flannel pajamas. Then he donned his bathrobe, stuck his cap on his head, and walked at attention down the gallery to the latrine. Five minutes later he was buried in the cot. He didn't hear taps blow at ten-thirty.

Marquales was completely baffled the next day by his chemistry examination. Luckily he managed to copy the answers to the first three questions from the paper of his neighbor. Then the neighbor saw him doing it, and shielded, giving him an aloof frown. "Pissant," whispered Marquales to the cadet, a thin boy with an Adam's apple like the prow of a canoe. Unfortunately the neighbor on the other side was of no use. He had been copying Marquales' paper.

Later it was disclosed that the examination went "on the curve." By that method Marquales made a grade of 85. His score would otherwise have been 60. The professor, a faculty Colonel, explained that since this was the first exam he was taking the lowest mark in the class and giving it 70 then grading all other exams in relation to that, by the help of a sliding scale. No one understood it. But three cadets made grades of 160 and everybody passed. Several pupils expressed the opinion they would appreciate it again and didn't mind being thrown such a curve.

That afternoon Hulitt gave his roommates a bad surprise, totally without warning. "I've been transferred, boys," he said.

They stared at him and Wintermine asked, "Do you mean you're leaving the room?"

Hulitt explained he had been assigned to the North Barracks by special order of Colonel Evers—the reason was that there were too many cadets in Hemphill Barracks and not enough in North.

"And they happened to pick you?" said Marquales.

"That's right."

Marquales and Wintermine spent two hours helping Hulitt move his gear. They met his new roommate, a yellow-haired boy of eighteen, a freshman from Albany, Georgia. The boy's nickname was "Red," because his last name was "Herrin." Hulitt began to call him by the nickname immediately. Marquales and Wintermine did the same, promising sadly to come over and visit.

[ 253 ]

Hulitt's absence made the room empty that night. Marquales and Wintermine sat at the study table face to face, nervous. They quietly talked about what a fine boy Ben was. They were friendly with each other and just before taps they agreed that now Ben was gone they'd have to make a stronger effort to get along; life was too short for quarreling and conflict of the kind they'd been guilty of in the past.

However, on the next morning, Tuesday, Marquales and Wintermine got into an argument. It began because Wintermine wouldn't move his bed to allow Marquales to sweep the room.

"You drove Hulitt out of here with your eternal fussing," said Wintermine at one point.

"You bored him to death," answered Marquales.

"I know damn well he left because of you. He practically told me so, and I don't blame him in the slightest. We didn't ask for you to come in here; you couldn't get along with your other roommate, and you saw—"

"What do you mean, he told you? He was transferred; he didn't tell you anything."

The argument continued. It gradually became more bitter. Finally Wintermine said, "Marquales, you're a low-down son of a bitch."

"You're not a son of a bitch, but your mother must be dumb to have hatched out such a character."

"Take it back!" said Wintermine. He stood over Marquales.

"Oh, shut your loud mouth," said Marquales casually.

"Get on your feet like a man!" shouted Wintermine.

Marquales stood up and hooked his thumbs in his belt. He stared Wintermine boldly in the eye and said, "I'd like to find out once and for all if you've got the nerve to do anything but blow."

Wintermine made a gesture with his left hand, shouted something, and punched Marquales a lopsided blow in the face. "Stop that!" said Marquales, his ears ringing. He held his face and felt blood coming out of his nose. He hurried out of the room to the latrine.

When he returned a few minutes later Wintermine was waiting, still pale. He told Marquales to sit down. Then he self-consciously

[ 254 ]

offered him a cigaret. They smoked for a few moments, neither looking at the other. Wintermine said:

"Robbie, here's what I want to tell you. Don't interrupt me because if you do I can't speak the way I want to.

"First of all I want to apologize for hitting you. You're not as big as I am and it wasn't the thing for me to do. No matter what you said, it was wrong. And I'm sorry I did it. Second, the truth is that we are roommates. We are here at The Academy together and in my opinion we ought to get along. Now I want very much to get along with you. I don't like fights and troubles with anyone though I'll never dodge them if they come my way. What I want—more than anything —is to do my work, play the game here as it should be played, and feel that I'm not wasting my college years making a constant jackass out of myself.

"Now Robbie, I think we can get along damn well if we'll both try. I have some favors I'd like to ask you. Then if you'll grant them, as far as I'm concerned there won't be any future trouble. And we won't always be at each other's throats, which is a pure waste of time and is uncivilized."

"May I interrupt?" said Marquales.

"Sure."

"Let me say I think your attitude is decent, Les, and I am happy to hear you say these things."

Wintermine made a gesture with his hand.

"No, I mean it," said Marquales. "I'm very surprised—pleasantly surprised, not that I mean that to be an insult. I think I've had you figured out wrong in the past, and I admit it."

Wintermine got up and shook Marquales' hand. They smiled at each other.

"Les," said Marquales, rubbing his swollen nose. "I want to make something of my college period, too. But I have a different attitude, that's all. It's not that I have no ambition. I realize how important scholastic work is and I'm going to start studying harder. For example, I cheated on a test yesterday. Hell there's no sense in that, even if plenty of other guys do it. You can't learn anything that way, and

[ 255 ]

it's just a waste of your parents' money to be here. See, I realize these things! And I will admit something else: probably it's annoyed you I haven't cared much about the military side of life here, considering the fact that you do, that you want to get rank next year and be a corporal. I confess I wouldn't mind being a corporal. It's just I've never run up against anything like this place; I haven't gotten used to it. Being told constantly you're a bastard by every upperclassman, the drilling all the time, the inspections, marching to classes, marching to meals, bracing all the time, going to bed early and getting up earlier. You piss by the clock, it's everything by the clock. And having to fold your shirts in just such-and-such a way, having to fold your *socks* —the routine gets me down, I don't take to such a way of life. Don't blame me if I haven't been as military as you, yet. Notice I say *yet*.

"Now this is a vital point—I realize the hopelessness of piling up a mess of demerits, being sloppy, and not doing the best you can. I'm here, so I'm here. It's probably good for my character in the long run, because it'll teach me self-discipline if anything will. As soon as I can work up a little enthusiasm for this system of life then I hope to change. Now don't think I'm groveling. All I'm doing is agreeing with you that we ought to get along, and trying to see it your way. In my opinion the only thing that's needed is patience on both sides. That's the idea. What was it Confucius said about patience?"

"I don't know. But I've *been* patient," said Wintermine.

"You'll have to be even more patient now that Ben's not here. He had a good effect on my no-countness, I think."

"Is this the time for jokes, Robbie?"

"No, it isn't, and I don't mean to be joking. If you want to know the truth, I think Ben's departure might be all for the best. Things were getting unendurable in this room and now the atmosphere might clear up, that he's gone and this has happened."

"What has his leaving got to do with it?" asked Wintermine. "This has been coming for a long time, Robbie. My endurance was exhausted long ago."

Marquales said, "I know I've ragged at you, Les. And I don't blame you for getting mad. We just haven't understood each other."

"Rudeness is one thing, rudeness and lack of co-operation—ragging is another. But never mind that right now. Let me go ahead and make my criticisms, such as they are, all in a bunch, and we'll get it settled permanently."

"Okay, go ahead."

"All right, Robbie. Now let me say I appreciate what you told me a minute ago. It was said in the right spirit of mind. You see a lot I didn't think you saw. But I'm going to speak as if you hadn't said anything. Because while you were out of the room I figured out what I wanted to say and now I don't want to get it confused, by missing some links in my chain of thought. Do you understand what I mean? I'm going to speak as if you hadn't told me what you did a minute ago."

Marquales nodded in agreement. Wintermine licked his lips and said in a calm voice, "Now we'll get down to business. Some of these things I'm going to say might strike you as a little hard to take—but I believe I ought to be frank and I will be. I'm going to tell you exactly how I feel, let the chips fall where they may.

"Robbie, I think we can get along fine if we'll both try. I have the following criticisms which as far as I'm concerned will make everything all right in this room. First, I must ask that during study periods you do *not* talk. The habit of talking during study periods must stop. As far as Ben was concerned I knew it would never have done any good to ask him not to talk during study periods. But you're a different type from Ben and I ask you not to interrupt my studies by conversation during study periods or at any time I am trying to study.

"Secondly, may I request that you be more tidy. It's a strain to live in a room with someone of untidy habits, because it adds to the responsibility of keeping the room in order. I mean this.

"Third, please do not borrow any more of my things without permission. I don't want to sound selfish, but the truth is you make it a habit to use anything of mine and say nothing about it. Also my cigarets. I don't want to sound cheap. But if you can't buy your own cigarets please don't borrow mine. I leave them lying around, and the first thing I know a full pack has turned into half a pack. Let's not have any more of this kind of thing. It's really more serious than it sounds, and I mean it. By the way, however, any time you ask me, I'm perfectly willing to give you a smoke if you're out and need one, and I want you to know that. I'm not stingy at all. It's the attitude that counts.

"Robbie, listen closely to this, because it's very important. I must ask you in *all* seriousness—do not talk to me about religion if your attitude is going to be as it has been ever since you moved into the room with me and Ben. Robbie, this is one of the most vital of my points. My religion is something personal with me, and that's the way it ought to be. I'm not interested in hearing you make sarcastic remarks about it. I must ask you once and for all that you keep your opinions on religion to yourself.

"Now there's one final thing. That is your attitude in general. I think you ought to change your attitude—especially toward me. Ever since you came into the room it seems you've been trying to see how superior you could act toward me. Now I don't know where you got the idea you're so important. Frankly, it's a sad thing to see in any human personality. I don't want to sound nasty, but I do think I have a kick coming. I believe I have a right to object to all the sneers and sarcastic remarks you've thrown at me. How can anybody put up with such things? I can't.

"Robbie, I think it's reasonable for me to ask that you turn over a new leaf. I really can't stand another sarcastic remark. That's what I was telling myself when you were away from the room a minute ago following our fight, if you can call it a fight. I said to myself: 'I can't take another one of those comments out of him!' And I meant it. That's why I hit you—and despite the fact that I'm sorry about it now, I don't see how any man could be blamed for doing it. Most people would have done more than merely cuff you. They'd have grabbed you and absolutely beat the mortal tar out of you.

"However, we won't dwell on that. I really hope that nothing like this ever happens again. All I have to say is just please change your attitude toward me and try to co-operate more about the room."

There was a long silence as the two cadets stared at each other. Marquales cleared his throat twice, but didn't speak. Then Wintermine said, "I guess I'm through. I hope what I've said hasn't seemed too nasty; but it's the way I feel and I had to get it off my mind. The idea was to be frank, even if it hurts."

Marquales smiled and said, "You were frank all right."

"Now go ahead and give *me* the works. Don't be afraid, put it as strong as you want to."

Marquales stood up. He said, "Les, I'll have to talk it over with my lawyers." He walked out of the room and went to the latrine on the floor above, where he washed his face several times.

"What can I do about it?" asked Hulitt. "I'm not in the room any more."

"Who wants you to do anything?" asked Marquales angrily. "Do you think I want to be protected like a baby? All I want you to do is tell me why you left the room."

"I was transferred. I told you three times."

"Wintermine said you left because of me."

"You're being nuts. Simply nuts."

"I don't believe you," said Marquales, staring at him. "So help me! You don't seem to be telling the truth, Ben. Could it be you've been acting as if you were my friend all these weeks when you didn't like me?"

"You're a character," said Hulitt, flushing with embarrassment.

"Is it true?"

"Of course it isn't."

"Well listen," said Marquales. "Don't think I'm whimpering about Wintermine because I'm not. He just happens to be larger than I am and it'd be foolish for me to fight him. I'd only get beat up. I came over here to have a conversation with you, not to ask for your protection."

"Les isn't such a bad guy," said Hulitt nervously. "He can be a good fellow if you get on his right side."

"He's the sort of good fellow you can get along with if he's physically afraid of you. Then he's peaches. But you should have heard him lay down the law to me this morning. First he was upset.

[ 259 ]

Then he saw I wanted more than anything to smoke a peace pipe. So he laid down the law. The jerk put down a list of rules for my conduct. I'm to be seen and not heard. I'm never to talk back to him. The subject of religion is taboo, and I'm to stop smoking his cigarets. Well, I'll never room with him. I'll rot dead before I will. Any fate would be better than that."

"Why don't you talk it over with him?" asked Hulitt. "Really—I mean it. Talk it over heart to heart."

"Ben, what I'm interested in isn't stupid advice. I'd like to know exactly why you left the room. And cut out the fabrication."

"I tell you they transferred me."

"They really did?"

"Yes."

Marquales laughed. "Well, by crap, they're going to transfer me, too."

Hulitt fidgeted, swallowing. "No," he said. "I asked for it."

"What?"

"I can't lie. I never could. Robbie, the truth is I did ask them to transfer me. Don't get your dauber up, let me explain. And don't tell Les, that wouldn't help anything. It would just make trouble. Now Robbie, the real reason I asked for a transfer was I actually couldn't study in the room. Arguments, arguments, more arguments! That fussing was really beginning to go to my brain. Isn't this school enough of a hellhole without having your own room be one?

"Robbie, I wouldn't tell you this except for the fact if you go around asking for a transfer they might mention it to you. Then you probably would get the wrong idea. You see, I had to give them a reason for wanting to move; otherwise they'd never have let me have the transfer. So I told them a white lie. Please understand how it was. I had to tell them I wanted to move because I didn't like my roommates. That's what I told them, but of course I like both you and Les. It's just you guys spend your lives in argumentation. Do you understand? There was only too much noise. Who could study in an atmosphere of continual quarrels? I'm a good-natured guy, I don't like to argue. Well, with you and Les, it just happens to be different. Do you understand what I mean?"

"I sure do," said Marquales. "Ben, it's funny but I thought you were my only friend in the school. I thought you were the only guy here who liked me."

Hulitt blushed a deep red color and looked away, his lips moving with embarrassment.

"Am I being too personal?" asked Marquales. "Excuse me. I apologize for being so personal. I know how embarrassing it is when someone you don't like comes up and says he likes you. It makes you sort of want to puke."

"You misunderstood me," said Hulitt. He smiled. "It's your old argumentativeness. Robbie, I guess you must have been born that way."

"You mean my revolting character, don't you, Ben?"

Hulitt twitched. "No. Argumentativeness. You just love to argue with people about anything—for the sake of a good argument."

"Crap my argumentativeness!" shouted Marquales. He tore out of the room, bumping his head against the door.

Hulitt called, "You don't understand, Robbie!"

Marquales walked on down the corridor, tears of self-pity blurring his sight, a homesick pain in his chest.

22 Maurice M. Simmons looked over the tops of his spectacles then fumbled them up higher upon his nose thereby enlarging his eyes by at least a third. He stared wondrously through the lenses for a moment, then the dawn broke. "Jove!" he said. "Well, Robert!"

"Hello," said Marquales indifferently. "How are you?"

"What a shock!" exclaimed Simmons. "You've come to visit me, haven't you?"

"I wanted to see how you're getting along."

"I was only just writing a little thing here," said Simmons, a burr of excitement in his voice. "You wouldn't be interested."

"If you're busy I can come back later."

"Oh not at all—just a mere incident, jotting down a few things. Nothing much, my diary, that's all."

Marquales lit a cigaret. "You still keep it every day?"

"Still smoking, eh?" replied Simmons. "You ought to cut it out. I knew a young man who used to smoke two packages of cigarets a day. He died, gasping for breath. His lungs had been clogged up with cigaret tar complicated by T.B."

"Sure," said Marquales. "I know all about that."

Simmons laughed, tossing back his head. "Robert, you're still possessed of your fraught tongue, aren't you? Well, now, there are worse things than the tobacco habit. I'd never make an issue of it when there are so many more important things."

"But I agree with you," said Marquales pleasantly. "Smoking is bad for the lungs. Doctors have said so. Of course, I don't smoke two packs a day, because I can't afford it; but even as it is sometimes I take a deep breath and there's a whistling sound in my chest."

"Well, how have you been getting along downstairs?" asked Simmons.

"I told you—this whistling in my chest."

"And why haven't you been up to see me?"

"You know when one of the cadets sees a pretty girl? He whistles just the way my chest does."

"By Jove!" said Simmons. "I happen to have written something in my D. five minutes ago about whistling at girls. Telepathy! I've never seen anyth—"

"Hey!" said Marquales, suddenly impatient. "Listen, Maurice, I have something to tell you."

"Yes?" murmured Simmons, hurt.

"I'll tell you this and then you can say whatever you want to. The truth is I'm not getting along with my present roommates. As a matter of fact I had a fight with one of them this morning and the other one moved out yesterday. Now I went to Pete Layne when I was rooming with you and asked him to shift me to another room. I didn't feel happy in here with you. But I got along with you better than I have with my present roommates. Or it looks that way, anyhow. Now I don't know how you feel about it, but you don't seem to have resented my moving out. How would you feel about my coming back?"

Simmons said, "Robert, I'd like to ask you why you left this room."

"What difference does it make. I don't know. I think it was because you got on my nerves."

"Did it occur to you that you got on my nerves?"

"All right," said Marquales. "I don't blame you. I just thought I'd ask."

"Why don't you like your present roommates?"

"There's just a chance they'll let me move to Company Ten," said Marquales. "They have an empty room in their part of the building."

"You can't do that," said Simmons. "They won't let you go to another company now."

"Yeah," said Marquales thoughtfully. "Listen, why don't you think over my proposition? We'll co-operate and get along."

"You mean about your moving in here?"

"Sure. Why not?"

"It would be impossible. I already have a roommate, and this room wouldn't be large enough for three."

"Don't be foolish, Simmons. You haven't got any roommate."

"No, Carlton is moving in here."

"What was that?"

"Carlton is joining me tomorrow. He already has permission."

"Then his room will be empty?" asked Marquales. "Or is that one of your pipe dreams?"

"Carlton is moving in tomorrow," said Simmons with dignity.

"What a stroke! But I can't believe it. It's too good to be true."

Simmons said, "Are you accusing me of being a liar?"

Marquales rubbed his hands gleefully.

"I am not a liar," said Simmons. "I have never told a lie in my life. Unlike many cadets here I always tell the truth. Think of such a person as Colton who tries to see how many lies he can tell every day. But as for me as long as I can do the things that interest me and live life the way it should be lived I do not tell any lies."

Marquales began to be suspicious. "Simmons, when you say you aren't doing something that's just what you're doing."

"*I've* got to *go*," said Simmons. "And this seemed to be a friendly visit."

"Wait a minute. You don't get out of here yet. Tell me once and for all whether Leroy is coming in here."

"He is. If you like, he's down the hall in his room. Ask him."

"What did you mean when you said you have to go?" asked Marquales.

"It's simply that I have an appointment with Dr. McClugh."

"Who's that?"

Simmons smiled and looked up at the ceiling. Ironically, he repeated, "Who's that."

"Don't be sarcastic, please. Just tell me who that is."

"He wants me to tell him who that is."

Marquales said, "All right, then. If Leroy isn't really coming in here, you think over my proposition about our rooming together again." He adjusted his cap and dropped his cigaret into the waste can.

"That would be out of the question!" called Simmons. "You left here because you didn't like me. Having made your bed now lie in it."

Marquales stopped. "Leroy *isn't* coming in here, is he?"

"I must go talk with Dr. McClugh," said Simmons.

"Okay, give him my regards." Marquales hastened out of the room and walked down the corridor.


Leroy was there, standing fat and naked by the radiator. When he saw Marquales he gave a yelp of surprise and put on a greasy bathrobe, blushing modestly.

"Are you moving to Simmons' room?" asked Marquales.

"What?"

"Are you moving?"

"Not until tomorrow, Robbie."

Marquales sighed deeply. "Thank the Lord. It's actually true."

Leroy stared at him.

"Hey!" said Marquales enthusiastically. "You've got religion?"

"Yes," grinned Leroy. "In a manner of speaking."

"What's the matter? Are you afraid Simmons will go talk to General Drawgrog about you?" Marquales chuckled and lit a cigaret.

"Me? Why Robbie, what would Maurice do that for? He and I are going to be roommates. He's my best friend and's forgotten all about the other stuff."

"Carlton, I maintain what you need more than anything is to have that big tail of yours beat."

Leroy smiled. "I get it beat all the time. Koble and McCarthy come in here after dinner every night and chop it. I swow I'm getting calluses on my tail. A string on each side."

"Pull up your skirt and let me see," said Marquales.

"Ore . . . goar!" said Leroy. "Robbie!" He rolled his head around, smiling with bottom lip pulled in.

"That flatters you, doesn't it?" asked Marquales. "You're proud of your great big butt, aren't you?"

"All I got to say—Robbie, they'll never catch Carlton Leroy in a bathing suit! I'd bust it!" Leroy threw open his mouth and laughed loudly, his red tongue pulsating up and down.

"You are not kidding," said Marquales.

"There's ONE thing I'm thankful about," gasped Leroy. "That's the fact old Jocko de P. got tired cutting my meat. He never comes around any more, only Ko—" Leroy suddenly stopped, gagging, staring popeyed.

"I thought so. I suspected as much."

Leroy said rapidly, "Couldn't find him, Robbie. I looked everywhere, so help me God! Jocko wasn't in the barracks. I went to the ball field. I went to the administration building. Then I came back to the barracks and he wasn't here so I had to leave that note under his door. But he got it all right, because I saw him reading it later on at the latrine. Then I said—"

"Oh, blow it out, bu-low it out."

"No—"

"Shut up, Lebo."

"Don't you want to give me a chance to explain?"

"No, dearie."

"I bet you tell that to all the girls!"

"Great God and all his triangles. Do you think that's funny? You're nearer to being a woman than a man. If I were you I wouldn't make jokes about it."

"What do you mean, Robbie? What have you got on your mind?"

"Leroy, you know perfectly well that you've got a whump like the fat lady in the circus."

Leroy puffed up his chest and said, "But I've got another thing she doesn't possess, and on that you may rely!"

"You've got a green little twenty-two cartridge."

"What Robbie? What was that you said Robbie?"

"I was talking about your pecker—and that's what it is, a pecker."

Leroy looked hurt, although he was smiling in a roguish manner. "Robbie, old egg, that's no way to talk. You shouldn't say a despairing thing about a friend, or he'll resent it."

"You're going to be rooming with Simmons, so you should say, 'Lord forgive you for your sins, but not me!'"

Leroy laughed. Then he became solemn. "I believe in God," he said.

"Is that a fact?"

"Don't think I'm not religious at bottom, Robbie, because I am."

Marquales puffed at his cigaret, enjoying himself. He looked about the room. "Maybe I'd better fumigate this place," he murmured thoughtfully. "With so much meat around God's probably set up housekeeping in the floor boards."

Leroy gasped. "You ought to be ashamed! I've never heard of such a thing—that's no way to talk, and though I might be wrong about some things, I know I'm right about this. Calling God a bedbug! You ought to be ashamed!"

"You're not religious," said Marquales. "You're dumb but you're not that dumb."

"Yes I am, Robbie. I am religious, and I wish you wouldn't talk that way. At bottom I'm very religious."

"Will you please stop bragging about your hiney. Haven't we gone over that territory by now? At bottom you're *not* religious—at bottom you're a pail of congealed pink lard."

Leroy laughed, but cut it short. "Robbie, whether you believe me or not I have the conviction there is a God."

"Are you sure?"

"I'm completely convinced. There's not even any point in talking about it."

"Let's talk about it; let's go into it. I'll ask you a few questions. You don't mind being cross-examined by means of to be held to a point of quizzical inquisitions, I'm sure, and I assume you are positive about your numerous nostramic beliefs and digitations. You don't really mind, do you?"

"No," said Leroy.

"All right, we'll look into it. First of all, do you believe the earth was made in *seven* days?"

"Yes."

"Do you believe in Adam *and* Eve?"

"Yes, I do."

Marquales rubbed his hands together, cigaret smoke fuming up into his eyes. "Leroy, did they both have navels?"

"Don't talk dirty, Robbie."

"This isn't dirty. There's nothing dirty about a navel if you take a bath now and then. It's just an innocent little nick in your tummy. Did Adam and Eve have them?"

"They were in the Garden of Eden."

"Well, why did they go out?"

"They ate the apple, that's why."

"Washington winesap?"

"I don't know."

"Tell me about their navels. That's the point—I mean, pit."

"Pit?"

"That's the pit, the navel. Or pits, the navels."

"What?"

"Tell me about Adam's and Eve's navels."

"I did."

"No you didn't."

"Yes I did."

"Oh no you didn't."

"What do you mean, Robbie?"

"You didn't say a word about Adam's and Eve's navels."

"I said they had them."

"All right, they had them. Now—"

"There's nothing wrong with that!"

"Of course not. But where'd they get them?"

"What?"

"Where'd they get their navels?"

"They were born with them, naturally."

"And who gave birth to Adam and Eve?"

"*What?*"

"You heard me—quit stalling."

"I'm not stalling."

"Listen, if Adam and Eve were born, who gave birth to them?"

"God made them. They weren't born."

"He made them with their navels?"

"Yes."

"Why?"

"So they'd look right, that's why."

"That's no reason, give me another reason. Come on, Leroy, think."

"I don't know."

"Listen, you don't know anything."

"Yes I do, too."

"Mention something you know. I'm curious to hear what you'll say."

"You oughtn't to talk against religion. I know that much. No decent person talks against religion the way you're doing."

"Maybe you've got something there," said Marquales, suddenly weary and stupefied. He walked to the door, opened it, then said, "Leroy, when I speak to you you know what happens?"

"No," said Leroy sullenly.

"I become a moron."

"What a sense of humor!" exclaimed Leroy. He shook his head, grinning as if faint from amusement. "You admit you're a moron."

"I sure do," said Marquales gloomily.

The sound of Leroy's giggling followed him down the corridor.

Pete Layne was not in his room but Marquales found him at the office of *Port Arms*. Tom Munro was also there. They were seated at the larger of two desks in the room, working together on what seemed to be proof sheets. Marquales stood uncertainly by the door.

"What is it?" asked Layne.

The freshman smiled and walked forward. "The usual thing, sir, a favor."

Munro said, "We're out of them."

Marquales laughed.

"And we're busy right now," added Munro.

Layne asked pleasantly, "What was it you wanted?"

The freshman said, "Sir, frankly, I'd like to move to another room, if I can get your permission."

"I'm sorry, but too many people want to move as it is."

Marquales thought, then smiled and took several steps forward.

[ 269 ]

"Sir, I have a strong reason to want to move. If you'll give me a minute I can tell you about it."

"But we know your reason," said Munro. "You don't really dislike your roommate, but the guy talks so much you can't get your lessons."

Marquales suddenly felt he should wait until he could see Layne apart from Munro. Nevertheless, he said, "No, sir! That isn't my reason."

"You mean to tell me you've thought up another one?"

Layne and Munro chuckled.

"No sir, I haven't thought up one. But there's a reason for my wanting to move."

"We haven't got time to listen," said Munro.

Marquales smiled and said, "Sir, I'm really serious, and if you'd only let me tell you I think you might agree."

"Okay," said Layne. "Tell us about it then."

Munro sighed.

"Sir, it all began—"

"There are two of us," said Munro. "You should say *sirs*."

"Yes, sir, Mr. Munro. Sirs, it all began during the first night of general leave this year. My roommates and I happened to carry Mr. Jocko de Paris home that night because we found him drunk on a sidewalk. Ever since then I've been more or less in a fix. Sirs, you remember the meeting of the Hair-of-the-Hound Club the other night? Mr. de Paris forced me into a card game, despite my—"

"I hear you boys cleaned up on Gatt," said Munro.

"Sir?"

"How much did you win?"

"I don't know, sir."

"What do you mean, you don't know?"

"I won a few dollars, sir. But I don't know exactly what Mr. Wilson or Mr. de Paris won."

"Yeah."

"Sir, I didn't want to be in that poker game. I didn't want to associate with Mr. de Paris either. He made me."

"Uh-huh," said Munro.

"You know how he is, sir. He's an awful bully. He bullies everybody." Marquales saw from the expression on Munro's face he had made the wrong remark. He hurried on, "Sirs, you asked me to the meeting. Then Mr. de Paris burst in and made me play in the card game. Mr. Munro, I appreciated your attempt to steer me out of his hands. And believe me I was sorry when Mr. de Paris made such a fool of himself by being so abusive you gave it up as beneath your dignity to bother about. I don't blame you—but it was hard on me. I hardly had a chance to see what the Club was like!

"Sirs, here is my point. I now live only two doors down the hall from Mr. de Paris. He's always coming in the room, borrowing cigarets, talking, asking me to go out with him. I can't escape him when he's that close to me. But I thought if I could move up to the top gallery into the room Carlton Leroy is leaving then I could manage to get away from Mr. de Paris' influence. I'm afraid if I don't then sooner or later I'll be in trouble. Believe me, I'm telling the truth. I'm not happy about Mr. de Paris' liking me, if that's what he does."

Layne nodded his head in agreement. "It sounds reasonable to me. I don't see why you shouldn't move if that's the way it is."

Munro remarked with a smile, "Pete, I think this sarcastic freshman is trying to pull our leg."

"Sir?" asked Marquales, putting a bewildered look on his face. "I'm telling you the truth, sir."

"No, you're not. Here's what you're doing and I don't like it. You're aware we don't approve of De Paris so you're trying to pretend you yourself don't like the guy. Why don't you admit you can't get along with your roommates?"

"Sir, it does look as if I can't get along with my roommates. But there's also the fact I'd like to move farther away from Mr. de Paris."

"Listen here," said Munro. "You don't have to tell me about De Paris. I know what kind of bastard he is, even though he's not an important man at The Academy in any sense, and shouldn't be taken seriously. He should be just allowed to rave all he wants—the right thing to do about a fool like that is to ignore him." Munro turned to Layne. "Pete, I haven't anything against this freshman, and it certainly is your business how you run your company—you're the captain of it and I'm just regimental brass. However I think this freshman ought to be kept where he is because he tried to deceive you about his reasons for wanting to move."

"Sir, I didn't. I swear it. My main reason for wanting to move is Mr. de Paris. Of course, I don't get along with my roommates. I admit that and it makes a difference; it makes me want to move out all the more."

"But you didn't tell us that a minute ago," said Layne.

"I was going to."

Munro shook his head slowly. "It won't do."

"Can't I move, sir?" pleaded Marquales to Layne.

"No."

"Why not, sir? I'm unhappy where I am, after all. Wouldn't you let me move to that empty room? What difference would it make to anyone? I really didn't mean to deceive you a minute ago, I just can't express my thoughts well."

"My reason isn't about that," said Layne slowly. "It's simply there are too many people who want to do it as it is. For all I know you might be telling the truth about De Paris. Although it doesn't seem likely to judge from your manner—and from the remarks Tom made on the situation."

"Don't let me interfere," said Munro. "It's none of my ash can."

"No, that's not it," said Layne. "The freshman can't move because so many others want to. We can't have people moving around like gypsies. Marquales, one of your own roommates moved yesterday, didn't he? And you failed even to mention the fact. Why? That looks suspicious to me. Do you know that Mr. Hulitt bothered me for three weeks about moving? What's the matter with you? You seemed like a nice enough freshman the other day. Can't you get along with anybody? The important thing is not to act like Jocko de Paris trying to see how many enemies you can make. That's the important thing in life."

"It certainly is," said Munro.

Layne continued, "Now I'm your company commander, Mr. Marquales. My captain's bars would be nothing but little bits of brass if I didn't take care of the men under me. I always try to do that. Nobody can say I haven't got you men's welfare at heart. You frosh can come to me when you've got problems—we'll sit down and talk about them."

Munro said, "In my opinion, not every senior officer will do that, Pete. Mister, you ought to be glad you're in Company Twelve."

"Yes, sir," said Marquales.

Layne went on, "Why not use your head for constructive ends? Do you see this silver star on my sleeve? It means I made 'A' in all my classes. But when I was a freshman I didn't use the small amount of intelligence I've got. I didn't have any silver star to wear, either. I was the kind who wasted his brains trying to fool people. But I recovered. And Mr. Marquales, see if you can do the same."

"Yes sir," said the freshman. "Then I definitely can't move?"

"No," said Layne. "I'm afraid not."

"Yes sir."

"Too many people already want to move."

"Yes sir. You mentioned the silver star a minute ago. Well, I planned to get it myself—my grandmother's very old and she told me to win her a prize. Frankly, sir, if you'd make an exception in my case I believe I'd stand a better chance to win the silver star."

"Great scott," said Munro in disgust. "Of all the bullshit."

"Mr. Marquales," said Layne sadly. "I must tell you once and for all that as far as I am concerned you will never be transferred from your present room."

"Is that final, sir?"

"Be a decent fellow and you can get along with your roommate."

"Wouldn't you relent, sir? I ask in all seriousness."

"Hey," said Munro. "Get the hell on out of here!"

"That's right," said Layne. "We're busy, and I've tried to treat you right. I'm sorry about the room, but it's out of the question."

"Yes sir," said Marquales. "Tha-ank you just the same, sir!"

Entering the main gate of Hemphill Barracks Marquales heard a familiar voice. "Halt there!" It was Carroll Colton.

The freshman stopped in his tracks, put his hands down along the seams of his trousers and stared straight ahead.

"I'm afraid I want to see you," said Colton. "Come along, please."

Marquales followed him around the first gallery. They came to Colton's room and he held open the door, looking coolly over the freshman's head. They went inside.

"Will you sit at the table, please."

"All right."

"Perhaps in view of the fact I am a senior and you a freshman you had better put *sir* on that."

Marquales stared at him scornfully. Colton wet his thick lips, then after a moment gave an elaborate shrug. He pulled a folded slip of paper from his pocket.

"Take this and read it. When you finish leave it on the table. Then kindly do not stay in my room."

"I won't."

"Please don't speak to me if you see me around barracks during the remainder of the term. I'm afraid you're not the sort of person I'd care to know."

"I won't."

"I'm quitting school at the end of this term. I'm going to live in New Orleans."

"It doesn't matter to me what you're doing," said Marquales.

Colton gave an angry sigh then walked out of the room. He slammed the door. For a moment Marquales sat in the chair. He had an urge to tear up the slip of paper, but he decided that was silly so he unfolded it and read:

Dear Robert M.:

I know you think it foolish, affected, insane to write letters, keep journals, or carry on conversation. You will laugh when Carroll gives you this note. However, do let me indulge at least one more time. May I?

You'll be uninterested to know I'm moving in a couple of weeks to the crescent city of the bayou territory, New Orleans, where I have a gracious wealthy aunt. With her I will reside from now on, and Port George can rot on its own terms. N.O. will be similar enough to quiet any homesickness. Thus I'll be gone soon and you'll never have the bad luck to see me again.

I believe you have a conscience: therefore I am writing you this. I believe you can feel for the suffering of others: therefore I am saying a few personal things to you. I want to see you realize what you tried the other night.

At that time you attacked my love for my father whose affection for me—throughout his long illness—has never wavered. You attacked my sentimental attachment to J. de P. You attacked my broken home and flung at me the charge of being a Wm. Poley. (What could be more insulting than to discard me as one of those who devour: uneducated, filth-filled hordes; those towhead snot-face guitar players of hell's tunes, strumming blood on their own taut entrails, slashed open by themselves. Insult of insults.) You behaved like a real savage; you were the Wm. Poley, not me.

There's much that I could say to you. I truly feel that you should realize the direction you are taking. I believe you have capacities. But I'm so weak all I can do is scribble a few lines. I believe it would profit us both for you to come visit me at least once before I leave. After all, there's no reason for us not to understand each other.

I will add one more thing. As for the homosexuality: that is entirely a figment of your imagination. I made an error in provoking you & encouraging you to believe it. My "writings" to Jocko de Paris were literary exercises. I am a literary man. And I happen to make close male friends, that's all, but I enjoy a woman just as anyone does. They're very exciting.

Well, perhaps this is in vain, but I would like to talk with you. Will you visit me this Friday night? Kindly put your answer on this sheet and leave it with Carroll.

with no anger,
PERRIN

Marquales took up a pencil and scrawled across the slip of paper, "Oh, you kid!" He thought for a moment then added, "Old boy, you're wrong, I have NO possibilities at all, and no capacities, either. Not me, son, I'M not THAT way."

There was a cough outside the door: Colton. Marquales left the slip of paper on the table and walked to the door, a melancholy sneer on his face.

"It's all yours," he said to the senior outside.

Colton understood perfectly—he looked relieved.

Marquales sat in his room, smoking a cigaret and brooding about the events of the day. At five o'clock, Wintermine entered.

"Hello, Les," said Marquales pleasantly. "I talked to my lawyers."

Wintermine strode across the room. He tossed a book into his press, upsetting a bottle of hair tonic. He cursed, then turned and looked directly at his roommate.

"I've had time to digest your criticisms," smiled Marquales. "I think all in all you were pretty fair in what you said."

Wintermine walked to him slowly, swinging his shoulders. He stood a few inches from Marquales, hands on hips. "Do you know something?"

Marquales swallowed.

"This morning, when you made that crack about your lawyers after I tried to talk seriously to you, when you made that crack and went out of the room—I almost got up and dragged you back in here and gave you the worst beating you ever had in your life."

"Now, Les," said Marquales. "You said some hard things this morning. I couldn't help it."

"I was purposely too easy on you."

"Were you?"

"Yes, you little squirt."

"To hell with you!" shouted Marquales. He jumped to his feet, grabbed Wintermine's shirt collar, and gave it a yank. Buttons spilled to each side, and Marquales, snarling with rage, clutched Wintermine's throat with his fingers, digging in the nails and squeezing vio-

[ 276 ]

lently. Wintermine recoiled, stumbling backward across the room, Marquales on him like a leech. They fell to the floor and Marquales lost his grip on Wintermine's throat. They rolled and tumbled over each other, clutching, punching, kicking, gouging. During it all Marquales was snarling out curses and roars of anger.

After a few moments a passing upperclassman entered and stopped the fight. He braced them and then made them shake hands. Neither was at all hurt, though there were later blue marks on Wintermine's throat, and a few scratches on Marquales' face.

The two roommates were perfectly polite to each other that evening. Marquales realized he had won a victory—and he was proud.

# 23

Wednesday and Thursday went by like all time between week ends at The Academy: like lightning. This was the fault of the daily schedule, which made one day unrecognizable from the other; a work week usually meant sixteen hours of life, not eighty. But Tuesday of this week had been extraordinary, and on Thursday Marquales did visit De Paris at the Infirmary: this was a long week, and as it turned out, very long.

Wintermine and Marquales, who had been carefully polite to each other, arranged Friday afternoon to go to Port George on leave together. Their departure was held back, first by Marquales' work on a theme, second by a surprise visit from Roger Gatt.

Marquales finished reading through his essay a few minutes before Wintermine returned from the canteen. The essay was hopeless. It had started with the assigned title, "My Favorite Spot in Port George." Marquales had written several idyllic paragraphs in description of the beauty of Port George Park; he pictured himself there surrounded by magnolias, a setting sun, and strolling couples. Then a prostitute wagged into the scene: her teeth were described as "black bloody stumps," her hair as "a greasy coil of filth," her soul as "the tortured symbol of the age."

Wintermine tossed a carton of cigarets into his press and asked politely, "Have you finished it?"

"Yes. But none of it's any good. It's too flippant."

"Let's go on to town, Robbie. You can write it Sunday."

"All right," said Marquales. He tore up the pages and flung them into the waste can. Then he and Wintermine put on their dress uniforms in preparation for general leave.

As they were about to depart the door of the room opened and Roger Gatt peered inside. "Pop to," he said.

The roommates shuffled to their feet and braced rigidly.

"Rest," said Gatt from the door.

"Hello, sir!" said Marquales.

"I've come to talk to you about something personal."

Marquales knew what Gatt wanted to talk about: the ninety dollars, thirty of which at that moment was jammed into the freshman's watch pocket.

Wintermine murmured, "Maybe I'd better go to the latrine for a minute."

Gatt stared thoughtfully from the door.

"Sir," said Marquales. "This is my roommate, Les Wintermine. Les, this is Mr. Roger Gatt. Of the football team."

"How do you do, sir?" said Wintermine. "Would you like me to leave the room?"

"Hi," said Gatt. "Leave the room? Oh, stick around, it's all right."

"We were just about to go to Port George, sir," said Marquales.

"You were? On general leave?"

"Yes sir. There's a movie we want to see."

"Is that right? Well, what movie is it?"

*"Pinocchio."*

"We're too young for other movies," explained Wintermine.

"I like a good show," said Gatt. "Who's in it?"

"This is a Walt Disney picture," explained Marquales.

Gatt walked on into the room, smiling.

"Another full-length cartoon," added Marquales.

Gatt nodded in a friendly manner. "It ought to be good, then. Most of them are."

"Yes sir. We were about to go in to see it when you came."

"I saw a full-length cartoon once—*Snow White.*"

"I saw that," said Marquales nervously.

"Where'd you see it?"

"Atlanta, sir."

"I saw it in Birmingham. Do you live in Atlanta?"

"Near there, sir."

"I live in Birmingham."

"I saw *Snow White* in Winston-Salem," said Wintermine brightly. "And I don't live there."

"Say, what did you think of it, Mr. Gatt?" asked Marquales.

Gatt stared briefly at Wintermine, then said, "What did I think of *Snow White*? Great picture. I saw it a long time ago, though."

"In Birmingham?" asked Wintermine.

"I hear *Pinocchio* is better than *Snow White*," said Marquales.

Gatt said to Wintermine, "I told you I saw it in Birmingham. Dry up if you can't understand the English language."

"Yes sir," said Wintermine quietly.

"I've heard people argue *Pinocchio* is better than *Snow White*," said Marquales. "I wonder if it is."

"It'd have to be pretty good," said Gatt. "I remember those seven dwarfs in *Snow White*. Very funny. It was a pleasure to see the picture just because of the dwarfs. They were actually funny."

"Oh, yes," said Wintermine, winking at Marquales. "That was the name of the picture—*Snow White and the Seven Dwarfs*."

"Uh huh," said Gatt.

"They were really funny!" exclaimed Wintermine. "Oh boy, I nearly died!"

Gatt chuckled in reminiscence. "You boys remember Dopey? What a name. He was the kid with baggy knees who never spoke. What a face they had on that character."

Silence.

Gatt said thoughtfully, "There were six other dwarfs besides him."

Wintermine was grinning at Marquales—he started when Gatt asked in a loud voice, "What were the names of the others, you?"

"Sir?" said Wintermine.

"Sneezy, Bashful, Sleepy . . ." said Marquales.

Gatt said to Wintermine, "You don't seem to know much, do you?"

"I beg pardon, sir?"

"What were the names of the others?" asked Gatt, turning back to Marquales.

Wintermine said, "There was one called Grouchy."

"I asked *him*."

"Sir?" said Wintermine.

"I asked him, not you, bud."

"Yes sir. I'm sorry."

"Oh," sighed Marquales. "Let's see. There was Happy . . . and one more. We've got Dopey, Sleepy, Bashful, Grouchy, Sneezy, and Happy. That's six, anyhow."

Touching the tips of his fingers on one hairy wrist Gatt counted off: "Dopey, Sleepy, Bashful, Grouchy, Sneezy, and Happy. What's the other one? Doc. And *Doc*. That makes seven okay."

Wintermine laughed.

"What's the trouble?" asked Gatt, frowning. "His name was Doc all right and don't tell me it wasn't. He was the leader."

"This is quite a conversation," said Wintermine.

"Les," said Marquales quickly. "There's nothing wrong with talking about *Snow White* is there? I mean, it *was* an interesting picture."

"What were you laughing about?" asked Gatt.

"I wasn't laughing," replied Wintermine. "Not really."

"Mr. Gatt," said Marquales. "Les didn't mean anything."

"Sometimes I just laugh," explained Wintermine feebly.

Gatt leaned forward. "Do you laugh when somebody chops your can?"

"No sir."

"Okay, then. See that you don't!" Gatt burst into laughter.

After a moment Marquales asked, "Mr. Gatt, about that movie. Did you like it, or do you think it was just for children?"

"Not necessarily," said Gatt. "I believe Mickey Mouse was in that picture, wasn't he?"

"No, he wasn't in this one, sir," said Marquales.

"I believe he was."

"I don't remember much about it."

"Yes, I remember now. He was in it. What's the name of his dog? The dog was in it, too. As a matter of fact, the dog was featured."

"Pluto," said Wintermine.

"Mr. Gatt," said Marquales. "What exactly happened to Pluto in this picture? I can't remember for sure if he was in it. Do you remember offhand what happened to him?"

"No."

Wintermine twisted uncomfortably in his chair. Gatt said, "Feel grapes running down your legs?"

"No sir."

"You look like it!" Gatt burst into another laugh.

"Shall I leave the room, sir?" asked Wintermine.

"Not yet."

Marquales said, "Mr. Gatt are you sure Mickey and Pluto were in *Snow White*? I don't believe they were."

"Now what difference does it make? You guys act like kids. What do you care about a bunch of cartoon animals? But since you want to know I'll tell you. There was a scene with Pluto all right. To balance him they had a wolf; you'll find they use a dog to balance off a wolf, or a wolf to balance off a dog. The two have a fight and that's the plot of the picture."

Marquales and Wintermine both laughed, briefly. "I'm telling you how it was!" said Gatt. "Goddamn it you said you were curious to know, and *I'm* telling you. I don't mind telling you. And what I said a minute ago wasn't meant to be funny, it was factual."

"Yes sir," said Wintermine. Marquales nodded solemnly.

Gatt went on, "They had money piled on a stage coach. Pluto was the driver taking them to Houston, Texas. Therefore the wolf was the outlaw trying to rob the stage coach. He did it. He got all the money off and rode away on his horse—but later Pluto caught him and took him to the sheriff's office—he planned to rob them there, too.

"But they threw him in a machine. The sign on the machine said, 'Third Degree, patented by Pluto.' A big hand grabbed hold of the wolf and banged him up and down on tacks that came along one by one on a belt. Then paddles beat him on the tail, driving in the tacks good. Later on after a lot of other treatments the wolf had acid shot over his ass then got away by being blown up the chimney with a 'wolf bomb.' He ran across the countryside scraping his butt on the ground, howling. That's how it was. But when you see one of these cartoons you've seen them all."

"Yes sir," said Marquales.

"It's *fun* to see them," said Gatt. "But a regular picture is more serious. I'm surprised guys your age would be interested in cartoons like this."

"They're for kids," said Wintermine, nodding.

"I don't think cartoons are just for kids," said Gatt. "Grownups can like them a lot, too, because they're funny. My point is cartoons aren't as serious as other pictures."

"Of course sir," said Wintermine.

Gatt stared.

Marquales asked, "Les, what time is it?"

"Four-thirty," said Wintermine. "We ought to go soon."

"What are you talking about?" asked Gatt.

Marquales said, "Sir, we've got to stop by the post office—are you going that way?"

"Listen, I came over here to talk to you about something personal."

"Yes sir."

"We've had a pleasant conversation for awhile and now's the time to bring up the subject."

Marquales said, "Maybe you could go with us to the post office and talk on the way over there?"

"I came about last Friday night," said Gatt. "You know."

"Sir?" asked Marquales, raising his eyebrows.

"The poker game."

"Poker?" said Wintermine, smiling. "Why, Robert."

"I'm talking to him," said Gatt.

"Yes sir. I'm *sorry*."

"All right. Maybe you ought to go on out now."

"Sir?"

"Go on down to the latrine and come back in ten or fifteen minutes."

"Yes sir," said Wintermine politely.

They watched him leave the room. Then Gatt said, "I lost ninety dollars to you."

"Was it that much?" asked Marquales.

"Yes. Don't you remember?"

"Yes sir, I remember now. It was exactly ninety dollars."

"All week I've been thinking about you winning such a lot of money from me. That's a fortune. Well, I thought I'd come over and have a pleasant conversation with you about it. But I have something very important to say."

"Yes sir."

"Well, here's the way it is. Today I got a letter from Birmingham. It changes everything. I don't mind losing money in a poker game, but this is serious. My grandma is sick. I got a letter from her telling me she can't pay her doctor's bills. The drugstore won't give her any more credit."

"Yes sir?"

"Poor Grandma," murmured Gatt. "I hate to think of her lying off there in Birmingham. Of all my kinfolks she's the only one I really like. You know how it is? When I was a little boy she used to be good to me."

Marquales said, "Sir, I thought your grandmother owned one of the Birmingham mills."

"Not her, she's been poor for years. It's my father who's rich. But he's no kin to my grandma. She's his mother-in-law. Most people don't like their mother-in-law and he's no exception to the rule."

"Sir, you mean to say nobody will give her money for medicine?"

"Look, don't talk that way. *I'll* give her money."

"Yes sir."

"Don't make those kind of remarks."

"I just asked, sir."

"You won ninety dollars off me. That's a lot of money. My father sends me a fair allowance but I have to think of other things. All week I've been wondering about that money."

"Yes sir."

"The point is my grandma needs help, understand? She wants me to send her some of my allowance from my father. But you won so much I can't. And I won't get my next check for two weeks. What am I going to do?" Gatt looked at Marquales with head bowed forward, eyes staring from under his fuzzy eyebrows.

[ 284 ]

"Sir," replied the freshman. "I don't know what you're going to do, unless you force me to return the money I won."

"Look," said Gatt, blushing. "Is it fair to win more than five or ten dollars in a poker game?"

"Sir, suppose the tables were turned. Suppose you'd won ninety dollars from me."

Gatt thought for a few moments, then said, "Here's the point: I *didn't* win any money from you."

"Yes," said Marquales. "But suppose you had?"

"I didn't."

"But if you had, would you ever give it back to me?"

"If your grandma was sick, yes."

"Are you sure, sir?"

"Yes, I'm sure."

"Mr. Gatt, may I say something? I hope you won't mind. But I think I ought to mention it. You know, Jocko de Paris told me your mother and father were dead. He told me your grandmother owned a steel mill all by herself and was rich. He said your grandmother was the one that sent you your allowance."

"Jocko said that?"

"Yes sir."

Gatt laughed, first quietly, tossing back his head. He began to rub his eyes as if there were tears in them. He laughed more and more loudly. Then he let out a roar and said, "There's something in my eye!"

Marquales stood up nervously in the center of the room. Gatt was peeking through his fingers. "A bug, a bug," he moaned. "Give me a cloth, quick."

Marquales hurried and got a towel from his press.

"Well," said Gatt, wrapping it around his head, "lead me to the wash basin, I can't see where I'm going."

Marquales closed his hand around the huge bicep of Gatt's right arm and led him to the basin across the room. Gatt moaned unhappily, cursing. He fumbled for the faucets then turned on both hot and cold, filling the basin with water. He began to flip handfuls onto his face and head.

"It's annoying to get something in your eye," said Marquales.

"It sure is!" replied Gatt, voice muffled by the towel. He rubbed his face dry. After a moment he peered out, eyes reddened by the water. "Well here's the way I look at it. I'm not going to argue."

"Is the bug out?" asked Marquales.

"Yes, it's out. Now listen, I never argue with anybody. If they want to argue they can pick somebody else, I'm not their man. Either I get along with somebody or I don't have anything to do with them, then if they bother me I break them in two pieces and mash the grunt out their can. I don't argue, get me?"

"Yes sir."

"But I'll say a poker game has limits. Anybody knows that, if he doesn't he ought to go to kinneygarden. You can't win a guy's last cent and leave him stranded. Especially when he needs the money for a good purpose."

"May I ask what the purpose is, sir?"

"My grandmother, bud. And anybody who says I don't like her and love her more than anyone in the world, anybody that says that, I'll mash the grunt out of them, believe me."

"Yes sir, but Mr. de Paris was of—"

"Leave Jock out of this, you. It isn't anything to Jock."

"Sir, my only argument is when you lose money in a poker game it doesn't belong to you any more."

"I told you about argument—but listen, did you ever think of the fact that I'm a senior and you're a freshman?"

"I didn't believe that mattered in this case, sir."

"What right has a freshman got to win ninety bucks off a senior? You tell me that and I'll kiss your tail in the middle of the quadrangle."

Marquales smiled and said, "You and Mr. de Paris and Mr. Wilson asked me to play, sir."

"Well do you know what Wilson said to me this afternoon? He said that as far as he's concerned I lost too much money. 'Roger,' he says, 'You had awful hard luck, old boy. My personal opinion is that that freshman ought to give you back about a third of what he won.' That's what Wilson said. But I need the whole ninety. You're a nice kid so give it back to me now."

"I haven't got it, sir."

"We've talked about this and now give here that money."

"Yes sir," said Marquales, tugging out the thirty dollars from his watch pocket.

"That's right," said Gatt, grinning and nodding. He slowly counted the bills, then looked up. "Bud, you're short!"

"That's all I've got, sir."

"We had a nice talk, didn't we? I'm telling you, fork out that money before I hit you one and knock all your teeth out."

"Sir, you wouldn't do that," said Marquales. He touched Gatt on the arm. "A whole week has gone by since the poker game. I swear on my word of honor this is all I have left. I'd give it to you if I had it."

Gatt looked down at Marquales' hand. The freshman removed it, and took a step backward. "Sir!" he said. "I haven't got it."

"Where is it?" said Gatt in a strangled voice.

"I loaned it, sir!"

"Who to?"

"Jocko, sir."

"You're trying to pull the wool over my eyes," whispered Gatt.

"No, sir!"

"Jock's rich, he wouldn't borrow money from you."

"Sir, I'll tell you how it was. This is what happened, sir. Mr. de Paris' brother died. He had to send home money for flowers; he couldn't go to the funeral because he's sick. I tell you that's the truth, sir. But I can get the money for you sooner or later if you'll just wait. I mean it, Mr. Gatt. I think you ought to have that money returned."

Gatt sighed, and shoved the thirty dollars into his pocket. Then he said, "I need that money today. You'll have to telegraph your father and make him send it back to you by telegram. We'll go do that now. Come on!"

"Oh, sir!" said Marquales.

**24** When Marquales visited the Infirmary Thursday afternoon he found Jocko de Paris in the non-contagious ward, a large room with twenty beds, most of which were occupied by sick cadets. Jocko himself was hunched over a single page from the Port George *Herald,* working on a crossword puzzle. His brown hair stuck out, tangled; his face was unshaved.

"Hello," said Marquales.

Jocko looked up and whispered, "Hi there, kid." He looked unhappy. His hands were dirty and stained from nicotine tar; the sheets of his bed speckled with cigaret ash.

"What happened to the voice?" asked Marquales in a mimicking whisper.

Jocko didn't seem amused. He rubbed his five-day beard and said, "Laryngitis. That's what she says."

"The nurse?"

"Yes, if you can call her that," said De Paris dully. "Sit down. I'm glad to see you."

Marquales sat in a chair by the bedside table. He grinned. "Jocko, I meant to come visit you before now, but I thought you'd get out. Wilson told me you just had a hangover."

"Once you get in you stay a week," said De Paris. "You ought to know that. Everybody comes in here has calomel. It takes a week to get over a shot of that poison. How've you been doing?"

"Jocko, I've been having bad trouble with my roommates. Ben Hulitt moved out, then I learned he didn't like me: I was the reason for his doing it. Then I had fights with Les Wintermine. On top of it all Layne wouldn't give me permission to move to an empty room. Tom Munro caused that. Do you know the reason?"

"No."

"Guess."

De Paris sighed.

"The reason was you."

"Me?"

"Yes, Munro has the idea I'm a friend of yours. Since he doesn't like you, he therefore doesn't like me."

"Aren't you a friend of mine?"

"But that's not the point. I was trying to say Munro did it for that particular reason."

"Never expose yourself to an enemy," said De Paris.

"I started to wait and ask Layne afterwards."

"Did you whip Wintermine in the fight?" asked De Paris idly.

"Well, not exactly; we had *two* fights."

"Why did you fight him if you can't whip him?"

"He started it."

"Why did you let him start it? If you can't whip a guy you shouldn't be dumb enough to fight him."

"How could I help it, he—"

"Let's drop it." De Paris scratched angrily at the armpits of his pajamas. "Something is biting me."

"Maybe you've got lice," said Marquales. "Layne and Munro would say so. According to them you're no damn good, I regret to say."

"Did they tell you that?"

"Munro did. He expressed the opinion you were a form of termite."

"So what?"

"Nothing."

De Paris looked at his crossword puzzle, indifferent. After a moment he thrust a fountain pen at Marquales. "Fill this for me, there's ink in the drawer. A pencil doesn't show on this thing."

Marquales took the pen and experimentally moved the plunger.

"Is 'eek' a word?" asked Jocko.

"I'm not sure."

"Nothing else will fit."

Marquales leaned over the bed and looked at the newspaper.

"Go away," said De Paris. "It's no fun if you get help."

"What's the definition?"

"It's silly to do it if someone helps. You go and fill the pen."

Marquales filled it, slushing ink down the side of the bottle.

"This is the word all right," said Jocko in a convinced whisper. He took the fountain pen and printed; Marquales watched the blue ink melt into the paper and come out on the other side:

## KEE

"Jocko," he said. "I've had a rough life since you've been in here."

"We all have a rough life. Don't gripe."

"I wonder why I ever came to this school."

"You'll quit wondering after you get through freshman year," said De Paris coldly.

"To think I could have gone to the University of Georgia and lived a life of ease!"

"This bores me," said De Paris.

"It bores me, too."

"There're bedbugs in here, I think. For the last three nights I've been bitten like a dog."

"You need clean pajamas."

De Paris snorted.

"Those look sort of dirty, Jocko."

"Of course they look dirty! They are! And I'll tell you why. The colored orderly gives us a bath in the morning, but Miss Frune stands and watches to see he does a good job. So we have to keep on our pajamas. And how the hell can you get a bath when your pajamas are on? All you can do is get your pajamas wet and dirty. One of these days I'm going to smile at that Ward Witch then pull it out of my pants. 'Here it is,' I'll say. 'All yours.' She'll pass out cold, with joy."

Marquales swallowed, and smiled.

"The orderly doesn't give us a good bath," said De Paris in his whispery voice. "I mean what he does isn't done right. That's because he's afraid of Miss Frune. Listen—he's a colored man. Miss Frune is always lecturing us in here about how prejudiced we are against colored people. 'You Southerners!' she's always saying, as if she herself was from Maine. The old fool got those ideas when she was working for the Salvation Army in Macon. Can you beat it? But the irony is the nigger being scared to death of her. And he's really a nice egg, too. He wants to be a doctor."

"You sure do need clean pajamas."

"Yeah," agreed De Paris, sinking weakly back into bed.

"Why don't they let you wash yourself?"

"We're supposed to be sick. But the ones in private rooms get a bath every day. And they take it themselves."

"Why don't you get a private room? Or did you already try?"

"Christ!"

"It was just an idea."

"I had an awful hangover, believe me. And now this laryngitis. But I'm getting out of here tomorrow, or I'll wring her neck. She can keep her private rooms for the ones that suck up to her." De Paris gazed around the room at his fellow patients; several stared back at him. Two cadets across the ward had interrupted a checker game to look—they held their heads as if to hear what De Paris was saying. Jocko turned to Marquales and asked, "Where's Junior Wilson? Have you seen him? He hasn't been around with my mail, goddamn it, and I'm expecting an important letter from my old man."

"I haven't seen him," said Marquales. "Not since Monday."

De Paris sighed and gave a shrug, then began to scratch angrily under his arms. Marquales smiled as Jocko's eyes slewed gradually around the room, finally resting upon a red-haired cadet in the opposite bed. De Paris' hands stopped in the middle of a scratch—and he stuck out his tongue. The red-haired cadet immediately grinned, and scratched sympathetically under his own arms.

"Hey, brute," said De Paris. "Go get me a glass of water."

The cadet rolled off his bed and came forward, wiggling his feet into a pair of bedroom slippers. "Fresh ice water, sir?"

"No," said De Paris, yanking at his sheet. "Stale ice water. Wash out the glass, you morbid brute."

The cadet turned and went off down the aisle between the beds Marquales murmured, "I see you've got the freshman trained."

"*You're* a freshman. But that guy's a sophomore recruit."

"Oh, is he? He looked like a freshman."

"They always look like freshmen. It's because they're not military."

"Where'd he go to school last year?"

"Yale."

"Really?"

"Harvard."

"He went to Harvard?"

"Princeton!" shouted De Paris.

Marquales shut his mouth.

"How do I know where the guy went to school?" asked De Paris in a whining voice.

"Okay, Jocko."

"Here I am penned up in here with all sorts of insidious worries on my mind. I'm worn out with boredom. Why don't you tell me what's been going on instead of making idle conversation? That crap about not wanting to go to school here—where this jerk went to school. Don't you realize the filthy General might kick me out of here two days from now? Why talk about such subjects, not that I believe he will kick me out, all he wants is for me to eat mud. You should tell me about Gatt and Corger. Did you know Gatt's been pestering Wilson, whimpering about that money—blah, blah, blah, his dirty old grandmother's sick and he's got to send her a present so she'll know he loves her, blah, blah, blah. The idiocy of that dumb brute beats me; it amazes me, he's so filthy dumb. He's so dumb he ought to have his head chopped off. Wilson's just as bad, though, the yellow runt. You should hear the way *he's* been talking; scared shitless. Where is that bastard, anyhow? I want my mail."

"I don't know, sir."

"What do you mean, you don't know?"

"Sir, I haven't seen Corger or Gatt or Wilson, so how could I tell you anything about them."

De Paris sighed. "Don't misunderstand me, Marquales. I appreciate your coming around to see me—me, a poor fellow who's going to be expelled in a couple of days. The point happens to be that I'm bored stiff. You don't know what it's like in here. They've really got

[ 292 ]

you at their mercy. You can't do a thing. Try talking to Frune—she doesn't even know when she's insulted. But she'll assume you insult her when you don't mean to. What are you going to do with a character like that? I'll be glad when I get out of here. Christ."

"I don't want to be boring," said Marquales coldly. "I told you about my roommates. Wasn't it interesting to hear the way Layne and Munro talked? You should have heard them, they said you were a nasty bastard nobody liked. Munro said the only thing to do in the case of a skunk like you was to ignore you."

De Paris stared thoughtfully at Marquales, then said, "They are the ones that should be ignored. Listen, I've come to the conclusion in the last few days that I waste a lot of time on unimportant cowards. Suppose you run into a bastard? The world's full of them. If you try to run down every single one, you'll wear yourself out. Besides what good will it do? Why bother about a yellow coward or a person of inferior mentality? You know what I mean—Tom Munro and Pete Layne are not only of inferior mentality, but they're cowards."

De Paris shoved the newspaper page off his bed, watching it slide gently to the floor. He looked up, "That's the way they are—give them a push and they fall down. But are they worth it? How much energy have I wasted on similar guys? Energy is a vital thing in life —you have only so much of it because the amount nature gave you is fixed. Throw it away and you get to the point where you haven't got any more."

"You called Munro's bluff the other night," said Marquales. "He was scared to death. It did me good to see you give it to him. What was it you said?"

De Paris smiled. "All I told him was, 'Here I am, Tom. I'll fight you if you want to stand up like a man.' That's all you ever have to say. Just vary that basic remark to fit the occasion. This simple remark will make ninety-five per cent show their yellow streak."

"What about the other five per cent?"

"If you call one of those babies, be ready to beat his ass."

Marquales said, "Jocko, you sure figured out Munro. I thought he was going to scream for help. But he really doesn't like you. To show off a guy that way will do one thing—make you an enemy. He really doesn't like you at all."

De Paris frowned, then scratched his stomach. "Look, you're tiring out what's left of my voice."

"Maybe I'd better go. What became of that water boy?"

"Sit down and I'll tell you something. What is all this stuff about liking and not liking? You don't even know what the expressions mean. Marquales, you'll have to use your head more if you want to get along in life. What does it mean to say Tom Munro doesn't like me? The point happens to be that I don't like him. Don't you realize Tom Munro would be crazy about me if I liked him? The fact is, what I like usually likes me; what I don't like usually doesn't like me. I'm not being conceited. It turns out that way all the time. Why is this? Because since I was twelve years old when I got my stepmother I've seen to it nobody decides whether they like me. I decide whether I like them!"

Marquales nodded.

"When I like someone they like me. When I don't like them they don't like me."

Marquales asked, "What happened to the guy that went after the water?"

"I know what happened to him," said De Paris. "You'd really better get on out of here because Frune has caught the guy. She's probably giving him the third degree now to find out who sent him. The bitch stands by that cooler just to see if any of the boys go out for water."

"I'll leave," said Marquales.

"She caught him all right. Or he let her catch him. Did you know Tom Munro and me used to be good friends? We did and I don't care if he says nasty things about me now. I understand him. There was a day when he used to tag along after me the way Al Wilson does. Then once Tom made the fatal mistake of saying something sarcastic to me. If there's anything I can't stand it's an uncalled-for sarcastic remark. Especially if it isn't funny in the first place. But what did he do but five minutes later make another sarcastic remark! That was the limit. Nobody makes two sarcastic remarks to me in a row."

"Did you whip him?"

De Paris laughed. "All you have to do is be able."

"I just wondered," said Marquales.

"And that's the way it turned out. I had him by the balls the other night because he was afraid of me. But Frune isn't and she'll come in here and cuss me out and it'll be all I can do to get the best of her. You gather I don't like this woman? She's so nuts she makes Sowbelly Simmons look normal. If there's one thing that makes me sick to my stomach it's a nut. They ought to take them out and shoot them. What good are they? But especially do I hate a female nut; that's the worst kind. You see, the trouble with Frune is for years she's wanted that thing without knowing what it was. It finally drove her crazy. That's what happens to women born ugly. An ugly man can go out and buy a piece. But an ugly woman can't do anything but f.f. themselves to death, the poor bitches—an ugly woman, believe me, is uglier than an ugly man, and it's no wonder they can't buy it. Who would ever go in for that line of work?"

"They have them in France," said Marquales.

"Those filthy French! Name any perversion you can think of: the filthy French invented it. France is the most disgusting, nauseating country in the world."

"Paris is supposed to be a nice city," said Marquales. "I hope to go there someday. My aunt went there."

"Did she come back with curly hair between her teeth?"

"You don't know my aunt."

"Listen, my dad was in France during the last war. He knows those frogs in and out. Take my word for it; they're no good."

"All right," said Marquales. "I better go now before the nurse gets back."

"Yeah, you better."

Marquales stood up and put on his cap.

"Go tell Junior Wilson I want to see him. Tell him to come here with my mail and to bring me a carton of cigarets."

"Okay." Marquales started to walk off.

De Paris called, "Tell Wilson to bring clean pajamas—and some flit for the bugs."

Several cadets in the ward laughed.

Marquales passed through the door. He'd gone a few feet when Miss Frune came into sight around a corner. She had the red-haired sophomore recruit firmly by the arm. Marquales saw angry tears in her eyes and felt sorry for her. He wondered if she were actually a virgin. He decided she was.

# 25

On Friday afternoon Jocko was still at the Infirmary. He had obtained his private room, however, and it was there that Marquales and Roger Gatt found him. He sat in a rocking chair by the window, wearing a silk bathrobe and puffing on a cigaret in a shiny aluminum holder.

"Knock! Knock!" said Marquales in a facetious voice.

De Paris gazed on out the window at the Infirmary lawn, his profile grinning. "Okay," he said. "Who's there?"

"Bessie."

"Bessie who?"

"Besame mucho."

Gatt guffawed. De Paris turned and murmured, "Cripes." Marquales noticed the laryngitis had disappeared overnight. Suddenly Gatt quit bellowing and jabbed his thumb into the freshman's back, whispering, "You shouldn't joke with him now."

De Paris had shaved, combed his hair, bathed, and put on clean pajamas. His fingers still had nicotine stains, but were freshly manicured. He grinned and arose from the rocking chair. "Hi there," he said. "Roge, shake."

Gatt held out his big right hand and De Paris took it. They smiled at each other: Gatt shyly, De Paris with charm.

Marquales edged around them into the room. "I see you shaved, Jocko."

"It was simple," replied De Paris. "I used a razor."

Gatt rubbed his own blue-black jaw: a grating sound resulted. "How do you feel, Jock?" he asked.

"Fine, keed."

"Jock, I was sorry to hear the news about your brother."

"What news?" De Paris glanced at Marquales, who said, "We were in my room talking and I didn't think you'd mind if I told Mr. Gatt about it." De Paris waved one hand, a somber expression on his face. "You fellows come on in. Make yourselves at home in my cell." Gatt looked at the floor in an embarrassed manner. Jocko meanwhile made a consterned grimace at Marquales—he became at once bland

[ 297 ]

when Gatt looked up and said, "If my brother died I'd hate it—I mean, I know how bad it must be for a member of the family to die. I haven't got a brother."

"Sure."

"How did you get this private room?" asked Marquales. "Even if it is a cell, which it isn't, it's better than the ward. I wonder how you got it. You look like you've had a bath, too. Does this room have a bath?"

Gatt murmured, "That's right, we should change the subject."

"How did you get Miss Frune to let you come in here?" said Marquales. "You must be a miracle man."

"It was simple," said De Paris quietly. "I told her I wanted to stay in the room with the other boys. The miracle would be if she'd let me stay in that stinking ward."

"How do you feel, Jock?" asked Gatt once more.

"All right. How do you feel?"

Gatt turned to Marquales, his face red with embarrassment. "We oughtn't to bother him."

"What?"

Gatt tugged at his collar, blushing.

"It's okay," said Jocko.

"No," said Gatt. "Kid, you'll have to get the sixty somewhere else. Jock's my friend."

"What's that?" asked De Paris. "What sixty? What could you be talking about, Roge?"

"I don't want to bother you when you're sick," said Gatt. "Then that trouble about your brother."

"I'm all right. The last few days have been tough, but I'm all right now. What do you want to talk to me about?"

After a pause Gatt said, "It's my grandma."

They waited. De Paris asked gently, "What about your grandma?"

"I was fooling the kid," said Gatt. "I didn't want him to think I was a dope, so I tricked him. I told him my grandma was sick. She's all right, but it's her *birthday* Sunday and I want to get her a present."

"That's nice," said De Paris.

"She was good to me . . . she was a sweet old lady when I was a runt. My aunt was mean, but not my grandma. I used to get picked on in those days. Everybody used to call me 'Rock Head,' and 'Black Gatt,' and 'Tom Gatt,' and a lot else. They used to throw rocks at my head and then say it wouldn't hurt me when I got hit. Jock, the women used to come to the house to talk to Grandma, then when she'd get out of the room they'd thump me on the head with their thimbles and tell each other the story how my head was made out of a rock and nothing could hurt me. But my grandma never did anything like that; she was always sweet as pie to me and I love her a lot."

"I see," said De Paris. "Therefore you want to buy her a birthday gift. But you can't because Marquales won all your money last Friday in the poker game."

Gatt nodded.

"How old's your grandmother, Roge?"

"She'll be seventy-six."

"I think I remember her last birthday. Didn't you send her a set of silver combs and brushes with the number '75' engraved on the backs?"

"Yes!" said Gatt. "Laurie was going to help me pick something out, but I did it myself."

"That was in April, Roge. This is November."

Silence.

"I was telling Mr. Gatt all about it," said Marquales. "You know, Jocko, how I got lucky and won ninety dollars from Mr. Gatt. He wants me to return it because it isn't fair for a freshman to win money from a senior—and also because of his grandmother. I see what he means. I returned thirty dollars already, but that sixty I loaned you for your brother's funeral—Jocko, I'll have to ask you to give it back, because Mr. Gatt is in a hurry."

"I'll be goddamn," said Jocko. "You want me to hand over sixty dollars so you can present it to Mr. Gatt. Does it occur to you I have other uses for my money?"

[ 299 ]

"Okay," said Gatt, rising from the chair by the door. "Kid, I figured you were stalling. You have to wire your daddy for that sixty bucks after all. Come on, let's get out of here."

"Wait," said Marquales. "My father won't give me sixty dollars. There's no telling what he'd do if he got a wire like that."

"Don't crap me," said Gatt. "You've got plenty of money."

"Jocko!" said Marquales. "Can't you help me out? No kidding!"

"Come on, you," said Gatt.

De Paris said, "Listen, Roge. Do you mean to stand there and tell me you're making this poor freshman give you back what he won just so you can have the cash to throw away on those Luck Street whores? I'd never believe you'd do a thing like that. By God, I'm shocked."

Gatt said, "Come off that, Jock. What you don't know is my grandma has her birthday in November, not April. Drop that line."

"What do you mean by this advice, Roge?"

"Act decent, you," said Gatt thickly.

"I'm not sure I understand such cretinous words, Roge."

Gatt stood up. "You don't know what I mean, Jock?"

"Roge," said De Paris, grinning earnestly. "I want to tell you something. Listen—this is interesting. I had a conversation about you with a certain fellow the other day. He was telling me some things, and now I want—"

"My grandma's birthday is in November!" said Gatt, his big face white, neck craned.

"All right," said De Paris. "Sure."

"NOVEMBER. Let that sink in."

"Roge, please don't get excited. I agree with you about it all the way. Just as you said, your grandmother's birthday is in November. I made an error. And of course you have to send her a present. We have no disagreement on this score at all. Now the other day I was talking— sit down, Roge, come on, sit down and listen to this. The other day I was having a conversation with a certain fellow. I want to tell you what I said to him. But first of all do you know what he said to me? Well, he told me Roger Gatt was no good. He said, 'Jocko, you're wrong when you say Roger Gatt is one of the nicest guys at The Academy. Roger Gatt stinks like an ape in the zoo.'

"That's what he said to me. Now this is what I told him. I said, 'Don't talk like that about my friend, Roger Gatt. He's twice the man you are. I've never known him to do a dirty trick in my life. Roger Gatt is a terrific athlete and a damn fine guy.'

"That's what I said to the fellow. I let him know where I stand on the subject of Roger Gatt. For my money there's not a better man to be found anywhere. I just want you to know that before you start jumping to conclusions. Now, Roge, when you start talking about making Marquales return the money he won fair and square it confuses me. It doesn't jibe with my high opinion of your character and it doesn't seem the natural thing for you to do. Understand, Roge?"

Gatt swallowed several times, his bewildered eyes focussed on De Paris.

"*Roge,*" said Jocko persuasively. "My suggestion is to return the thirty dollars you forced out of this poor kid. Now what do you think? Really, I mean it. What do you think?"

Gatt asked, choked, "Who was the guy said I stink like an ape in the zoo?"

"I promised him I wouldn't mention it."

"I wonder who he was."

"The guy will have to remain anonymous. I couldn't give you his name without breaking my word—and that's one thing I never do. But Roge, the important thing after all isn't this guy. I just mentioned him to make a point. The important thing is the principle involved in making the freshman give up the money. There's a big ideal here—the ideal of fair play. Let me ask you: what would people say if they heard you were forcing this helpless freshman to give back his money? Would they approve of such an unfair thing?"

Gatt exclaimed, "Wilson did! Albert Wilson."

"Roge, you know Wilson didn't tell you to rob the freshman."

"He said I'd gotten a dirty deal in that card game losing so much money. And he told me, 'Roger, you had awful hard luck, old boy. My personal opinion is that that freshman ought to give you back

[ 301 ]

about a third of what he won.' That's what Wilson said! But I need the whole ninety on account of my grandma's birthday. Her birthday is on Sunday and it's already Friday. I should buy her something tonight or it'll be too late."

De Paris nodded his head thoughtfully. "*Wilson* said the freshman should give up a third. Well, perhaps Wilson didn't mean that. I'm sure he's friendly to Marquales."

"No he isn't," said Gatt. "Wilson said the freshman might have cheated to win that ninety dollars. But I don't believe the kid cheated. I was watching him."

"Well then," said De Paris quietly. "Maybe the kid should give back the money after all, if Wilson advised it."

"Yes," said Gatt. "He should be a good sport and realize he's a freshman, and that it was a friendly game, and that my grandma has a birthday. That's all I ask. I don't see why he can't understand that."

"Then your mind is made up," said De Paris.

"Yes. Now Jock, there's something else."

"What? Do you want interest on the ninety dollars?"

"Interest?"

"Did Albert Wilson say you should draw interest?"

"Jock, I want you to tell me who the guy was that said that about me."

"Roge, I told you I can't give away his name."

Gatt said, "I want to know."

"Sorry, but I won't tell you."

"Look here, Jock, I'm asking you who that guy was."

"And I'm telling you I won't say."

"You're upset on account of your brother. That explains how you're acting this afternoon. But I want to know who that man was."

"Well," said De Paris, as if deliberating.

"Come on!" said Gatt. "I won't tell him you told me."

"No wait, Roge, I have an idea. Look, why cause trouble? Suppose I go to this guy and demand that he retract his insulting remarks. Then if he doesn't apologize I'll give you his name. Is that all right?"

[ 302 ]

"No," said Gatt.

De Paris was thinking. He suddenly cracked his hands together and said, "Roge, by God I'm going to do it! I didn't think I would, but I'll tell you the name of this guy—and what's more I'll tell you something else he said."

"All right."

"But first I'd better tell you why I changed my mind. You remember you sympathized with me about my brother. Well, I didn't know what to say because my brother *isn't* dead. Roge, the fellow who called you these names was the man who sent me a letter saying my brother was dead. That's his idea of wit."

Gatt was silent.

"It had such an effect on me I had to come to the Infirmary. But that wasn't all. His practical-joker letter said we'd lost all our money and I should send a hundred dollars to help pay expenses. I only had forty so I borrowed sixty from Marquales. But you know about that.

"Roge, try and imagine how I felt this morning when I got a sarcastic letter from my father asking me not to write him while drinking. My brother is actually in the best of health, thank God, and the family doesn't need any measly hundred dollars."

De Paris took a green check from his bathrobe. "Here's my father's check for one hundred bucks, dated yesterday."

Gatt stared, puzzled.

"Well," said Jocko earnestly. "What do you think of such a trick? Isn't it low and dirty? Isn't it the work of a yellow coward? It certainly is, and he must pay for his cowardice! Roge, I am going to tell you what he said about you. I sure hate to do it because he said an awful thing."

Gatt replied shyly, "Jock, I'm glad to hear your brother is all right. What did this guy say about me?"

De Paris hesitated, then said, "I told you he called you an ape."

"Ha," said Gatt. "What a wow."

"Roge," said De Paris. "He also told me you had carnal relations with your grandmother."

"I did what?" asked Gatt hoarsely.

"This fellow said you once raped your grandmother."

Gatt turned white. Then he laughed. "What a wow! Who is this guy, a dope? He hasn't got any sense at all. What was that he said again?"

"That you screwed your helpless grandmother."

"Ha, ha!" laughed Gatt. *What's his name?*"

"I'll tell you," said De Paris. "But first I want to endorse this check over to you. I'll sign it payable to demand of Roger Gatt. You're getting ten extra dollars so give Marquales back forty instead of thirty. That'll make it even."

Gatt took the check and looked at it.

"It's for a hundred," said De Paris. "Give the kid forty."

Gatt slowly counted off forty dollars from a large roll of bills. "I've only got eight bucks left."

"Cash the check at any hotel, then you have plenty."

"All right," said Gatt, a vacant look on his face.

"Okay, Roge, that settles it."

"Jock, did that guy who fooled you really say that about me and my grandma?"

"Yes, he did."

"Okay." Gatt started to leave the room.

"Hey!" called De Paris. "Don't you want to know his name?"

Gatt turned, face gray and his eyes bulging out like blue marbles. He moved his lips silently.

"Albert Wilson," said De Paris. "Go kill that bastard."

They heard Gatt walking away down the hall. The freshman got up to shut the door and De Paris said, "Are *you* stupid."

Marquales whirled around, smiling.

"Don't look at me like a dental ad."

"I know," said the freshman. "It was dumb."

"You don't know your butt from a bear's ass."

"Jocko, I had to come over here with him."

De Paris said, "Because of you we're up Snot River without a paddle." He stared out the window, disgusted.

⌈ 304 ⌉

Marquales said, "Thanks for helping a fool. I'll get out of here now. Gatt's money is on the table."

"Keep that forty dollars!" said De Paris. "Get yourself screwn twenty times."

"It's yours," said Marquales.

"What are you talking about? In all seriousness, do you think I gave that morbid brute anything? Don't judge other people by your own weak brain."

"The check wasn't good?"

"It's my father's check. His check is good. But I endorsed it with the handwriting I had in third grade. I'm going to report to General Draughton that the check is stolen. I'll wire my old man to make the bank refuse payment. Let Gatt try to cash it and I'll have him arrested and booted out of school."

"That's wonderful," said Marquales. He sagged down into a chair.

"What's there to be sarcastic about?"

"No, I mean it's wonderful."

"Just what do you mean?"

"Well, I thought you weren't doing anything but trying to murder Albert Wilson. This new angle is a surprise."

"Are you weeping over that dog? Don't you see he turned on us?"

"Yes, he was afraid of Gatt. So am I. Aren't you?"

"Marquales, you act as if you hadn't the least idea what went on in here a minute ago. It's because you don't understand Roger Gatt. You assume he hasn't got any sense. And you're wrong. That ape is very crafty. It's his stock in trade to play dumb. That's how he fools people."

"It is?" said Marquales.

"There are two possibilities," replied De Paris, frowning. "First, Gatt believed us. Second, he didn't. He is not dumb enough to swallow what was told him. For that, we have you to thank. And therefore, it's the second: he didn't believe us.

"Marquales, your story about my *brother* was as stupid as the one Gatt told about his grandma. Now if he didn't believe what you said, he naturally wouldn't believe what I said.

[ 305 ]

"Besides—he and Albert Wilson might have their heads together. My opinion is Gatt knew all along Wilson didn't really say anything dirty about him. Gatt knows it was his friend Jock who was saying those things. Did you see the looks he gave me?

"But even if I'm wrong, even if Gatt believed everything, then why should it make any difference? Suppose Junior didn't do anything but just tell Gatt to get thirty dollars out of you. Wasn't that a bad enough mistake? Didn't it cause the whole thing? Wilson deserves to get his ass beat. If Gatt doesn't do it you can be sure I will.

"If Junior had had the nerve to tell Gatt the money was lost and once lost forever lost then none of this would have happened. We wouldn't have this ape over here blowing his breath in our face and yapping about his goddamn money. He'd never have asked for it if Junior hadn't encouraged him.

"Or Corger, maybe. I wonder how he fits in this? He must have his hand in, the mean-hearted bastard. Just because he's heavyweight on the Boxing Team he thinks everybody's afraid of him! How long would Corger last in the ring with Joe Louis?

"Marquales, do you remember that blank look on Gatt's face when he said Wilson hinted the game wasn't fair, that you cheated? What about it? Suggestive, isn't it?"

"I don't know," said Marquales. "Maybe Gatt made it up."

"I believe it means Gatt knows the game was crooked."

"I don't think he did. He would have acted different."

"Don't underestimate him, that's a fatal mistake! More people lose out through underestimating their enemies than from any other reason. It's a lot better to overestimate. Then you can't go wrong. Suppose I'd stupidly assumed Gatt believed the crap about my brother. I haven't even got a goddamn brother. But suppose he believed it. He'd go whip Wilson and probably mangle the piss out of him. So what? Junior deserves punishment and we'd be spared the trouble of giving it ourself. More important maybe Gatt would be expelled for doing it, which would solve the whole thing. But what if it didn't work out that way?

"Suppose Gatt was sitting here all the time aware that I was lying

[ 306 ]

about Junior. Then wouldn't he lay for me and leave Wilson alone? I don't want that big bastard hanging around me foaming at his mouth. I took out insurance, and here's where you see the difference between being smart and having brains. My insurance is that check. I can fall back on it and ruin him that way."

De Paris paused for a moment, breathing heavily. Then he said, "However there's another possibility. Gatt might not even try to cash the check. If Corger is in on it or if Wilson has talked then Gatt sure won't try to cash the check. He'll have enough sense to know there's something wrong. Besides Corger wouldn't let him; Corger would know. That's looking at it as pessimistically as possible. But if you think I haven't got a hidden ace up my sleeve you're wrong. Do you know what I'll do if it turns out that way?"

"There wouldn't be much to do," said Marquales.

"There's always something to do. A man with brains is never trapped. Tomorrow morning I'm getting out of here—Miss Frune promised. I intend to go see Wilson right away and talk to him. Then I can find out what's what. If I learn that Corger and Gatt are wise, then I'll head right up to see the General. I'm supposed to learn my fate from him tomorrow anyhow, which means I'll have to eat more dirt.

"But I'll trick that goddamn old bastard if it kills me. And I believe I can do it. See, I'll confess everything to him. I'll confess I was playing cards the night before my talk with him last Saturday. I'll say: Oh General, I was a bad boy and I want to confess it so I can get on the straight path. Then I'll give a frank, honest smile and confess I lost a hundred dollars to Gatt. This subtle touch will make the whole thing look on the level, whereas if I said I *won* money the old bastard would doubt me. If I dare to go crab about a lost gambling debt he'll assume the business must be on the level and that I really mean to reform and accept Jesus Christ as my saviour.

"Get the subtlety of it. What would happen when I told him that? He'd investigate about the poker game. Then he'd kick Roger Gatt out of school and he'd probably kick Wilson out. But he'd let *you* off with a special order because you're a freshman. And he'd let me off with a special order because I told him the honest truth. Gatt would have to turn over my check which would be the evidence. That would ruin him and the thing would be so complicated General Draughton would never believe the original story even if Wilson and Gatt told him. You and I'd end up walking punishment tours for the next sixty days. But Gatt and Wilson would be expelled! And we'd have Gatt's money!"

Marquales said weakly, "I sure hope it doesn't turn out that way."

"If it does and you have to get a special order, then don't blame me. Your sins will find you out. Marquales, all you had to do when Gatt asked you for that money was tell him you'd sent it home. What could he have done then? You've got to use your brain otherwise you won't get by in life. You didn't use your brain and you showed a yellow streak. Marquales, it is nerve and brains that make the world go around—not the law of revolvement, or the law of piss, or whatever it is. See, instead of rattling off a clever and marvelous subtle lie that would confuse Gatt you lost your head and gave him thirty dollars then tell him a dopey lie about *me*. So you come over here and put a hot griddle under my ass. I swear it's enough to make me want to take a swat at you."

"Jocko," said Marquales. "Wait a minute. If I'd told Gatt I sent the money home he'd have made me wire for it. He wanted me to telegraph my father as it was. Jocko, if I wired my father for sixty dollars *this* would happen sure as night follows daytime: my father would fly into a rage and call General Draughton on the telephone from Georgia. He'd say: Sir, what in the name of hell's bells is going on down there at your school. So the General would investigate. He'd find out about it all. And you and I and Wilson and Gatt would be expelled before we knew what hit us."

"That's ridiculous," said Jocko coldly. "If you handled it in a truly intelligent way nothing like that would have happened.

"Marquales, the world is full of people like you. You're not dumb but you're not smart. You're not yellow but you haven't really got any guts. Your conversation gives me an unpleasant feeling."

"I'm sorry," said Marquales.

De Paris smiled. "I actually like you. You're not bright and you are more or less yellow, as I said—think differently if you want to. Anyhow, you're a good kid at heart and I just wish you hadn't gummed up this whole thing."

"Maybe I better go now," said Marquales.

Jocko laughed nervously and yanked at a cord that hung over his bed. "I'm going to call Frune in here and make her give me a lemonade."

"Then I know I'd better leave."

"I've got her all futzed up. She does everything I tell her." De Paris grinned, showing his white teeth. "If I don't get out of here soon I'm going to call her in one night and give her a ride."

Marquales nodded his head and walked toward the door.

"She'd love it," chuckled De Paris. "The poor old hag."

At that point Marquales left. Jocko was yanking at the string, a gloomy scowl on his face.

Hurrying back to Hemphill Barracks Marquales wondered if he dare warn Albert Wilson. As he approached the front gate, however, he saw Wilson getting into a Port George taxicab with Harold Koble and Philip McCarthy. The taxi passed within ten feet of the freshman; he smiled and saluted.

"Glug, glug, glug!" yelled McCarthy, holding up his hand as if drinking from a bottle. Koble waved one of his apelike arms. Albert Wilson looked the other way.

Wintermine was waiting in the room. He was impatient at the long delay, but remained polite. Marquales explained Gatt wanted to borrow five dollars, that they'd gone to Jocko for it.

"De Paris will never see that money again," said Wintermine. "Not that I care."

He and Marquales went on to Port George. They had a poor dinner in a Walgreen drugstore and talked politely with each other. After dinner they went to see *Pinocchio*. At eleven o'clock they returned to barracks and went to bed. It was a dull, awkward evening.

# 26

Wintermine crawled out of his cot and walked barefooted to the window. He said, "Robbie, your pillow's on the floor."

Marquales answered sleepily, "I thought it was a girl."

"What?"

"I was dreaming about a nice, stacked-up girl then the bugle blew. So I threw her out of the bed."

Wintermine banged shut the window and stood stretching for a moment. Then he took off his flannel pajamas, turning his rear toward Marquales. He laid the pajamas on the study table and put on socks, shoes, underwear. After that he faced about, and grinned. "Are you going to get up today?"

Marquales yawned in reply and lazily watched Wintermine put on trousers and shirt.

"You're going to miss another two-minute steel if you don't get up."

"Was it reveille I heard a minute ago?"

Wintermine smiled artificially. "Don't you feel well?"

"No, I don't," said Marquales. "I feel like something covered up by a cat." He pulled the blanket over his head.

Wintermine didn't reply. Marquales heard him dressing. Then suddenly breakfast call sounded.

"Now you've got two minutes to make the steel."

Marquales threw off the blanket and hopped from the cot. He quickly shed his pajamas and snatched up his gray cotton shirt. He began to put it on.

"No underwear today?"

"They blew the call too soon!" said Marquales. "Those skunks."

Fully dressed, Wintermine walked to the door. "Good luck," he called.

"Thanks," said Marquales. When Wintermine had gone he added, "For nothing, you bastard."

As he was stuffing in his shirttail a freshman orderly appeared in the door. At first Marquales thought it was Wintermine come back, then the orderly said, "Hey, you, what's your name?"

"Marquales."

"Marquales, you're wanted in the Guardroom."

"Guardroom? What for?"

"I don't know. But in dress uniform with gloves and waist belt."

"Don't you know what they want?" asked Marquales.

"You'd better hurry," smiled the orderly. "You're going to be taken to the General's office for examination."

Marquales came forward, holding up his trousers. "Are you sure?"

The orderly grinned.

"What do they want me for?" asked Marquales.

"I couldn't say, chum."

Marquales stared at the skinny orderly for a moment then removed his trousers and kicked them across the floor. He took off his cotton shirt and got out his dress uniform. At that time the bugler sounded two-minute steel. Marquales hurried into dress trousers and dress blouse. The orderly helped him buckle the blouse collar then he slipped on a pair of fresh-laundered white gloves. His own waist belt was soiled so he borrowed Wintermine's. "All right," he said weakly. "Let's go."

The orderly grinned. "Your cap."

"Oh," said Marquales, grabbing the cap. "Look, I want to stop by the latrine."

"Whatever for?"

They reached the bottom gallery as Company Twelve left the quadrangle. It was the last company of the battalion. Marquales watched the third platoon cut through the rear gate toward the mess hall, freshmen all marching in a brace, stiff legged. He had done it himself so many times, yet never seen it.

"Am I going to miss breakfast?" he asked.

"I guess you will, bub," said the orderly.

The cadet Officer of the Day waited in the Guardroom. "Is that Robert Marquale?" he asked.

"Yes sir."

"Marquales," corrected the orderly.

"Is it Marquales?"

"Yes sir."

"You shouldn't agree with me if I get it wrong, Mister."

"Yes sir."

"Let me see the top of your cap."

The freshman took off his cap and held it out.

"Why didn't you clean it? You didn't even comb your hair." The O.D. pulled a pink comb from his blouse. "Give me the cap; I'll take care of it for you. You go to the basin and wet down your head."

Marquales held the comb under running water then pulled it through his hair. He heard the O.D. say, "I'm taking him." Then in a louder voice, "You're going to see the General."

"Yes sir."

"Did you tell him? I said for you to keep your mouth shut."

"He thought I was kidding," lied the orderly.

Marquales asked, "Is my hair all right now, sir?"

The O.D. smiled at the orderly, "What movie star does he resemble?"

"I know—Stan Laurel."

"Alfalfa," said the O.D.

"I think he looks like Ben Turpin," said the orderly. "Remember him, with those eyes?"

"Turpin had cockeyes. But give Alfalfa one brown one and one blue one and change the color of his hair and you couldn't tell them apart."

Marquales laughed nervously. "In my opinion I look like Rin-tin-tin." Gritting his teeth, he started back to the mirror to re-comb his hair.

"Never mind," said the O.D. "We've got to go. Here's your cap."

The orderly was giggling. "Am I in charge of this hostelry?"

"That's enough back talk," said the O.D. "You freshmen come on guard duty and decide you're Admirals."

The orderly accompanied them to the front entrance, still giggling. There the O.D. turned over the key ring, then he and Marquales waited outside the bars while the skinny freshman locked the gate. He went back in the direction of the Guardroom doing a tap dance.

"Look at him," said the O.D. to Marquales. "Is it any wonder you freshmen get in trouble?"

"No sir."

"Just because I treated him decent last night and gave him some of my coffee he thinks he can act like this. I guess I'll have to cut his ass this afternoon when we go off guard."

They marched down the sidewalk in front of Hemphill Barracks, then cut over to the asphalt driveway and headed toward the Administration Building five hundred yards away. The sun had just come up and most of the campus was submerged in fog. To the right a sudden noise rolled across the grounds—shouts of conversation and tinkling silverware; "rest" had been given in the mess hall.

"They're eating," sighed the O.D.

Marquales didn't answer.

The Junior Officer of the Guard was waiting for them on the steps of the Administration Building. When they approached he said, "Is that the freshman? Hurry; Aloysius will be here in a minute."

"Okay," said the O.D.

"Is that the freshman?"

"Sure it's the freshman."

"He goes in the reception room."

"I know where he goes. Come on, kid."

Marquales followed the O.D. up the steps, his feet dragging. They passed through the front door and entered the foyer.

"Wait," said the O.D. "I'm going to give you your instructions now."

"Yes sir."

"Mister," said the O.D. quietly. "You're going to be interviewed by General Draughton. I don't know what it's about. But it must be serious. They wouldn't call for you at a time like this if it wasn't. Now you're going to wait in the General's reception room until he gets here. He'll be here soon—you heard what the O.G. said. And there are some other cadets in there waiting too. But you're not to talk to them. Understand?"

"Yes sir."

"Captain Morris is going to be in the room to see you don't. I warn you from personal knowledge: he's a West Point graduate. And he hasn't had his breakfast either."

"Who is he, sir?"

"You know him. Captain Morris."

"The gray-haired one?"

"Yes. And he's to keep an eye on you in the reception room. So you sit there and don't say anything. Just wait until the General and Cadet Colonel arrive. Then wait until Corger asks you to go into the private office."

"Yes sir. I will."

"All right, here we go."

They walked on into the north corridor. The O.D. suddenly halted again. "Christ, I forgot to tell you the most important part."

"Yes sir," said Marquales hoarsely.

"Listen, when Corger calls your name here's what you do. It's like when you go before your Company Cadet Committee for not squaring a corner, or for missing a two-minute steel. First put on your cap. Be sure it's level. Then you go in: Corger will be holding the door. Take *ten* steps forward. Then *halt,* do a *right face,* and *salute.* Hold the salute until the General returns it. When he does remove headgear with your left hand. Then, *stand at attention.*"

"Yes sir."

"After you take off your cap say, 'Sir, Cadet Marquales, Robert reporting for examination.'"

"Yes sir."

"Now you're a freshman. That means Corger will brace you when you get in there. But don't wait for him to start. Go in standing up hard. I doubt if Corger will brace you much—since the General is there it'll probably be just a form. But you'd better stand up hard, though."

"Yes sir."

"Now repeat what I've told you."

Marquales said, "I go into the room, take ten steps, do a right face, salute. I wait until the salute is returned. I remove my cap with my other hand; then say, 'Sir, Cadet Marquales, Robert reporting for examination.' I stand at attention. All the time, I brace."

"Good. Be sure to do it right, or they'll blame me."

"Yes sir."

"And remember not to talk in the reception room."

They walked on down the corridor and finally stopped in front of an oak door, on which was the brass plate:

---

# GENERAL A. L. DRAUGHTON, U. S. A.

---

"Sir," said Marquales. "Can you give me an idea what it's about?"

"I don't know," said the O.D.

Marquales whispered, "You don't, sir?"

"You go in now," said the O.D., shaking his head. "Do everything I told you."

Marquales reached for the doorknob. The O.D. gave him a pat on the arm and said, "Keep your chin up." Marquales looked away, a pain in his throat.

"Thanks."

He opened the door. Three gray-uniformed cadets were sitting on a sofa. Marquales turned to close the door and a voice ordered, "Take that place by the window."

Marquales faced around. On a straight chair a few feet away was Captain Morris in U.S. Army uniform.

"I said, Take that place by the window."

"Yes sir."

Marquales looked down the room. Harold Koble, Philip McCarthy, and Albert Wilson were the cadets on the sofa. They stared curiously as he walked by and took the seat at the window. He put his hands in his lap.

"All you men, remain silent," said the Captain. He looked back down at the copy of *Reader's Digest* perched on one khaki knee.

Five minutes later General Draughton entered the room. He nodded briefly at Captain Morris, who had arisen. Cadet Colonel Larrence Corger hurried from behind the General and held open the door to the private office. Marquales saw a black desk, fireplace, gray rug, and globe of the earth. There was a large oil painting of General John J. Pershing on one wall. Then Corger shut the door.

A Negro waiter from the mess hall came ten minutes later with the General's breakfast on a tray. Ten more minutes passed, then Corger put his head out of the private office. "Koble, McCarthy, Wilson," he called.

The three cadets got up from the sofa. Marquales saw General Draughton behind the desk. The General was leaning down to a coffee cup, lips shaped as if about to kiss. Then the door closed and Marquales listened. He heard nothing. For the next half-hour he looked out the window at the parade field.

The door opened and Harold Koble came out, followed by McCarthy. They walked at attention and both were pale. Albert Wilson came last. He wept. His mouth was deformed into a wretched pucker, tears dropped out of his eyes and fell on his uniform. He gave Marquales a blank, watery stare.

Corger appeared in the door and said, "Captain Morris—the General would like to see you, sir."

"Righto," said Captain Morris, dropping *Reader's Digest*.

The door closed after him. Corger, Marquales, Koble, McCarthy, and Wilson all stood in the reception room, waiting, the silence broken by sniffs from Wilson, who continued to weep. Then the Captain strolled out of the private office putting on his brown army cap. "You three junior classmen, come along," he said.

Marquales was left by himself in the reception room. But only for a short time; Corger soon reappeared and said, "You're next."

He began counting, feet tapping across the gray rug in the private office. After ten steps he halted and did right face. He saluted: then his eyes came to focus. There was General Draughton behind the desk four feet away.

"Stand up, you!" said Corger from the door.

For a moment Marquales thought Corger meant the General. Then he realized his error and retracted his chin, throwing back his shoulders, keeping his hand against his eyebrow, spatulate. He heard Corger scuffling toward him, then the moist chant into his ear. Monotonous, "Pull that chin in, drop those shoulders, get a wrinkle in that neck." Marquales braced violently, staring at the General's gray head which was in his line of vision. The old bracing pain cut into his back, chin, neck, and shoulders as Corger chanted on—". . . fracture that liver . . . wrinkles in that jutting snout . . . want highways on that map . . . stand up like a stone . . . pull it back . . . pop . . . stand up . . ."

During this, General Draughton lazily returned Marquales' salute.

"Number two!" snapped Corger. "Down with the flag."

Marquales completed the salute, whipping his right arm down to his side.

"Get off that headgear!"

Marquales took off his cap.

"I want to hear you pop off," said Corger. "Pop off! POP OFF!"

Choked by the violent brace the freshman said, "Sir, Cadet Marquales, Robert reporting for examination."

"At ease," said General Draughton, nodding to Corger.

Marquales sagged and let out his pent breath. With the back of one gloved hand he rubbed perspiration from his eyes. Corger walked from around him and presented a sheet of paper. The General stared at it, holding steel-rimmed spectacles before his eyes. "Sit down, Larrence," he said.

Corger took his place in a straight chair by the window. He was clad in full-dress uniform. He had a senior saber buckled to his side. A silver star was on one sleeve, four black service stripes on the other. His hands were in white gloves made of a silk and cotton mixture; the crimson sash fitted his waist tightly and without wrinkles; his gray trousers were heavily creased; and his shoes had been polished to a creamy black.

Marquales watched him cross his knees and adjust the saber so the sheathed tip rested on the rug. Corger slowly raised his hands back to his large biceps and covered a part of the braid with the gloves. He then gave a cold stare to the freshman, who shifted his eyes to the portrait of General Pershing over the fireplace. The painting was in dark colors on a canvas one yard square.

"Well, sir," said General Draughton hoarsely. He laid down the sheet of paper, sighing. "We'd better get at it. What arrangement does your family make with you for spending money?"

"An allowance," said Marquales.

Corger said, "Mister, say *sir* to the General. What's the trouble with you."

"That's all right, Larrence." The General turned to Marquales. "How much do you get?"

"Sir, two dollars a week."

"About nine dollars per month? Is that all?"

"Yes sir."

"Do you find it difficult to manage on this?"

"Sir, I have to buy pencils, ink, paper, haircuts, and other things," answered Marquales in a whisper.

"So there's very little left for entertainment?"

"Yes sir."

"Have you made any debts at The Academy?"

"Yes sir, I made one."

General Draughton's eyebrows went up.

Marquales said, "I borrowed two dollars from Cadet William Poley, sir. A freshman, sir."

"No," answered the General impatiently. "I mean, considerable debts."

"No sir."

"Have you tried in any manner to get extra money?"

"No sir."

"But you are dissatisfied with your allowance?"

"Yes sir. I think so."

"Very well. Are you familiar with the regulations of The Academy as found in the GRAYBOOK?"

[ 318 ]

"I believe so, sir."

"You *are* familiar, or you are *not*. Answer yes or no."

"Yes sir."

"Then you understand The Academy doesn't sanction mingling on a social basis between freshmen and upperclassmen?"

"Yes sir."

"Are you acquainted with the cadets you saw just then in my reception room?"

"Yes sir."

"Who are they?"

"Sir, Mr. Harold Koble, Mr. Philip McCarthy, Mr. Albert Wilson."

"Are you acquainted with Cadet Peter Layne?"

"Yes sir."

"Cadet Munro?"

"Yes sir."

"Cadet de Paris?"

"Yes sir."

"Cadet Gatt?"

"Yes sir."

"Have you behaved in an improper manner, insofar as your position as a freshman is concerned, with any of these upperclassmen?"

"No sir."

"Have any of them behaved improperly toward you?"

"No sir."

"Does The Academy endorse drunkenness?"

"No sir."

"Gambling?"

"No sir."

"Answer in a *firm,* audible voice."

"Yes sir."

"The Academy approves of gambling?"

"No sir."

"I believe I understood you to say 'Yes sir.'"

"I meant I'd speak louder, sir. The Academy is against gambling."

"You're correct. Does The Academy approve of secret clubs?"

[ 319 ]

"No sir."

"Now," said the General. "Let's see how well we understand one another. Have you recently drunk alcoholic beverages?"

"Beer, sir."

"I didn't ask you what you drank. I asked you if you drank."

"Yes sir."

"Have you gambled recently?"

"Yes sir."

"Have you attended the meeting of a secret club?"

"Yes sir."

"Name your gambling partners."

Marquales hesitated. General Draughton said, "I warn you. Don't try to deceive me."

"Sir, it's just I don't want to be an informer," said Marquales, stuttering.

The General's lower lip came down and twisted to one side. He stared contemptuously, waiting.

Marquales said, "Mr. Wilson, Mr. de Paris. And there was Mr. Gatt."

"The element . . . of the tattletale, as you express it, is not connected in any way with this examination. I advise you not to make any more flippant remarks."

"Yes sir."

"Do you understand me?"

"Yes sir."

"Personally, I loathe an informer."

"Yes sir."

"I had one sent to prison years ago in the Philippines.

"Yes sir."

"The informer gives *unsolicited* information for reasons of spite or desire for financial gain."

"Yes sir. I see."

The General stretched his long arms and began a yawn, which he repressed; for an instant this gave him an odd, bleary look. "Now," he said. "When did this gambling take place?"

"Last Friday a week ago, sir."

"Where?"

"At a Port George restaurant. The club meeting place."

"What's the name of this organization?"

"I'm not sure, sir. It's the 'Hound' something or other. I don't remember exactly because I was there just a little while."

"Would it be a name like 'The Hare from the Hound?'"

"I think that was it, sir."

Corger spoke up. "It was the Hair-of-the-Hound, General. I believe the freshman knows it. This type of vulgar name sticks in the mind."

"Why?" said the General.

"I beg pardon, sir," said Corger.

"Why do you say the name sticks in the mind?"

"You're not familiar with the etymology of the expression, sir? I believe it comes from an old Irish saying. The drunkard, upon awakening with an alcoholic hangover, treats his illness by drinking more alcohol. This he calls taking 'the hair of the hound that bit me.'"

The General said, "Then it's H-A-I-R and not H-A-R-E?"

"Yes sir," said Corger, directing a scornful glance at Marquales.

"Sir," said the freshman. "I forgot the name. It was careless of me. But the restaurant was called *Neddie's*."

"No matter," said the General, rustling at some papers on the desk. "It's not important. Are you a member of this club, Cadet Marquales?"

"No sir."

"Are any other freshmen members?"

"No sir. They don't let freshmen in."

The General paused. "You were invited to attend the meeting?"

"Yes sir."

"Who invited you?"

"Mr. Layne and Mr. Munro, sir."

"Splendid. Why?"

"I was working on the magazine, sir."

"What?"

"*Port Arms*, sir."

[ 321 ]

"I am aware of the name of the magazine."

"Sir, I was working there. Mr. Layne happened to mention the club then he asked me to come. I was hesitant, but Mr. Munro more or less insisted, sir."

The General said, "Cadet Marquales, your duties with the magazine could not have prompted an undue advance from these two seniors. It follows that the fault for this invitation must lie with either yourself or them."

"Yes sir."

"Well?"

"How do you mean, sir?"

"Answer the question."

"Sir, I'm not sure what you want me to say."

Corger said, "Answer the General's question."

"Never mind, Larrence!" barked General Draughton. "I'll conduct this inquiry."

Corger flushed.

"Now," said the General. "If you didn't understand my question I'll repeat it. I merely want to know with whom the fault lies for your mingling with upperclassmen at this club. Was it your fault or that of Cadet Layne and Munro?"

Marquales said, "It must have been my fault, sir. If I'd behaved right, they wouldn't have thought to ask me."

"Thank you," said the General. "Now I'll sum up what we've learned from you. First you say you have not ingratiated yourself with any upperclassmen. You told me that when you first entered this office. Yet you were invited to the hideaway of an upperclassman group; you mingled freely with them there, drinking and gambling with them. You're aware the GRAYBOOK forbids such a club as this Hair-of-a-Hound, yet you attended. You know not to drink and you drank. You know not to gamble and you gambled. Is it true you not only gambled but also cheated?"

"Sir?" said Marquales.

"I am waiting."

The freshman swallowed as if very surprised by the question. Then he said in a small, humiliated voice, "I did cheat, sir."

"Then you also lied to me. A moment ago you told me you haven't sought to increase your income by any means at The Academy."

"Sir, I meant that this was—"

"You are guilty of five offenses by your own testimony. These are: gambling; attending the meeting of an illegal alcohol club; ingratiating yourself with upperclassmen; cheating; and lying. What penalty goes with each of these?"

"General Draughton I didn't lie to you."

"What penalty goes with each of these offenses?"

"A dishonorable discharge, sir."

"You're correct."

"I was drawn into the game, sir. I didn't plan to increase my income or anything like that."

"In what way were you forced into this game? At the point of a loaded revolver?"

"No sir. I was merely a freshman and I wasn't in a position to refuse to play when asked to do so by upperclassmen, sir."

"If upperclassmen ordered you to thrash an old woman, what would you do."

"Sir, the two things aren't equal."

"Are you contradicting me?"

"No sir. All I mean is they asked me to play."

"Did they force you?"

"No sir."

"Cadet Marquales, I can promise this attitude is not doing much for you. Frankly, each of your five offenses demands an immediate discharge from this school. I thought of being more liberal. However, such petty quibbles make me lose my patience. Are you interested in continuing your career at The Academy?"

"Yes sir."

The General sighed and shook his head. "I assume someone must have had a bad influence on you. Didn't you come to Port George with your mother last July and talk to me about enrolling?"

"Yes sir."

"I remember the lady. What would she say if she saw you now?"

"She'd feel bad, sir."

"I have no doubt. What will your mother say if you come home with a dishonorable discharge?"

"I know she'd be unhappy, sir."

"And what about your father?"

"He'd be even worse, sir," said Marquales in a low voice. "He was in the last war."

"He was?" said the General casually. "An officer?"

"Yes sir," said Marquales. "A major. He rose from the ranks."

"Very swift promotion," said the General, musingly.

"He was injured by poison gas," said Marquales.

The General nodded.

Marquales smiled. "He still likes to be called, 'Major Marquales.' Dad wanted me to go to West Point as my mother mentioned to you this summer. But I thought The Academy would be as good."

The freshman wondered what his father would say if he should hear these remarks. General Draughton coughed and stared curiously over the desk. "What was your father's unit?"

"The Rainbow Division!" snapped Marquales unwaveringly.

"Well . . ." General Draughton coughed again. "I daresay no institution in the nation has the facilities and personnel of the Point; everything is available there, the training procedure is carried out with perfection, no narrow-minded people interfere. In short, you are mistaken when you call The Academy the equal of the Point! But as a second choice, you could have done worse. You never thought of Annapolis?"

"No sir. Not at all."

"Why not?"

"I don't like water, sir."

The General threw back his head and laughed loudly. Then he said in a dignified voice—"Annapolis is a splendid institution. I won't say a word against it for those who like that kind of thing. But

[ 324 ]

no matter. We are far off the subject. Let me ask you this—what will your father say when he realizes how you've bungled here?"

Marquales gave a sickish smile. "Sir, if I was home he'd probably . . . be so angry . . ."

"That he'd give you a sound thrashing?"

"Yes sir."

"Perhaps that's just what you need?"

Marquales didn't reply; he bowed his head as if slightly angry and greatly humiliated.

"All right," said the General, leaning forward. "I want you to tell me everything pertinent about this gambling affair. If possible I'll be lenient with you—your inexperience should be taken into consideration. But I want the complete facts. I want to know how the gambling started, who arranged the cheating. I want to know everything that's happened consequently, and who has been involved."

"I'll tell you all I can, sir," said Marquales earnestly. "The first I heard about the gambling was at dinner that night. This was the first I knew about it. Mr. de Paris told Mr. Wilson to go reserve the card table and said I was to play with them. The first I knew about the cheating was when he slipped me extra cards under the table."

"All right," said the General. "Then this cheating was definitely done through you with Cadet de Paris' guidance?"

"Yes sir." Marquales hesitated. "Mr. de Paris told me earlier in the evening I should follow his lead and we'd ruin Mr. Gatt. I didn't know what he meant, but as soon as he slipped me the cards from his extra deck I understood. I did what he wanted."

"You used those extra cards to cheat?"

"Yes sir. I did."

The General shook his head. "Go on."

"Sir, during the game I won ninety dollars. Then we went on back to barracks. The next day Mr. de Paris split the money three ways. Me and Mr. Wilson and himself. Then nothing happened until yesterday, sir. I was in the room when Mr. Gatt came by and told me he wanted his money returned. He didn't say it was because the game was unfair; he said it was because his grandmother was sick and

[ 325 ]

couldn't pay her doctor's bills. He told me his father didn't like the grandmother and he had to have the money because he wanted to help her. But I knew she was rich and that Mr. Gatt's father was actually dead years ago. I told him, then he said he wasn't going to argue and the reason he wanted the money was because he was a senior and I was a freshman.

"I couldn't give the money back because I only had a third of it. But I gave him thirty dollars and asked him to go with me to the Infirmary to see Mr. de Paris about the other sixty. I told him I'd loaned it to Mr. de Paris. He said Mr. de Paris was rich and wanted to know why I'd ever loaned the money to him in the first place. So I told him the reason was Mr. de Paris' brother died and his family had lost their money. He seemed to believe me—maybe because the story was so unbelievable he couldn't imagine anybody being such a bad liar as to tell it. Then we went over to the Infirmary."

Marquales paused, then continued: "Sir I made it clear to Mr. de Paris what was going on. He told Mr. Gatt it was the wrong thing to make someone return the winnings of gambling. He asked Mr. Gatt if any cadet in school would approve of taking dishonorable advantage of a freshman. Then Mr. Gatt said Albert Wilson had given him the idea in the first place.

"Mr. de Paris became very angry at Mr. Wilson. He told me later it was all Mr. Wilson's fault and that if Wilson hadn't lost his nerve Mr. Gatt wouldn't have come and asked for the money. So he told Mr. Gatt how he'd heard Mr. Wilson say a dirty thing about him. He explained that my story about his brother being dead was a practical joke Mr. Wilson had played. He said that was his reason for talking about Mr. Wilson behind his back. Then he told Mr. Gatt what Mr. Wilson was supposed to have said.

"Sir, Mr. Gatt was put into a great rage by this. He was so angry he wanted to go right out and look for Mr. Wilson. Then during all the excitement Mr. de Paris endorsed him a check for a hundred dollars and made him return the money he'd gotten from me, plus ten dollars to make up the difference. But the check wasn't endorsed the right way. Mr. de Paris meant for it not to be any good."

[ 326 ]

"Yes?" said General Draughton. "What were Cadet de Paris' intentions concerning this check?"

"He meant to report it stolen, sir."

"What was the idea behind that?"

"He wanted Mr. Gatt expelled, sir."

"I see. What was the remark Cadet de Paris quoted Cadet Wilson as having said?"

"Sir, it was a filthy comment about Mr. Gatt and his grandmother."

"I see. But until Cadet de Paris did this, Cadet Gatt and Wilson were on friendly terms?"

"Yes, sir."

There was a long pause, then the General asked, "That concludes what you have to say?"

"Yes sir."

There was another pause. General Draughton sighed. "I'm afraid it'll be necessary to expel you."

Marquales looked him in the eye. "I deserve it, sir."

"I'd hoped your testimony might clear you of a few offenses. But you're even more deeply involved."

"Yes, sir," said Marquales.

The General glanced at Corger. "How do you feel, Larrence? Do you think it would be sufficient to give this man a severe punishment order?"

"No, General," said Corger. "In my opinion, he must be expelled. A special order would be out of place."

"Yes, it would," said the General. "Larrence, will you step down to Evers' office and bring Cadet de Paris here."

"Yes sir," said Corger. He walked out of the room.

The General said, "Cadet Marquales I want you present at this interview. However, do not inadvertently give any information to Cadet de Paris."

"Yes sir."

"Keep a blank expression, if you understand me."

"Yes sir."

"Go take the place by the window."

Marquales crossed the room and sat where Corger had been.

A few moments later Corger and De Paris entered the room. Jocko glanced at Marquales, then stood erect before the General. He saluted, whipped off his cap, and said coolly, "Sir, Cadet Jacques de Paris reporting for examination."

# 27

"At ease," said the General, his blue eyes glittering.

Jocko relaxed and folded his arms.

"Cadet de Paris, I believe you can help us this morning. We face several problems which I've been attempting to solve by aid of the freshman you see across the room. I regret to say his memory seems weak. I hope yours is better. I dislike a careless memory."

"Yes, sir," said De Paris, nodding.

"Cadet Marquales has insisted on answering my questions by inquiring why I asked them."

Jocko pursed his lips. "I won't do that, sir," he murmured.

"I hope not," said the General. "Do you remember our talk a week ago?"

"Yes sir. I've had several nightmares about it."

"I'm afraid this isn't a chat. Leave out extraneous details; we're not concerned with your dream life, but with facts. Understand me?"

"Fully, sir."

The General asked, "What did I tell you a week ago?"

"You said my attitude was bad. You told me I was on a week's probation and if my manner didn't change I'd be sent home."

"I haven't made up my mind about you," said General Draughton. "But I will, soon. Are you acquainted with the regulations of The Academy?"

"Of course, sir."

"We'll find out if you are. Does The Academy approve camaraderie between upperclassmen and recruits?"

"No sir."

"Have you failed in this respect?"

"No sir."

"You know the cadet sitting by the window?"

"Yes sir."

"How well?"

"He's in my platoon, sir."

"Do you know him better than other freshmen in your platoon?"

"Yes sir. He rooms down the gallery from me."

"Can you offer an opinion on his character?"

"I don't think so, sir."

"If I asked you if he were truthful what would you say?"

"I couldn't answer that question, sir."

"Very well," snapped the General. "Have you drunk recently?"

"Yes sir. I have."

"And did you gamble?"

"Yes sir."

"When?"

"About eight days ago, sir."

"Where?"

"A restaurant in Port George, sir."

"What were the circumstances?"

"I was at the meeting of an unregistered cadet club, sir."

"Give me the regulations concerning such clubs."

"If they're discovered, each member is expelled, sir."

"Are you a member of this club?"

"Yes sir."

"With whom did you gamble?"

"Albert Wilson, Roger Gatt, and Robert Marquales, sir."

"But you haven't been familiar with this freshman?"

"I fear I told you an unintentional lie about that, sir."

"Yes you've broken many regulations. Who won at the gambling?"

"Marquales won ninety dollars from Gatt, sir."

"No one else took in any profits?"

"No sir. Wilson and I broke even."

"You've lied once. How do I know you're not lying again?"

"General Draughton, when I answered your original question I didn't realize I'd been guilty of familiarity toward a freshman. He was at the table that night, but I paid no attention to him and it was not my wish he come in the game."

"I see. And you say neither you nor Cadet Wilson profited."

"It was a wasted evening for us, sir."

"Who originated the idea of gambling?"

"Wilson, sir."

"Who invited the freshman to attend the club meeting?"

"Sir, it was either Pete Layne or Tom Munro."

"What beverage were you drinking that night?"

"Ale, sir."

"What were the others drinking?"

"Ale, beer, whiskey, gin, and so on, sir."

"Were there women present?"

"No sir, it was stag."

"You've had meetings with women present?"

"Yes sir. There were three or four co-ed meetings."

"Co-ed? College girls?"

"Whores, sir."

"I see," said General Draughton.

"Yes sir," murmured De Paris.

The General said, "Cadet Marquales won ninety dollars."

"Yes sir."

"Didn't Cadet Gatt resent losing such a large sum?"

"Not that night, sir. Afterwards, he certainly did."

"Tell me what you know about it," said General Draughton. He sat back in his chair and mopped at his forehead with a handkerchief. "Take all the time you need to give a full picture."

De Paris shifted his position on the rug, then said coolly, "It will only take a short time, sir. The game was on Friday. I woke up feeling ill Saturday; you remember I had a talk with you that morning. Sunday I collapsed and was sent to the school hospital by the Officer of the Guard. On Wednesday I was visited at the Infirmary by Albert Wilson. He said Roger Gatt had been talking to him about the game; Gatt did resent having lost so much money. I didn't pay any attention, assuming it was just a natural complaint. But Friday afternoon, yesterday, Gatt went to the freshman and asked for the money returned. This put Marquales in trouble because he'd sent his winnings home. He came to me for temporary help and I advanced him the amount in order to save him from a beating. That was yesterday. This morning I was suddenly called over here."

[ 331 ]

General Draughton was still mopping his face. "I asked for details," he said. "Not a summary."

"I know, sir," answered De Paris casually. "But I thought I should sum up the whole thing for the sake of clarity. General Draughton, I realize something serious must have happened. I don't know what —but I want to clear it up. As a matter of fact you'll be very surprised when you hear what I have to say about my own connections with this trouble. And I say that not even aware of exactly what this is about. I already know what I should tell you. Actually, it has been arranged in my mind since yesterday afternoon, unless I am greatly mistaken about the meaning of this interview."

General Draughton put his handkerchief down into the pocket next to the rows of multi-colored ribbons. He folded his arms and sat, listening.

Jocko de Paris' voice rolled on smoothly. "Sir, my behavior has been bad this fall, and I realize that I now will be expelled because of it. That much is certain; but before I leave The Academy I would like to set my record in order, if I may. I don't want to leave incorrect ideas behind me. Although I've done enough to be expelled on four or five different counts there are a few decent things I've done, and I believe they should be mentioned.

"As ironic as it may sound, new vistas have appeared before me since my talk with you last week. Smile if you like, sir. But please remember the gambling came before my conversation with you. I don't mean to say I enjoyed that conversation. Sir, it was extremely humiliating. No man wants such an experience. If he says he does then he is a hypocrite. But I realize you were right—my behavior this fall has been extremely bad. And this poker game—which took place the night before my talk with you—was the climax to eight weeks of it. I wish you'd spoken to me twenty-four hours earlier. Then I wouldn't be standing here now."

"Please come to the point," said General Draughton hoarsely. "These remarks are not pertinent."

"Sir I hope you will be generous enough to allow me to contradict you. I firmly believe what I've just said to be most pertinent. I insist you understand my position. I ask that you see what my attitude is. It's essential you see my point of view has undergone a change."

"This lecture about your moral health is irrelevant," said the General wearily. "I'm not interested."

"That hurt," said De Paris, looking at the floor. "I'll go ahead and give you the details you asked me for, sir."

They waited. Corger by the door, standing with folded arms; the General behind his desk; Marquales perched on the chair by the window. Finally De Paris looked up and spoke in a matter-of-fact voice:

"Gatt came by the freshman's room yesterday afternoon and asked for the money. At first he said it was because his grandmother was ill and penniless. Marquales recognized this story as a lie. Then Gatt took the position it was unfair for a freshman to win money from an upperclassman. Marquales was frightened and wanted to turn over the money. However he couldn't because he'd sent it home for safekeeping. Gatt insisted. Then the freshman decided to come to the Infirmary and ask me to loan him the ninety dollars for a few days— I suppose because he was aware I have money."

The General nodded his head in comprehension. His eyes were half shut.

De Paris said, "However that might or might not be what happened. I'm inclined to believe it because it's what the freshman told me. I don't know what character this freshman has. I did hear him tell a lie once, and I'll talk about that later—but he was very excited when he did it so perhaps it shouldn't be held against him."

De Paris hesitated. He shifted his feet on the rug and stretched his shoulders, hunching them up for a moment. Then he said:

"Now to start at the real beginning, sir. The first I knew of Gatt's desire for a refund was when he and Marquales walked into my room at the Infirmary. I was taking a nap when they arrived; I woke up to see the freshman standing over my cot with a frightened look on his face. He said, 'We've come to visit you.' Then I noticed Gatt lingering in the doorway. It certainly didn't look like a social call, and I suspected the truth at once. Marquales soon blurted it out confirming my suspicion, telling me he'd sent home the ninety dollars, begging me to loan him the sum so he could return it to Mr. Gatt.

"Sir the proposition struck me as ridiculous. I thought it unsporting of Gatt to behave that way and I also thought it strange he was in such a hurry to get his hands on the money. Later I found out what the rush was about. But that isn't important, so I won't mention it. I went over—"

"I want all the facts," interrupted General Draughton.

"But sir it isn't important," said De Paris. "It doesn't have any place in the story."

"I'll be the judge of that."

"All right, sir. I hate to reveal this, but Gatt later mentioned he had a date with a woman known as Katie. He said the date was going to cost him a lot of hard cash."

The General took up a pencil from the desk. "What's this woman's full name?"

"I don't know, sir," said De Paris. "I've only heard the boys speak of her casually. She's supposed to be a hire-by-the-hour private secretary for one of the 'hotels.' This Katie is one of the numerous people on the establishment's payroll. She's not exactly a secretary."

"I see," said the General. "What's the name of this place?"

"Hotel Delmore."

"A regular hotel?"

"No sir. It just fakes at being one."

"What's the address?"

"Fifty-four Vanderbilt Square."

General Draughton scribbled on a pad then looked up, his face bland.

De Paris said, "Well sir, I told Mr. Gatt how I felt about what he was doing."

"Go on."

"What happened was a shock. I'd always liked Roger Gatt, but he showed an awful temper when he heard me disagree. He stuttered, trembled—for a moment I thought he meant to jump at me, sick in bed as I was.

[ 334 ]

"All I'd done was attempt to reason with him. I pointed out that although gambling is an un-honorable occupation it should be done with honor if done at all. I tried to say it in a tactful way, but he was furious. So then I said, 'Roger, what would your fellow cadets think of this?' I asked him if there was a single man in school who'd approve of what he was doing.

"He said yes. I told him I didn't believe it. So then he came out with the surprising fact that Albert Wilson had originally put the idea in his head. He told us Wilson said the freshman should give back the money.

"You see, Wilson really hates Gatt. But he's afraid of him therefore he tries his best to court favor. Undoubtedly that's what he was doing when he advised the money be taken away from the freshman. He knew Gatt secretly wanted to do it and must have thought he could get on his good side by telling him to go ahead. During the poker game I remember he flattered Gatt constantly, then as soon as Roger's back was turned he cursed him. Nothing really bad, however. The usual sort of hedging around.

"But now to get back to yesterday afternoon. What Gatt told us about Wilson had a great effect on the freshman. I saw him turn pale, and then he asked Gatt was he sure Wilson said that. Gatt told the freshman to shut up, and of course Wilson said it. Then Marquales told *Gatt* something. He told him that Albert Wilson had cursed him. However, Gatt wouldn't believe it, maintaining Wilson was his buddy. And at that point the freshman told an awful lie. In venom words he quoted Wilson as saying during the poker game that Gatt had once thrown down his own grandmother . . . and raped her carnally.

"Gatt was amazed. He didn't seem to understand what was said. The freshman told him again, this time using even more vulgar language. General Draughton, I hope you won't mind my saying it, but I'll quote the remark exactly, in order to tell the complete truth. What he said was this: 'Mr. Gatt, your true and faithful friend Wilson told me you once *fucked* your grandmother.'

"Well, sir, Roger Gatt reacted like a madman. He jumped to his feet, saliva came dripping out of his mouth. He stood there paralyzed, spit hanging on his chin, eyes popping out of his head. I was astonished at the sight—and since then I've seriously wondered whether Roger Gatt is normal mentally. But the freshman wasn't satisfied to let it go at that. He went on, inventing more things Wilson was supposed to have said, even worse things.

"Of course Marquales was angry at Albert—yet his hatred seemed far out of proportion to the facts. It was almost as if he had some unknown reason for wanting to get revenge. I said I once heard that freshman tell a lie, and this was the time I had in mind. But he was terribly upset and I'm sure he didn't even know what he was doing. This ought to be considered in his favor, and I would like to add that I've never heard him lie or do anything wrong on any other occasion than this.

"But it backfired on him. Gatt was so torn up by his remarks he grabbed him by the throat and began to shout for the ninety dollars. Marquales went limp and Gatt had to hold him up to keep him from the floor. Then I got out of bed and crossed the room in my pajamas. I laid a hand on Gatt's arm and said, 'Roger I'll give you the money. But you'll have to promise me something.'

"He let go the freshman and looked at me. I said, 'Pledge me your word of honor not to bother Wilson. Then I'll give you the money. The freshman can pay me back later.'

"He said, 'No. I'm going to get Wilson.'

"I told him in that case I wouldn't give him the money. He argued briefly, then pledged me his word of honor not to do anything to Albert.

"I made one more effort to reason with him. I asked him for the last time did he think it fair to force a man to return honest winnings.

"He stared at the freshman and then said a strange thing. He told me Marquales *cheated* in the poker game.

"I saw it was hopeless. But I told him there was no cheating in the game because if the freshman cheated I'd have seen him. Gatt mumbled in reply that the freshman was smarter than any of us thought. So I gave up the struggle and endorsed a check to him for one hundred dollars. He gave me ten in change, and he and the freshman left my room."

De Paris cleared his throat, then said quietly, "Sir, that's all I can answer as far as your questions are concerned. However there's some evidence about myself that I have to give. It's about the check I endorsed to Gatt. It's also about the conclusion I came to yesterday afternoon. I frankly believe you should know this if my position is to be understood."

General Draughton was sitting forward in his chair, listening intently. He stirred as if waking up, then said in a hoarse voice, "Time's getting short."

"Yes sir," replied De Paris.

"However, I want to hear everything you have to say."

"Thank you, sir," answered De Paris, taking out a handerchief. He blew carefully into it then announced:

"General Draughton, I have one motive for telling you this. If I leave without saying more my position won't be clear. I believe I owe it to The Academy to say this. It might seem out of place at first but later on you'll see the connection, I think. There's something I later want to tell you about the check I gave Gatt. But first this other thing, which is just as vital.

"Sir, my expulsion will be a blow to my father. But at the risk of embarrassing you I'd like to say my father's friendship for The Academy will grow stronger, not weaker, as a result of this. He rose from nothing to become one of the nation's most influential men— and such an individual as that will see the truth. He'll know I deserve just what I'm getting."

General Draughton frowned, rat-tat-tatting his fingers on the desk.

De Paris went on coolly, "I think you might be interested to know I had a letter from Dad the other day. He was telling me about his quarrel with Mr. Patrick Webster. It seems a couple of weeks ago Mr. Webster ran an editorial in his Chicago paper against military academies. Before the threat of war, he favored them. Now that the country's need is greater than ever he changes his mind. His editorial hints they should close up West Point and suspend the R.O.T.C. This

Webster is a renegade! He acts like the personal friend of Adolf Hitler. I have a clipping of his editorial over in barracks if you'd like to see it, sir."

"I read it when it appeared," said General Draughton. "All this strikes me as very irrelevant."

De Paris smiled. "Sir, it's just that I'm long winded. I was telling you how my father quarreled with Webster—the real argument is one involving the principles of democracy and freedom. I've always said Webster runs a great newspaper, but his ideas are crazy. Military academies don't cause wars, they just win them."

"Will you come to the point?" asked General Draughton.

"I was telling you about my father's argument with Webster. It seems Dad went to him and asked if he wouldn't get his weight behind something—The Academy needs a new hospital which Dad's been trying to fix up; I don't know whether he's mentioned it to you or not. At any rate Webster refused, then the *next* day printed that disgusting editorial. All I wanted to say, sir, was that my father wrote me in his last letter he thinks he can take care of the hospital even without Webster and the other renegades, who used to co-operate but are now isolationist cowards."

"*Just what* are you trying to say to me?" asked General Draughton.

De Paris answered in a loud voice, "Sir I thought you'd be interested to hear me tell you that when I get to Chicago I'm going to talk to my father and ask him to increase his efforts for The Academy! Damn it, I want you to know how I feel! I realize I deserve what I'm getting and I won't let you think taking disciplinary action against me is going to hurt The Academy!"

"Calm yourself," said the General.

"I wanted you to know the news about the hospital," said De Paris passionately. "I wanted you to know my own feeling about it. That's all I'm trying to say! If it strikes you as out of place, I'm sorry."

"You are gossiping," said the General. "You're not giving me news. You're gossiping about something none of your business in front of these other cadets. Now, since you've dragged forth the financial problems of The Academy I'd like to say that sufficient

[ 338 ]

money for the new Infirmary is in our treasury. I'm not sure it will be used for that purpose, but it is there! Never before in the history of this institution have funds been so ample. City, state, and national governments have been extraordinarily helpful. Various individuals have offered their services in the most generous manner. Of course, your father, as is well known, has been one of these. In the past, he has done much. But as I told you last week this has nothing whatsoever to do with your career at The Academy."

"I agree, sir," said De Paris, crestfallen. "What I've just told you is maybe unnecessary. But I wanted you to know how I felt about it. Sir, I didn't mean to gossip about the affairs of The Academy—that was a mistake."

"It surely was," said the General.

"And I shouldn't have brought my father into it. I meant well, but I can see it doesn't have any actual connection. I'm very sorry, sir."

"We'll drop it," said General Draughton. "Didn't you have something more to say in your defense?"

De Paris replied with a gloomy smile, "Not in my defense, sir."

"How do you mean?"

"I'm not trying to defend myself," said Jocko quietly. "Under the circumstances that is impossible."

The General said, "I'm ready to hear anything you have to say that will throw light on your recent actions."

"Well sir, I do want to explain about the check."

"What check are you talking about?"

"The one I gave to Gatt, sir."

"What about it?"

"It was uncashable, sir."

"It was?"

"Yes sir. I endorsed it in six-year-old handwriting and spelled my name wrong."

"Why did you do that?"

"Because I feared my own weakness."

"What do you mean?" asked the General, leaning back in his chair.

[ 339 ]

"Sir, yesterday afternoon I realized the whole thing had gotten into such a mess that you should know about it. But I was afraid I'd never have the nerve to come and tell you. I wrote out the check wrong to have it hanging over my head. I wanted to be forced to tell you the complete truth. And I knew the bad check would cause me a great deal of trouble with Roger Gatt; I knew he'd be infuriated and I knew to save myself from him I'd need your protection. Fearing my own weakness, I endorsed that check wrong so I'd have to tell the truth.

"Sir it would have been hard for me to come in here today and tell you I've gambled, drank, been a member of an illegal club, and associated with a recruit. But because of our talk last week I realized the only thing to do was bring this mess into the open. I knew I was coming here this morning to find out your decision on my error last week when I acted like such a fool about not cleaning up my room for inspection. I meant to tell you the whole story, with the threat of this bad check hanging over my head to make me do it. An accident—whatever it was that happened last night—has prevented me from doing this as I wished, of my own free will. Instead, I've been summoned here and examined in a way that makes it look like my remarks were forced out of me. But sir, that check is my evidence of good intention.

"General Draughton, as I've stood here and talked to you this morning, the irony of my situation has been enough to make me wring my hands with frustration. You'll undoubtedly agree that if I'd come here and told you this as I planned the whole thing would be different. But whatever it was that happened last night put me in the position this morning of being the criminal at the dock—rather than the honest man speaking of his own free will."

De Paris stopped, swallowed, and looked down at the floor. Finally he raised his eyes. They contained tears. He went on in a trembling, nearly inaudible voice: "Sir I said I realize the situation. There's no hope of my getting another chance. I've done so many bad things I'm certain to be sent home. But sir despite all the facts I nevertheless stand here hoping you'll consider the idea of granting me a conditional pardon—in the light of what I've just told you. Give me any special punishment. Restrict me to campus. Make me walk punishment tours for the rest of the year. But, General Draughton, I ask you please don't ruin my life by expelling me."

There was a long silence. Then the General replied, "It certainly took you a long time to get that said. Of course I'm willing to think more about your case. I never make up my mind until I learn everything."

De Paris said, "Thank you, sir."

"However this check that you seem to think so important . . . it was successfully cashed despite what you said."

De Paris looked up quickly. "Sir I'll be glad to have the bank send it to you and you can see for yourself how I endorsed it. I'm amazed anyone would cash it."

"It has no importance," said the General. "Now that you've finished what you have to say, I'll point out that your facts clash violently with those given by Cadet Marquales."

De Paris looked bewildered.

General Draughton said to Marquales, "Did Cadet de Paris cheat in this game of poker?"

"Yes sir," murmured the freshman.

"I do not understand, sir," said Jocko.

The General turned to Corger. "What did Cadet Wilson tell us this morning?"

Corger answered, "Sir, Wilson testified the gambling was dishonest and that De Paris did the cheating."

Jocko said quietly, "This doesn't make sense, General Draughton."

"Why not?"

"I'm surprised you believe I'd cheat at a game of cards, sir. I receive an allowance from my father of one hundred dollars a month. This doesn't represent my total income—I get many surprise checks and at any time I need extra money I just drop my father a post card. I have five thousand dollars in a Chicago bank under my own name. Why would I be such a fool as to cheat in a card game? The idea doesn't make sense and after all I've said it's humiliating to hear such a thing."

"Cadet de Paris," said the General. "This has gone on long enough. I'm sure you've said all you can in your own defense. I believe at this point we should conclude our interview."

"Very well sir," said De Paris. He squared his shoulders and looked firmly at the General. "Have you come to a decision, sir?"

"Yes. I'm expelling you."

"I was afraid you would, sir. I knew there wasn't much chance for me." Tears rolled out of Jocko's eyes down his face. In a broken voice he inquired, "Sir, do you want me to go get my things from barracks? I mean, to get them packed?"

"You leave on the next train out of Port George," replied the General. "Your belongings will be sent after you."

De Paris stared from narrowed eyes at General Draughton, then slowly put his hands on his hips and said, "Do you really mean to expel me?"

"I told you my decision," said the General.

"And I demand an explanation," said De Paris, his face white.

The General smiled. "On what grounds?"

"Isn't it my word against two filthy liars—Wilson and the putrid freshman there?"

General Draughton said, "My boy, your cleverness was insufficient to extricate you. Five cadets provided the details of this case and their evidence agrees conclusively. You, more than anyone else, have been troublemaker. Your remarks this morning consist of a flow of vicious lies. I have been aware at each point that you left the truth. Now, are you so far gone you lack the courage to take your punishment like a man? Or do we get more tears?"

De Paris gave a harsh laugh and wiped one glove across his face. "I want to make a statement," he said.

"Speak up, then."

"Okay, I will," said De Paris, his mouth twisted. "I'll ask you some questions and give you some answers. Look, General, do you think I don't know why you bawled me out last week? Do you think

[ 342 ]

I don't know why you're expelling me out of here and why you led me along in this thing like a goat? Just for spite you've trumped this thing up for your own dirty reasons. You think my father isn't going to help you any more—and he wasn't, until I asked him. That's what you don't know, and I tried like hell to tell you. My father really intends to help, despite Paddy Webster. Dad doesn't have to do everything he says. Now I don't really care a great deal about being expelled—I'll just go ahead and join the Air Corps like I've been wanting. But my father will be so angry about this that all you'll ever get out of him in the future will be a loud fart in your face."

General Draughton listened to De Paris with an expression of polite interest. Then he arose and said, "All through with that statement?"

"No!" said De Paris. "You're the one that's all through."

"My boy," said the General. "There's something I feel you ought to know. Perhaps it'll clear up your confusion and make you regret these coarse, foolish words, if such a thing is possible. Larrence, I want you and Cadet Marquales to hear this also, since you've had the misfortune to have just witnessed that exhibition.

"Cadet de Paris. I spoke to your father yesterday on the long-distance telephone from Chicago. He mentioned to me his continuing desire to assist The Academy. But I gathered from his attitude he wanted me to repay him by giving his son special privilege. It seems he had a letter from you, Cadet de Paris, in which you complained of what I said to you last week. So your father calls and suggests a bribe. I will not accept a bribe. I'm too old to start such a thing. And I would like to add that if Mr. Roy de Paris wishes to withdraw his support—The Academy will be better off without him."

"You're lying!" shouted Jocko furiously. "Dad's on a hunting trip in Canada!"

"Larrence," said the General casually. "I want you to put this hysterical fool on the next train out of Port George."

"Yes sir!" snapped Corger.

"Now remove him from this office, Larrence."

[ 343 ]

"Why don't *you* try it?" yelled De Paris. He curled his lip in a sneer of contempt. "Look at him shake—the old bastard's yellow!"

Corger walked forward and said, "Let's go, you."

Jocko sprang into a crouch, his fists up. "Corger, get away!" he shouted. "I'll kick the shit out of you!"

"Larrence," called the General. "Punch him."

Corger came on, blank faced. He did a skip on the rug, and his arm flew out, striking De Paris a blow in the face. Jocko fell against the General's desk and sprawled unconscious, bleeding from the mouth and nose.

"All right, get him out of here," said General Draughton hoarsely.

Corger pulled De Paris to his feet and dragged him across the room. Jocko's eyes were rolled upward, his mouth open.

The General turned to Marquales. "Go to your barracks."

"Yes sir," said the freshman.

"Don't speak about this."

"No sir."

Marquales paused in the doorway and saw General Draughton sit down heavily in the swivel chair. The freshman walked on through the empty reception room to the north corridor. A few feet away, Larrence Corger was pushing Jocko's face into a water fount, apparently trying to bring him to his senses. Marquales tiptoed away in the other direction.

# 28

Marquales waited until nearly time for the special formation before opening the envelope. He then sliced open its back and took out three crisp ten-dollar bills. There was also the message:

Dear Judas:

I hope we meet again some day. It would be nice to see you, really. In the meantime I hope your conscience doesn't torture you about what you did. There are worse things than cowardly selling out the best man you ever knew. I'm enclosing your reward.

sincerely,
JOCKO DE PARIS

Marquales smiled and tore up the note. Two weeks later he bought a portable radio with the money.

The three battalions slowly assembled in the Armory. General Draughton waited on the rostrum, a weary, grim look on his face. He was flanked by Colonel Evers and Cadet Captain-Adjutant Starkson.

An absolute hush came upon the regiment as Starkson stepped forward and read from a scroll of brownish-white paper:

*"November —, 1940. The Academy. Port George. Special Order Number Five. Subjects: Cadets Koble, H. B.; Wilson, A.; McCarthy, P. L.; De Paris, J.*

*"Whereupon with the reading of Special Order Number Five it becomes effective immediately that the enrollments of the above-mentioned cadets be obliterated from the records of The Academy. These men have been guilty of extreme and wanton violation of numerous regulations of The Academy. Their reward is dishonorable discharge.*

*"The following twenty-eight cadets are hereby placed under arrest and stripped from whatever cadet rank they might now hold. After a period Special Order Number Six will be issued. This will establish*

*definite punishment for these men and until such order appears they will hold themselves in readiness for expulsion. These men are:*

"*Caffre, Wilson S.; Caffre, William B.; Carmichael, L. M.; Fulton, W. T.; Garby, J. O.; Georges, B. A.; Harrison, G. W.; Horace, B. B.; Jackson, R. C.; James, S.; Karlson, T. F.; Kauffer, C. N.; Lawrence, H. S.; Lawrence, B. T.; Layne, P.; Morrison, S. C.; Munro, T. K.; Nash, W. S.; Norton, A. B.; Nunally, M. M.; Olsen, S. C.; Parker, F. H.; Richardson, W. W.; Richey, U. V.; Thomas, F. I.; Wallace, H. H.; Walton, T.; Willcox, S. C.*

"*Signed, Larrence E. Corger, Colonel of Cadets.*

"*Approved in full and signed, Colonel A. P. Evers, United States Army.*

"*Approved in full and signed, General A. L. Draughton, United States Army retired.*"

Starkson whirled around and saluted. He stepped briskly to one side. General Draughton slowly walked forward and rested his yellow-gloved hands on the balustrade. He spoke in a deep, hoarse voice:

"Gentlemen of the cadet corps!"

The General paused, then said rapidly, "I haven't made up my mind whether to expel the twenty-eight cadets cited in this order, but at the moment I feel their expulsion probable. The most generous punishment would be restriction to the campus for sixty days with all tours and room confinements served. This last was suggested by Colonel Evers. Personally I do not feel that lenient.

"Gentlemen, as originally written Special Order Number Five expelled six cadets, not four. At the last instant it was altered, two cadets being removed. These are Cadet Roger Gatt and Cadet Robert Marquales. Cadet Gatt is being allowed to resign from The Academy. Cadet Marquales will remain here on probation.

"Cadet Marquales is to serve all punishment tours and room confinements for a period of ninety days. During this time he is restricted to campus. There can be no excuse for the upperclassmen involved in the trouble that brought about Special Order Number Five, but the freshman has been a cadet only two months and is relatively inexperienced. If his attitude warrants reconsideration at the end of his restriction, charges against him will be looked into again. Pending a satisfactory examination he will be excused further punishment duties. Otherwise he will then be expelled from The Academy.

"Orders for his restriction will be contained in whatever action is taken against the twenty-eight cadets now placed under arrest. Of them I will say they have been the members of a secret club. Such organizations are prohibited at The Academy. I would like these men and the entire regiment to know I will not hesitate, if necessary, to expel anyone discovered in such a group.

"I have said in the past how I feel on the score of secret cadet clubs. The Academy is a military institution; as such it does not have odd bands of men forming themselves into clubs or fraternities. There is no place for such activity here. Any club formed must have a purpose for existence other than itself.

"You gentlemen are automatically the members of a club. I refer to The Academy. This large club is broken into smaller segments: your three battalions, then your sixteen companies. Even at that point it does not stop. You have your platoons, which have their men and officers. And in your platoons, squads.

"I would like to point out that we have any number of clubs. Clubs in the ordinary meaning of the term. There is the Boating Club, the Camera Club, the Nature Club, the Y.M.C.A. Club, the Glee Club. There are many other such organizations. Our Society of the White Pen, for literary aspirants. Our Society of the Silver Star, for men of scholastic leaning. And there are our numerous honorary groups.

"We also have our athletic units. There is first the intramural division. Those of you who have no great athletic skill may join the ranks of the intramural teams. You may play on any of the several Basketball Squadrons. You may join the Volleyball Team, the Touch Football Team. You may join the Rifle Squad. You may become a member of the school dance orchestra. You may attach yourself to our military band.

"I can mention more. There is gymnastic work on the Tumbling

Team. Our swimming pool is at your convenience. You may join the Aquatic Team itself. I think of the Track Team. We have a group interested in aeronautical design.

"Now gentlemen I've probably overlooked many of the clubs that can be joined at The Academy. Needless to say, they are innumerable. But each, you will notice, has a purpose; all operate for a specific reason. Why is it with such a number of clubs to be joined certain of you men have seen fit to form a *secret* club? I fear the answer is obvious.

"There are thirty men at The Academy who have banded together and formed an organization with the name—'Hair-of-the-Hound Club.' I regret to say many members of this group are among our most distinguished cadet leaders. They hold high cadet rank and make excellent marks scholastically. They are leaders in other ways —athletes, representatives on the boards of cadet societies.

"They banded together for this purpose: to break the regulations of The Academy. That is what they had in mind and that is what they have done. They rented a private room of a Port George restaurant and there they have been retreating on each week end to drink alcoholic beverages, to reduce themselves to stupefaction, and to gamble. I learned that the members of this club once rented a large house for the purpose of a gala celebration at Jamaica Shore. They carried with them several kegs of beer and a large amount of whiskies. For additional entertainment they invited fifteen young women of a disreputable variety.

"During my examination this morning of Cadets Wilson, Koble, and McCarthy I learned of the existence of this illegal club. I soon acquired a list of the membership. I wish to point out to you that this is another illustration of the maxim that errors are uncovered, if not at once, then sooner or later. If other such clubs at present exist, or if any men have thought of forming such a club, kindly bear in mind what has happened to this one.

"I find it incredible such a thing as this Hair-of-the-Hound can exist here. You see the results of it: twenty-eight of our most distinguished cadets are to be served special punishment orders; six other cadets have had their lives directly marked.

[ 348 ]

"I want it known that of all the cadets involved in this affair the burden of greatest responsibility falls on one single man. This youth has behaved in a reprehensible manner throughout all the disturbance.

"Cadets Gatt, Koble, McCarthy, and Wilson last night disgraced The Academy by indulging in a public brawl. This brawl was fostered and nourished by the lies and arrogance of Cadet Jacques de Paris, who is also expelled. As a result of this brawl one of the cadets involved has suffered a serious brain concussion. He was unconscious for six hours last night; his sense of hearing has been permanently affected. I refer to Cadet Roger Gatt.

"The brawl last night was begun by Cadet Gatt. For this reason I must dismiss him from The Academy. I am not, however, entering this dismissal in terms of dishonor but will allow him to resign. Cadets Wilson, Koble, and McCarthy finished the brawl—by means of the most vicious methods possible. They conducted themselves like ruffians not Academy cadets. They were half intoxicated at the time of the brawl, and they have given this as an excuse. They told me they were drunk and were only attempting to protect themselves. Drunkenness by no means constitutes an excuse. Cadet Gatt was unconscious and lying helpless on the floor long before these gallant men ceased to beat his skull with their bottles and chairs. These men violated an important regulation in ever having entered this bar in the first place. They violated another in having drunk liquors. And, their uncouth brutality makes their discharge mandatory. I am expelling Cadets Wilson, Koble, and McCarthy in dishonor from The Academy, along with the despicable cur, De Paris.

"Gentlemen, I understand human nature, for I myself am human. I know you are young, that you look for excitation. However, I point out that the world is full of the shattered bodies and crushed spirits of men who have been unable to master themselves.

"It is necessary to subdue random urgings to a central purpose— only in this manner can life have meaning. I am a soldier, not a philosopher, but any good soldier has something of the philosopher in him. We know that the Being we call God is the Father of spiritual life. We also know that the way we handle the physical selves entrusted to us is a direct reflection of our understanding of Him. Gentlemen, I ask you: what more could God desire than that man should protect, not destroy, what has been given; that man should make himself healthful and strong, that he should develop to the utmost his physical being?

"We offer aid toward this at The Academy. I will not hesitate to say that I do not know of any other institution in America that can give you a more solid basis upon which to construct your life. Here you might learn to achieve the self-discipline without which an individual existence is blind chaos. Here you might learn the spiritual cleanliness which makes a man rise in the morning prepared to meet the day, secure in the knowledge he is a decent individual with no need to bow his head to anyone. Here you might widen the scope of your intellect and acquire from our instructors the culture of the ages."

General Draughton paused for a long time, arms stiffly down to his sides. Then in a voice choked with emotion he continued: "Gentlemen, I have said this before and I will say it again now. No youth can pass through four years of The Academy and not end as a man. We expel the failure; I present our diploma only to a man. Think of that word; listen to it. *Man*. A simple monosyllable, but it has great force. Nothing is stronger than this word, for without the quality it signifies, the life of the race, and your own, is rendered utterly futile. Let adversity fall upon you. Fools insult you. Illness strike. Your head will be unbowed and your courage as sure as the turning of the globe—if you are a man."

The General quickly turned and stepped down from the rostrum. His gray head was visible over the rows of cadet caps as he strode out of the Armory. Starkson then dismissed the regiment.